MW00632376

THE ETERNAL MACHINE SPECIAL EDITION

DARK STEAMPUNK FANTASY

AELINA ISAACS

Book Cover and Illustrations by Lianne Peterson @fantasyspritestudio

CONTENTS

DEDICATION

To all those who find comfort in the darkness, this is for you.

PREFACE

Please read before starting The Eternal Machine.

This is an adult fantasy fiction novel with mature themes such as sex and violence, which are described in graphic detail. Mature themes include descriptions of physical abuse, loss and intense injury. Chapter 'Fresh Hell' may be especially triggering for some.

There is a glossary in the back which includes spoilers.

There are now three prequels, Children of Iverbourne, Prince of Sylvan and Princess of Terra. For this special edition, scenes from Princess of Terra have been included along with a bonus heated chapter featuring three characters.

I recommend reading the novellas after this novel if you don't want spoilers, but the chronological order is in the back of this book and they *can* be read first.

Visit https://linktr.ee/aelinaisaacs for the playlist, full color maps and more.

IVERBOURNE

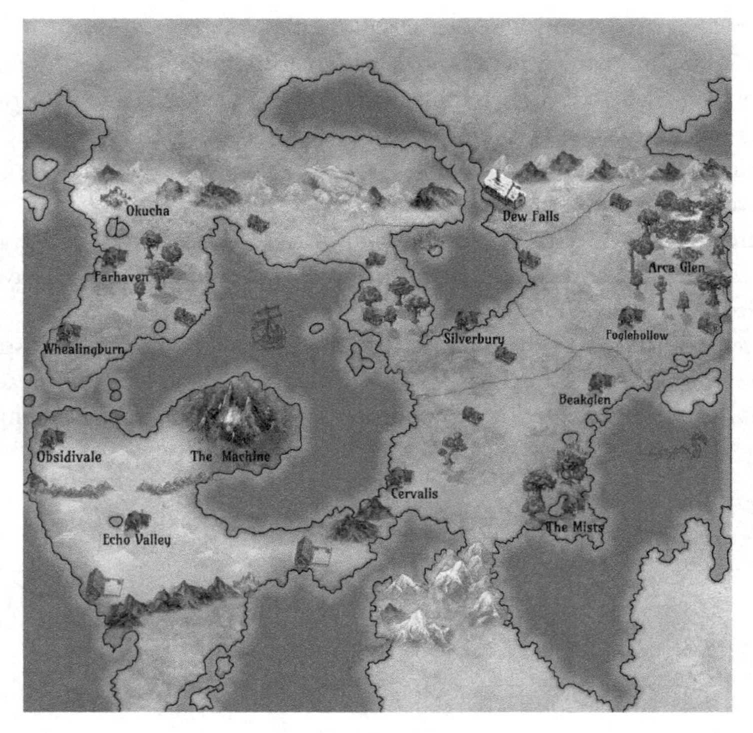

Lyth's Map, circa 16,095 A.C (After Creation)

OLD LANGUAGE

The Old Language derives from Hebrew, some words have been adjusted to fit the story.

Shomer - Guardian

Meggido - The impassable mountain borders separating Iverbourne from the North

Zemer - A talented musician

Tzel - Shadow of Death

Te' Omin - Two bodies, one soul

Akar - Troublemaker

Mazzikin - Demon

Im hayiti chai et chayay mehahatchala, hayiti motse otkha mukdam yoter.

If I were to live my life again, I'd find you sooner.

THE ETERNAL MOUNTAIN

As decreed by the Four Ancients after the Civil War of Iverbourne in the year 15,095 A.C.
The High Court of Iron will preside over The Eternal Mountain and take charge of the criminals inside. Only the High Lord can recommend inmates to the prison and must delegate all High Fae to work on The Eternal Machine.
The Eternal Machine shall restrict Aether vented to the lands above from the depths of the earth. The Five High Courts are responsible for monitoring the Aether usage of their inhabitants.

TO BETRAY AN ENEMY

The Eternal Mountain, Iron Court
16,095 A.C

Chaos slumbers here, festering in bloodied rust and coals. Wandering cinders threaten to ignite the simmering anger brewing from the work camps surrounding me. Prowling disorder is sure to follow as I strut into The Trenches.

I walk with my chin held high and the coal forges flanking my sides crackle with distaste. Copper shines from almost every available surface, but everything else is covered in soot, sweat, and blood. Purple smoke billows from the blacksmith's fires, whirling over my head as I reach the end of the grand cavern. Hundreds of blood thirsty Fae eyes burn on me, and every step is carefully placed.

I halt before The Machine and lift brass and leather goggles onto a lilac nest of curls. I study the massive undertaking of ancient technology, watching its spider-like copper arms weave into the abyss below. Copper gears tower to the top of the stone chasm, making the labor camps behind me minuscule in comparison.

Metal cranks together, belts purr, and purple smoke fills the air above, never ceasing.

I trace along the cliffedge, passing treacherous ladders which lead down into the deepest trench reserved for the Keepers, elite security and the only engineers allowed so close to the beast. While inspecting for malfunctions or leaks, the gauges on my leather and tech-covered wrist spin out of control. The lingering familiar stench changes, sweetness replaces death hanging in the air. Exhaust vents huff speckled night now instead of the usual purple haze.

My handcrafted gauges never agree with the ones on the wall, those only tell you what they want you to see. Regardless, ambient Aether is high enough I can tell without tech there is a leak. I shake my head, then pull tangled goggles and knotted hair back down. I creep further along, the darkness is thickest here in the heart of the Eternal Mountain.

Threatening to swallow me whole if I dare take a step too far.

A low, whistling tune escapes my lips, one my inmates know well. I halt and my dirty fingers flick down the green third lens on my goggles, revealing the jammed gear in clarity. Bright red, followed by a tendril of smoke. Kindling ready to burst into flames.

"Idiots." I sing playfully, letting the anticipation build for another moment before facing the crowd. Pressurized magic threatens to combust and the crackling smoke rolls thicker. My melody halts, as do the cautious footsteps behind me. A devious grin escapes and my tall boots spin in place, the leather pouches and straps along my sides swing with me.

Disgust rests with every creature. Most of the crowd consists of males and only a few females watch me approach from the distant edge. I make what has been called 'demonic' eye contact with every Fae as I evaluate the group. My small form wanders through the heated bodies, assessing. Playing. Only High Fae inmates are reserved for working in the labor camps near the Machine.

In a place far from here, High Fae are Power. High Fae are Magic.

But, we are not in a place far away. We are right here.

We work for The Eternal Machine, the beast conjuring magic and fueling the lands. Crimes of all kinds are welcome in this mountain, but you leave your magic behind. Rather, it's taken from you. Not that I know what that feels like.

Minutes pass, the only sound is made by leather boots and a whining engine.

And then, I halt before my target. The foreman. A Grasshopper before a Bear. I snatch a dark matted beard and yank him down, tough knees meet rock. Dull emeralds shine for a moment, his jaw works as he scowls at me. I lean forward and my soft face brushes against his filthy cheek, then my full lips meet a pointed ear.

A lover threatening sweet nothings.

"Darling, what's this?" A wicked smile lights my features as I pull back to bask in the crackling smoke reflecting in his eyes. I release his furred face, then pat his cheek harshly. I wipe away the ash left by his surly cheek on my own with the back of my hand, and the sickly sweet scent of Aether filling the air rushes into my nose.

I have to humiliate him.

He, along with the others, need to hate me even more than they already do.

They need to fight.

"I'm sure this is a misunderstanding." I taunt, words dripping with poison. I waste no time returning to the front of the group, tired of this show. Unsheathing the dagger strapped to my right thigh, its dark obsidian blade shines as I twirl it between my fingers with precision. I caress it with long fingers and bring the black blade to my pale lips upon turning, leaving a smiling kiss on the tip for all to see.

The Bear narrows his eyes, shifting his gaze to me. If I didn't have everyone's attention before, I certainly do now. I'm sure even through the goggles they can all see the darkness in my eyes, lacking pupils and emotion. Nothing can hide that.

"Rumor has it some here are shirking their duties, tampering with our beloved Eternal. Why let all this go to waste," I gesture behind me to the cloud of smoke, a whining spikes the air as belts threaten to snap. I note which eyes narrow at my statement. "Especially when you can't use it anyway. So much power, so close."

I giggle offhandedly, despite the fact the restraining tattoos on my wrists began painfully simmering minutes ago. I'm sure their ink is burning as well by now, the only thing these Fae and I share. "If a rebellion is what you want, you can have it. However, I'm sure most of you remember how that went last time."

My first kills, all that time ago.

"This is your last chance. Tell me what you know, and I may put in a good word with our High Lord. Or I can kill you all." I pace, shrugging at the idea of waiting at all. "I'm sure Commander Knothall will find me replacements quickly enough."

Silence and consideration. The privilege of the waiting sun above tempts every being. Some have never experienced its warmth at all, or the land it gives life to. I raise an open palm and prepare the whistle, assuming no one will believe the lie. We all know better than to make deals with Fae.

Or, so I thought.

"It was I, Keeper." The once quiet foreman pushes his way to the front of the crowd and glares down at me. Murmurs fall across and are quickly silenced as he continues. "For far too long have we tended to endless fire, for too long have we forged the backbone of this world. For many of us, we do this for crimes we did not commit. You know it well." His primal voice reaches every Fae. My dark heart thunders, warmth surges through the dead parts of my soul. I admire his courage, his dreams.

Even if it's my job to shatter them.

He isn't entirely wrong, most of the criminals here are no more than the wrong race, unable to crawl above with the fortunate. My neck burns and stomach twists, the last act is ready. A group of fifteen is gathered close around The Bear, their boisterous voices meld together in agreement. They are tired. They are done.

"Your difficulties are The Eternal Machine's blessing. Your crimes, see them as a second chance. As ... an honor. Be thankful you're not dead." My sharp whistle of death strikes out, and the masked army of guards waiting in the shadows make their move.

Screams fracture the cavern. Those who aren't with the Rebels find themselves on the sidelines of a malicious masterpiece, my exact precision has prepared a bloodbath for us all. Sixteen inmates are on their knees before me and the scent of burning flesh is ever present for our last act. I glance down at my right wrist, numbly watching the ink boil under my skin. Too much magic is in the air.

A young Fae female catches my eye. She is on her knees in the back, staring down what I suspect to be her pale lover in the crowd on the sidelines. Neither look afraid, they just watch each other with blank faces. Cloaked figures hold a knife to almost every treacherous throat, leather plague masks hide their faces. How strange, that they didn't stick together. Then again, this is prison.

My target, however, beholds no leash.

"Without your toil, who would run the Machine? Who would say, keep your family above ground?" My voice is childlike, beaming as I give the foremen my complete attention. "Last I checked, Firthorn, your family committed no crime. Unless you want to change that of course, I can have it arranged easily enough."

My dagger is no longer a plaything, already waiting for his pulsating throat by the time he lunges from his knees. A single callused hand wraps around my neck, lifting my boots off the ground.

The Bear can break me in an instant. He doesn't squeeze, just holds me there. I make a show of pressing hard enough into the hollow of his neck to draw blood, the other hand slips a treasure into his rumpled shirt pocket.

Blood trickles down the blade, meeting my leather wrapped forearm. I give him my best genuine smile before whistling sharply once more. I try not to think of the implications of what happens the moment my tune escapes. Firthorn's head attempts to turn back, but is stopped by my small hand.

My so-called demonic eyes shut tight, the sound of fifteen bodies hitting the floor slam into my ears. Firthorn drops me the moment it's over, his defeated gaze trained downwards.

"What are you all standing around for? Get back to work." I land on my feet, throwing a shout at the group of survivors, less than half remaining. Leather masks splashed with blood wait for my command, still standing guard over the bodies. "As for this one, throw him in the pit." I jut my chin to the darkness creeping from behind the work camps, unable to look at Firthorn's once again dull green eyes.

I rush to fix the damn Machine. My gauges busted a long time ago from the excess Aether in the air causing them to spin out of control. This is a chaos of a different breed, one I don't like. One that I am quite good at creating.

I scale down the closest ladder, dropping onto the grates of the keeper's trench. A groan escapes as I instantly regret the shock my thighs absorb, already sore from being dropped onto the rocky floor above. I flip the master switch, slowing the Machine down before I have any more damage to fix.

Luckily, I'm just as good at fixing things as I am at breaking them.

I retrieve the leather roll from my back, unrolling it to reveal The Tools of the Unusual. The obsidian wrenches, pliers, and chisels shine under the hot machine glowering above me. My fear of what lay below the grates left a long time ago, and luckily I know exactly where the malfunction is. I knew where it was long before my grand performance.

With thick hide gloves protecting my small hands I grab a chisel, then climb up into the copper framework of the enormous main engine. A carousel of machines work together as one, spinning the mechanical fingers into the core of the earth. Gears turn, belts run, and Aether is vented to the world above.

The shining limbs, nearly fifteen feet long each, weave through the magical atmosphere rising from the depths. Some say the Ancient Fae live down there still, hiding away from their creation. I don't give much credence to such things, but I don't put it past the Ancients to be watching us from somewhere. A limb dances behind my back, brushing against my leather vest. Even as I make my way to the jammed gear, the metal continues slowly turning. The Machine can never be truly stopped, just slowed down. So many inmates have tried to destroy it, and still try, but there is nothing that can bring it to a halt. I wouldn't even know what would happen if it did. I'm sure there is a flicker of power in the lands now with this inconvenience.

The red hot gear threatens to burn my arm as I reach through the framework with my chisel. With a sharp hit to the onyx stone blocking the crank, hidden from curious eyes above, it breaks free. Anything else would've been magma by now. I climb down and pick up the impossibly cool black stone laying on the metal walkway. Standing at the edge of the grates, I peer down past the ends of the spinning copper arms. Past their reach, into the deep darkness of the world. I drop the rock and watch it float down.

For several moments I stand there, lost in thought. I shake my head and turn back to finish patching up my mess. By the time I climb out of there and back into the work areas, it's the end of the night shift. The coal forges are still burning, and a new batch of inmates replaces the ones I had just terrorized. I leave just as proudly as I had walked in, ignoring every stare, and leave small bloody footsteps in my wake.

Screams and the scent of decay drift to me with an unwelcome sense of familiarity. I've put many of the Uncontainable down here, which lately number quite a few. Once peaceful Fae turned insane and blood thirsty, one of the side effects of living in an underground world for too long. I shudder at the thought of what monsters were here before my time, Fae and otherwise.

The spiraling rocky steppe leads further down, threatening to scratch deeper under Iverbourne than the last abyss I had just visited. No one dares go farther than The Pit, the farthest prison cell, and I have no intentions of doing so today. Cold dampness tightens around me while leather boots reach their last stop. I unlock the door and crack it open, then find a rather lashed Firthorn seated cross-legged in the mud. The Pit is no more than a hole in the stone wall, a freezing place to rot in. I step in and we are in dangerous proximity, the stone door behind me shuts us in together.

"You did well, Firthorn."

He evaluates me for a moment in silence before rising to tower over me. His jaw is set tight and the dull glare is hidden beneath long, knotted hair. I spy where I had cut him earlier, a shallow slice now half covered in filth. Both of his elongated, brown furred ears twitch with his solemn tone. "How many?"

First I cross my arms, then widen my stance and swallow, heat prickles my neck as I do. "Fifteen. It was quick, I assure you."

He pulls at his beard absently, his faded green eyes narrow at me. "There will be more." Firthorn says plainly. His friends, the ones he stabbed in the back. Closest thing to friends you can have here, anyway. I understand it for what it is. Truth, not threat.

"I know. You better keep one eye open." My voice is sharp and he lets out a purr of a chuckle, stirring my stomach. He evaluates my small stature, eyes pausing on the arsenal of daggers on both thighs. Fury lights my veins as he underestimates me. Just like everyone else.

Firthorn reaches into the pocket of his torn tunic and unfolds the photograph I gave him. "Where did you get this?" Humor leaves his voice, now shaky and wavering. I have peeked at the picture enough times in the last day to have them memorized.

The two girls with rounded ears and magic swirling in their bright green eyes. His eyes. I can't look at it again, not now. They look too much like him. "Knothall had kept it when you were interned. Favor for a favor."

He looks up from the photograph and for a moment, there is no anger on his face. Confusion, perhaps? But, hope is there, without a doubt. I draw in a breath, I unstrapped both dagger sheaths while he was distracted, my weapons always more prepared than my soul is. "High Lord Ragnis fulfilled his bargain. You wanted to see your family again, there they are."

I am ready for him again.

His dark throat contrasts against crossed, small pale hands, each wielding a dagger, ready to take his head off. The stance I hold is sickeningly familiar to my first murder. In all reality he holds the upper hand, but he does not lay a hand on me this time. Ragged breathing sweeps over the room, his thundering heart calls to my own pounding chest. The joints in my knee whir as I brace myself, provoking anxiety. If he notices, he says nothing. He further presses the thickness of his neck to my blades, raising a charcoal brow.

Daring me. Testing me. He stands over top of me, my daggers are no more than a toothpick in comparison to him. He encroaches further and bite my lip as blood stains my right blade. "Don't shoot the messenger."

No smile, no games. I am not the hero in this story. I am the villain. He could kill me right now, and have every right to dance on my grave.

My voice softens and my hands drop. Truth, not threat. "Did you really think they would've let you leave?"

We are still pressed to the other, blood and mud shared between us. He lifts my brass and leather goggles, my loosened purple hair tangles up in the contraption as he sets it upon my crown. I sometimes wonder what it's like to stare into my darkness. He doesn't flinch, strands of greasy walnut fall over his relaxed eyes while he memorizes every part of my face. The whisper he lets out is more fatal than if he had killed me.

"I hoped. Is that too much?"

He wants me to tell him it gets better. I haven't gone out of my way to comfort a fellow inmate in years, all feelings and friends bring in this world is hurt. I try to put myself in his shoes, but it's impossible. I've never known the outside world. I suppose it's better never knowing freedom, than to have it taken away. Always this place, this Machine. Insanity lives in the corners of my sharp mind, waiting for the day all this bloodshed finally breaks me. Over two centuries strong, and I haven't yet.

"Yes, it is." My purple tufted ears prick at the sound of my knees whining as I pull out of the mud. Once again, if he notices, he doesn't say anything. I yank my goggles back down and turn away, leaving him and my vulnerability behind. Anyone else I wouldn't put my back to them, but he had his chance to kill me more than once already.

"What is your name, Keeper?" Firthorn's crooning stops my footsteps on the first stone step outside the door. I glare over my shoulder at him, throwing off the curly strands hanging onto my goggles.

I didn't know he existed before today, my work has kept me away from the labor camps. The Aether Labs have been my life as of late. Knothall personally arranged for the inception, I had only received the photo and instructions late last night.

My only mission was to plant the problem and single out the largest male there. It wasn't hard to figure out who that was.

"I'm not someone you want to know." I decide, hand tightening on the throwing dagger at my right hip. A second of tension passes.

"I'll be the judge of that." A dark smile taints his hoarse voice, the echo of his promise follows my pained footsteps to my home waiting above. He's free to work in the chaotic heated camps among the remaining Fae he betrayed, his only reward for becoming enemy number one.

IS THAT A THREAT?

The Eternal Mountain is a massive black spot upon the world, or at least on the map I have of Iverbourne. The crisping illustrated texts in Commander Knothall's library describe the Mountain as a towering volcanic rock, with constant thick black smoke pouring from the sparking peak scratching the clouds.

After the War, the Ancients pulled the Mountain from the sea. Caverns and chasms took root inside to provide a prison for all those who brought harm to the world, which at the time were infinite.

Endless stone labyrinths and darkness keep thousands of us inmates company. The infestations of factories and laboratories throughout the Mountain supply the world above with industrial goods and metalwork. There are many forced laborers here, not just the Fae blacksmiths who toil closest to the Machine. Keepers like myself mainly work in the Aether labs neighboring the Eternal Machine's chasm, engineering new technology for the Fae High Courts of the world above.

The armory and blade smiths possess their own work camps, their caves are settled between the Aether labs and upper caverns. Only Goblins and Lesser Fae who are excellent craftsmen work there, and under no circumstances are they to be bothered. Other creatures have earned their place beside High Fae like me, but we are just treated the worst, and number the most. In the outside world of Iverbourne, Fae rule the world with an iron fist, squashing all those they consider lesser. In prison, everyone has a chance to get even.

As Lead Keeper, it's my duty to tend to The Machine and ensure its safety. Through any and all means necessary. Paperwork and bloodshed are my lifetime companions. Every once in a while, I'm able to sneak into the other labs and work on some new airship engines. The hulking beasts are a glorious challenge, but with the latest dramatics and false rebellions, I've been too busy. Parchment and oil, metal and leather. That's my only reprieve from the malevolent role of Lead Keeper, the most hated inmate in the Mountain.

I am perched high above my personal lab, the oak tables below me are filled with clutter and random works in progress. The metal loft is close to the granite ceiling, holding my few possessions and a makeshift bed tucked against the wall. Sitting along the open edge, I caress the top of my feathered companion's head and rub the end of my blistered thigh. Virgil rustles his dark body and tilts his head downwards, spying Knothall entering below. I hadn't removed the sockets hugging both my thighs, so I strap my left prosthesis on first, hurrying through the leather straps and brass buckles.

I repeat the process on my right thigh, wincing as the contracting muscles relentlessly send pain through me. Next I roll the loose linen pant legs back down, snapping the cuff at the bottom tight to the metal ankle joint. All ready to put my knee high, chewed up black boots over top. So many layers, so much time.

Any other day, I might drop onto the Commander and cause a tussle. I am sore enough today and think better of it, taking the spiral stairs with caution instead. I pause and lean on the wooden cane I have waiting at the bottom for a moment, gripping tight as I amble over with sheer annoyance. I find relief at an iron stool at the longest industrial surface. The master table.

The oak and iron table marks the center of my catacomb, stretching long enough to seat twelve but never has. One side of the room holds my loft, study and work tables. On the opposite side is the kitchenette and bathroom. Knothall waits for me to get settled and arches a gray brow, the lines in his face pull as he evaluates my filthy state. The Commander is not as tall as Firthorn, but much more frightening than the foreman. When you've been the leader of a prison like this for over a thousand years, your heart turns glacial.

We must truly look like father and child, though my shomer has always insisted I call him otherwise.

"You look as if there might be a rebellion." I cross my arms and pout, taking in his usual array of weapons along with a few additional blades strapped to his chest. Maroon eyes narrow, but a tug pulls at the corner of his thin lips. Silver tufted, short pointed ears twitch and he glances at the closed oak door. Strong voices bellow past, then he pushes out a breath when they quiet.

"Amwren isn't working today," I say, grasping the long wooden pipe next to me on the table, half burnt herb still in it from earlier. I puff on it, using a match to light, and pass it after a long drag. He takes it and inhales deeply, watching the smoke blow out for a moment.

"We have visitors coming tomorrow. Ragnis will be looking forward to creating fresh hell for entertainment," he warns. I groan and run a hand through my hair. The thought of the High Lord of Iron visiting is not a pleasant one, our grand dictator always loves to cause trouble. I tap the table with a finger, wondering if he'll fetch me for some personal torturous entertainment. Ragnis hates me just as much as the inmates do, he blames it on me being Knothall's 'pet'. The clock on the wall draws my attention, the traders will be arriving soon.

"Visitors? What are they selling?" I smirk, but his expression doesn't change. Visitors besides the usual traders have been an uncommon occurrence. Ragnis himself usually only visits on the monthly payday, which is chaotic enough, but he hasn't been here in four months now. Sometimes his Queen visits, but only when he does, and she is even more bloodthirsty and bored than the bastard lord of fire. If they both come and bring visitors, Slate will be hell. Even more so, anyway.

"You should stay here tonight, Lyth. I'm sure the remnants of the rebels will be looking for you." He rubs his temples, exhaling with his entire chest. Long, dark gray hair is tied back, pulling at skin that hasn't seen sunlight in over 1200 years.

"I can handle myself," I bite out. Another underestimation of me. He glances at my boots, then back up to my face. I shift my gaze to Virgil resting on his perch, hiding my disgust at Knothall's pity. The Commander rises without a word, then leaves me only to pause at the door. He rests his scarred and callused hand on the iron knob.

"I know. At least take that thing with you, he could do with stretching his wings." He nods in the direction of my now sleeping crow who ruffles his feathers at the thought of having to move. Virgil isn't stuck here like me, but he's never tried to leave. He's grown a bit now though, since I first found him. I can still remember Knothall firmly saying no, but somehow the crow never left.

"If you insist." I throw a wicked smile at him, but I falter after he leaves. I remove my goggles, retie my waist length hair into a side knot, then slip my brass goggles back down. I look around for a moment at the simple lab, the warmth of the lanterns beckoning me to stay. I tap my cane on the stone floor, contemplating. Perhaps Knothall is right. I indeed have training and experience, but it's all trapped in a small body. Easy pickings for anyone who tries hard enough. It's not like I haven't been attacked before, and survived.

No.

I won't start hiding. Not now, not after everything.

Before rising from the table I unlock a rolling drawer, retrieving the Tools of the Unusual. I lay it out and remove a wrench, then slide it into my side pouch. I push out a breath after locking the rest back up, then straighten my spine. With a quick whistle, Virgil reluctantly hops onto my shoulder, nestling against my neck after he settles. "Good boy."

Dirty fingers stroke beautiful feathers of darkness. I bask in the moment with him before leaving the wooden cane, and safety of the lab behind.

The sharp path from the cavernous under workings I've left behind leads into a magnificent chasm, the small tunnel expanding into a world of stone. Sickeningly red faelights hover above the trail, leading the way to the heart of the Eternal. It's not a particularly long walk to Slatepoint, however shards of rock have already begun to chew at my boots. I just traded for these boots a few months ago, and I already need new ones. One problem at a time, I suppose.

Smaller paths diverge from the main road, leading to cave holes dotting distant rock walls, the Darkedge villages. Menacing spiked towers overlook the inmate's residential catacombs and the sight still sends terror through a small part of me. The Keepers living there take out their frustrations on inmates for fun, and because they can. Despite my authority over them, they've never wasted an opportunity to jump me, and it's taken more and more Fae each time. Virgil takes off from my shuddering shoulder, catching stale air in his wings.

Faelights brighten as I approach the desolate village of Slatepoint. I click the green lens on my goggles up and out of the way not that the darkness has subsided somewhat. Another benefit of black eyes, I can't see well in the darkness of the maze I left behind. The end of the road is dotted with small canvas tents, left behind by the various traders who are allowed to visit once a day. They usually begin to tease us with their wares at the night shift change, which happened hours ago. A few Fae merchants linger in their stalls, but most of them are deserted in favor of the tavern, no doubt.

Hopefully, Umber will still be here to join me for a much-needed drink. The sapphire Fae is one of the few things that makes life here tolerable, tinkering in my precious spare time is the only other hope I hold onto. Slatepoint can be considered a village, it beholds dark pleasures and an opportunity for trouble, anyway. Jagged gravel crosses under a menacing archway, then the path gives way to smooth granite. Sheer borders of angry, towering black rocks wrap around the miserable town.

My scuffed footsteps pause at the last tent before the archway. I roll my eyes at the strong, curved High Fae stretched out in a hammock. Umber's canopy is small compared to the rest, a tent housing one table and simple goods. Her hammock stretches along its open back wall, tied between rickety posts that definitely should be snapping under her weight. I browse different loaves of bread and scraps of junk, deciding on a more simple loaf.

"You are disgusting." A lulling voice taunts from the hammock, followed by gray eyes narrowing at my figure.

Ocean skin erupts from the hammock, the rough and tough Fae crosses the distance between us in an instant. A long moment of tension and hard stares crawls before we both break, laughter shaking from tightened chests. Umber's strong hand claps my tired shoulder, almost taking me off my unsteady feet.

Umber steadies me while I curse her out, gray Aether shining bright in her round eyes. I don't envy the telltale flash of emotion unrestrained High Fae have to deal with, their colorful and sentient magic makes them terrible liars.

"Hard day?" She reaches into her pocket, then drops a satchel into my hand and closes my fingers around it. I scan the area, taking the wrench out of my pocket and slipping it into her own as I do. "Lyth," She protests.

I pocket the herbs and shake my head. "It will never fail you."

She nods and tucks away a loaf of bread into my pack. "Drinks?" She asks with a grin, stretching her arms overhead as she shakes out her blue curls. Gazing at Umber is like looking at illustrations of the sea in the books from Knothall I've come to treasure. Her playful eyes are usually bright gray, clouds lining what I imagine the ocean to be like.

"I thought you would never ask." I muse. We cross under the arch together, staying close to each other's side.

Dark red flags with the Mountain insignia wave along sharp border walls. Masked guards pace along the jutting spears of stone, observing everyone inside. Training rings for letting out frustrations and hashing out bloody duels are interspersed around the outer edge of Slate.

Shouts emerge from them as we pass by, along with the occasional curse when the jagged rock floor slices into flesh. Knothall and I train here several times a week, in front of everyone to see. He never lets me win, I just happen to be much quicker than the old Fae. Centuries of training can't hurt either, after being hurt the first time he vowed to never leave me defenseless again.

In the center of Slatepoint is an auditorium of sorts, a concave circular stone that spans nearly one hundred feet in diameter. A raised walkway with crumbling pillars of rock and a shoddy roof encircle the bowl of black stone, slow moving inmates occupy the circular, open air hall. I keep my focus away from the throne waiting in center stage. Outside of the auditorium, cobbled structures hold a few pleasures, the foundations almost pass for buildings. We head straight for the most crowded one, and usually the most troublesome.

There is no roof on Steammire, our lovely treasure of a dive bar. The flagpole above the splintered front door is thrust into crumbling bricks. Black gears are burned against the red fabric, waving for all to see. Chaotic conversation pauses as I enter the place full of Lesser and High Fae. A stool at the center of the bar looks most promising, and I waste no time claiming it. I order mead from the usual disgruntled fire imp and scan around, boredom masking my face as I do.

Quite a few burned wrists are present in here, along with simmering tempers. Soot is still fresh on the groups of High Fae recovering from their day shift in their camps. They wait for me to terrorize them some more, so I dismissively wave a hand. "Don't stop on my account." I break from their silent stares, resting a hand on my dagger as I throw back the supposed mead. Brain buzzing before I slam the mug back down, I call for another.

Umber raises her brows at me, shaking out her frizzed, short curls as she sits. "Seems like you pissed off a few folks." She whispers, then drinks, glancing around the room. Murmurs of curses filled with my name thicken the air and my skin crawls with the hatred poking at me. Umber shifts in her seat, scowling right back at those uttering my name.

A stare from the darkest corner burns into my back, and after several minutes I can't take it anymore and have to glance over. White eyes pierce me at once, filled with blood lust and anger. A lean High Fae male with a bloody hand print dried onto his bare chest. The lover who left his partner to die alone. I found it odd that one Fae chose to be honest, and the other chose to be a coward. Seated with him are three other males from today's shift. After tense moments of neither of us looking away, I accept defeat and stare down at the stone bar instead.

"It doesn't take much." I remember to answer Umber after a moment, swirling my drink and finding it doesn't taste good anymore.

"Let's go for a walk." Umber glances at the corner still watching us, her voice an edged whisper. Tired hips protest leaving so soon, but I don't want to be here anymore.

We both keep a hand on our weapons, my engraved dark dagger and her elegant sapphire encrusted sword, and leave without a second glance.

Back in Umber's quiet tent, the Fae rests on a stool and I lay stretched out with my eyes closed upon the hammock. Both of us are silent for some time. I think about the first time I met Umber, she erupted from the hammock just as she did today, eager and intense.

But, that intensity is lost on her today. "Tell me what happened." Umber pleads, voice trembling.

I sigh. I hate mixing my life 'down below' with the relatively good times I have up here with her. "I had to take care of something today." I reply after a moment, opening my black eyes whilst turning my small face to glare at her.

"You're going to get yourself killed." Umber takes my hand, squeezing it tight as she leans closer. Her eyes flare with an intensity I've not seen before, and I have to look away.

I exhale quiet honesty. "What choice do I have?" The Keep's lights flicker in the distance, teasing me with the closeness of freedom. The impenetrable barracks is the only way in or out of the Mountain, the last checkpoint before a miles long tunnel. “I wouldn’t even know how to live out there, even if I could leave.” I add, voice far off as I recall a dream I had as a child.

Umber turns my face to hers with a gentle finger and thumb, her usual roughness gone. Her free hand gently caresses my cheek and I fight the urge to lean back. Something’s wrong. Silver eyes flash, filling with Aether as an opaque cloud of sapphire mist surround us. “Lyth, I could —”

“If you’re trying to stay hidden, I think this may just bring attention.” A rough voice reaches us, shattering my already fried nerves. Sarcasm cuts through the fog and I roll my eyes at Umber, recognizing Firthorn’s voice.

After a moment of pause, she leans back and reels in the clouds and sickly sweet smell of Aether around us. The dizziness clouding my mind disappears with it. Magic fumes always give me a terrible headache, or dizziness at the very least. The only active magic I’ve encountered besides Ragnis’ tortuous fire is Umber’s air magic, just as beautiful but less deadly. There is the Aether from the Machine and it fuels the engines we work on, but it’s just a ... substance, in its raw, mined state. A very finicky material, but a material all the same. Only when coursed through a Fae’s veins does it come to life.

“If you’re not here to buy something, then leave.” Umber hisses, scowling at Firthorn waiting on the other side of her tent. Firthorn puts his hands up and shrugs, watching me leave the hammock and approach him. The only thing between us now is the table of wares.

“May I help you?” I cross my arms and widen my stance, looking up at him with a raised chin. The filth and blood from his admittedly rugged face is washed away, leaving a sly smile hiding under the madness of his beard and free flowing hair. Small braids hide behind his ears and the back of my neck heats. Stay focused.

“I came to thank you.” Firthorn straightens and crosses his arms, briefly glowering at Umber before looking back to me. “And to return the favor, I’m warning you.”

The threat sends my blood running, his voice full of anger and promise. I push my goggles up into a tangle, revealing the abyss swirling in my eyes. “Is that a threat, inmate?”

Firthorn’s brows narrow, his jaw clenches tight. “Go home.”

The Keep’s horns let out a bellow, rumbling the chasm and shaking loose pebbles from the ceiling. I exchange looks with Umber, her last call if she wants to leave. When I turn back to Firthorn, he is already gone.

Sleep doesn't find me easily, and when I do drift into shapeless dreams, I am met with the same terrifying blank nightmare I have every night.

For two decades now, I've been haunted by a terrified voice, hiding in the darkest recesses of my mind and always just out of reach. The whisper begins with desperation, whining becomes a whimpering. Darkness swallows my soul and senses, hiding the voice calling out to me.

"*Findmefindmefindme.*" The begging whisper turns uproarious, the edges of my now lightening vision curl into tendrils of smoke. The breaking light threatens to reveal who is tortured beneath the curtain of darkness in my mind. But, they never are.

FRESH HELL

A headache is my constant companion the next morning, the throbbing worsens as my chattering lab assistant briefs me. A petite Lesser Fae with rose skin, and wings. Beautiful, iridescent wings that brighten even this dank place. Different from the leathery type some Fae hold, these look like glass.

"Amwren, will you fetch me some coffee, please?" I interrupt her midway through a discussion of the materials list, rubbing at my temple with a soft voice.

"Of course, Keeper." She bows her chin, ever respectful. She's one of the few people in here who treats me as a person, but I suppose that's because I treat her the same. Amwren leaves me in the study area, nestled into the nook under my loft bed. She flits over to the small kitchen, quiet as a mouse.

I study the paperwork in front of me, then take off my goggles and run a hand through my knotted hair. Sleep and a bath has eluded me and I can't help but think my mind would be running much more efficiently with both. The numbers make no sense as ink on parchment melds together, dancing nonsensically in my mind. Input and output values dictate my life, it's up to me to adjust the vents in the earth above accordingly so the territories receive appropriate amounts of Aether.

"*Findmefindme*." The hoarse whisper from my terrors burns through the chaos of my mind. After taking a moment, I attempt to decipher the reports with a slightly clearer head.

The output values for the Machine are increasingly high, starting in the last week. The amount of Aether released is ... beyond astronomical. Far too much to be just from my shenanigans, and it's not an error. Errors don't happened with the Machine. I cross check and find a set of coordinates listed in one box instead of the entire twelve it belongs in. My fingers leave the data in search of the map, and I shudder after touching the glacial mountains to the east. Vents in the Southeastern hemisphere are outputting almost twice the allotted amount, and for a week straight now.

How did I *miss* this?

Amwren joins my side with a steaming cup of coffee, after handing it to me she perches on the table beside me. "Something wrong?" She asks softly. I pass the papers to her and sip the black coffee, watching her face as my soul awakens a bit. Reports regarding the Machine are never diverted from me, and my brows narrow as the gears grind in my head.

"The south east?" Her voice rises an octave and her wings flutter at the same time her elongated ears fold down. Lesser Fae typically hold much longer ears than High Fae, naked and bare compared to the fluff most of us don.

I shrug my shoulders, watching her scrutinize the map. "Nothing there, not that I'm aware of anyway. According to my maps it's a glacial wasteland." I tap the Southern Mountain, but Amwren's eyes rise to the land of The Mists above. "When were these delivered?"

Amwren tears her eyes from the map. "This morning, the Commander delivered them while you slept. I must say I was a bit surprised, I don't see him often anymore." Sadness lingers in her voice, a tone I recognize. He has become distant from all of us in the past few years, leaving many to live in this hell alone most of the time. Really, ever since *her*.

This further drives my suspicion Knothall has been secluding himself for a reason, but why?

Amwren scoots closer to me, her wings flutter and send a few papers aloft. "I heard that Ragnis' visitor is from The Others' Court."

"The Others?" I glance at her with a raised brow. I only know of the territories forged in the treaty, after the War ended and the Ancients crafted the Eternal. Without it, our world would've fallen apart.

I pore over the map of Iverbourne again, tracing the realms. Iron Court was physically torn apart from Borealis after the war and sheer red canyons to the east divide Fire Fae from the remaining continent. Everyone in the desert is landlocked, doomed to live in the scraps Iron gives them. Iron Court itself is rich beyond belief, profiting from our forced labor and giving nothing back to their struggling people. The only way out of the desert is through Echo Valley, and to save enough money for an airship trip out of there will take a lifetime.

Not that I've thought about it much.

Borealis Court rests across the sea to the north of Iron, the only Human lands remaining after the war. Iron will always look over the water and lust after the land they once traversed, and destroyed. I never hear much about Humans, other than they despise Fae with a passion, and are hunted endlessly by Water Fae. They've only begun trading in the past few years, and with extreme trepidation. For good reason.

Sylvan and Terra Courts rule the upper mainlands of Iverbourne with age old disputes raging ever since the treaty over territory lines. These days, Sylvan mercenaries hunt lesser beings for sport, and there has been a decades long famine plaguing the lands of Earth Fae. Iverbourne is brimming with conflict and threatening to break. A beautiful land, choked and snuffed out by greedy Fae.

The southern lands are ruled by the Hallowed Court, Air Fae. They are quiet folk, or must be as I've never seen one in the Eternal. Water and Fire Fae overwhelm the population here, but there are some Terrans here too. Hallowed marshes and hillsides stretch far south, stopped only by glacial wastelands and mountains. Similar impassable ranges rise along the northern borders of Iverbourne, trapping the people together and separating the northern lands from us. A land I don't even know the name of, for it's a blank spot on all my maps, and Knothall's.

I rise and begin to pace, biting my cheek as I think aloud. "Something's not right. To override the output vents, it would take," I pause and turn to Amwren who is overlooking the output values. She sets them down and gestures for me to come closer. Amwren points to the mountain range residing in the south, below Hallowed.

"When I lived in Hallowed," She swallows, dark eyes glistening, "High Fae visitors, claiming they came from these mountains, visited us. Fae that didn't fit in anywhere else. The Court of Others."

I shift my gaze from her trembling lip to the map. "Sounds like it wouldn't be too bad." Amwren closes her eyes and shudders, the red scars along her face and shoulders catch my attention. The rose Fae's voice is near silent, my tufted ears need to perk to catch her words.

"They stole children. And, my kind. Wherever they went, the disappearances were so immense." Her voice breaks, tears fall down her face. My bulky arms wrap around her thin shoulders, careful not to touch her wings, and I fold her close to me.

After her breath returns, I ask the question. "Why did they come? To Hallowed?"

Stained glass wings tremble, eyes widen. "I don't know, after meeting with our High Lady a bargain was struck, one so powerful she forbade it to ever be spoken of again. After that, they were taken. All of them." The Fae sobs into my chest, heaving with the sadness of her people.

Later that afternoon, I pay a visit to the Machine, leaving Amwren to finish up in the lab before she returns home. The Fae has been my assistant for decades, and Knothall's before that. More than an assistant, she is my engineering mentor, friend, and the closest thing to a mother I'll ever have. Knothall is my protection, and she is my humanity. She's never really talked of her past before, and to this day I don't know why she's here. The terror in her eyes when she spoke of the Others curdles my blood.

Heated glares watch me stroll past the floor to ceiling forges and my shoulders rise. My limp is more noticeable today and I curse under my breath. There are only a few alive who know of the incident that took my legs, but it's hard to hide the physical pain I feel every day. It's only a matter of time before my vulnerability is fully revealed, and I resolve to refuse the next instigated rebellion. If I can.

Firthorn works at the last round forge closest to the keeper's trench, hammering a scythe into shape on his anvil. He is bare chested, thick arms shuddering as his hammer meets steel. I stop and widen my stance, waiting for him to pause. He turns, revealing the slick muscles composing his wide back as rests the blade into the coals again. He faces me again and tears down his soot-covered goggles, then raises a brow. "What?" Firthorn snaps.

I don't really know why I stopped, but the sight of him makes me want to forget this world, inhale the charcoal resting on his dark-haired chest. I tear myself from my muddied thoughts and will annoyance into my voice. "Have you seen Knothall?"

The Bear gestures in the direction of the looming Machine. "He's inspecting." He states and straightens his shoulders, eyes wandering over my small stature and threatening to see through me. "See you tonight." He reminds me, his threat bordering on seductive promise.

I give him an eye roll before sauntering away, heat lingering over my neck and through my core. It's been too long since I've thought of anyone that way, and I don't know why it's him that has my heart thundering. I climb down into the trench, taking the ladder all the way down instead of repeating yesterday's stupidity. Knothall waits at the inner edge, arms crossed and stony face watching the lengthy gleaming arms probe into the dark below us.

"I think you owe me an explanation." I scowl, coming to his side. Knothall continues staring into the abyss, face hard and blood throbbing in his neck like he's run a marathon.

"Do you remember the day you became Lead Keeper?" He says, completely still and voice empty of emotion. I straighten, glancing back at the empty space behind us on the stained metal grates. The sound of a head rolling echoes in my ears.

"Of course I do." I say quietly, pricking Knothall's silver ears up.

"You killed my mate that day." The Commander of the Eternal Mountain faces me and drops his arms, his aged voice now wavering and broken.

I lift my goggles up and bite my cheek, tone dropping an octave. "Rohana? She was their leader," I rub a dirty hand down my face, "Why didn't you-"

He raises a hand and cuts me off. "It does not matter now." Knothall's scarred jaw sets tight once more, his usual firm tone returns. "She entrusted a task to me. The time has come for it to pass to you."

I tilt my head at him, aghast. How does it not matter? The first person I murdered happened to be my *shomer's* lover, mate. Whatever that is.

"Does this have anything to do with the southeastern territories?" I question with frustration. His eyes alight for a moment, then he nods.

"Your next assignment is in one week. Be ready, that's all I can say." The next shift of Keepers make a ruckus into the camps above, sending my heart into a race. They actively cause trouble and torment the inmates for pleasure, and they work in groups as opposed to Knothall and I's shifts accompanied by no one. We both glare at the ladders and I fight the trembling biting at my skin. With blood boiling and my anger threatening to lash out at him, I settle for pushing out a breath and pulling my goggles back down.

"Will I see you tonight?"

"Yes." He bites out, turning back to the abyss beside us. I leave without another word, leaving him standing over the edge.

The walk is slow, but I don't care to put myself through any more pain than necessary. My mind swims with images from my first kill. Rohana. The darkness swallowing her face and body, as well as any chance of my being a decent Fae. In the beginning, I convinced myself I did what needed to be done. Protect the Eternal at all costs. But, over time, guilt has eaten away at my soul. Not just because of Rohana, but of the countless other lives I've taken since then, most of them wrongly accused. The world would be a lot better off without Aether, and that constant thought makes it hard to keep it contained.

Somehow, living in a place like this hasn't hardened my heart. *Yet.* Perhaps on the outside, but on the inside, everything I do sickens me and rents my soul in two.

A streak of red and blue tears me from my thoughts and I look up to the Keep, the way out I desperately desire. An unmarked, dark blue airship is maneuvering alongside the familiar blood red ship beside it, both drifting down inside the towering walls of the Keep and out of sight. The thought of seeing Ragnis is reason enough to stay home, but I would be dragged out anyway. He would send someone for me, his favorite plaything.

Slatepoint is filled with filthy creatures from every depth of the prison, far more crowded than yesterday. The ever constant trader's canopies are deserted, leaving me empty and disappointed. I frown at Umber's tent, checking the time on my wrist. It's far too early. The traders must've been turned away today, another method to fuel chaos.

Steammire's crowded, drunken chatter does not cease when I weasel my way past the threshold and between stumbling creatures. The familiar imp at the bar is preoccupied with two goblins and I wait wordlessly in my seat. The imp never speaks to High Fae, or so I've heard. He doesn't give me any problems, but I did hear he killed two Fae to earn a ticket here. Where goblins, imps and everything not Fae or Human originate from are a long lost legend, one I try to solve every now and then. Knothall's library is lacking and gossip only gets you so far, however.

I tap my finger gently on the bar and scan the room. No rebel lovers here. When the bartender turns his attention to me, I set coins on the bar in silence, receiving a full mug of honeyed mead in return. Red leather wings flit off to another customer before I can thank him, the sweet beverage a rare treat. I throw down the drink without hesitation, the rare sugar quenches the indulgent side of me. The hairs on my arms suddenly stand up and panic spreads across me, spiking my heart and freezing my veins solid.

Someone is watching.

I casually glance behind me and scan the voracious crowd, not finding any immediate danger. A group of High Fae is bellowing together, drinks in hand and smiles across their faces. I shake my head, unable to fathom their happiness in this place. Every payday that Ragnis doles out worthless coins to every creature here is a joyous one, for some odd reason. Seeing how it's been a few months, they must be expecting back pay. What fools.

An ominous feeling yanks me from my seat. I sneak a look between the rowdy patrons who still pay me no mind, then dart out of the bar. Virgil crows at me from the flagpole, taking off for the Keep after catching my eye. He can leave any time he likes, but the looming tunnel beyond the Keep is quite terrifying for a small bird to navigate through. I like to think he stays for me, but only the Ancients know. I pause my pained step to lean against a stone pillar resting outside of the smooth, inner circle foundation.

Faelights hover high above, bloody warmth lights the stage and illuminates the gossiping creatures lingering around the outer edge. No one steps past the pillars and into the bowl, yet. The massive stone below remains empty, except for the dais in the middle. The raised slab of blackened stone holds a single throne. The walkway around the auditorium fills further, the frenzy between creatures across the cavern builds into constant bellowing. Bodies bristle closer to mine and a cold shudder has me searching once more to no avail.

Horns blast, echoing from the direction of the massive Keep overlooking us all. The Keep rests a half-mile outside Slate's rocky border, but the quaking sound thrums my ears as if the horns were right beside me. A small arch in the impassable borders to the right holds a heavily guarded trail, snaking towards escape. Inmates from every slimy crevice and dark hole slink out at once to gather in the center, filling Ragnis' waiting stage. Tattered clothes, sunken faces and fidgeting are common among everyone present.

One more feature binds us all, the barbed black tattoos on our wrists. We have all committed crimes deemed miserable enough to band us together.

I do not move, carefully keeping an eye on those emptying the bar behind me. Virgil is perched on the flagpole again, watching the scene unfold. Red faelights glisten on his dark feathers, it has to be an omen. A crow covered in blood light, watching a vicious High Lord approach his prey. I turn my attention to the lone throne crafted of iron, vines, and roses snaking around the seat. I spy an unimpressed Knothall guarding the empty dais. Firthorn stands several rows ahead of me, I recognize his walnut hair braided down the length of his broad and leather covered back.

The Bear argues under his breath with another blacksmith from the Trenches, their anger-fueled conversation catches my attention. The pale Fae beside him glances back at me and I find the familiar eyes of the jilted lover narrowing. Firthorn follows his gaze and catches me strengthening my stance. My knuckles turn white from gripping the familiar dagger handle at my thigh. Firthorn turns away expressionless, shaking his head to the jilted lover.

Another low bellow erupts and everybody collectively turns to the right. Masked guards part from the archway of freedom, their unit moving in complete synchronicity. Waiting in the shadows, always precise and ready to strike. The dripping warm elegance of the Iron Court enters our midst, throwing my heart into a permanent run.

We have been kneeling for five minutes before the throne, and the pasty High Fae child lounging upon it. The High Lord absentmindedly plays with an orb of fire, small flames dance along his freckled hands. To his right stands a near white High Fae female, her glacial glare soaks us all in with intent. Her right temple is shaved and tattooed, the rest of her hair sweeps into white waves down her back.

The Commander stands beside the mysterious guest, and on the other side of the High Lord stands the Queen of Iron. The ambitious Fae contrasts her husband in so many ways. Burning orange eyes hold more years than his spritely bright red, her black hair contrasts his bright amber curls. Ragnis thrives on games and torture, where she thrives on pain through politics, and power. Always power, for both of them.

Ragnis and his Queen are dressed in brilliant red silks, adorned with rubies and finery beyond our grasp. Our guest is in simple black leather pants and a white long-sleeved tunic, bound in a black leather corset. Business, not pleasure.

The child finally looks up, surprised, at the entirely packed Slatepoint. Not only is the center stage full, but the entire circular walkway holds untrusting eyes, inmates watch the scene from every angle. A devious smile spreads across his dimpled face. "Oh, you're all here." The flames in his hands die as he shifts into an upright position. The Queen scans across our filth, seeming rather pleased.

"There seems to be a few missing, Commander." She muses to Knothall, tilting her head and smiling at him with perfect white teeth.

"There was an attempt to overthrow The Eternal Machine. The traitors were dealt with, of course." Knothall gestures for us to rise, his voice strong.

A simultaneous shift echoes through the cavern as every creature and Fae turns their attention to me. Hundreds upon hundreds of eyes, all of which burn with nothing but hatred. Everyone knows who the Lead Keeper is, who would've dealt with it. I'm already the scapegoat for every inmate's problems, add my Empty Fae status to that and I'm a walking target.

I hold my chin high and fix my eyes on Ragnis as I pass through the crowd of snarling inmates, and they part reluctantly. I focus on my heavy steps, not stumbling or falling. I can't show weakness, not right now. But of course, Firthorn's body is a hard stone in the river before me. Instead of stepping around him, I pause behind the obstacle.

The lover from yesterday's rebellion snarls at Panrauth's side. Firthorn himself remains silent and unmoving when I take his braid with care. "Darling, you're in my way." I tease, voice loud enough for the audience to hear. Panrauth doesn't respond save for the flickering of his jaw, but the Fae beside him approaches me with haste.

"Go fuck yourself, Empty Fae *whore*." He spits on my boot, evoking a raised brow from me, and a gasp from the crowd. The next movements take all of seconds.

Releasing Firthorn's hair.

Unsnapping the orb flask from my belt.

Poising my thumb on the lid and whipping it up *right* in front of the bastard Fae's face.

"I think you owe me an apology." I wink and release a smile that matches the wickedness in my voice. The explosive concoction is an impractical defense, unless I want to blow myself up as well. Perhaps if my patience is tested enough, it won't seem so impractical anymore.

Firthorn spins on his heel, breaking his silence as he rests a firm hand on my shoulder. I shake him off, giving him a murderous scowl. "Keeper, put that *thing* away." The Bear warns. Murmurs and shouts erupt around us. Does he really think I am stupid enough to release a fucking bomb in here? The idea is quite tempting, I must say.

My last resort is only a distraction. The pale Fae has his grinning attention on Firthorn coming to his defense when I pull my blade. Steel meets flesh, flaying open the side of the pitiful male's face. The orb is strapped back to my side as the Fae drops, blood spews across the shaking hands clutched to his face.

"You ... fucking bitch!" He howls.

He isn't afraid of death, but this, this is worse. I really should have killed him, but seeing him in pain and humiliated on the ground, jeered at by the other criminals, is much more satisfying. I wipe the blood from my blade before sheathing it, then step past Firthorn who moves in silence from my path. I cross the now silent stage and kneel before royalty and their guest, rising only when Ragnis' delighted giggle meets my ears. I stare into twin pools of blood, noting the guest and Queen surveying me in my periphery.

"Treason has no place in The Eternal Machine, High Lord. I will continue to tend to our blessing in honor, and duty."

Ragnis claps enthusiastically and rises from the throne, then skips to me. Perhaps I gave enough of a show, he will be entertained. Standing on the dais, he is only a few inches taller than I, but I am no child. I have lived here long before he slaughtered his father, claiming the throne as his own. Passing the bastard throne from one cruel, unrightful king to another.

Ragnis likes striking fear into his charges by throwing curve balls, even to those he claims to trust. The Eternal Mountain is the burden of the Iron Court, the punishment bestowed upon them long ago by The Ancient Fae. Those who ruled before Ragnis chose to kill first and ask questions later, unbothered by the inmates . Ragnis likes to make a show of his power, even to us, the slaves trapped inside the Mountain.

"Oh, I rather like you, *Lythienne*. I don't doubt you for a moment." The freckled child draws out my name, caressing my cheek with a flame doused finger. Burning flesh fills the air and I struggle to remain still against the fire licking my skin, the lithe hand cupping my face. I find relief only when he reaches up to pull off my goggles, the searing pain retreating for a precious moment. The High Lord examines them, clicking the multiple lenses back and forth, fiddling with the vials on the leather straps.

A mask of boredom rests on my face, silence fills the chasm as he toys with my most prized possession. After a long pause, he stares directly into my dark eyes. It's been too long since Ragnis put me through any pain, and through me, Knothall as well.

I'm overdue.

I lift my chin higher as he tosses my goggles over his shoulder, sending them crashing onto the stone behind him. The sound of fragile glass *shattering* deafens me and I try not to grind my teeth together. Ragnis' smile never falters as he snaps his fingers. My goggles burst into a pitch black flame.

I know he wants me to defy him. After the day I've had, I most certainly want to. He bears no restraining tattoo though, he can do magic here, same as his Queen and bored guest. They are High Fae, and all High Fae are privy to magic. Except for me.

I want to look at Knothall, the one who crafted the goggles for me decades ago. They were a game changer here, providing me a curtain to hide under and the ability to see in this fucking mountain. Instead, I look past Ragnis, at his guest. Deathly beautiful, akin to a finely made blade, lethal and cold.

"Oh, where are my manners?" The High Lord gestures to the Fae and she joins him in a few long strides. "Allow me to introduce you all to your new commander. High Commander, I should say. No one can replace you, Knothall." Ragnis gives Knothall a sly grin. "Just another helping hand."

Several gasps escape behind me and all attention turns to Knothall. Commander of the Eternal since the Mountain was formed over twelve hundred years ago. A Fire Fae sent away for misdeeds so grave they were never spoken of again. Knothall is unbothered, bowing his head to his new superior who stands before me with Ragnis. I move out of the way and join Knothall, a stone at his side.

The icy fae smiles at the gathering. Tribal inkings arc around her shaved scalp, their detail much easier to appreciate this close. I hadn't noticed the saber strapped to her back earlier, the handle studded with rare opals catches my eye. She walks among the inmates, looking down on each set of untrusting eyes. "I am Eros. You now answer to me. I'm sure we will get on quite well." She drawls, swaying her hips as she meanders, taking in her new charges with apathy.

"Who are you to command us? " A shout echoes. Eros' head turns in the direction of insolence, finding a dirty pink Fae. Amwren. Glass wings shake, threatening to shatter, but she doesn't look away. "It's you, isn't it?"

Eros doesn't need to say anything to establish her dominance. With a broad smile and snap of her fingers, black smoke rolls from her fingertips and in an instant, Amwren is gone. One moment she is there, and the next her body erupts into fine black powder, wafting away toward the Keep. Just ... gone.

"Does anyone else object to my ... observations?" Deafening silence swells around Slatepoint. I swallow my tears and look up to a pale Knothall with a tight grip on his sword. The Commander is terrified, a look I've only witnessed twice in my entire life. Ragnis' enthusiastic clapping fills the chasm, slapping our souls. The Water Fae I taunted before lingers near the distant Steammire. Blood fills his face, neck and violently shaking body.

I *really* should have killed him.

Before departing, Ragnis announces offhandedly there will be no pay given this month. Only silence and cold stares are shared among the crowd. Knothall escorts the High Lord and Queen to the Keep, and Eros stays behind to slink through darkness.

Hours later, I sit in the bar with the silent imp. Virgil rests upon my shoulder as the gears in my head turn, trying to make sense of the latest game. It's early morning now and Steammire is empty except for a few stragglers. One of them being Firthorn, who comes in and sits beside me.

Without a glance, he orders a mead, then downs it in one go. The imp has another ready and this time Firthorn turns to me, then raises his glass. I raise my brows and smirk, clinking my cup against his. We both drink, then release the air trapped inside our lungs. Virgil lets out a displeased crow and flies out to resume his post on the flag outside. Firthorn narrows his brows whilst watching the crow, then focuses on me with renewed purpose.

"So, Lythienne is it?" A hungry smile fills his broad face, lust pulls his usual wall of indifference into curiosity. Now *this* is a look I don't get often, especially from someone like him. I bite my lip, shooting him a death glare and glorious eye roll. "I prefer Lyth. Less *fancy*."

I can't remember the last time I laid with a male. My experiences thus far are nothing to write home about. If I had a home, that is. Being alone is easier than dealing with the filth here, and the need to feel release is not one that passes me very much anymore. The warmth that surges through me when I look over the thick blacksmith beside me changes that fact very quickly.

"Just Lyth?" Dark brown arms rest on the bar and he looks over me with interest, waiting.

"I have no family name. And that's all I wish to say about it." I say harsher than I intend, but he doesn't seem to mind. The lingering silence between us has me questioning what I thought I saw in his eyes.

After a few more minutes of quiet, I turn in my stool to leave. His low tone perks my purple tufted ears, pausing my movement. "Panrauth. Firthorn is my family name." I bit the inside of my cheek, surprised he would divulge his first name to me.

"Well, that just seems like a mouthful. Perhaps someday I can call you Pan instead." I give him a real smile, the one spreading across his own face giving me courage.

I will never use his name here. Panrauth's laughter rumbles low in his chest, his glazing eyes seeming to dwell on the thought of it. I need to ask him, even if I don't want to know the answer. "Why are you speaking to me? After what I did to you ... " I shake my head, unable to finish. He studies me and I become stone when his rough fingers caress the lines on my face where my goggles once rested.

Instead of the passionate touch I crave, his momentary gentleness twists into something dark and firm, and once trailing fingers hold my face in place, squeezing my cheeks. "I'm curious, how can such darkness hide in such a tiny ..." Heat pricks my face at his snarling tone, his threatening fingers grasp my cheeks tighter. "*Insignificant* body, and not be crushed by everything around it?"

I yank away, but only for a moment as Panrauth takes my chin once again with firmness, forcing me to look at him. I blink away the burning in my eyes and push my lips into a thin line. The Bear holds his judgment on me whilst his other hand wipes tears from my round, warm cheeks. His thumb rests on my trembling bottom lip, pressing on the fullness.

With all my *insignificant* might, my open palms slam against his pointed ears hiding under knotted hair. A shout rips from his broad chest and I escape his grip, spitting words at him while he holds his head. "How do you know I haven't been already?"

I storm out of Steammire and the tears don't stop running until I reach the entrance back to the catacombs. Virgil lands on my shoulder before I enter the darkness, drawing some comfort to me. Until she starts. The hoarse decades old whisper in my head screams, blocking out every other noise and begging with such intensity, it might throw me under.

Virgil rustles his feathers, talons dig into my shoulder as his beak brushes my face, looking behind us and in front again. The tunnels are eerily quiet, it's a few hours before shift change but it's usually not *this* still. The crow steps onto my other shoulder, letting out a nervous squawk. There are no faelights here and without my goggles, I cannot see, but Virgil can. I retrieve both daggers strapped to my thighs, hoping they will be enough. Pointed ears twitch at the sound of footsteps approaching.

Four sets. Two approaching from behind, two from the front. Fuck. Pebbles are no longer crunching. I've never had this many come after me before. I debate taking out the explosive flask, but all that would do in here is collapse rock onto all of us, possibly even the entire lower labyrinths. A singular match lights inches from my face. Adrenaline surges and it takes everything inside me to pause, planning the best way to attack and not focus on the death waiting before me.

The white eyes of the male I humiliated earlier come to fruition, his wicked smile catches flickering shadows. The blood over his bare chest is just as visible as the pleasure spreading across the predator's face. He caught the pesky fox in a trap. The wound I gave him earlier is already healing, angry skin turning pink and closing up.

"How very brave, you brought some friends." I say, squaring my stance. I shoulder off Virgil who flies back out towards Slate. The Fae brings a finger to his cracked lips, his smile unnerves me to the core.

The match goes out.

Darkness falls as I do, blades slice out behind and in front of me. My left blade penetrates deep into a shoulder, right meets the air where the leader once was. Echoing screams ring my skull from the Fae I downed. Relentless arms take my waist and I throw my head back, slamming into a thick skull. Warmth spills onto my neck and shoulders but the attacker doesn't let go.

"*Fuck*, she's a fighter." A deep voice rumbles in front of me, laughing at the dismay the attacker behind me holds. I squirm in the tightening embrace and widen my shoulders, twisting to the right with a subtle movement.

"I'll take this." The taunting rumble in front approaches closer, and I swear I can smell the familiar charcoal from earlier. My daggers are yanked away from me, along with the rest of my weapons.

"Bitch gave me a *fuckin'* bloody nose. How do you like this, sweetheart?" The teasing from behind stops my blood cold. A hand brushes sticky warmth across my cheek, and a flicking tongue enters my ear.

"Haven't you heard, I'm into that kind of thing!" Fire shoots from my lungs and I slip down to the right, throwing my elbow into his abdomen. I stumble into a wall, the cold stone is electrifying and steadies me against the concussion ringing through my brain. There are no footsteps, and no one makes a sound in the darkness. I can't see, and they can. I have no weapons, and it's still three against one. I am entirely fucked. I can only think of one thing to do.

Ancients, if you're listening, I could really use some help.

Cold hands wrap around my throat, squeezing the air from my small being before lifting me away from the wall. Hands claw, my legs aim for the face below me. It's no use, the vengeance-fueled lover slams me into sharp gravel, knocking the world away. Air escapes from my chest, warmth oozes from my head and my soul disappears temporarily.

They waste no time seizing the opportune moment. The leader sits on my chest, pinning my arms down with skeletal knees. The other two males hold down my head and feet. Cold steel presses against my cheek, focusing my awareness on the poisonous voice above me in thick darkness. "Father will be quite pleased, two pits straight to the depths of hell."

The tip of his blade caresses my brow, then runs down my cheek and over my lips. Steel parts the fullness, drawing blood from my trembling bottom lip. The knife lifts and I move to jerk away, but the hands holding me down are immovable. Steel scratches my temple, causing my thighs to kick out in surprise, and the sound of metal scraping rock flattens my ears. A sadistic laugh echoes from them as they realize what was taken from me long ago, in a cave not so different to this.

"Well look at that, not so strong after all, are you?" The deep voice from my feet turns my blood cold. I snarl and attempt to kick him in the face as my pants are torn off, the straps to my sockets are next. Pain sears through my thighs, hips, and entire being as the sound of my metal legs thrown against the wall ring my ears.

Tears fall, at last.

"Vengeance never tasted so sweet." The Fae on my chest licks my cheek, delighting in the wet tears and blood mixed together he finds there. Tilting the blade upon my face, the tip of steel rests on my tear duct. Stinging, threatening to do more than just break the skin. I can't focus on either horror, I am done.

There is nothing else to do. A chest heaving scream echoes through the tunnels, then the tip of the blade sinks deep into my eye socket. Burning pain shoots through my skull, plummeting my mind and body into a seeping, glacial cold.

Am I still screaming, or does sound not exist anymore?

The meticulous Fae scrapes around my eye socket, careful to not damage the precious treasure inside. Pain is now a foreign word, his blade keeps close to the bone as it carves through my face. Something oozes down my cheek, meeting the pool of tears and blood underneath my broken skull. Sickness twists my entrails temporarily, then is replaced by ... Bliss.

True darkness is coming, at last, to bring me some relief. Suddenly the hands at my feet and head are gone, as well as the fight inside me. Taunting giggles and laughter echo from the world above. Another small flame flares above my cheek, revealing the last horror waiting for me.

An eyeball, black through and through, staring back at me with tendrils of ligaments hanging from its root. Then, the face of a bloodthirsty Fae and echoing sadistic laughter takes me under.

What Are Stars?

The evil here isn't enough to dim those bright silver eyes. The female High Fae may have lost her magic, but she would never stop fighting. Defiance filled every pore in her body.

I stood over her, a weapon waiting to strike. The other Keepers and I seized the rebels after a long and bloody battle, the dead from both sides littering the camps above and the trenches. We managed to capture her and her closest consorts alive, ready to execute them with fine dramatics.

Knothall shouted for us to wait, his deadly voice booming from the camps above. The Commander skidded to a halt at the edge of Keeper's Trench, stopping dead in his tracks as he took in the scene taking place along the dangerous lower edge.

"Rohana, what in the hell are you doing?" He growled at the beautiful Fae on her knees before me, staring her down with intense fury. She smiled at him, the wrinkles at her eyes pulling up with the fullness of it. Knothall locked eyes with me, anger fueling his face.

It was swift, clean. Her limber body and smiling face tumbled off the edge into the darkness below. The other rebels are dispatched and follow her down into the Aether void. I looked up to Knothall immediately, expecting praise. My mentor trained me every day for this moment, defending the machine.

Little did I know, he had left the moment my blade ended her life.

The dream ends with a notorious shout, pushing me off the edge and into darkness.

"Find me."

Pain is a surefire way to remind you that you're still alive. Pain in the heart, body and soul.

Terror fuels my movements. I throw myself upright and regret it in an instant. My prostheses aren't there to stabilize me and a terrifyingly dark world swallows me as I fall. Callused hands catch me as I roll off the wooden surface I lie on.

"Do not touch me!" I snarl, confusion and fear overwhelming me. I swing and push at the arms that now hold me, my tired hands meeting a leather strapped chest.

"Lythienne, stop." Knothall's stern voice centers me. My weak punches stop and he holds me tight in his arms like he did when I was a child. The first time I teased death. "You're safe."

Heaving, ugly sobs leave me, releasing centuries of hurt hidden inside. Pain twirls my mind into a sickening dance, heat spreads across my face as I cry. The river of tears do not care about the pain, and my sobs bury into his chest until I fall out of consciousness with my *shomer's* arms tight around me.

The next time I awake it's still dark, but I am in my own bed. The only movement I make are my ears twitching, evaluating who else might be here with me. It's silent, the smell of oil and parchment orients me.

After a moment of struggling with exhausted arms, I push myself up, moaning as I take in each pain and ache. Thank the Ancients, the only place that doesn't hurt is my pelvis. Of course, who would want to fuck an Empty Fae? The thought brings bile up my throat and I focus on feeling my thighs hidden under the blankets.

The stubs are lacerated and lonely without any socks, or sockets. Both legs hurt like a fucking bitch, but the throbbing in my forehead reminds me of my newest problem, a circulating pain made worse by every small movement. I can't tell if they took both my eyes, I only remember the one staring back at me. Truly, a portal to hell.

As I reach for the bandages around my eyes, someone clears their throat, perhaps five feet away. Too close for comfort. "I wouldn't do that if I were you."

I recognize Firthorn's disapproving voice at once and *scowl*. Goosebumps spread across my skin and heat warms my neck. "Get out, you are not welcome here." I try to sound intimidating, even if I am anything but at the moment.

"The healers recommend keeping it covered for another day or so. You're not ready yet." I don't hear any footsteps approaching, just his rumbling voice. How didn't I sense him?

"Did you not hear me?" I reach around me, feeling for something to throw at him. All I find are blankets and a smooth stone floor. I pause my jerky movements upon realizing my bed isn't on the loft above, but on the lab floor. To make life easier for the cripple. Anger spreads over me further and I wince at the pain of my eyebrows narrowing together.

"Yes, I *heard* you. Trust me, I would rather do anything else than watch you." Firthorn's warm presence settles beside me suddenly, his breath tickles my ear and sends a shiver through me. I am sure I heard him last night, but I can't imagine Knothall letting him live if he was. Unless the Commander doesn't know.

"I don't need your pity. You made your position very clear last night, why watch over me when you could finish the job?"

The Bear chuckles, a dark roar echoing off the walls. I wonder if his eyes are lit up in delight at my pain. "You don't need anyone's pity." I pull away instinctively from his disgusted voice creeping along my neck. Footsteps trace away from me and his voice is distant, unbothered. "Take it up with Knothall. You have been my assignment for three days now."

Three days since the attack. I must've slept through most of it. Only four days until my assignment. Fuck.

"And I must say, it's rather boring." Firthorn taunts from across the room, my nose perks up at the smell of herbs floating towards me. Before I can ask, smoke tickles my face and teases me. I reach my hand out and he places the wooden pipe directly in my palm. His touch causes my shoulders to rise.

"I'm sorry to disappoint you, but I don't mind your being uncomfortable." I muse and inhale deep, the throbbing pain in my face and legs dulls into manageable aches after a moment. Silence creeps between us for several minutes. We share the pipe and he ensures to place it firmly in my hand each time. I search my memories for definitive proof he was part of the gang, but he interrupts me.

"I think the day you stop fighting, is the day you disappoint me."

I bite my cheek and sigh. Shivers escape and I pull the blankets closer around me, then give into vulnerability. Maybe he'll make another move if I do. "Take them off, please," My lips and voice tremble, "I don't want to be in the dark anymore."

Boots scuff and stop for a moment. His large hands pause at my shoulders to notify me of his presence before he brings them up to my neck, stopping at the bandages. "I turned the lamp down." He remarks, and I wince as he begins to unwind the bandage, his rough hands fumbling as he does.

As the last wrap comes undone, a gasp escapes me. I blink, adjusting to the dim shapes and shadows around me. The shape of my bed is resting against the wall, a large chair and a low table with a dimmed lamp beside it. The study area is now a tidy infirmary. Panrauth's ragged breathing washes over my shoulders, the Bear still kneeling behind me. If he's been watching me for three days, he definitely could've killed me or taken my other eye while I was sleeping. Unless he wanted a conscious participant, but that doesn't sound right either.

"Come here." My words aren't entirely audible, but he obeys. The Bear comes around to kneel on the floor in front of me, his hair and beard hide him in the shadows. After a moment of adjusting, I notice a streak of pink on his otherwise dark and blurred features. He studies my face and I avert my eye.

"Do you want to see?" He asks flatly. I shake my head, cursing under my breath at the movement.

"No, I ... No. I just want to know what happened. To my other eye." I already know what happened to the first one.

"The healers say it will heal. The attack was," Panrauth rubs at his neck, "interrupted, before any more damage was done. Your vision should return in another day or two." He flexes his jaw and not so subtly glances down at my thighs covered by blankets.

"For fuck's sake, what is it?" I manage, then swallow and blink away burning tears.

"Knothall is repairing them. It will take a couple of days." He says simply, then stands and holds up a fresh bandage, raising a brow as he does. I nod, words caught in my throat.

What am I going to do for two days? It won't take long for predators to smell their opportunity. Panrauth's hands are gentler than before. He wraps around my swollen right eye socket, leaving the other free to see. After he's finished, he wanders to the big chair and falls into it, rubbing his temple and leaving distance between us. I lay down and pull the blankets back up, noting the mid-morning hour on the clock.

His gaze burns into me and after a few moments I can't take it anymore. "Quit looking at me like that."

Panrauth snorts. "Like what?"

The chair creaks as he leans forward, arms resting on his legs. I prop up on an elbow and scowl at him. "Like you might be my friend."

His lips push into a thin line and he watches me for a moment before admitting, "I find you interesting. I've known since that day in the pit you aren't my enemy." He fiddles with his beard and I stare him down, waiting. "What I said before, it came out a *bit* more intense than I meant it to be." Panrauth pauses, rubbing his neck. "This place, you have been here for who knows how long, and yet you still have so much fight in you."

Not anymore.

"I've been here for 236 years. My entire life." My eyes turn down to my lap and he pushes out a long breath. "I bet a year doesn't seem so long now, does it?"

"One day is one day too many." He mutters.

"Yes, this is true." I sniff and he settles back in the chair, crossing his bulky arms. I roll away from him and clutch the blankets. It's quiet for a few minutes until Panrauth whispers from his corner.

"Do you remember the surface?"

"No." I clench my jaw, pushing the word out of my mouth. "Whoever my parents were, they took one look at my emptiness and sent me here." I pause as he shifts in his chair. I am telling him more about me than anyone before, and I can't seem to stop myself. "Knothall will tell me anything I want to know." I trail off for a moment, unable to speak without breaking. I know he will let it go if I don't want to continue. But, I need to say it.

"I have no idea who my parents are. Where I'm from. What powers I might've been privileged with. I never wanted to know. The only thing I know about myself is my first name."

Panrauth heaves out a heavy breath and I watch his shadow settle on the wall. After a few moments, he speaks with softness. "It doesn't matter who you were. The only thing that matters is who you are going to be."

I don't say anything, just pull the blankets over my head and wait for sleep. Instead, I am met with nightmares.

White eyes with blood dripping from the tear ducts fill my dreamscape. The jilted Fae stands over me with numerous dangling black eyes in his fingers. He wields my dagger, then launches it into my heart. Panrauth's laughter rings through the tightening cave walls, and the whispers of a desperate pleading mix with the grating sound.

"Find me!"

I wake with a scream caught in my throat, rough hands shake my shoulders. "Lythienne." Panrauth's desperate voice yanks me into reality.

He kneels on the bed in front of me, knees on either side of my legs, eyes wild and hair in a tussle around his face. Panrauth loosens his grip and slides onto the floor, beside the bed. The rise and fall of my chest is even again after a few minutes of silence and I clutch the blankets closer around me. My old nightmares are tangling with new ones. I will never find sleep anymore. Not that I did much before.

Panrauth absently braids several locks together near his ear, the furred brown points twitching as he brushes across them. His rough hands are more nimble, slower than usual. "When I was a boy, my mother would take me to the tallest oak in the forest," His voice is soft and for a moment his hands and words pause, then continue. "We would lie in the treetops for hours, she taught me everything about the constellations and old legends of Iverbourne, before the war."

"What do they look like?" I bite my cheek, thinking of how absurd the question is. "The stars?"

Pan reaches a steady hand out to mine, still grasping a handful of quilted blankets. After a moment I take it, finding comfort in the warmth waiting for me. I look over his face, alight with that unfamiliar expression. Hope.

"They are glittering specks of silver and gold, splashed against the darkest velvet skies. On clear nights, you can see both moons trailing across the sky, lighting up the lands."

My eye glistens and I smile, lying back with his hand still in mine. I attempt to sleep once more and try to imagine what stars look like, and the world they hang over.

WOULD YOU KILL FOR IT?

I awake in a tussle of blankets and pillows, my only companion a gut wrenching headache. I groan and rise on an elbow, shaking the bird's nest out of my face. Brows draw together at the sight of drool on my shirt, drawing pain across my forehead.

I sit up fully and peek over to the stretching master table and kitchenette beyond it. No hulking bear to be seen. I rub at my bruised thighs and notice my old wooden wheelchair parked beside the mattress, rusted brakes on. A scrap of parchment rests on the seat.

Take a shower, you run hotter than the machine. I'll be back this evening with food.

-P

I smirk and lift my shirt up, inhaling the smell wafting from underneath. A breath whooshes out and I mutter, "Guess a shower can't hurt." After pulling myself up into my chair, I find a packed pipe on the table and cannot hide the growing smile as I indulge myself. As I smoke, I think about Panrauth. I've decided he couldn't have been part of the attack, but he definitely knows something.

The small granite washroom has wooden bars installed along the walls, resting beside the toilet and bathtub. I haven't used them in quite some time, they remain from my days before prosthesis and during the adjustment periods when I was growing. I'm usually not upright without my prosthesis on in case of emergency, but today I'm glad for the accessibility. I strip down and transfer from the chair to the edge of the tub, pausing as I check the temperature. It's already filled and my curious fingers dip into clear lukewarm water.

Someone was quite generous this morning.

I sigh and sink into the water, then my broken nails scrub greasy hair and layers of soot off my skin. Grime and evil refuses to wash away, clinging to every molecule of my spirit. I stay under until my lungs ache, then shoot above the surface and gasp for air when the burning is too much.

I catch my reflection in the mirror after I dry off, the sight halts my hurry. Naked and seated in my chair again, simple beauty shines from under all the scars marring my complexion and the blood clinging to my soul. I run long fingers through my bright purple hair, tresses light and free of knots, a few shades lighter than before. The shade reminds me of glittering Aether straight from the Machine, specks of blue once hidden under the soot are revealed now.

Like how I imagine stars are.

Color fills my otherwise pale cheeks at the sight of the pink scar originating above my left eye. It travels through my brow, over my eyelid and down my cheek, then arcs sideways to my ear dramatically. For a scar to remain after days of Faerie healing, the interrupted slice must've been deeper than the initial injuries to my other eye. The right side of my face is near perfect, the angry swelling around my eye socket is already coming down. He even left my eyelid behind. Two sides of the same face, completely different.

Father will be quite pleased.

I shudder at the surgical precision the Fae possessed. I don't even know his name, or anything about him. The memory of the lover's last moments burns my spirit further.

Staring each other down and willing silent words across the distance, the steel blade pushes against her throat as he watches from the sidelines. Blood drips to the floor, the guard waiting for my order to finish her.

The hair on my neck pricks upwards. Perhaps I deserve it, every bit of evil that's happened to me. I am only an insufferable Keeper, squashing any chance those inmates have at ever even smelling magic again. Is magic that wonderful? Is the shimmering Aether worth dying for?

I snarl at the mirror, then smash my fist into the glass and hundreds of shards shatter around me.

Eros lounges on the master table, ankles crossed and dangling over the edge while she waits for me. I wheel up to the table, cursing myself for fucking my hand up too as it protests the splintered wheel of my chair. I can't even remember the last time I used this contraption, if I had known it was going to be needed I would've given it an upgrade. Blood is already seeping through the fraying bandages, ready to drip from the clenched hands I keep at bay in my lap.

"May I help you?" I ask, tone flat.

The epitome of fabled winter hops down and circles around me, tracing a glacial finger along my shoulders. Goosebumps spread across my arms as a small giggle escapes from her. "When I heard you were still alive, I just had to see for myself. You've made yourself into quite the legend around here." She settles in front of me, then leans back on the table and faces me. I shift in my seat as her playful gaze evaluates me, raising her white brows as she does so.

I am quite pathetic, dressed in ripped black leggings, an old pair I hemmed at the thighs. A gray short sleeved tunic flows over my muscled shoulders, and a simple linen wraps around my eye. The everyday obsidian carry is strapped to my right thigh again, my left leg holds a plain dagger. I gave up on carrying the explosive orb around, it's useless down here. Unless I want to take down every creature in this place with me, which is quite tempting at this point. The attack was the time to use it, but I didn't. I'm not ready to give up.

I continue to stare at Eros' face, waiting in silence for her to get to the point. She taps her foot twice before twirling at her white tresses, curiosity spreads across the predator's sharp features. "For someone who has," she pauses, eyes cast upwards and searching, "protected the Machine, as well as you do, it should be no surprise. Being Knothalls pet can't hurt, either."

I wince at the word *pet*, she twists it with the same amount of disdain that Ragnis does. Eros leans down and places both hands on the arms of my chair. Snow white straight tresses flow down between us, blood throbs against her slender neck. I unsheathe my right dagger and press the black blade against her flexing artery. She narrows her brows and tilts her head, exposing her throat and daring me to do it. I bite my lip and press the blade firmly but her body encroaches further, delicate lips brush against my ear.

"You certainly deserve power. I wonder, what would you do with it?" A shudder threatens to break my hold on her. Blood splashes in thick drops onto my lap, mixing with my own crimson mess from my shaking bandaged hands. "You have the scent of a killer. Would you destroy the world with me?"

Eros leans back, ears flicking at the sound of my heart racing as she awaits my answer. The small slice at her neck reveals a thick, dark blue and intoxicating blood. The sickly sweet smell overwhelms my sinuses the same way magic does, and it's then I realize a crucial fact. I am staring into the eyes of a beast who leaks pure Aether. She is no ordinary Fae, her oily blood is something I've never witnessed or read of in all of my life.

My blade loosens and free eyelid flutters when her hand raises, hovering over my right eye. Focus returns to my left eye as a soft blue mist flows from her hand, similar to Umber's, but more elegant and precise. Sizzling pain jolts me in the chair and the fog from her hand retracts with haste. The scent of burning flesh floats in the inches between us.

"Prisoners can't have magic in their bodies. Not that I would want any from you, I know better than to deal with faeries." I snarl, heart reeling and hand readjusting on my dagger. In all reality, it will do me little good against this force of nature.

Her thin, white brows scrunch together as her hand ponders in the air neighboring my face, but lacks magic. "Do you really?" Eros whispers with excitement on her tongue, then her fingers move to my crown and trace along a free lock. "I could give you everything, darling. We would be unstoppable."

Stone overtakes my body, heat licks my neck and teases between my thighs. What the *fuck*? I open my lips, unsure what to say. Eros' offer is quite tempting, and I am tired of fighting the inevitable dark side of myself. With her I could ...

"Don't you crave Aether flowing through your veins? To be like everyone else? For the hate to end?" Her seductive words break me from my moment of consideration.

I straighten and bring my lips an inch away from hers with renewed fury rushing through every inch of my being. "I would rather die as myself, than to live as anyone else."

Wide, white eyes flash with Aether and transport me to the caves long enough for my heart to stop beating. A smile tugs at one corner of her full lips, her breath pushes onto my trembling bottom lip. "Good girl." She whispers and leans back, quite pleased. With a snap of her long fingers, a flurry of white specks waft through the air, sucking her into a swirling vortex.

A singular fleck lands on my nose and I shiver under the minuscule cold, then hold out a hand to catch another small crystal. This must be snow. Virgil lets out a squawk as stray flurries rustle his feathers, disturbing the otherwise unbothered bird.

Panrauth returns late in the evening, finding my lab filled with smoke. The mechanism I had been tinkering with earlier after Eros left shutters across the stone floor, heat caressing its erratic metal carcass as it travels across the lab.

"Lyth?" His voice booms against rock, my ears fold down against my neck at his echoing thunder.

"So nice of you to *finally* arrive." I snark at him from the floor, slumped against a cupboard in the kitchenette. Panrauth rushes over from the entry, his raised shoulders drop when he finds me nursing a half burnt pipe. His wild hair is braided back and even his beard has plaits now. I pat the floor next to me and he obliges, setting down his satchel beside him. I pass him the pipe and we share it, silent for a moment.

"I didn't mean to be gone for so long. Knothall added a few tasks on my way out." Pan states whilst watching me push out a ring of smoke. We are shoulder to shoulder, the unfamiliar touch should send panic through me, but it doesn't. I lean into his warmth, instead.

"Eros was here. Waiting for me after my bath." My words are quiet, questioning. Apparently the watch Knothall set up for me was inadequate at best, and my gut tells me it was intentional. My heart protests the idea of my shomer putting me in harm's way, but so far he hasn't proved otherwise. All Knothall has proved is the fact he's hiding things from me.

"The Commander and that witch have been thick as thieves from what I heard in Slate. No challenge has been called." He shrugs, finishing off the remaining herb in the pipe.

I rub my neck, my worry deepening. "Yet." I remind him. Knothall will never let such a dangerous, unchecked variable disrupt his Eternal, regardless of his plans. I shudder and my ravenous pit rumbles. I can't remember the last time I ate anything. "Did you at least bring food?"

Panrauth laughs heartily. "Yes, I brought us food." He retrieves a cloth bag from his satchel, revealing the buttery loaf hidden inside. I straighten, but our bodies don't separate. He breaks a chunk off for both of us, and we collectively moan as the freshness hits our tongues.

"How was Umber?" I press a bite under my nose and breathe in deeply. He smirks, looking at me sideways. I never noticed the light green highlights in his otherwise dark beard, and there are even some strewn through his hair.

"She was ... Umber. Almost ripped my head off until I told her who the bread was for." Panrauth pulls out a pouch from the satchel and hands it to me, the smell of herbs wafts out at once. Excitement spreads, then is quickly replaced by worry. I set the herbs beside me, my mouth turning down.

"What did you tell her?"

"That you pissed off the wrong people." Humor is attempted, but the guttural sound in his voice breaks the facade. I can't disagree with him. I tempted a wounded beast, not once, but twice. It's been a long time coming, and I should've been more prepared.

"Umber's a good friend. She'll be fine." I stare across the room, my eyes glazing over with too many thoughts.

We sit on the cold stone for several minutes, neither of us very hungry now. The malfunctioning contraption finally gives up, the echoing rattle ceases as well. Pan leans a little heavier on me and wets his lips, words wanting to tumble out but too afraid to escape. His emerald eyes meet mine and his broad jaw tightens.

"What is it?" I creep my hand across his thigh and bring it to rest on his knee. Testing the waters.

But that's not what's on his mind. "Who took them from you?" He surprises me, but the primal question brings warmth to my growing desire.

"Stragglers from our great performance." A sly smile plays at my lips. Pan lays his hand out beside mine on his leg, palm up and open for me to take. I thoughtlessly trace the deep labor lines there, finding solace. Until he speaks.

"The first time." He manages to clarify through gritted teeth.

"*Oh.*" I focus on his skin, running my long fingers up and down the veins rising from hardened muscle. The feeling of someone's skin touching mine is not one I am familiar with, and the sensation is addicting. I raise my attention to his face, and he watches me with those eyes that have glimpsed stars. I know he will let it go if I choose to be silent.

I am tired of being silent.

"Believe it or not, I wasn't always such a hard ass." I smirk, continuing my trail up and down his forearm. His warm skin gives me strength. "When I was eight, Knothall had a bad batch of inmates working at the Machine. I didn't know as much then, hell I wasn't even allowed to leave his quarters until I was around six years old. My world opened to include this lab, Amwren's lab at the time. Knothall commanded me to stay in the lab with her and focus on my studies,"

I gesture around us, a small smile fills my face as I remember the first time the winged Fae attempted to teach me the basics of machinery. I was always full of energy and could never sit still, but once my hands found work, I never stopped tinkering.

"I wanted to be with him. I knew he wasn't my father, but I was lonely. He was always leaving me behind. So I snuck out and went to find him," I shrug softly, "at the time, the thought of leaving the lab, defenseless and small, wasn't a dangerous one. Somehow, he managed to keep me sheltered and hidden away with the inmates, away from evil."

Our bodies are melded so closely I can feel his heart racing, and his twitching ears must hear mine too as his thick fingers wrap around mine and grip tight.

"Needless to say, I never made it to the Machine." I swallow, avoiding his face. "By the time they found me, it was too late. The healers couldn't do anything, not without magic anyway." I wipe at the tears falling and sniff, the knuckles on my other hand blanch from holding on so tight onto his. The first time I had wished for Aether in my life, and the last.

"I never knew." He whispers.

I laugh darkly. "Why the hell would I let anyone know my biggest weakness?"

Panrauth grabs my chin immediately, gentle but firm. He lifts my watering gaze and I stare into simmering green begging to come to the surface, restrained by the power of this place. "Lythienne, you are not weak. What you are lacking is not proof of weakness. It is proof of your strength."

Pan caresses my chin with his thumb, moving up to trace my right brow. He leans in, kissing my forehead with a soft tenderness. "This too."

I shiver against him, his lips turn up against my skin before he pulls away. I bite my lip and smile. "I suppose you can be right. Sometimes."

"I'll take what I can get." He murmurs and gives me a small smile, then winks at me in the most subtle of ways. *Fuck*, I am hungrier for him every moment I spend in his presence. "So, then what? Obviously it didn't stop you." Pan says with a hint of something warm in his voice, perhaps pride?

"No, not much does it seems. I healed and learned to live on contraptions for legs, then Knothall and I trained, and never stopped. I wouldn't be left defenseless again." I rub my left temple and shake hair from my face, drawing sarcasm into my words. "Which worked out splendidly, centuries of work down the drain."

"Three against one is hardly a fair fight." He mumbles, releasing his grip. I shift on the floor and push out a breath, heat pricking my neck as I digest. Did I hear him right?

"I didn't realize Knothall was such a busy body."

Pan watches me over as his truth comes out. "Knothall didn't find you. I did."

Cold settles in my gut. "And what did you find?" I ask, moving from massaging my temple to my thigh. He reaches across me and grabs the satchel and pipe, packing it in silence. "That bad?" I huff out.

"You're in pain." He says matter of factually, then hands me the pipe and another match. Virgil squawks from the corner and peers through a singular sleepy eye at us. Pan puffs slow and long, watching Virgil for a moment, then points the wooden stem of the pipe at the bird. "That demon bird of yours," He shakes his head and passes the pipe to me,

"After you left, I wanted to clarify things." Pan rubs the back of his neck, glancing at me with shame coloring his face. "I was on my way back when the damn thing started dive bombing me. I was going to give it a good thwack," I raise my brows, smiling a little, "then I heard you." He fiddles with his beard, rubbing the hair between his fingers. I wipe off a dirt patch on my pants, keeping my gaze averted.

"Your voice ... In all my years, I have never heard anything like it. One moment I was drunk off my ass, fighting with a damned bird, and the next I was standing over three bodies. And yours. I thought you were dead, I didn't know."

Someone got away. I bury the terror rising in me, and instead focus on him. I raise my trembling lip, meeting his strong face. The wetness in his eyes surprises me. He grasps my hand again and I inhale sharply. "When I brought you to Knothall, he told me to go back. After some searching I found your prosthesis, but they weren't functional anymore."

My ears ring and I pull away from him, then bury my face in my palms, allowing pain to sweep over my right temple. Ragged breathing is the only sound through the stale air. I had it all wrong.

"There was a moment in the tunnel. I was convinced you were there." I remain hunched over, admitting truth. "I thought you hated me, you have every right to. After what I did to you, your friends-"

"Lyth, look at me." Desperation fills his voice and I tear my face from wet hands. Tears fall into his dark beard and silence. His gaze dashes across my face for heavy seconds. "Who you are, and what they make you be, they are two different people." I wipe away the tears from his cheeks, my hand finds rest on his furred jaw. He takes it, kissing my palm with care. "I meant what I said, about us in the pit."

A small smile pulls at my lips. "I know you do." I am sure of it now. Panrauth isn't my enemy. Not anymore.

"So, are you gonna tell me what happened there?" He nods to my other bandaged hand, covered in blood and soot, and to the oily blood staining my lap and shirt.

"Nothing I can't handle." I jut my chin to the wheelchair waiting along the wall opposite from us. "I don't want to use that right now. Will you," I bite my lip and push out a breath, "will you carry me to bed? I'm tired."

He bows his head and slips an arm under my thighs, the other behind my back. I wrap my relatively small arms around his neck and we rise in a smooth, fluid movement. I admire the braid running down his crown, ending at his waist. Pan raises a brow haughtily, catching me studying him. I look away with haste, ignoring the warmth spreading through my nerves once more. Pan kneels, then sets me down delicately on the bed.

He sketches a bow after standing. "Anything else, my lady?"

Fear entwines with my question. "Are you leaving?"

Panrauth crosses his arms and stares down at me. "Do you want me to?"

"No." I blurt out, his brows raise at my quickness. "I don't want to be alone. Please." I look down at the purple and black quilt Amwren made for me, shame filling me with the last word.

"If you wish, I will not leave your side. Until you get sick of me, that is." I know he's serious, despite the teasing. I manage a nod, then bite my lip and keep my face turned down.

"I have a few things to do. Sleep now, I'll be just over there." He gestures to the master table in the middle of the lab.

I lay down, pulling the blankets up around my face when he takes his leave. I close my eyes and listen to the sound of paper rustling, followed by a gentle tap of fingers and a forced out breath. "Thank you for saving my life, Pan." Goosebumps run across my skin, not only at his name, but as I realize that was exactly what he did.

Papers pause and thick, warm air pushes down on me, the silence continues for another moment before his whisper reaches me. "Thank you for showing me what it means to fight again."

I smile, removing the bandage from my face. It's uncomfortable to lie on, and I don't really need it anyway. What I said to Eros, it's true, for this too. I don't want to hide any part of me anymore, scars and all.

SHE'S DEAD

A new terror.

I am lost in the dark tunnels, crawling in shards of rocks and without my prosthesis. Repeated flashes of a blinding white light illuminate mutilated body parts along my path. When I reach the dead end, Knothall is waiting with Eros in his lap.

A throne of blood and iron is shared between them, blood gushing from their dais and spreading through the tunnel. Immediately it covers my hands and legs, the warmth sickens me and twists my entrails. The winter Fae leans into his ear, whispering with upturned lips. Blood fills my lungs and I drown in the sea, screaming for someone to find me. They both laugh, watching me pull under the tide.

I jolt awake, the dagger under my pillow in hand as I swing out, but a rough hand stops my wrist. Panic swells across, warmth and adrenaline filling my entire body. Before I can stop myself, I throw all my energy into headbutting my enemy. I meet darkness and a heavy weight pushing on my side.

"That would've felt great." Pan's gruff voice pulls me from my nightmare and I slump, he releases my wrist. The bed creaks and the lantern on the side table flickers to life within a moment.

He's bare chested with wild hair undone, voice teasing. "I thought you were done trying to kill me." He sits back on the bed, beside my bare thighs.

"Bad dream." I mutter, pulling up the blankets around my hips.

"Do you want to talk about it?" The Bear rests his arms on his knees, running a hand through his hair.

"No."

"I can't hear you." Of course he can hear me. We are two faeries sitting next to each other. "Look at me." He orders after a moment.

I huff and look at him, wondering what the dancing shadows across my face behold. An empty eye socket and a pit of darkness. "*What*?" I bite out, warmth pricking my neck.

A gentle hand encompasses my right cheek, his careful thumb caresses my face. My wrinkled brows soften and I study his handsome face looking at me. Really looking at me, like no one else ever has. "You are more beautiful than any star I have beheld, Lythienne." A deep smile quirks up a corner of his lips, his eyes brighten.

We sit there for a moment, staring into each other's souls. Neither of us look away, memorizing every bit of the other's face. I can't take it anymore. I want to be loved, and I feel like he can love me, or pretend to.

I throw my arms around his neck and for a moment he is completely still, hands unsure what to do. Lavender hair tumbles over his bare shoulder, lifting him out of his stupor. He grasps my hips and pulls me onto his lap gingerly. Walnut hair falls over my own shoulders when he holds me close, the warmth of our bodies meld at last.

Two bodies, one entirely too small and the other entirely too big, holding tight to a chance at pleasure, at feeling something other than pain.

I run a hand up his broad back until fingers tangle in his soft hair. I lift my face from his firm shoulder to study his work worn features lit under the warm lantern glow. My careful fingertips travel across his jaw, raking through his beard. It's fluffed now, free of ash and sweat.

Pan lets out a soft moan while I explore his beard, chest vibrating with a purr. His length twitches under me, pressing on his pants and begging to be let free. My curious hand travels down his throbbing neck and chest, palm coming to rest on his pounding heart. His dire grip on my hips tighten, drawing more need from me. "Lythienne."

Ears twitch at my name on his lips, he draws it out with a tenderness I don't recognize. I sigh when his traveling hand breaks from my waist and reaches up my back. The rough hand wades through my hair, his hungry eyes watch as the purple locks fall onto the pale skin of my bare shoulders. My thin tank top is nothing under his gaze and I tremble again, the nerves in between my thighs on fire and calling to be touched.

I want him, all of him.

Courage swells and I lay a hand on his face, then gently lower my lips to his.

The Bear brushes loose strands from my forehead and lays a careful kiss between my brows, avoiding my lips. He gives me a weak smile, his mouth pushing into a thin line after he confesses. "I can't." His fingers at my neck loosen and my face falters. I immediately pull away from the pleasure that didn't want me back. How could I let myself believe I could have him, that he wants me just as much?

"I understand." I murmur. Pan's strong figure stiffens and his hand is firm behind my neck once more, keeping me in place.

"No, you don't." His eyes are fierce, unflinching. "I haven't been with anyone since ..." Jaw muscles flex madly, keeping the last words buried inside.

I am a fucking idiot. I didn't even think about it. The moment he says the words, I am reminded of his voice warming at the thought of reuniting with his family.

"I'm sorry, I didn't even think ..." Of anyone but myself. I avert my glistening attention and bite my cheek, shame filling me. Once more he tugs my face to his, tough fingers gentle on my round chin.

"I have to get back to my girls." He says, tearing a hole in me.

"And their mother?" I ask before my bravery fades. His warm hand leaves my round cheek at once.

"She's dead, and that's all I wish to say about it."

I sleep through the last few hours of morning, every startle and jerk is met by strong arms lulling me back into an otherwise deep slumber.

When I awake, Pan's chin rests on my head. One arm is snaked around my waist and his free hand sweeps through my hair. I listen to his heart thunder under my cheek, eyes closed. The same way we fell asleep, or I did, at least.

"Good morning," I yawn, glaring down at the drool on my twisted shirt. He chuckles, the rumbling in his chest awakens the sparking need in my gut. Pan kisses my forehead and sighs, breathing me in.

"All I want is to hold you." He whispers, clearing the grogginess from my mind. "I don't know what's right, I didn't expect to feel like this again. This feels like a betrayal to what we had." Pan breaks a little, his once strong chest heaving under me. I nuzzle into his thick neck, hiding in his beard and contemplating the right words. I wonder if he stayed up all night, thinking about her.

"Will you tell me about her?" I ask quietly. Based on the rounded ears of his daughters in the picture, their mother must've been Human. The lab is silent for a long time, his chest unsteadily rises and falls with my relaxed body half sprawled across. I don't know if I've ever felt this safe and comfortable, and a small voice inside warns me to not let my guard down too quickly.

"Her name was Weylin." Her name captures the air in his lungs, and after a moment of recovery he continues in a whisper. "She tended to the earth like a child, caressing each leaf and speaking to every animal as if they were her best friends. And the most beautiful dark skin, the girls get that from her."

"What are their names? Your girls."

"Estienne and Mirah, they're twins." He sighs, voice trailing for a moment. Even I know twins are quite rare among faeries. "They will be ten in a month, on the summer solstice. Must have stolen fire right from the sun they did, quite a handful."

"I wonder where they get that from." I tease and sit up on an elbow, he holds a small smile but sadness lingers in his eyes. "I don't think it's too much, anymore." I run a hand through his bushy beard, admiring how my skin that's never seen the sun hides under the hazel hair along his jaw.

"What do you mean?" He tilts his head.

"To hope. When I'm with you, that's what I feel. You bring me hope."

"Will you wait?" He asks, heart thundering against me, threatening to burst. I ponder his question and both of his muscled arms tighten around my figure.

"I will wait, as long as you keep your promise. You won't leave."

"I will always be by your side, Lyth. You have my word."

"Good." I pull away and he releases me, his body takes up the entirety of my bed.

A blacksmithing beast. Pan crosses his hands behind his head and my gaze pauses on his dark haired chest, the numerous muscles composing his thick torso dare me to follow the ripples downwards. I make it to the slight v of muscles above his pantline before I notice Pan watching me with a tight jaw, his body has no trouble wanting my own. The obvious bulge in his pants presses on the tight seam of his trousers and I find myself staring, wondering what it would feel like to be filled with it.

I look away, flushing at my shamelessness. I catch his wild eyes pause on my full breasts falling out of my discombobulated shirt.

Ice replaces the desire in my heart, he's frowning at the scars there, a multitude of blisters left over and over again by a vicious Fire Fae. Ragnis' Aether kept them from healing normally, and over time the angry scars the size of coins have piled on top of each other. I scoot to the edge of the bed, finding the dimly lit table beside us very interesting.

"I have a plan. I'm going to help you, but you'll have to do everything I say. *Exactly* the way I say it."

Pan sits up hastily, grasping my hand. "I've never been so excited for a female to boss me around."

I tap my spoon against the metal bowl, watching between the clock and the door. Pan strokes Virgil who is perched on the master table and I rest on a stool at the kitchenette island.

"He's coming," Pan muses.

"Well, he can't come fast enough." I bite out, shoveling cold porridge down my gullet. Pan strides over and leans on the island with an amused look on his face.

"Aren't you going to eat?" I ask over a mouthful.

"Oh no, I raided the cupboards about the time your snoring was unbearable." Pan grins with deep sarcasm.

I bite my lip and cheeks warm. "I do not." He arches a knowing brow, a smile tugs at his lips. I fling a spoonful of porridge at him as the door opens, causing me to barely miss.

I jerk my head up to Knothall, breathless and red faced at the doorway. Pan casually walks to the opposite side of the island, crossing his arms. Knothall walks over to us and releases a breath upon taking me in, a large leather duffel bag slung across his back. "You look well."

I laugh wholeheartedly, not caring if my face protests. "I look like shit, shomer. But I appreciate the sentiment." I straighten in my seat and Knothall rolls his eyes, relief washing over his wrinkled features. He regards Pan for a moment under a hard gaze.

"Firthorn, you are needed in the armory and blade smith's. *Now.*" Pan dips his chin and glances at me sideways before leaving. I bite my cheek, I've never called him shomer in front of anyone but Amwren.

Knothall sets the bag on the island beside me, then unbuttons it with care. "I'm sorry it took me so long," He pushes out a hurried breath, "I thought you would want these." He gestures to the gaping bag and I reach in, pulling out the left prosthesis first. I pause and look up to him, then back down at the magnificent prosthesis in my hands.

I caress the calf, a lightweight metal finished with a pale cream that matches my skin. I manipulate the knee and ankle joints, marveling at how the leg flexes easily. I press my ear against the smooth surface on the upper calf, listening as tiny gears click together. I gaze up to my mentor with tears in my eyes. "These aren't my old ones."

He sniffs and removes a simple socket composed of an unyielding dark material I'm not familiar with out of the bag, along with a sock and liner. "You do not attach these with a strap." He explains and I tilt my head at him, brows pulling together as I silently watch. "They work by vacuum seal. The sockets are modeled after your old ones, but if they don't fit we will have to hurry with a new set."

"Will you help me?" I ask quietly, pulling up the fabric of my linen shorts. He kneels, first sliding on the thick socks over my thighs. The ends are bruised but healing, I assume they were injured when my other pair were ripped off. A shudder rolls through me as he situates the liner over top next, a soft cushioning material that caresses my entire thigh. Another long sock rests over the liner, and I pull the hem of my shorts up to hug my upper thigh.

I remember the first time we did this, a year after my attack. I couldn't walk on my own and the first pair was so heavy, but for a painful moment I was able to stand on the stone floor, not crawl. With Knothall holding my hand, of course.

"Are you ready?" The Commander asks. I nod and he slides the socket around my residual limb, the pressure builds and sends a moment of pain through me. Luckily it's a comfortable, snug fit. With a whoosh of air the socket seals around the liner and sock. He repeats the process on my other leg.

"That's it?" I ask, it doesn't seem very practical, no straps or anything to hold it in place.

"Are you doubting me? I had my best engineers on this." He scoffs, rising to stand.

"No, I apologize. Thank you." My cheeks warm and I place a hand on either side of the upper leg, then pull it onto the socket. A near silent click purrs under my fingers as the prosthesis seals around it, but with less discomfort. I release my hands and let the beautiful weight hang. I swing my leg back and forth, the knee joint purrs with movement. "It's so easy. There is no resistance."

I pull on the other prosthesis and swing it, a little too hard. I smash it into the counter and curse at the shock wave, slamming a fist into the table. I glare at a smirking Knothall, then a small smile escapes when I find his own. "Thank you."

"I want you to have everything that you need." He states, laughter fading into seriousness once more. My hip muscles are already awake with a passion to move, and then sleep.

"For what?" I ask, head tilted. He nods to the bag and puts a finger to his lips. I reach in and find a note, then unfold it.

Change of plans, your assignment is tonight.

Take Firthorn with you and only what you need. My last assignment to you is to deliver this package to the High Lady of Hallowed Court.

Tell no one of your mission, come to Slate and be ready at shift change.

I don't know if I ever told you, but I love you, Lythienne.

You made life here worth living.

-Shomer

Tears splash onto the parchment and I jerk my attention up to him, or where he once was. I read it again, caressing the last passage. The lab closes in on me, thick air squeezes out of my chest. I close my eyelids and inhale deeply through my nose, then exhale from my mouth. I shake off my feelings and attempt to stand on my own.

I shift out of the seat and lean heavily on the table while my hips and thighs remember how to be knees and legs as well. With slow movements, I transfer more of my weight to my legs instead of my muscled arms. My sore thighs welcome the fresh cushioning in the sockets that envelope my entire upper legs. I push out a breath and straighten, releasing the table from my grip.

I waver and my heart sputters, these prostheses are lighter and more agile than my old ones. The ankle and knee joints vibrate wonderfully with each movement, providing much more range of motion than I'm used to. I step forward and put way too much weight into it.

I fall flat on my face, my now scraped arms barely break my head's contact with the stone. "Fuck!" I growl in frustration, rolling onto my back. I won't be able to use these on my own yet, not without a cane. How in the hell am I supposed to enact an escape plan?

I sit up with a groan, the elbows of my tunic are chewed up from the stone floor. I spy my old cane hanging by the stairs and grin, an invention coming to mind. I pull myself up using the nearest stool with a string of curses and use the counter to limp along. I make my way to the old thing, a stump of wood with a tip on the bottom. I take it and inspect its length for a moment, then slam it down on the table and get to work.

It's late afternoon by the time Pan returns, covered in soot and carrying two leather bags. He plops them next to my own packed bag on the counter obnoxiously. I'm facing away from him, standing at the soldering table. I can feel his gaze burn up and down my figure, the hair on my arms stands up under his evaluation.

I am wearing a thick dark tunic, and over top rests a leather jerkin and baldric strapped with vials, knives and tools. Two more knives are strapped to me, one at each thigh. The familiar leather pouches lay on their belts on my wide hips. Multiple purple braids run down my scalp and flow down to my waist.

"Well, hello there." He chuckles, coming to my side. Pan gestures up and down to me. "You look prepared for battle."

I laugh, he does as well. Black breeches hug his thighs and a charcoal tunic hides under a leather jerkin darker than my own. A baldric is slung across his chest as well, empty though at the moment. Pan reaches a hand out to me and I grin, then step back and swing the hollow steel cane out in front of me. I press a button as I do, the thin estoc blade unsheathes to meet his throat. "Now, that is a statement." He laughs, pushing the blade down with a finger. I retract the blade and flip the cane, setting the cushioned tip on the floor.

I smile wide, though my face falters when I speak. "Our plan has been moved up, tonight. Apparently Knothall has plans of his own."

"I know, take a look." Pan leaves my side and wanders to the bags. I walk over, trying not to rely completely on the cane. He opens the two bags, revealing one for him, and one for me. Pan removes a folded up crossbow and quiver with eighteen bolts. A dark wool cloak rests inside the bag and covers his other gear.

I raise my brow at him and nod at the crossbow, a Human invention. "Know how to use that thing?"

"You may find I'm a bit more of a badass than I let on." He chuckles darkly and I rummage through my own bag while he gears up. My own has a matching wool cloak, other supplies and a small cotton satchel. Pan putters in the background, packing his near empty bag with his own possessions and stack of parchments. I reach into the bag, reading the note tied to the inconspicuous satchel.

This will reveal their true nature to you. It's a different world out there.

The writing is beautiful, an elegance I haven't come across before. I dump the contents into my hand, revealing a small crystal ball. I weigh it in my hand and scrutinize the milky color, unsure of what it's made of. I've encountered two new materials I've never seen in the Eternal now, and an unfamiliar energy radiates from the orb. Pan pauses at my side, he narrows his brows and reads the note I hand him. Exactly the size I need for a new eye.

"There are water skins and matches over there," I nod to the master table, "in the drawer, along with some other things that may be useful." I toss him the key from my pocket and walk away before he can answer.

"The mirror would be quite helpful right now." I mutter to myself, sweating profusely, then let out a deep exhale. Just get it done and over with. I press the crystal into my eye socket, wincing as the pressure builds before it enters fully. The moment it rests in my face, a cooling sensation spreads and my headache dulls considerably. My wrists itch and I scowl, the tattoos. The eye must be charmed somehow. It's better than nothing, and I can deal with a little discomfort.

I step out of the washroom to find Pan closing his bag, his giant body fully strapped with weapons and more dark leathers. He straightens and I grin at the ferocious bear lurking under his braided hair and wild beard. "Well, how do I look?" I strike a pose which elicits a rumble from him, echoing off the walls.

"Absolutely terrifying."

We spend the evening planning our route through the territories, first crossing the sea to Cervalis, the port of Hallowed Court. That is, if Umber agrees to help. I have a feeling that's what she wanted to tell me that day, that she could help me leave. Pan taps his finger on the map at an empty spot, south of the Great Tree of Terra. His eyes glaze over with faraway thoughts and I squeeze his hand, he smiles for a moment before his lips turn down once more.

Pan stands and evaluates me, hands at his sides. "We should glamor you, Lyth. Your eyes will be a dead giveaway out there."

I straighten and cross my arms, brows furrowing together. "No. I told Eros I would rather die as myself than be anyone else, and I meant it." Warmth runs over me as the thought passes he might not want a target on his back. I look back at the map, tapping Cervalis. "We can part ways here. I understand your concern, but I can't hide anymore."

The muscles in his jaw flex and he pulls at his beard. "Sick of me already?"

I sit down on the stool behind me, my hips already tired. "No, of course not. I can understand why you wouldn't want to be seen with me, though. I almost forgot," I pause, rubbing my neck as anger builds, "I forgot that I will be the only High Fae out there without magic. I'm used to it here, no one has access here,"

I gesture to the door, "they all hate me for it, but there's nothing they can do about it." My anger drops to a whisper. "Nothing else they haven't already done."

Panrauth kneels before me, taking my hands in his. My pale hands are so small in his tawny grasp, my own calluses seem like nothing compared to his smith hands.

"I told you I would stay by your side until you wished me away. If you do not wish me away, do not push me away." He tilts my chin up so I'm staring into his emerald eyes, he into my black and white. "If you don't wish to be glamoured, that is your choice."

Courage surges over me so quickly I can't stop myself. "If you kiss me, I will do it."

Surprise lights his face, then a smile lifts one corner of his lips. "Lythienne, you are a wicked thing." He grasps my waist and tugs me closer to the edge of my seat and I rest my hands on his face, unable to contain my unsteady breathing. I run a finger down his cheek and look up through my lashes, biting my lip.

Pan releases a soft rumble and his lips crash onto mine, taking my breath away. He bites my lip, pulling it in his teeth. A satisfied moan escapes me and I wrap my arms around his neck, his hands snake around my entire waist until his body encompasses my own. I slip my tongue into his waiting mouth and this time he groans into me, then brings his lips to the hollow of my neck.

We both lose track of time, one kiss transforming into hunger filled writhing and passion. Every part of my deprived body his hands touch burns with longing. I can't release his broad shoulders from my desperate hands. Nails dig into his skin and his grip is bruising. We are two feral beasts and for a moment, guilty hope creeps across me.

"Pan," I manage to whisper out as his lips tenderly caress my pointed ear, "I want you so much." I sigh, hoping he will change his mind. Tell me that he wants me too, that he doesn't care anymore. His wet lips trace back up my neck and leave me with one more perfect, lingering kiss on my trembling mouth.

"Think of it as something to look forward to, when you get us out of here." He murmurs, letting out a primal grin. The small, wise part of me speaks up once more. Don't count on it.

"Will you still want to kiss me? Or did you just because I asked you to?" I hold my breath.

"I'm ashamed to say, I've thought about kissing you since the moment you brought me to my knees by that fucking machine." My heart flutters and I run a hand down his leather strapped chest, a sigh of content leaving me as I do. For now, that's enough.

"Leather do it for you?" He chuckles, laying a kiss to my forehead once more and resting his hand in my hair.

"It sure does." I inhale his charcoal and earthy smell, the moment anchors me to hope. The watch on my leather and tech wristlet buzzes, indicating the time striking six. The heat cools immediately between us.

"Let's get out of here." Pan rises, pulling me up with him. "You have the keys, right?"

We need time to walk, and Umber needs time to get here. "Yes, but we have to wait." I clutch the pouch on my left side. The keys to our freedom. He nods and slings two bags over his shoulder.

I sling my own on and pick up the cane waiting by the door, then take one last, long look at the lab. The loft I called home for so many years, the tables I learned how to be an engineer at. I never thought it would be hard to say goodbye, but it is. I swallow and open the oaken door.

Virgil flies out past me and Panrauth Firthorn walks behind me, and I leave the safety of the lab for darkness once again.

FALL TO RISE

The tunnels are no longer pitch dark to me, even without my goggles. The crystal eye provides a sketch outline of my dark surroundings, illuminating enough of my environment to traverse through. The loose, jagged stone hampers my walking, even with my cane.

Pan makes no complaints as we slowly make our way through the lower labyrinth to the chasm above that Slate rests in, and he doesn't offer an arm to assist me. We walk in silence, passing some disgruntled Fae along the way. We turn into the main tunnel leading away from the labs and as we near the exit emptying into the cavern, I stop dead in my tracks as hair pricks on my neck. My skin runs cold and my chest caves in, like the walls suddenly closing around me.

We were really this close to the exit?

If I look hard enough, will I find my blood staining the stones beneath my boots?

"Lyth?" Pan rests a gentle hand on my shoulder, saying my name as a precaution before touching me. A shudder rips through me and I take his hand at once. We walk through the remainder of the empty tunnel together, our hands clutching the other tightly. The bloody red faelights leading the way to Slatepoint bring me energy. I glance at The Keep, my heart rattles its cage.

It's nearly shift change, many creatures pass us on their way to the labyrinths we've left behind. Their sneers and stares don't go unnoticed, however Pan at my side deters them from doing anything else. After the arduous trip, we come to a stop in front of Umber's empty tent. My stomach drops when I peer into the lacking canopy.

"Maybe she's just not here yet —" Pan offers, swiftly interrupted by galloping footsteps thundering from behind us. Before I can turn fully, a solid thud hits the arm Pan has outstretched. He snarls, his usual composure failing, "Watch out."

Umber's silver eyes connect with mine, her bewildered face crumples at my state. She evaluates my newly scarred face and the cane, then scowls at Pan as he lowers his arm. Umber hugs me gentler than I ever thought possible for her. She begins to speak but I put a finger up.

"Not now. I have a favor." I whisper, holding onto her shoulder with all my might. She nods, glancing between Pan surveying the area, and back to me.

We sit at the loosely crowded bar, the usual red imp flits between quiet patrons. Umber and I slug back mead and leave, noting how many inmates are present as we do. Half capacity at best, it would be better if the place was busier. Umber and I casually stroll along the walkway encircling the inner foundation, evaluating the scene.

Eros lounges across the iron throne, speaking to a Keeper and a crimson Lesser Fae smith. Her head doesn't turn but her white eyes watch Umber and I, her icy glare cuts through me. It's eerily silent in the chasm, even the cushioned tip on my cane seems too loud.

"That's her." Umber states more than asks in a whisper, startling me. I nod, facing her when we pause. I evaluate the imposing walls on the Keep side, Umber watches the opposite.

"Have you heard of her?" I ask quietly, scanning the guards pacing the raised borders of Slatepoint.

"Yes, she's quite something from what I hear." Umber's deep tone drips with poison and I catch her watching Eros with tight lips. I glance over my shoulder to find the Fae staring right back at her with a menacing grin. A horn rumbles the chasm, declaring the beginning of night shift. I notice a guard disappear from view, and another while the sound erupts. I hold my breath, willing the universe to allow Panrauth to make it out of this alive.

I elbow Umber, disturbing her standoff as I gesture to the commotion gathering around the archway at the forefront of town. Knothall enters Slate wearing a hard face and battle gear. He leans against the first pillar circling the center stage, his eyes set on Eros.

She straightens on the throne, waving off the creatures beside her as sudden interest takes hold. Inmates stream in, far more creatures arriving than were here just moments ago. Eros stands, chin held high whilst she stares Knothall down. I recognize the hardened look resting on her savage features, one I hold quite often. A mask. Why is it there?

"Eros, I challenge you for the title of High Commander." The Commander's challenge echoes across the chasm, the thunderous tone folds my fluffed ears down. He unsheathes an epic great sword from his back, gripping the hilt with steady hands. Eros' face is stone, but hot white flames roll tightly around her body, an armor of Aether.

The walkway around the auditorium fills and Umber elbows me, subtly gesturing behind us to the exit. No guards patrol across from me on the high border walls. The ones on the ground are approaching the center, oblivious to their fallen comrades. It's time to go, but I can't look away. A Keeper announces the rules of the duel. There are only two.

No magic.

Fight to the death. As in, no surrender, no mercy given.

The saber unleashes from Eros' back, then points directly at Knothall while her flames die out. They brace themselves for a moment, then lunge across the inner circle. Umber doesn't wait for the clash, she physically drags me to the narrow arch leading to the Keep. I recollect myself and shake her off. The masked guards are just twenty feet away from us now, more than half the distance between us and our first obstacle to freedom.

"Keeper, what is your business?" One of the ten calls out, and I smile.

My step is sure, the cane in my hand light. I flip the cane in my hand just as a bolt slices through the air and meets the skull of the guard closest to me. I swing the cane out, unsheathing its blade which immediately finds the vulnerable neck of the guard closest to me.

Shouts erupt but fade into the jeering and rambunctious crowd surrounding the duel behind us. Dark, poisonous clouds roll from Umber and sneak under the remaining guard's masks, tortuously choking their life out.

In a matter of bloody moments, we leave nothing but bodies in our wake. Several beheaded leather masks lay beside pierced and choked out bodies. I straighten my resolve as the sight reminds of Rohana.

Swords clang out in the distance and the shout of a struggling female brings cheers to the crowd. Panrauth's dark figure waits for us on the ground, on the other side of the archway. This is it. Our last obstacle is the Keep, we can get out.

We can do this. I break into a run and neither companion protests, the crunching stone leads us upwards on a curving trail that hooks to the right. I grind my teeth and my hips scream, but I can't stop now.

A deafening pained roar from Slate erupts, shaking the chasm and sending small rocks hurling past us. Every fiber of my body screams to watch my shomer fall, but I can't. I would turn back if he's still standing. If he needs me. And I need to focus on what waits in front of me, our run slows to a walk as the looming castle waits before us.

Umber casts clouds of mist around our dark figures already camouflaged by the black stone flanking the narrow roadsides before we get much closer, providing a thin cover. Large red flags wave on wooden poles along the barracks upper walls and in front of us waits an open portcullis, the bars shaped into iron vines.

Pan's crossbow is primed, Umber had said there were two guards outside this entrance. The magnificent Keep is deathly quiet, only the sound of flags catching heated wind raises my hackles. Virgil flies over us, circling the area. The bird can leave, he is so close, but for some reason chooses to wait.

I move under the portcullis first, staying close to the wall and keeping my step light. Airships and weigh stations fill the massive gatehouse, Umber's balloon ship is docked on the end closest to us. Masked guards lay everywhere across the grounds, but no blood is shed. *Anywhere*. I can't tell if they're alive or dead, but my gut doesn't like this.

"It's a trap." I whisper to Panrauth beside me, his face is hidden by his cloak hood. We pause, unsure whether to come out of the dark safety of the entry. Umber releases the clouds from us and focuses them on herself, then quickly checks the guard closest to us as Panrauth covers her with the crossbow.

"He's still alive, he's ..." She looks up to me, drawing her blue brows together. "Sleeping."

"We can't waste anymore time, let's go." Panrauth orders. He and I break from the wall, Umber is already sprinting towards the ship.

A wooden ramp is down and I climb onto the mediocre deck, then shoulder off my gear into a corner. I quickly find the rigging keeping the sail secure and let it loose. I know a little of sailing from the air mariner's books Knothall has and from the stories I've demanded from Umber over the years, but everything is easy on the ground. Once we're in the air, it's a whole new game.

Umber scurries on the ground outside the ship, releasing the ropes holding us to the world of the Eternal. Panrauth finds a control panel behind the steering wheel and cranks the engine up. A bright orange fabric draped over the circular framework above Umber's wooden basket of a ship stretches taut as Aether gas billows against it.

Umber jumps on as the ship lifts and I pull the ramp up, then bolt it into place when she immediately marches for Panrauth at her steering wheel. "Know how to drive one of these?" She asks him gruffly, her silver eyes flashing bright. Airship engines are powered by their Captain's Aether, despite her ship's small size these engines are quite powerful. Umber doesn't flinch under their increasing draw on her magic, and I stare at her in awe for a lost moment.

"I may." Pan says, crossing his arms.

"Then get your own." She growls, then turns up the gas more and takes the wheel.

Once we're high enough, the ship darts into the gaping tunnel that leads out of the Mountain. The lights of the Keep fade behind us as sudden inertia presses me into place against a railing. Within a terrifying moment, I regain senses of my body and slump onto the floor for fear of falling over the edge as Umber speeds through thick darkness. My schematics about the Mountain says the tunnel is over twenty miles long, but at this speed it won't take long to reach the exit, and the shield covering it.

"You know how to pick them." Pan groans, kneeling beside me.

Lanterns tucked into the four corners of the airship alight with a soft glow, just enough so I can dimly make out my surroundings. I ignore Pan and retrieve the silken bag tucked into my hip pouch. I dump its contents into my hand and when my fingers brush Pan's key, a shock jolts my arm and I drop it onto the deck at my feet. How Knothall obtained these from Ragnis is beyond my comprehension. Only the High Lord of Iron possesses the keys to every inmate in the Eternal, and I don't see Ragnis letting me leave. Unless Knothall made a deal, which I don't put past him. Regardless, I won't squander this opportunity.

Panrauth squats beside me and picks his key up, studying it with furrowed brows. Short obsidian daggers, my handle is encrusted with diamonds, his is composed of vines and branches. A leather tag is strung around each, mine is unreadable, his has P.F burned into it. The blades that mark our enslavement, the key to break the bond. Bonds made in blood can only be undone by spilling more blood.

"We're almost there, if you're gonna do it, do it now." Umber warns. The shield is the last precaution, an invisible force of magic spreading across the epic, yawning mouth carved into the mountainside. Anyone with a tattoo can't get past the field, cast long ago by the Ancients themselves. I whimper, my bracelets of enslavement burn red hot as we near it. Pan's marks are as well, but his face doesn't change.

"Now?" I shout, raising my knife filled hand as the shield presses on the airship, jarring us to a stop. Engines whine and the balloon's framework creaks, groaning under the sudden impact.

"No, wait." Pan orders fiercely. The glittering field wraps around the ship, moaning and splintering wood threatens to implode in the abyss of the tunnel. The red desert beyond is just barely visible through the veil, the stone bridge below us into the Mountain is visible.

"Now!" He yells as the shield envelopes the ship completely, forming a bubble.

I slice through my shirt into my shoulder and the dripping blood releases me from the pact made the day I entered. When I was only an infant, the first time my blood spilled. A rush of burning, gritty air enters my lungs, crawling into every crevice inside my body. Freedom burns with a passion. A blinding green light erupts and shakes the ship, throwing me backwards. The force field disintegrates around us, feathered cloaks of glittering darkness waft through the air. From the corner of my eye I spy a black speck of wings escaping from the Eternal.

Good boy, fly away.

The explosion of green dims just enough to reveal emerald flames licking Pan's manically laughing body. The unnatural fire spreads to the fabric above, the Bear is unable to contain his excitement, or his Aether.

"What the fuck!" Umber shouts, rushing to put out the flames. I rush forward and take the wildly spinning wheel in attempts to steer us away from the red cliffs cutting through the desert. Panrauth's joy ends but it's too late.

We make it only a few miles away from the Mountain before scraping into sheer rocks and smashing into the red ground below.

THE HERMIT

ECHO VALLEY

As decreed by The Four Ancients after the Civil War of Iverbourne.
The remaining land of Iverbourne will be divided by the Four Elements, and the remaining Human Territories will remain untouched.
Each High Court will preside over their own assigned territory and be responsible for contributing to the greater good, dependent on their region and Aether capabilities.
High Lords or Ladies will furthermore be chosen by the Aether flow in the original royal lineages of each territory, only the strongest shall rule.
NO EXCEPTIONS.

YOU CRASHED THE FUCKING SHIP

Cold bites my skin and I groan, then rub at my head and shake off the endless pleading in my mind. I open my eyes and slowly remember the new mess we're in. I am still on the ship, or what's left of it. I look around, panic growing when I find the deck is empty.

My stiff body protests and I pull myself up using a shattered railing, then peer over it after I stand. A nest of branches cradle the ship, fresh leaves and pink flowers budding on them. They practically glow, the sweet floral scent reminds me of Aether. Perhaps that is the smell of magic, the light fragrance of flowers. I strain, spying a frizz of blue on the night covered ground along with a hulking dark figure.

Even from here I can hear it.

"You crashed the fucking ship!" Umber bellows. A blast of bright silver meets emerald green and the florescent colors tussle together, clashing against the pure black sky. I roll my eyes, then collect my belongings before calling to them over the side, my cane in hand.

"If you're going to fight, at least bring me down so I can watch." Their lights dim and I can see their faces again, both scowling up at me. Pan's expression softens when he sees my amused face and he lets out a smile. A solid slap reverberates across his cheek, and I gasp.

"Don't look at her, you could have killed her!" Umber shouts, fists clenched.

He rubs his jaw, the storm of emeralds around him rumbling again. "Yes, I could have. Would you like to tell me more things I already know?"

I perch on the edge and whistle, and they look up just as I jump. Crisp air rushes past me and is invigorating, tickling my body. The glee only lasts until Pan catches me, dropping to a knee under my weight. I straighten and push away from him, then lean heavily on my cane.

"What happened?" I ask. Umber opens her mouth but I hold up a hand, resulting in her face twisting into an intense pout.

"I knew the release would be intense. I figured I would use it to our advantage." He shrugs, rolling his shoulders back. "Might keep them busy, scrambling to keep the rest of them in, instead of looking for us."

I look to Umber and raise a brow, she just rolls her eyes and mutters about her ship. "Your nightlights are going to get us caught, can you turn them off or something?" I warn, and they exchange confused looks. "You were glowing ..." I rub my neck, realizing how it sounds.

"No, I was just kicking his ass." Umber glares at Pan. I rub my chin and take the weight off my cane. Momentarily. Pan taps his right temple, reminding me of my new eye, and the note that came with it.

"So, I can see magic?" I question, to which Umber shrugs.

"The only physical indicator of Aether I know of is the eyes. If you see anything else, it's usually suggested you run. So I would say, yes. You're seeing auras, or surrounding Aether." Umber decides with a confident smile. "So, what color am I?" She asks, excitement barely veiled.

"You are dark blue, most of the time, it changes. Firthorn is forest green, most of the time."

Umber's silver eyes flash as she stares at Pan immediately. "Firthorn?" She asks, which draws Pan's brows together.

"Is that a problem?" I ask, glancing between the two.

"Just funny sounding is all, just like the rest of him. You sure know how to pick them."

"Funny, he says the same thing about you." I tease, but she mutters and storms off to investigate the wreckage, leaving us alone.

Pan takes my hand, squeezing tight. "Last names out here are like first names in there. Better just stick to Pan."

I nod, an uneasy feeling settling in my stomach. "I thought about what you said. You're right, it's reckless to not glamor my eyes."

He kisses my knuckles gently before releasing my cold fingers. "Alright. Who do you want to be?" Brilliant unrestrained flames of green Aether dance in his eyes.

"Surprise me." I say, closing my eyes before his aura brightens. His Aether washes over me, cold and sweet floral air caresses my face.

We gather only what we can carry. Pan and Umber split the extra supplies between them, each adding to their own possessions. Pan and I change from our dark armored garb to simple earthly linens. My crop top rests above my navel, my pants are loose and cuff at the bottom with a snap.

Pan's chestnut tunic is taut against his broad shoulders and chest, simple tan breeches replace the black ones from before. Umber is the most fashionable among us, she wears a beaded blue tunic with gray breeches. She is dressed the same as before, but night falls on her differently than the darkness of the Mountain does.

Late night and threatening morning hours compose our grueling trek across red sand, the most vile substance. Sneaking into every crevice, grinding at the joints in my ankles and knees. We travel along the base of the cliff ranges, using the towering monuments as cover. I frown, even the clouds are dark. No moons or stars tonight.

"*So,* where exactly do we go now? Can't exactly walk to Cervalis from here." I ask no one in particular after some time.

"Lucky for you, I know a gal in Echo. She'll take us, for a price." Umber answers me with a proud tone, shaking out her hair.

"I brought the rest of the tools, will that be enough?" I think of their unbreakable strength, charmed to bring good fortune. Surely they will bring wealth to anyone who sells them.

"Yes, I think so. It might take all of them though, if she knows who you two are." She slows her step and Panrauth strides ahead of us casually, leaving Umber and I semi-alone.

"Do you still want to go?" I ask as my gaze meets hers. I wonder what color my eyes are.

"Why wouldn't I?"

"I thought Echo was your home."

She scoffs. "No, no. Echo is like your mountain, but with sand and starving children. They fight for scraps just as well as the rest. I'm from Hallowed, hence the Air magic."

Gears spin in my head and I furrow my brows, focusing on boots in sand. "You said it's more than a full day's trip from the Mountain to Cervalis, over the sea. Why would you do that so often?"

She is silent for a minute, and when she does speak, her voice is surprisingly deadly. "Do I need a reason?" I don't reply, just amble along in shock. I open my lips after a few moments but she is first, spitting out rather gruffly once again. "We'll never get there before daybreak, it's at least another couple miles."

My cheeks warm and her face is unapologetic, staring at Pan ahead of us instead of me. He stops and turns on his heel, then strides back to us. I stop walking and Umber continues in a hurry. My ears are laid down flat against my neck and judging from his tight lips, I'm guessing he heard everything.

I shrug off my pack and hold it close to my chest. Without a word, he slides his arms under and behind me, only lifting me off the ground when I lean back. I wince as the weight of my dangling legs pulls on my hips, but I don't complain.

Pan's aura is a comforting pale green and wraps around us both, fending off Umber's seeping dark blue trailing behind her. Eventually Pan catches up to her and they walk in silence, and I don't say anything either. Umber's tone surprised me, she is the last person I expected to treat me that way.

After a long period of silence, Pan looks down to me and smiles gently, then kisses my forehead. At that moment, exhaustion takes over and I go down without a fight.

My face is warm and dusty air tickles my nose. I awake in Pan's bulky arms, but keep my eyes closed. I don't want to talk to Umber yet, and it feels nice to be held. They are mid-conversation, and Umber's desperately low voice spikes my interest.

"You need to tell her."

"It's *not* her problem." A threatening rumble emits from the warm body holding me, and I fight my ears from perking.

"No, but it's *ours*. Do you even know how bad you left things?" She hisses, and for a moment, I don't think he will respond.

"I know," he shifts me in his arms, "I *know*, I'm going to fix it." Umber huffs in protest, but Pan stops her. "It's not her job. She gets to live now. That's all I want, for her to *thrive*, not just survive."

They turn to the left, we must've reached a break in the cliff side at last. Pan shifts me again, he must be so tired. I open my eyes reluctantly and find him grinning down at me. "I appreciate you sleeping the whole way. I only had one headache to deal with instead of two." I grin and move to get down, but a groan escapes as stiffness radiates through my body. "Wait a moment."

He kneels and I shift my pack onto my back, then take my cane in one hand and his sure grip with my other. I stand, my hips and hamstrings rebel against every movement. He raises his dark brows and I nod to him, wincing when I shift my full weight from him onto the cane.

"There it is." Umber says in awe, pointing to the distant village ahead of us. A cobblestone path cuts across red sand, rising from a seemingly random point in the desert and leading to a decrepit town. The place glimmering with color contrasts the unending wasteland surrounding it. The sight of Echo stirs the nightmarish voice inside me, already whispering to be found.

SO, THIS IS NORMAL

The town is open with no borders to keep anyone in, or out. After minutes on the cobbled road, I learn Echo Valley isn't randomly placed there. Skeletons of great buildings and thousands of weather Fae bones litter the roadside, feet of red and orange sand covering their carcasses. Gusting wind reveals bits and pieces of what I imagine was once a picturesque town. I swallow fear, wondering why two neighboring towns suffered such different fates. Echo Valley isn't anything spectacular in itself, but at least it's still inhabited and above ground.

Orange flags with a valley range hang on random buildings, and airships with the same insignia are docked on the distant end of the village, their colorful sails catching sun. As we approach, I notice many of the buildings are just glorified canopies. Some places are brown cob houses baking in the heat with thatched roofs.

Others are crumbling cobblestone, those seem to be the businesses. In every crevice between buildings are moving skeletons, most of which are children of every age. Some Elder Fae join them, but all of the beggars poke their heads in the sun to plead for food as we pass by.

The sight rolls my stomach, but not as much as the two young males fighting to what appears to be to the death. Over a scrap of dried meat, stolen by a stray child during the scuffle. There is no order. Homes and desperate vendors are strewn along the winding paths that narrow the deeper we traverse, the town more of a labyrinth than the Mountain is. It appears they just built on an empty spot and kept going with the road.

Chatter grows as we near the heart of the village, and a group of young pixies fly past us. I've never seen them in person before, miniature versions of Fae like Amwren. Umber grabs the last by his wings and I flinch at the action. The pixie frowns and Umber holds out her hand. The tiny winged being, hardly bigger than a crow, begrudgingly drops Umber's side pouch into it. The thief lifted it so quickly, I didn't even notice, and I was walking right behind Umber.

It must hurt, to be grabbed midair by the wings. Thief or not.

We reach the impressive center, a behemoth clearing situated around an Oasis of deep blue water. Flat stones run around the edge, stacked four feet high and providing a molecule of shade underneath its slick slick border. Several High Fae are seated on the rocks, peering in and admiring their reflection. Large water wheels turn, churning and dumping fresh water into a separate rectangular pool, which is surrounded by females with buckets.

The Fae argue and fight over who will get the most of the dirty water, tainted by all the filthy bodies reaching desperately into it. No one touches the crystal clear water in the Oasis pool, the crystalline surface undisturbed. Not even a ripple, as the wind is dead here. Leaning over the Oasis are lumbering smooth trees with broad leaves.

Smaller ones shoot up everywhere around the square, providing shade to those lounging under them. A circular mosaic to the left of the clearing catches my eye, at least twenty feet in diameter. The collage stone area is painted in different colors and insignias, and I recognize the symbols as each element of the lands. Water, Earth, Air and Fire.

A group of Fae stand up a tall maypole in the center of the mosaic, red streamers flowing loosely in the breeze from the towering beam. The circle is empty at the moment, save for a few creatures sitting on the benches around it. Umber stops suddenly, halting my step and study of the circle.

"I will meet Captain and make the deal. Meet you back here in one hour. With Beltane, I can guarantee we won't be leaving tonight." She points to a cantina bustling down the way. "The Crew likes to party." I cross my arms and nod, voice hiding. She saunters away into the crowd, towards the small port.

There is too much noise, and too many people to keep tabs on. A kaleidoscope of colors melds together between the Fae auras and fantastic decorations strewn about the village. I need to focus on one thing, or I'll pass out from the stimulation. It's too much.

"What is all this for?" I gesture to the orange and red banners hanging in every available space, then to the beaded outfits many wear, the silken fabric akin to flames dancing in the sun.

"Beltane is the solstice between spring and summer." Pan stands guard close to me, his voice calm and even as he scans the area.

"Have you been here before?" I look up to him with a raised brow. After studying the place once more he looks down, giving me a small smile.

"Yes, on business. Occasionally pleasure."

"Oh?" I shift my tired weight and he offers an elbow. I loop my arm through and he walks us over to an empty bench at the mosaic.

"You'll see." He promises. Several red skinned Lesser Fae enter the mosaic, along with a High Fae, and a human. The group sets down hard leather cases, unfolding the simple folding stools slung across their backs. I sit up, watching the round eared fellow with intent. I've never seen a human before, only read about them and heard stories. Humans never make it to the Eternal, let alone in Iron territory, before they are sold off or killed.

He's handsome, a limber body with curling light hair. He doesn't seem much different than Fae, other than his rounded ears. He even has an Aether aura, but it's different from those of the Fae. A gentle charcoal rests around him, a pool of warmth spreading from the gray aura. The musicians chat among themselves and laugh, paying no mind to the gawking cripple watching them.

Pan's watchful gaze disrupts me and color rushes my cheeks. "What?"

"Nothing, nothing at all." He smiles at me, but sadness lingers in his strong face and voice. Every hair on my body stands up and ecstasy washes over me when the only music I've ever heard begins.

I don't remember standing or taking a few steps closer, the strings on the instruments must've called me. Without my cane I unsteadily watch the human strum his lute, watching the bond between him and his instrument. The band's music sweeps over me, thrumming my heart to life and bringing a stupid grin to my face. When the musician does tear his attention from the beaten up lute and finds me, I'm immediately lost in two deep oceans.

The closest I've been to this feeling is when I'm thrust elbow deep in a new invention, or getting a wretched prototype to work right, finally. Books can never describe the sounds that simple lute makes, multitudes of strings working together in harmony to create the haunting music. Melodies drifting in from the guitar, vocalist and canvas drums add to the effect, the notes melding together and rising across all the gathered creatures. The language the red Fae sings in is unfamiliar to me, but the tune is chillingly beautiful just the same.

Children dance around the maypole, skipping across painted stones, and the upbeat tempo beckons others to join. Flower crowns adorn most of the females, and I realize there are many races that live here. Pixies, Fae and some short, pointed ear folk. Several couples waft in, spinning each other and laughing.

For a moment, everyone forgets the squalor they are surviving in. Only light faces and smiles are allowed here. Joyful whispers filled with the word *Zemer* flow through the air, an unfamiliar word that warms my heart for some reason.

"Would you care to dance with me, dear Keeper?" Panrauth waits at my side, his steady hand is outstretched to me.

"I don't know if I can." I place my small hand inside his and bite my lip.

"Luckily, I'm good enough for the both of us." He chuckles, pulling me closer to him. His comforting pale green aura surrounds us while we sway in place, all the people and noise drift away, leaving just Pan and I. I lay my head under his heart and sigh, listening to his even and slow heartbeat. He's practically holding me up, leaning over so my small arms can reach his neck properly.

The Bear and the broken Grasshopper, attempting to dance.

"Ready?" He asks and I arch a brow, tilting my head. He grins before I can answer, his hands grasp my waist and lift me up. I squeal, grasping onto his shoulders while he spins me around. Joy spreads through me and the music slows, both of us are laughing when he sets me down.

"Let's go on an adventure." He declares and takes my cane from the bench, handing it to me. I nod, glancing back once more at the music continuing without us. The lute player watches us in silence, his figure surrounded by a cloud of darkness. It has to be an aura, or the chanting crowd would be screaming.

I can't shake the feeling of multiple eyes trained on me as we weave in and out of covered vendors. They are all selling hard, the holiday must be good for business.

"So, what happens on Beltane?" I ask as we browse a dried flower tent. I've never celebrated a holiday before, they were too trivial to even learn about in the Mountain.

"For most solstices you can count on excessive drinking, dancing and," he chuckles, "frolicking." I roll my eyes at him and he trades a stack of parchment from his bag for a simple flower crown, adorned with small white and purple flowers.

"Where I'm from, we thank the Ancients for new life and beginnings, and ask for help with the season. It's mostly the same in other places." He places the crown on my head, a disapproving brow turns down. Pan removes the crown and holds it in his hands. Aether fills my nose as the purple flowers turn dark, and green vines with thorns encircle them. He holds it out to me, smiling nervously, perhaps the only time I've seen him unsure thus far.

"That's better." I say, taking the crown and placing it upon my frizzy sand filled braids. I smile and he puzzles over my face for a moment before we continue on. He is silent until I speak again. "So, I'm assuming I'll have to pry your story from you. I've already gathered you're an Earth Fae. Does that mean you're *from* Terra?"

We come upon a nearly empty side street and turn down it, walking with easy steps. "Yes, I was born in Terra lands, close to the court." He says shortly and annoyance rolls in my brain.

"Umber is from Hallowed, so that's why she has air powers?" I know how Aether works, but males love to hear themselves talk. Perhaps he'll divulge something useful, or open up a little. We pause in the midst of the empty alley and he faces me, arms crossed tight across his chest.

"Your magic hails from the lands you are born on. No matter where you go, you take those elements of your land with you. Some Fae take it quite seriously. They only breed with others born with the same elemental magic." He shuffles his feet. I wonder what Aether is created by combining different elements, or if the child takes after the strongest parent.

"Like Sylvan?" I ask, and he nods once. "Why does it matter where your magic comes from? I've seen auras of every color today, even the human's."

"Luckily, Echo doesn't care who you are. Everyone here is just looking for somewhere to belong. A village of misfits if you will." We begin walking again, and a heavy confectionery scent wafts our way.

"What color was it?" Pan asks quietly after a moment, my ears have to perk at his words. The Human. Of course he would want to know.

I stumble a bit, righting myself with the cane before Pan tries to steady me. I flush and keep walking. "It was gray. Soft, like charcoal. It was nice to look at him." A sigh escapes me, and I pause my step to clarify. "A relief, I mean. Colors are too much. I'm not used to, well, everything."

We stop where our path crosses a filled main street. Panrauth gives me a half smile and I reach for him, grasping his shoulder with care. "You're not telling me something, Pan. I've tried to let it go, but I can't."

"What do you mean?" He stiffens under my touch, then softly pulls away. Anger flushes my cheeks. He still isn't going to tell me what's going on. I don't want him to know I was eavesdropping. I was really hoping he would just tell me, and the small voice I had pushed away in the lab taunts me with an 'I told you so.'

"Never mind." I shake my head, stepping away to follow the road to our left. "I need to rest. Let's go back." We follow the winding path back to the Oasis, and for once, Pan has a hard time keeping up with me. I won't let my guard down again, Knothall is right.

I can't trust anyone.

Umber enters the crowded heart of Echo just as we do, slapping a heavy hand on Pan's shoulder. "We have a ship, a place to sleep and a party to attend."

Pan shrugs her hand off and scowls at her. "I don't fancy the idea of a party."

"I, for one, need to blow off some steam." I say, if only to antagonize Pan.

Umber grins wickedly and nods to the open cantina, a crowd of Fae leaking into the street outside it. "I'll meet you there."

I nod to her and watch her disappear again, this time to the opposite side of town, beyond the mosaic. I check my watch as the burning sun crisps my skin, mid afternoon. Pan keeps his watchful gaze on me. I avoid looking at him and scan around, catching the blonde human leaning against a distant cob wall.

Watching. *Waiting*.

I need to find out what he wants, and Pan is getting under my skin right now with his bullshit. "Why don't you go ahead, I'll meet you there?" I jut my head in the direction of boisterous laughter erupting from the bar down the way.

"Why?" He asks gruffly, the already stretched tunic pulling under his flexing shoulders.

With nothing clever in mind, I give him a small smile, willing softness into my voice. "I want to be alone for a while."

He holds my gaze for a moment, then his face falters before he heads for the bar with a rumbling growl, taking me off guard. Both of my friends are hiding things from me. I need to get to Hallowed, with or without their help. Even though I no longer work for Knothall, I promised him I would do this. If there is anything good about me, it's that my word is my bond. I haven't looked at either of the packages tucked away in my bag, yet.

One is for the High Lady, and one is for me.

I sit on a shaded stone edge of the Oasis under a broad leafed tree, watching the water wheel crank. I stare at my reflection, finding an unfamiliar face in the water. Cold green eyes are framed by sand filled purple braids, the crown of thorns resting atop. The scar is still prominent on my left cheek. If it hasn't faded by now, it won't at all. I frown and take the crown off, then set it beside me.

The female staring back at me is not one I care for.

A curly mop of blonde hair and playful eyes joins the reflection, grinning at us both. I lift my head, locking eyes with the human. He hyper focuses on my eyes and scarred cheek. I can't look away from his rounded ears and sun kissed, freckled face. Carefree lines at his eyes and lips are permanently turned up. I had expected to find myself in danger, but instead I find him comforting.

Until he speaks, that is.

"Well, never thought I'd meet the fabled Keeper of Death." He taunts. I can't hide my amusement at the moniker, narrowing my brows and tilting my head with a grin. He isn't supposed to know who I am, not with my eyes hidden.

"And who is that?" I muse. He takes a purple braid and lets it flow between his fingers. I reach for a knife, but think better of putting it to his throat and settle for caressing the blade with my fingers instead. "If you don't want to lose any fingers, I suggest keeping your hands to yourself."

The aura around him darkens immensely and the deep dimples in his cheeks pull up a wide, wicked smile. His intoxicating presence leans closer to me and the Oasis spins. "Lovely locks. Quite the giveaway." He whispers, then pulls away with a long lashed wink. Danger wrapped in a beautiful body indeed. I regain my senses and straighten.

"My *hair*?" I search around for more purple hiding in the overpopulated streets, not finding any. Shadows settle further around us, blocking my view and threatening to trap us together. Nobody notices us, children still run through the square, females fight for water, and music drifts from a far corner.

Black and white eyes shoot back to his wild grin, and his slender shoulders roll back. His right ear twitches and catches my attention. Humans can't move their ears. The scar tissue on top is precise, obvious now to my curious gaze. I'm not sitting with a powerless human. I am keeping a being of darkness company.

Eros is the only other Fae I know of with powers beyond the four elements. Burning 'Winter Aether' can definitely be classified as something Other. Staring into his sapphire eyes, the thought smashes into me there is so *much* I don't know. This creature, he is pure otherworldly darkness. Something I know everything, and nothing about.

Every muscle urges me to run, find the others and hide at the ship. I point the dagger at him, throwing off my playfulness and arching a purple brow. "Why are you watching us?"

"Technically, I was watching you." A chuckle emits from him, the sun glints off my black blade and reflects in his eyes.

"I didn't realize I'm so popular."

"Not everyday you meet an Empty Fae, especially one capable of so much death." He shrugs, then stretches his slender arms overhead. He wears plain clothes, his thin orange tunic half undone and revealing carvings on his chest. Sand stained baggy pants with tight cuffs adorn his bare feet. Without my eye, I would've thought he was a handsome young desert Fae. With his ears cut off.

"You seem clever enough you wouldn't poke the snake, then." I keep my guard up as his warm shadows encroach, the darkness swallows us entirely and no attention is drawn to us. *Still.*

"One would think so. There are quite a few who would pay a pretty coin for your head, though." The musician leans close again, giving me another wink as he bounces on the stone edge. My body is not on the same page as my mind, desire building with each handsome smile from the dangerous being.

"I suppose you're inclined to oblige them. Rats like you need to pick at the scraps." I bite out. He lets out a carefree laugh and holds his soft stomach. Not rumbling darkness like Pan, but more akin to my giggle when I threatened inmates.

"I haven't decided yet. Humans are *supposed* to despise anything to do with the Machine." He muses, shaking blonde hair away from his face.

Perhaps I shouldn't have shown my hand, but the words tumble out red hot. "You are no Human. That, I am certain of."

His smile fades and he takes my blistered wrists with firm gentleness, studying my skin now free from the ink that used to live there. I don't pull away from his warm touch and after a moment of evaluating my wrists he releases me, raising a brow when he finds my scowling face again. "You are no ordinary High Fae, of *that* I'm certain of." His playful, threatening voice rests in my soul.

I rise, my hips are stiff but I don't use the cane to stand. I stare down at his rebellious face, laced with devious playfulness. He grins wide and snaps his fingers, and his shadows swallow him in an instant. Without a trace, he's gone.

I scan around, someone must've noticed. Bickering continues at the waterhole, evening settles on the rousing drunkards and music continues at an upbeat pace. No eyes catch on me muttering about trickster faeries either, and I decide a drink is exactly what I need.

THE WICKED BOY

Fast tempo music spills from the lute player perched on a stool outside the cantina, different from the one full of shadows. An orange and black monkey rests on his shoulder and I watch it clap along to the tempo, a long fluffed black tail wrapped around the young Fae's neck. Another thing I've only read about, animals. Besides Virgil of course, but I haven't seen him since we escaped from the Mountain.

Perhaps Knothall adding books upon books to my training will prove helpful, facts on parchment is all I know of this new world. A world I never thought I'd see, information I once deemed pointless.

I squeeze past a circle of dancing Fae in the street and pass the threshold of the bar. A woven orange tapestry drapes overhead for a ceiling and more colored tapestries line the three cobbled walls. The front of the place is open, brown pillars lining the entrance. Tables are arranged haphazardly along the outside and inside, situated wherever they fit.

I find a stool at the end of the sturdy wooden bar, choosing to rest on the side closest to the exit. The endless noise and countless bodies distracts me from attempting to read the chalkboard menu hanging above the fluttering gold Fae bartender. I huff when I finally make out the letters, then realize there are too many choices.

Streaks of gold paint lay across the bartender's body, the amber beads covering her chest and pelvis match the shimmering of her thin wings. My heart flutters, her wings are so beautiful and remind me of Amwren, which splits my heart. She looks me up and down with a raised bald brow and bare elbow leaned on the bar in front of me, her soft voice cuts through endless chatter as she leans closer.

"What's your poison?"

I shrug and fiddle with the tech on my wrist. "Surprise me." She chuckles, then leaves as she prepares my concoction. I watch her flutter behind the bar, in awe of how fast she works. Glimpses of her eyes bring me comfort. Most Lesser Fae have no eyelids, their large, almond gray eyes unnerve most people, however I find it comforting. The eyes of my childhood. I scan the area while she shakes a metal tumbler, the noise laying my ears down.

I find Pan's behemoth presence situated in the farthest corner, huddled around a table with a leather winged Fae and a dark skinned female High Fae. My breath hitches at their hands, entwined together. They laugh uproariously, the winged Fae elbows Pan closer to the female. Pan's giant body leans against the thin High Fae and her green eyes bat up at him. It's like watching a group of friends get together, no time passing at all. Fire burns a hole in my stomach and I narrow my brows, breaking my gaze when he wraps an arm around her.

What a fucking *bastard*. I have no one to blame for myself for letting my guard down, I knew better.

I *know* better.

The bartender sets down a glass filled to the top with a red liquid. "Thank you." I say, then pick up the glass and inspect the bizarre drink. I wonder if she's ever been thanked, but the smile escaping from her tells me just as much. The world is about as kind to Lesser Fae as it is to me. She smiles and perches on the island beside me, reminding me of Amwren once more.

"You'll forget your troubles rather quickly. I advise you to take your time, Keeper of Death." She whispers, and my eyes lock onto hers.

"And how is it you know who I am?" I spit out sarcasm and sip on the drink, sighing as the sweet elixir runs down my throat.

"Most of us *lesser* Fae have heard of you." She muses, fingers fiddling with the beads on her thin fabric of a skirt.

"And which team are you on? If you don't *mind*, I'd like for someone to not try and kill me right now. Try again later." I snap and don't let her finish, liquid courage burns my throat and soul. The music, bastard male and boisterous creatures are too much, turning my voice into a snarl.

Her elongated fingers grasp my own, her cool touch surprises me. "You are safe here." Giant gray eyes glaze over and her words extinguish the flame building inside me. "I was once in love with a Fae from The Mists, perhaps you knew her."

My breathing stops and I shakily set the drink down, then take her scrawny hand into both of mine. The paleness of my sunburned skin is heightened when compared to all those who dwell under the sun. "How?" I ask, my eyes warming. The Fae smiles and flutters her wings with a small rustle, looking around us before speaking.

"I met her many, *many* years ago. Well before your time. She was a traveling spinster, selling her goods throughout Iverbourne. So elegant," she sighs with longing, "the moment I set eyes on her, our bond fell into place. I *knew* she was mine, and I was hers."

I want to ask what that *means*, but wait. Knothall called Rohana his mate, but I don't know much about it. Books about love are not in high demand in the Mountain. Obviously, my luck with romance isn't great either as I notice Panrauth nuzzling into the female's neck out of the corner of my eye.

"Wren stayed here with me after that, it was the happiest time of my life. We ran this place together, she sold tapestries and I kept the town drunk." She chuckles softly, the brightness in her distant eyes dim. The weavings, they're all Amwren's.

I wonder when she learned how to engineer, she taught me everything I know about mechanics. I assumed that her life before the Mountain was full of gears, and shame fills me. I should've asked about her life, pressed a little harder. Knothall probably passed on his knowledge to her, to keep her out of the smiths or other labor camps.

The colorful fabric around the place pulls me into a trance, until the Fae speaks with such solemnity my blood runs cold. "Until The Others came." Amwren didn't tell me she saw them outside of Hallowed, too. The Fae grips my hand tight and I ground her, swallowing the building lump in my throat.

"They were 'recruiting', looking for Lesser and High Fae alike to join their cause. They came here, and Amwren," she breathes her name. I wonder how long it's been since she's said it fully. "Wren was terrified. She *told* me something wasn't right. She saw them taking children off the streets here ..."

The Fae gently pulls away from my hand, shaking her head as her wings tuck into her shoulders. "She went feral. It was horrific, I didn't know she was capable of that much bloodshed."

I can't imagine delicate, beautiful Amwren hurting a fly. I shake my head. "That doesn't sound right."

"It *wasn't* right. They took her alive, and at the time I wished I killed her myself. Until I received my first letter, that is."

I have a sneaking suspicion which trader would've snuck letters in, or out. I look around the bar, noticing Pan and the female gone. Umber is dancing outside with a handsome dark male, their bodies are melded beautifully under firelight from the ravaging bonfire. She's only been trading in the Mountain for fifteen years though, I wonder who smuggled in letters before that.

I turn my attention back to the bartender, unable to comprehend Pan's whereabouts right now. "So, what did she say?"

She smiles, opening and closing her wings slightly. "At first, they were just love letters between us. However, after a few centuries, all she seemed to talk about was a pesky girl, always getting into trouble." The Fae lifts her hairless brows and my cheeks warm. "She told me how you treated her. You made her feel alive in there. I'm sure even you know what that means to us."

"Amwren means the world to me, she was one of the few who treated me like a living being." She was like a mother, I want to say. Tears threaten to come out with that statement, though. "How have you done it? Being so close to the mountain? I would have gone insane."

She ponders, ignoring the impatient patrons hollering behind her for a moment. "What makes you think I haven't?" She throws me a weak, knowing smile and flutters off the bar. I reach out and catch her wrist, a little *too* hard.

"You know, right?" My drunken, heavy tears can't wait any longer. She wordlessly leaves me and tends to her customers, not looking back at my puddle of sadness. I look down at the bar with shame and wipe away tears, then drink the rest of my half empty glass in one go. Alcohol swims in my veins and I regret the bold move. The now pulsating noise and lights inside the place rattle my drowning brain, too much to bear.

Too much.

The room tilts and the floor sways under my brave legs, the intense spinning of my world threatens to take me down. Umber's frizzed sapphire catches my periphery and I stumble to a stop when I realize she's up against a wall. Half naked with a muscular, dark Fae thrusting into her, glowing white vines snake around his bare arms and neck. They can't *actually* be fucking.

Can they?

I shake my head and leave the bar, the street is now fully crowded with bonfires and half naked bodies. Umber isn't the only one 'frolicking' in public. I practically swim across the path in the direction of floating airships, the only landmark keeping me above water. Pan is there, waiting for me, I *know* he is. What I saw before, it has to be nothing. He asked me to wait for him, and I promised him I would. That means *something*, right?

He must've left the wanting female behind and took off for the ship. Along the sandy street sides bodies come together, using every surface possible to become one. The auras pulsating from individual and coupled Fae throw a rainbow of color against the pitch dark night, admittedly breathtaking. There are no stars again tonight, but this is truly beautiful, striking my heart.

My cane shakes and I pause, regaining my labored breath as my exhausted and inebriated body protests my day of adventuring. Aching moans and whining cries fill the air, the music of souls joining together. Red and green auras are speckled with a small purple and gray. Orange and yellow are less common, but present just the same. The overpowering Aether fragrance following me spikes with each coupling. A hungry growl rolls from the bench on the path beside me, which sends a startling quake through my chest.

Peering through two thick combined forest auras, I find Pan near naked, pants down around his ankles, and pounding into the bare female from the bar. I can't look away from the sight. She is on her back, hips bucking up into him and her full, dark breasts pressing against his bare chest.

Long nails *drag* across his back, his teeth have her neck pinned down. They climax as one, bodies shuddering and shouting with pleasure. The brightening Aether around them is astoundingly and disgustingly gorgeous. A power wave of sweet magic slams into me and I'm thrown backwards.

Wind knocks from my chest, simultaneously cracking my heart. I narrowly avoid hitting my head, a soft cry leaving me. A couple to my left glares at me in confusion, then continue on with their business like I'm nothing.

I roll onto my hands and knees and push myself up with shaking arms. Despite the burning in my muscles and heart, I hurry to the hovering ships. The alcohol clears from my pounding mind, anger fueling every step I take. Pan's voice calls from behind, but I don't stop, and he doesn't follow.

I have no idea which ship to board. Surprisingly, there are more than I anticipated, from slumbering beasts akin to sail boats, and small balloon crafts like Umber's. A groan of frustration hauls out of me and I stomp in frustration at the edge of the small, sleeping port. With caution I peer over my shoulder and my heart twinges at the empty path. I thought he would chase after me.

Say something, *apologize*. Anything to show he cares for me, at all. Obviously, I *am* nothing.

I bury my round face in my hands and slump against a cobbled half wall marking the docking area. We never agreed to be anything. There is no real, *exact* reason to be angry. But he asked me to wait, and I told him I would. I thought for sure the longing in his eyes was more than the lust he held for me. Love is a wicked thing, and my heart has been trying to tell me all along.

He called me a wicked thing, when I asked him to kiss me. He knows I crave love and used it against me, so he could be free. I would call his whole story a lie, if it wasn't for the photograph, the proof of his desperation. I am so deprived of love, I jumped at the first kindness shown to me. Palms and cheeks warm with wetness, tears mixing with sweat and sand.

"Well, you certainly don't look so frightening now."

I startle and swing the blade out of my cane, swiftly locating the creature in a human body standing over me. My blade touches his throat and his light blue eyes darken for a moment. The shadows surrounding his plainly dressed figure dim as well. The swirling darkness has specks of shimmering white hidden throughout, brilliantly contrasting against the abyss of an empty sky beyond his figure.

Obviously he possesses magic far beyond my knowledge, I have a feeling he could kill me *very* easily. We stare at each other in silence, sharing unreadable expressions. I'm curious why he's following me. After a moment, I sheath the blade and lay the cane down in red sand beside me, not taking my eyes off him. Aether rolls around his body, leaking down to the ground now in a river of star filled night, pooling around his feet.

"What are you?" I muse, not expecting a real answer.

"You're no fun, you're not even going to try and puzzle it out?" He whines, bouncing on the balls of his feet with freckled hands shoving into his pockets.

"I'm out of wits today unfortunately, I have a long journey tomorrow, and I would appreciate it if you took your games elsewhere." I muse, tucking my knees into my chest.

"Yes, so I've heard. Captain says we're taking some classified cargo to Cervalis first thing, isn't that *grand*?" The male is too enthusiastic, waving his arms up at the ships and grinning, his face full of mischief.

"I should've guessed the crew would include a trickster or two. You know Umber then?" I ask, watching his shadows creep across the few sandy feet between us. They almost seem curious, tendrils of friendly night which are much more timid than their master.

"*Ai*, trickster I may be, but we all need to have a little fun." He laughs, raking a hand through his hair. The movement draws shadows back inside his body, leaving behind a thin armor of darkness flowing over his skin.

A half smile escapes me and I shrug. "Sounds like something a trickster would say. You still didn't answer my question though."

"Oh right, Umber, that stick in the mud? She used to be part of the Crew, back a few years ago. Gave it all up for her own ship, but I heard that didn't end well." He raises a light brow, his bare feet inch closer. I roll my eyes and grin, hiding my surprise at the fact Umber gave up a stable crew for a life of trading in the Mountain.

"I had nothing to do with that, just along for the ride." I muse. He chuckles and gestures to sit beside me. I keep my eyes on the empty port ahead of us. "Free country, or so I hear." He sits cross legged to my left with a half smile revealing dimples, but my dark humor leaves silence between us.

Umber said the crew liked to party, but I didn't see him at the cantina. *Or* the mysterious Captain. I wonder why she's never mentioned them over the years we've known each other.

"That High Lord of yours though, not so much."

"What did you say?" I ask, attention snapping to his distant blue eyes.

"*Oh*, I assumed you knew. Want to hear a story then?" He asks in a giggle, twirling a finger in the air. Tendrils of black shadows form before my eyes, emitting from his long freckled fingers. I look around, finding we're still alone. I'm not sure if anyone can see his magic, or they just don't care.

"Once upon a time, there was a land of trees and snobs." He begins. I open my lips and he glares at me, silencing my protest. Smoke elegantly forms a scene in the air over our feet and I focus on the forest coming into focus. Muscles relax while I watch the pictures move, revealing a tragedy. A magnificent tree looms with a castle built into it, meadows and small trees surrounding the great tree.

"There once lived a boy who did not want to be King. He was rather spoiled, doing what he wished, *whomever* he wished." Green auras joining, bodies writhing together in the *street*. Moans echo through my brain and boil my blood. I watch the picture change in silence, face masked from the pain of my stupid heartache.

A young male climbs down from the castle, running away to the woods. The smoke rearranges to show a cottage. A garden forms beside the quaint place, a woman standing in the plants. She opens her arms to the male, they embrace and he sweeps her off her feet, carrying her inside.

"One day, the King grew ill, and the lands turned barren. It was time for the heir to rise, the Aether of the land choosing the most careless of his offspring. The wicked boy did not care if the crops died while he snubbed his duty, he chose his human bride over his people."

The garden wilts, trees die, leaves are shed and branches snap. Animal carcasses litter the once beautiful forest, and the stench of death tickles my nose. I tear away from the picture to glance sideways at the blonde male, his sapphire eyes glisten as he watches the next scene unfold. Three armored Fae arrived at the cottage, astride great furred beasts with curling horns. The smoke flashes red, bringing me back to my nightmare of Eros and Knothall watching me drown.

"The wicked boy fought his kin, refusing to go home and forsake his simple life." The couple flee from behind the cottage, the woman holds two small children against her as they run. The male attempts to slow down the onslaught but it's no use, the lovers are caught. A brother falls at the hands of Pan, and the other beheads the woman while she holds her children. Three bodies fall to the ground, the small children hold their mother's head and wail.

"The boy killed his own brother, the choice of human blood over his own kin permanently seeping into the ground of Terra and angering the Ancients. The wickedness killed the king's heart, sending him into a fit of crazed rage. The Queen could not survive his wrath, and since then the lands have been plagued by famine and sickness. The wicked boy's children were sent to live in the grand castle, and he was thrown into the Eternal, at the behest of his sister."

Pan falls to his knees, his children wordlessly scream as they're taken away atop a snarling goat beast, a brother holds a sword to Pan's throat. I look away, eyes brimming with burning tears as heat spreads over my neck.

"I think that's enough," I whisper. The smoke drifts down, settling on the sand. I rub away the burning on my face and evaluate the once devilish male, his softened face overlooks the unending horizon. "Why are you telling me this?"

I don't bother to ask if he's lying, it makes *sense*. Umber's pleading words, the rounded ears of his daughters. The reason Pan was in the Eternal at all. I'm going to fix it. That's what he told Umber, and he used me to do it. I've tortured and murdered countless innocent Fae, for the sake of following orders, can I really blame him for doing whatever it takes to get back home?

There is one particular thing that doesn't sit right with me. Why would they send away the rightful High Lord, knowing it would destroy the land and forsake their people? Are humans that hated in Iverbourne?

"I suppose I would want to know who I'm traveling with. I can't put my finger on it, but I feel like I should help you." A sly grin plays at his voice and I look sideways to find his sun spotted cheeks full of color.

"You *just* met me." I narrow my brows in disbelief, rolling my shoulders back as I will ice into my tone. Iron soldiers would be here already if we were sold out. The gears in my mind turn as I attempt to gauge his motive.

"Do you believe in fate?" His voice is kind, no humor tainting his question.

I've never thought about it before. Everything that happened to me was determined the moment I opened my eyes. I always thought of myself as a mistake of the Ancients. Is that my fate, to live as a series of mistakes?

"I don't know. Honestly." I rub my neck and push out a breath. "I do know I never thought I would make it out of there, and I have to believe I did that for myself."

The tight darkness around him softens further, the soft gray when I first met him playing the numerous strings upon his simple lute. "I think you'll find life is full of happy surprises." He murmurs, the dark sky is changing to pink on the horizon before us, orange and yellow warms the great distance.

We sit there for several moments in silence, watching the sun come up.

Eventually, he asks, curious and gentle, "Why did you let yourself be glamoured?" His scarred ear twitches as he tilts his head, watching every part of my exhausted face while he awaits my answer.

"Are you going to tell me why you cut your ears down?"

He scoffs, pressing a dramatic hand to his chest. "What makes you think *I* did it?" I stammer in attempts to recover, but he saves me from myself. "A band of Purist bastards found it fitting, I suppose." He chuckles, smile fading as I keep him in my unyielding stare.

"It was this, or watch them kill my best friends in front of me. Unlike *your* friend, I have far more respect for humans." He mutters, shaking his hair so wild locks cover his ears once more. My heart thunders, guilt courses through my veins. How could I ever think he did it to himself?

I think about Pan, the smoke images replay in my head. Novak is right. If Pan truly loved his wife, he would've let her go. Humans and faeries can never be together in this world. She would still be alive, if he let her go. At the very least, he would've never been separated from his children.

"Can you remove it, the glamor?" I ask, curious how powerful he is.

"Of course, what do you take me for?" He cracks his fingers and makes a big show of stretching, only to touch a careful and incredibly warm finger to my brow.

The headache of sweet Aether fades, replaced by heat and a sudden wave of salt rushing my nostrils. I sigh in relief and rise with stiff muscles. "I suppose if we're going to be stuck together, I should know your name."

The beautiful male grins, standing only when I'm fully straightened. He bows deeply, eyes flashing to an intense deep blue, then back to bright sapphires so fast I can hardly comprehend the change. "Novak, at your service."

I roll my eyes at the mop of hair covering his face, readjusting my pack on my back. "Well, Novak, make yourself useful and show me where I can pass out."

BETTER LUCK NEXT TIME

I sleep fitfully for the last few precious hours of dawn, tossing and swinging in a hammock in the spacious crew's quarters. Eventually, I roll right out, smashing onto the hardwood floor of the ship's lower deck.

I curse under my breath, thankful I'm the only one in the quarters, I think. Umber and Pan never returned from their activities, nor did any other crew member come down after Novak showed me to the sleeping area. He had offered his room if I wanted privacy, but I didn't dare step past the innocent looking blue tapestry door.

I pull out my sand stained bag resting under the hammock and scan the area once more, then get to work. First, I pull sockets onto lined and socked thighs. The contracting muscles in my legs and hips protest at only having a couple hours break. Perhaps our next stop will be longer, *wherever* that is. I shouldn't say *our*, at this point I have to accept the fact that I will be alone.

After both prostheses are attached, I slip the loose coffee brown pant legs back down, then button the cuff tightly at the bottom. I decide to keep the cropped linen top on and throw my jerkin over it, re-situating my favorite belt of leather pouches around my hips. I tie knotted hair into a rough bun off to the side, the purple fringe tickles my eyebrows and cheeks.

I shove off the floor and stretch my arms overhead, my back cracking. Heavy footsteps, multiple pairs, trace along the deck above. I eye the ladder centered in the lower deck and drag myself up one steep rung at a time, the blazing sun meets my face and pleasantly blinds me. I close my eyes and breathe in deep, inhaling the smell of hot sand, a freshly oiled deck and sweat ruminating from every crew member, the sounds of a chaotic ship emanate around me.

"*Oi*, you're in my feckin way." The squawk wakes me up from my moment and I find a thick bodied Lesser Fae waiting at the top of the ladder, rather put out. Leather wings are tucked in tight behind her, her large gray eyes are drawn together into a scowl. I stutter out apologies and climb onto the deck with haste, moving out of her way with a stumble.

She chews on a toothpick, otherwise unmoving while she scrutinizes me. Tattoos snake along her shaved head and continue down her bare arms and chest, a torn bralette attempts to corral the fullness there. I straighten, we are the same height so I lift my chin.

"At least one of ya's was on time." She chuffs, then moves on down the ladder using one arm, the other holds a sloshing barrel upon her dirty shoulder.

I wander around, exploring how the large ship reflects the early sun, so much more magnificent than at nighttime. Taken straight from books about pirates and mariners, the epic galleon holds towering masts and great golden sails. The mahogany beauty belongs in the rough seas, not in the middle of a desert. At the helm of the ship rests a glorious steering wheel, making Umber's look like a toy.

The crew members are already at work, grumbling among each other and complaining about their late comrades as they tend to the rigging and gather the last of supplies from the 'grounders.' A green Lesser Fae loosens the sails above, and on the ground a dusty brown High Fae unties the knots that hold the ship down, white vines encircle his neck and bare arms.

The male looks like the one I saw last night, but his inky hair is longer than I remember, and he's wearing glasses now. That is something I would've noticed, as not many Fae wear them. At least, not in the Mountain. My observations disrupt the male who pushes up his dirty lenses, giving me a nervous stare before continuing on. I decide technology is better company. Behind the steering wheel waits a brass display of switches, calling for me to tamper with the shining buttons.

I approach casually, not finding anyone at the helm. My cane is strapped away and I take my time, eager to adjust to these new prostheses without my cane as much I can. I caress the control panel, attempting to decipher the unfamiliar text. Levers and knobs beg me to turn and pull them, find out what they do. The last invention I tinkered on, a new type of Aether engine for the Water Fae, is more powerful than any made yet. What they intend to use it for is another question, one I don't want to know the answer to. A smile meets my lips when I ponder the feeling of a wrench in my hand.

"I wouldn't touch anything, if I were you." A melodic voice greets me from above. A bean pole of a High Fae lounges in the nets that run from the deck to the beams and rigging above. A rather large brown hat with colorful feathers rests on the face of the mysterious pirate.

"Oh?" I cross to the railing opposite the Fae and lean, arms crossing as a mask of boredom rests on my face.

The *thick*, bloody aura pouring around the Fae chokes me and I push out a forced breath. A thin hand pushes the hat up slightly to reveal sharp, sparking red eyes evaluating me. For a moment I see Ragnis, and air returns to me only when I realize it's *not* him. The hat settles back onto long raven hair, revealing a creamy angled face. The picture of female roguish perfection, and the opposite of what 'true' Fire Fae are supposed to look like.

The Fae rolls herself off the net, catching a rope in hand as she swings down, landing on black pointed leather boots. She dusts off her shoulders which are covered in a trailing leather jacket. "Gear heads aren't allowed near that." She nods to the control panel and looks me up and down, hands at her sides and face expressionless.

"To be fair, I was admiring the craftsmanship. And I take that as a compliment, by the way." I bite out the words at the end. The Fire Fae smirks and rubs her chin. She walks towards me, much taller than I and perhaps even Pan. A porcelain hand extends between us and I stare at it, confusion drawing my brows together. I hold out my hand, unsure what to do.

"It's called a handshake, dummy." She grasps my hand firmly and before I can grip back she releases me. "You may call me Captain. There are three rules on this ship. No brawling, no drinking and no back talk."

I nod, crossing my arms. "Fine. Where are the others? Pan and Umber?"

"It's not my job to look after your companions. I don't care if it's one or three stowaways, as long as I get paid." Captain holds out a hand expectantly. I sling my bag down on the deck, then kneel on a vibrating joint. I unstrap the roll attached to my pack and stand, handing it to her.

"These will never break, under any circumstances. I was never able to take advantage of their charm, but I've heard out here they will never encounter a problem they can't fix."

Captain's quick hands snatch the tool roll and she marvels at the obsidian tools inside. She bows mockingly, then strides away without another word. Her thick hips shake a falchion blade at one side, and a bag full of coins I'm assuming at the other. Apparently the *whole* roll will be payment for our journey.

I cross to the side of the ship closest to the village and overlook sleepy streets beginning to stir. Half and fully naked bodies are laying everywhere, in places there are more than two together. The bright auras that lit up the night are drowsy and faded by the intense sun. Beltane knocked this place out. I wonder if it's like this every night, or just on the holidays. A village of misfits could quite possibly party every day, but I doubt it.

At the half wall separating the village from the port, Pan and Umber are approaching, trailed by a male High Fae looking rather annoyed. The same from last night, sans glasses. I casually look around the deck and find another Fae eerily similar, now on the deck, the one with dirty lenses. *Twins.*

Umber rubs her forehead and Pan looks down as they near the ship. At least he's *dressed* now. I decided last night I wasn't going to make a big deal out of it. He saved my life, and for that I am eternally grateful. The idea of us becoming lovers is pushed far from my mind, now. Much easier to say and harder to do, especially when his sullen gaze meets my own fiery, glamorless eyes.

A light hand pats me on the shoulder, pulling me close. "Shall we kiss and make him jealous?" Novak's devilish voice is *quite* tempting. I want nothing more than for Pan to feel an inch of what I did last night.

No, *no.*

Pretending like nothing happened at all could be much more fun.

I face Novak, dismissing Umber and Pan walking onto the ship's ramp. The handsome Fae grins, hair falling over his eyes with no shadows or darkness to be seen. Too many dark freckles and sunspots to count lay across his cheeks, much like how I heard stars are. "Thank you, for last night. You're still an asshole though."

Novak holds his stomach and laughs, the stocky female I encountered earlier pauses as she walks by. "Well, I might like ya more now." She chuffs, then makes her way below deck with another barrel. Novak grins and pats me on the shoulder again, then takes off for the nearest rigging attached to the sails above.

Umber nods to me, muttering about cursed faerie wine and waving her hand lazily as she retires to the crew's quarters below. Pan settles at my side, figure drawn in and exhausted. I ignore him and watch Captain flick switches, enage a lever behind the steering wheel, my curiosity piquing as I do. As she pushes the lever forward, the ship lifts precariously with a rumbling hum flowing under my boots.

Whatever is powering the behemoth must be below the ship.

The massive sails overhead catch and the gold fabric stretches taut, a black faerie skull and crossbones are splashed onto every sail. Captain barks orders at the crew, her eyes spt fire and flames lick at her shoulders. Novak is perched in the crows nest above with his eyes closed, hair catching the wind and a peaceful smile resting on his face. No one else's eyes are lit up with Aether to power the engines, none that I can *see*, and I now have a newfound healthy dose of fear for this Captain.

She shouldn't have access to this much magic, *no* Fae does.

Within minutes we race away from the port, the speed something I didn't expect. The pirate ship doesn't float as Umber's did. We are thrust through a heated sky and clouds, my stomach teases my throat with bile. "Lythienne," Pan draws out my name, a rough hand brushes against my arm.

I take a casual step back and rest a shaking hand on the railing, then wave around us with my free hand. "Can you believe it? This makes Umber's ship look tiny. Don't tell her I said that, though." I chuckle, avoiding his cold eyes. I stare over the edge at the distant lands fading, replaced by a horizon of sea. I lean on the beautiful mahogany fully and rest on my pale arms, burying simmering anger.

Pan rests beside me, putting no distance between us. Skin on skin is no longer comforting, and my skin crawls as flashes of him pounding into that female race across my mind. "I need to apologize." Pan rumbles, waiting for me to look at him.

"For what?" Cheer drips from my voice, taunting him. Perhaps I won't be able to let it go so easily after all.

"What do you want me to say?"

"I don't want or *need* you to say anything. You're the one who said you needed to apologize." My neck burns and I focus on the clouds we sail through, the vertical golden sails beneath us catching wind.

Parallel Aether engines are attached to the dark hull, blasting fire and smoke behind them. The craftsmanship and power is remarkable, they rival even my last greatest work. The amount of Aether needed to thrust this behemoth through the sky still puzzles me, but a different problem *demands* my attention. Pan's stare burns me alive and I allow silence to fill the air between us for a minute, then *finally* turn my smiling face to his broken features. Hair dirty and knotted, exhaustion plaguing his eyes, he looks like the male I met in The Pit.

Broken and filthy.

His lips open a few times, words struggle to come out. Pan stares down at the sea that peeks between the clouds. He *still* isn't going to speak, tell me the truth behind everything he's hiding. Why I am *nothing* to him.

I can't help it, a breath leaves me before my words sting him. "Look, we didn't make any promises to each other. You saved me, and I saved you." I don't relent, taking in another deep breath and calming my voice. "When you asked me to wait, I thought that meant something. Obviously not." I bite out the last words, struggling to play it off.

Pan rakes a hand through his hair, fingers catch snarls before he stands. He glowers down at me. I rise and lift my chin, crossing my arms. "I don't even remember her name. She meant nothing to me." The words are so empty, like forced lines he recited.

"It looked that way." I mutter, cutting him off.

"I wanted to get my dick wet. Is that what you want to hear?" His primal tone reverberates through me, his shoulders draw back.

"I want the truth, Pan. That's all I'm asking, I don't even care about her, I care that you're hiding from me." Anger turns to pleading and hurt, shame fills me as

I let my guard down once more. For a moment there is so much rage in both of our eyes, I feel like we're back to square one, ready to rip each other's throat out.

"I'm afraid that if I fuck you, I will never want to stop." Panrauth's rugged face is stone, jaw *grinding* from under his thick beard. Confusion and goosebumps spread across me and I take a step back.

"I'm afraid if I start loving you, I will never stop. If I start loving you, how long will it be before I lose you?" His aura is the same pale green it tends to be around me, his words however, throw daggers into my heart. "I was so fucking drunk, she looked at me, and all I wanted was you. To love you. I thought I could convince myself I don't want you, and if I was with someone else, I could finally stop thinking about you every *fucking* minute of the day."

My arms drop, eyes burning with humiliation. I can't listen anymore, but he doesn't stop. I don't understand, this is his choice. I am *ready* for his love, or was ready, that is. He has no one to blame but himself for being a coward, afraid of risking pain for my love. I can't tell him any of it. My ears fold down as he hurls his last words at me.

"Every time my cock *pounded* into her and she moaned, I imagined what you would sound like. What it would feel like to be with you. And then, you really were there. I ruined it perfectly, all the fuck over again." The Bear practically spits words at me, his neck throbs under his beard. Even his arms are shaking, hands in fists and veins bulging along his arms.

My voice is a whisper in the wind, but it cuts through the air like a knife. "You're *pathetic*, Pan. You had my heart in your hands and you stomped on it because you were *scared*? Come up with a better excuse for your next damsel in distress." Tears burn down my cheeks and I march away from his broken face.

Captain, Novak and most of the crew are watching, paused in their business and silent. I storm off, holding my chin up and ignoring everyone. I flee below deck to Umber, who is already fast asleep in the hammock above mine.

DON'T WE ALL?

For several hours I lay sulking in a rickety hammock. Folded ears listen to Umber snore and small hands clutch the package with my name on it. How can something so *small* contain so much foreboding, so much potential to change my world?

Another body rests in a hammock at the opposite end of the quarters, just as silent as I have been. I've seen fleeting movement several times, but nothing else. The crew walking above and wind beating the ship teases my ears, occasionally I can hear Captain shouting and the thrumming of a lute. It sounds like what I imagine fun to be, what I've glimpsed sometimes with Umber.

I sigh and tap the box with my fingers, staring at Knothalls writing. I can't face Pan again. My plan to play it off ended miserably, my heart laid open on the deck and bleeding for everyone to see. The fucking idiot, raging about wanting to love me but can't. He's his own obstacle, and that isn't my problem. The ridiculousness of it stings my heart further.

I tuck the unopened box away, trading for a ration of bread from my bag. My stomach twists around it within seconds. I haven't eaten properly in almost two days, my last meal not entirely wholesome to begin with. I glance at the occupied hammock before standing, then wander through the quarters in search of food.

Thick canvas hammocks line the deck, broken only by a central kitchen area and side rooms. Several permanent bedrooms rest on the edge of the quarters, the simple fabrics covering door frames are noticeably different from the more private wooden door to the washroom. Novak's blue tapestry door is the finest, and two light purple fabrics across the deck catch my eye as well. Captain holds a grand cabin underneath the helm. I couldn't help but peek in earlier before I met her at the steering wheel.

I stand before the wooden cupboards and start opening doors. The first two have bulk dry goods, and the third is filled with glass jars. A long growl irritates my stomach and I groan. "I wouldn't touch anything else, if I were you." An annoyed male voice crawls across the deck, one of the white vined Fae sitting up on a hammock. The male rubs at his temple and *glares* at me. The twin Umber was with last night, the one with the markings of a warrior.

"I was just hungry." I put my hands up, drawing my brows together.

"You'll wait for dinner to be served, just like everyone else. It's the only free meal you'll get on this ship. Captain will have your fingers." The twin releases a rumbling dark laugh, then rises with a stormy blue aura and violet eyes. A Water Fae, and a powerful one.

I scowl, leaving the kitchen in haste. He meets me midway to my hammock, stopping in front of me. The brashness and confidence rolling from him is oddly tempting. My boots halt before him. "Do we have a problem?"

Hard eyes such a deep violet stare directly into my soul, taking me further off guard. Inky hair rests in shaggy coils over his scarred face, the sides of his scalp are cut short. The dark brown Fae crosses muscled, white vine tattooed arms and juts his sharp chin to the deck above. "When I found that sack of shit this morning, he was still drunk on the side of the road. Get your ass up there."

Small hands loosen and I blink, opening my lips but unsure what to say for a moment. "I thought Captain said it wasn't her problem if they came or not."

"It's not. Nor is it mine. I've just heard promising things about you, and I hate to be disappointed." Muscles flex in his neck while he evaluates me with a shrug. His hungry eyes pause on my full breasts pressing on the linen top, and my soft navel peeking out. A wicked grin erupts from him when my cheeks heat and I involuntarily bite my lip.

Ignoring the warmth spreading from between my thighs, I roll my shoulders back and put on a mask of boredom. "And who are you?"

His left brow arches, pulling at a hairless scar running through it. A warrior indeed, his clean shaven jaw is littered with scars. The largest runs over his brow, eye and straight down to his jaw. I see so much of myself in him, so much of the toll life can take on a strong Fae. The tense muscles across his chest are dressed in a navy tunic, embroidered with fine silver. A sword hangs from the baldric at his side, along with a belt strapped with other various blades.

He lifts a broad shoulder. "Nobody important. Just doing my job, hoping shit goes back to normal."

What a fun game we are having, he is indeed someone important, that much I can tell.

"Don't we all?" I tease in a low tone.

This Fae has a story, and a body lusting for my own. I step closer until my breasts brush on his chest, my hand caresses the bare skin peeking from his half done shirt. A strong, thundering heart meets my touch, threatening to spill its strength into me. My heart flutters and I look up through my lashes, biting my lip which draws a fatal grin from the Fae.

What *is* this feeling?

He arches a thick brow and parts smiling lips, a sure hand grasps my waist and yanks me close. A twitching shaft meets my hip, flooding me further with hunger. We are interrupted by Panrauth's heavy step landing onto the deck, the disruption jolts me from my trance. Pan pauses long enough to give me a disgusted look, then continues to an empty hammock and unpacks in silence.

Color fills my cheeks and I take my leave wordlessly, then head for the deck above. I probably would've just fucked him right then and there, without thinking twice. The pull that Fae has on me is dire, and apparently I impress him as well. And I don't even know his *name*. I focus on Cervalis, pushing away frustrating thoughts of coming so close to release and pleasure, once again. I check the time on my wrist and pace the deck above, three hours left. I have no real plan, how to get there, and what to do after.

Now that is the question, who will I be? I reel myself in and push out a breath.

I'm sure The Others will come across our path, or Ragnis will come calling. If he even cares at all, that is. This is not a problem he, or any previous High Lord has dealt with before. Before leaving, Pan and I agreed to travel together on foot, leaving the city for the Mists. Cervalis is only a front, the grand trading center is only the business side of Hallowed, the Mists hold the High Lady. I have no idea where Umber fits into that, or Pan for that matter, now.

I pause on the deck, unsure what to do with myself. Captain lounges against the wheel, her fiery eyes lock onto me and she smiles. She tips her hat to me and I stride over to the helm, then stand beside her. Dusk meets us as the sun greets the horizon and the clouds are painted with purples and pinks. I cross my arms and overlook the sea of colors, breathing in the salt lingering in the air.

I'm reminded of the smell when Novak lifted the glamor from my eyes, and comfort follows the memory. Behind us, night creeps, no stars though. The clouds are soft and vibrant up here, any sea visible below is just darkness breaking through the atmosphere. The golden sails catch the last bits of sunlight, the numerous epic fabrics billowing proud in the wind.

"It's magnificent, truly a stroke of genius." I breathe. Captain smiles, her aura a soft and inviting pink now. "How do you do it? It's so much heavier than a regular airship." I tilt my head at her, then look behind us at the trail of light Aether smoke as my cheeks warm in her silence.

"Come here." She calls to me, hand held out. I stare at her for a moment before gently taking her thin hand. Captain pulls me over to the wheel with a soft tug, then sets my hand on the warm, dark wood.

I bite my lip and attempt to veil my excitement. "Are you serious?"

Captain chuckles and sets her feathered hat on my head. I grip the wheel with both hands, the wind's freedom washes me clean. She leans on the railing near me, her gaze amused and sharp features turned up in delight. "You know, I could use an extra gear head around here."

I glance at her, arching a brow. "I think I may be more trouble than I'm worth."

Captain smirks, rubbing her chin. I watch the crew putter around the ship, the twins are chatting with lesser Fae. Novak is high up in the crow's nest, playing his lute and catching eyes with me. I am more at ease every time I see him, he is always smiling. And surrounded by darkness. Such a contrast, if I didn't have the crystal eye I would've just thought he was a roguish young Fae who liked trouble, smiling his way through life.

My cheeks warm again and I focus on the sea of clouds, avoiding Captain watching me gawk over Novak. Apparently a lack of sex makes you quite hungry for *everything*, but I crave the comfort I've found already in Novak more so than anything.

"This may be true, you do seem like a troublemaker, as Oaken says." Captain brushes dirt off her shoulder and tilts her head, curiosity plain on her face. "Tell me, what is the story between you and the High Lord?"

"We helped each other get out. That's all." I say shortly.

"Is it?" She asks, glancing at Pan and a dark purple Fae arguing fiercely on the lower deck.

"Why do you care?" I ask, turning away from the wheel to glare at her.

"I'm just nosy." Captain smirks, and I catch her glancing at Novak when she takes the wheel back from me. I rest on the railing she once occupied and regard Captain with an even face.

"I suppose you agree that Panrauth should take over?"

"It's not a matter if he *wants* to, he has to. Abdicating the throne to his sister so he can run away doesn't change the fact that the Aether of the lands chose him."

I narrow my brows, pondering her statement. "So that's why the lands are dying, because they reject his sister?"

"I pinned you for being a bit more of an intellectual, you know of the treaty, yes?"

"Well yes, but it doesn't say what the consequences are for disobeying." I mutter and she softens, her porcelain face thoughtful.

"He has no choice. He serves his people, or he fails them. Hopefully he makes the right choice. What affects Terra affects the rest of the territories, and my business."

I stare out at the now twilight sky, lost in thought as the horizon captures the bleeding sun.

"The question is, what are you doing?" She rests a hand on mine, the warmth emanating from her brings back memories of Ragnis. Whereas her skin remains comforting, his would flare and spark, blistering my face. Usually it was to punish Knothall, make him watch his pet suffer in pain. The memory sends a shudder through me and I rise from the ornate railing.

I watch Novak, now seated at a game table beside the lower deck edge. The Fae with glasses laughs heartily across from him, Novak's arms are wildly swinging in the air as he tells a story. "I have absolutely no idea what I'm doing." And I truly don't.

I am ravenous when dinner is served. I am unable to complain as the feast is a miraculous sight. Resting on the highest deck at the prow of the ship is a masterpiece, a stretching dinner table akin to the industrial surfaces in the lab. The great length of wood is covered end to end with random clustered platters of food, nothing matching and the food equally contrasting. I've never seen so many colors, inhaled so many flavors or *dreamed* of the combinations before me.

I can handle *this* overwhelming of senses.

Captain and Novak are seated at each end of the table, the other crew members I've only seen in passing are gathered as well and boisterously chatting. Everyone is present, except for Pan and the purple Fae he had been with, and Umber.

Novak pats the empty seat beside him and I oblige, sitting on a rickety stool. I glance at the twins, bickering over who will deliver a shipment. The only identical thing about them is their faces, but even those features are interrupted by scars and glasses.

They are both young like Novak and I, each bearing white tattoos of vines across their faces and bodies. The tendrils spread across nearly every inch of deep brown skin bordering on charcoal shades, the tattoos even overlap in places. I've never seen anything like it. Bright violet eyes filled with mischief rest in both of them, and their oceanic auras join as one when they are close to the other. The warrior one I met earlier, his side of the aura is much more intense than his brother's. With their fine embroidered silken tunics and clean cut figures, they belong in a court, not gallivanting on a pirate ship and fucking in cantinas.

Fluttering in after me are a couple of lesser Fae, neither with wings, instead horns protrude from their foreheads. Silent and simply dressed, they don't appear to be servants, but aren't as outspoken as the rest of the crew. Umber trails behind them with a heavy step and sits beside Captain, bringing her mouth to Captain's slender raven tufted ear. Umber's lips barely move, but Captain hangs onto her every word.

I break from my staring and decide on a platter full of green leafy bits with colorful vegetables on top. I'm not sure if I will even *like* fresh vegetables. Everything in the Mountain is either dried or canned, and usually served cold. I poke at circular slices of green, and little red globes.

"Why don't you both go?" Captain asks the twins, rather annoyed as she stabs into a bite of steak. Umber is filling her plate now, grinning at me, and I return the smile. She looks like the usual Umber now, not the one I saw in Echo.

"It's much better with this." Novak's soft voice pricks my ears. I face him, his freckled hand is outstretched and holding out a small bowl which contains a thick white sauce. My cheeks warm and I take it, then gingerly pour it over top of the produce.

"What is this?" I whisper to him, still catching glances from around the table. The grumbly female begins to complain obnoxiously about Sylvan's sky high price for fish.

"Supposedly, when you throw a bunch of healthy things together, it's called a salad," Novak shrugs his shoulders and steals a bite from my plate, "I just call it pretty feckin' good."

I smirk at the near swear and try a bite, the crisp flavors are indeed delightful. In minutes my plate is cleared, and I add a little bit more of everything from the other platters. The twins continue their bickering, Captain's gaze falls on me every now and then while engaged with Umber.

"So, do you all usually fly together?" I ask, meeting Captain's watchful eye once more. Novak snickers and leans back with his hands behind his head, eyes focused on Alvis swatting Orion upside the head.

"Novak has been first mate since this ship launched, and unfortunately, these two are the best in the business," Captain gestures to a grinning Novak, then to the twins offhandedly. "Despite the headache they give me."

The one without glasses sticks his tongue out at her, white tattoos glowing subtly as he does. The other brother rolls flashing eyes, then pushes up his dirty glasses. At last, both of them give me their full attention and I straighten subtly in my seat. The scarred one speaks first, dipping his chin and placing a hand on his chest. As if our confrontation never happened. "Alvis, pleased to meet you."

Perhaps food softened his attitude, and his hunger for me.

His brother adjusts his glasses once more and shakes inky coils from his face before doing the same. "And I am Orion, the better of the two." He grins, elbowing his brother in the ribs. I've never experienced so many shows of respect, but no one in the Mountain gives or receives the fist to chest gesture I've heard about.

I smile and nod to them both, my voice quiet and cautious. "I'm Lyth."

The bristly female pipes up. "Te' troublemaker is more like it." She smirks at me, and I'm unable to tell if she's teasing or not. I roll back my shoulders and move my food around.

Novak flings a spoonful of food at the Fae, hitting her scrunched up face with perfect precision. "Oh, Oak. Don't be such a party pooper." The Fae's square face flushes red and she rises like a kraken from the sea. Potatoes slide down her face and a glorious leather wingspan catches wind behind her, stretching over fifteen feet.

I bite my lip and look around the table, the twins are both lit up in delight, snickering away. Even Captain is smirking, hiding under a tilted down hat. Umber doesn't even try to contain her laughter.

"Ya little shit." Oak scowls, taking a handful of cake into her hand, making her way to Novak.

The handsome Fae blanches and he scoots his chair back, rising with his hands up. "Come on Oak, it's just a bit of fun."

She hauls after him, yelling profanities and chasing him around the table. He makes it around once before Alvis trips him, causing Oak to haul upon the musician and shove a fistful of sweets into his face. We all break into an uproarious laughter, my stomach muscles burn and tears flow from my black and white eyes.

Novak rises from the scuffle with a wild grin, licking at his lips dramatically. His happiness is infectious, you can *feel* the entire crew loosen up around him, their auras light up the crisp night air. Novak *himself* however, is surrounded by an aura darker than the abyss in the mountain.

Oak takes her leave, muttering about insolent kids while ruffling her wings back into place. Novak sits beside me again, the numerous dimples in his cheeks are still present. For a moment, I am struck by his face, framed by shadows and night. How can someone so happy be surrounded by so much darkness?

I give him a delicate smile and lean back, my stomach and heart beyond satisfied. I think about the note I received with my eye, seeing people for who they truly are. I find myself wanting to know more about him, and feel empty when I realize he'll be leaving with Captain. Novak seems quite mischievous to be a first mate, but it's obvious their crew is extremely tight knit.

What I imagine a family to be like.

The table settles down after a while, the aches in my body and mind compel me to pull the small wooden pipe from my side pouch and pack it with herbs. I remember Captain's rule about drinking, then pause and glance up at her. "Is this alright?"

The Fire Fae shrugs. "As long as you share with the class. I could give a shit about that," She nods to the pipe in my hand, "it's alcohol that turns you into a beast." Captain focuses on the sky with distant, soft pink eyes. I contemplate her words while familiar smoke finds my lungs, caressing my spirit and leaving a gentle softness in my body.

Novak is absolutely giddy by the time he gets the pipe, puffing on it with a grin before passing it down to the twins. "Are you ever *not* excited?" I muse to him.

"No." Captain replies with firm content before Novak can answer me. I shift my attention from Novak to her, arching a purple brow. "Is that a bad thing?" Captain challenges.

"No, it's nice." I say light heartedly, fully meaning it. Novak smirks and leans back in his chair, resting freckled hands behind his head. I find myself lost in thought, watching him talk to the others. Alvis' watchful gaze breaks my staring, and I find Orion watching me minutes later.

Alvis hollers to Novak with a grin. "Play us a song."

Novak groans, rubbing a hand on his stomach. "I'm not sure I can, your dinner is impeccable, as always." I chuckle, keeping my gaze on the night sky riding by.

"What's so funny, Keeper?" Alvis taunts, commanding my tightened gaze to his. Orion shifts beside his brother, nervously rubbing his neck. Captain straightens the feather on her hat.

I lift a shoulder. "Nothing, I just assumed males only knew how to do two things, fuck horribly and kill with mediocre talent."

Silence creeps for ten seconds, then is followed by unending laughter. Novak *literally* falls over in his chair, holding his stomach. My cheeks warm at Alvis' wide grin and subtle wink, he leans back and places his hands behind his head. "You may be pleasantly surprised to find what other talents I have."

Captain clears her throat, claiming silence. "Alright, enough children."

Novak rises in silence, suddenly taking to pacing the deck and muttering, a full cloud of visible abyss overtakes his figure, definitely not *just* an aura. My heart jumps at the sight, similar to the shadows he held in Echo, but these are visibly out of control and swallowing him whole.

Captain's flaming eyes fixate on him, her strong voice stops him cold. "Hey, kid."

Novak rolls his shoulders back, then his head whips to Captain. Shadows shoot to the ground but soft black irises remain, drawing stiffness from Alvis. Orion had removed his glasses and is now rubbing his face with a vined hand.

"What?" Novak approaches Captain nervously, gentle voice now hoarse like he's been screaming. The sight of him trembling at her side unnerves me, I haven't seen him like this before. His eyes are black, and he fidgets with the hem of his tunic.

"Play us your song." Captain asks with gentleness, a smile spreading across her beautiful sharp face.

Air visibly leaves Novak and he gives her a weak smile in return. With a wave of his shaking hand, controlled tendrils of shadows appear, ushering in his lute from nothingness. Orion stands and pushes his chair over to Novak, the rest of the table remains silent while the musician settles. I search Umber's eyes, she only presses a finger to her lips. She must know something, Novak said she used to be on their crew.

Novak rolls his shoulders back once more and finds peace at last when his fingers meet the strings of his instrument. The feeling I had watching him in Echo sweeps over me again, his music causes everyone around us to fade away. The song he plays is the same, too. Our eyes connect and I watch the darkness fade away in his, revealing bright sapphires.

A smile quirks up one side of his dimples, like he's playing for me. Just me. His leaking darkness dissipates further, until all that remains is a handsome, broken Fae.

The entire crew watches him play, silent and enjoying every tune and melody he gives. Even the Lesser Fae hold smiles, swaying in place with their arms slung around each other. Alvis and Orion are standing side by side and I can't help but notice the shine in Alvis' eyes as he watches Novak play. Captain watches Novak intently as well, then claps her hands when he pauses his playing. I join in immediately, drawing color to his tanned cheeks.

Captain can never be the uncaring fire Fae she is supposed to be, this crew is her family.

After another round of herbs and light banter I check my watch, 45 minutes until landing. The Lesser Fae whose names I still haven't learned left about ten minutes ago, leaving the 'Crew of Misfits' as I've dubbed them, above. "So what's the plan?" I ask Umber.

Umber shifts in her seat, her playful features drift to a serious calm. "I'm coming with you." A small breath of relief releases from me. I glance at Novak, my courage building to ask him, but Alvis speaks first.

"Where are we going?" Alvis asks Umber with mild amusement. Umber gestures to me, rolling her eyes with annoyance at Alvis. The warrior twin turns to me, rubbing his chin and grinning handsomely.

"I have business in Hallowed Court." I say, flat and simple.

Novak whistles lightly and Captain straightens the long, colored feathers on her hat, listening intently. "Hey, that's where we're going. Let us tag along." Orion chirps.

"So, we *are* both going then?" Alvis elbows his brother's side, and their bickering continues. Captain excuses herself, groaning about indeed more trouble than they're worth. Umber follows after her, glancing at me sideways with a half smile. She seems to have quite a few friends on this side of the pond, and quite a few secrets.

We need to have a little *chat*.

"Wanna play a game?" Novak inquires, a smile dancing across his face. Rounded ears poke out from beneath his crazy mop of hair. Wearing a loose blue tunic embroidered with black thread, the buttons are half undone and reveal a glimpse of angry, age old scars hiding behind the fabric.

"What kind of game?" I ask, unsure if I can handle any more games in my life.

YOU'RE LYING

"So, you see, you always have to be three steps ahead," Novak dramatically knocks my king off the board, beating me for the third time in a row. "Something *you're* not very good at."

I scowl at him, the intoxicating aura wrapped around us has distracted me for the past thirty minutes. Whether he intends to or not, I become light headed anytime I stay in his charcoal aura too long. Perhaps his playfulness is truly a facade, no one holds that *much* power without using it for malicious intent. After what I witnessed earlier though, I don't know what to think.

I growl and flip the board over, sending the dark and light wooden pieces flying. I cross my arms and sulk, looking away from him. Novak lets out a deep sigh of annoyance and twirls his finger. A wisp of dark smoke catches the board and pieces, arranging the game neatly on the table between us. He rests his elbows on the cracked wooden game table and knits his fingers together, resting his chin on them.

"Go again?"

"I wonder what you would even do without magic." I mumble and take the first move, the engines beneath the ship change frequency and we decrease in altitude dramatically.

"Probably look a hell of a lot better than you do." Novak laughs before moving his pawn two squares ahead. He's one to talk, those scarred ears flick as his happiness bellows across the deck.

What color was the fluff that used to grace those pointed ears? Were the tips long like mine, or short like Umber's? Slender like Captains, or stout?

I reach across and shove his shoulder playfully. Novak falls to the ground and makes a big show of his writhing pain. I can't help but smirk as I rise, then offer a hand and pull him up as Panrauth approaches. Novak and I are standing side by side near the railing, a lantern overhead warming the board and our faces.

Novak brushes himself off and sketches a magnificent, *deep* bow to Panrauth. Pan crosses his arms and narrows his eyes, the forest green aura around him is storming. "Should I start calling you High Lord now, or later?" Novak's dimples show as he smiles wide, keeping his strong teasing gaze on Pan. His tone is similar to when we met at the Oasis, and I realize it's *his* version of a mask.

Mine is indifference, his is dark and threatening humor.

Panrauth snarls, and for a moment looks as if he might throw Novak overboard. The Bear rests his hand on the sword at his side instead. He's geared up for travel, his clothing different from what we took from the Eternal. Dark green leathers replace the black ones he left with, now matching those of the Fae he was talking to earlier.

Novak puts his hands up. "Sheesh, so *sensitive*." He saunters off, looking over his shoulder at me before slinking away with visible shadows dragging along the deck behind him.

"You're making great friends already." Panrauth scowls down at me, hand still on his sword. I cross my arms and lift my chin, loose lilac blowing around my face. The wind gusts and cuts through my shirt, which suddenly feels very thin as his eyes wander over me.

"What is it, Pan? I'm not in the mood to fight with you."

In silence, he walks towards a door under the helm of the ship adjacent to Captain's cabin, motioning for me to follow. I push out a shaky breath and stalk over, entering a small pantry filled with vegetables and other goods. Pan shuts the door and faces me. Now, we're alone for the first time in days.

"I will be leaving with Brooks when we land in Cervalis." He's cold and flat, hands open at his sides. That must've been the Fae he was with.

"I didn't say you could leave. You said you would stay until I got sick of you." I say lightly, but his stone cold expression doesn't change. No movement or emotion radiates from him, at *all*. "Listen, it was a ridiculous fight, we both said things we didn't mean. I ... I still want you to come." I plead, heart racing when I realize he's serious.

"I meant every word I said. You weren't there." His shoulders loosen and he rakes a hand through wild hair. The overwhelming aura around him darkens, filling the room with such a dark green it's almost black. "So don't act like it's an easy thing to get over. My mistakes cost a life, the life of a woman I loved. I told myself I would never fall in love again-"

The thinness of my voice cuts through the air crystal clear. "You love me?"

Panrauth's hardened facade breaks, the storm around us calms to a sea of pale green dancing around our bodies. I step closer to him and raise a small hand in the thick, short distance between us. He opens his lips and emerald eyes soften, the air catches in my chest as a rough hand reaches for mine.

Then drops.

"No, I don't. You were my ticket out." His entire stature stiffens again, voice firm and striking my hand down. The storm around us returns with a passion, except it's not just his aura swirling around us. Pure black seeps from me like an angry river and tangles with his green.

Have I always had an aura? Is this what it looks like?

"You're *lying*." I whisper with shaking anger tainted by traitorous tears.

"Lyth, what are you doing?" He asks frantically, eyes wide as he stumbles backwards, taking his storm with him. My own angry aura crawls back to me, vibrating around my body with an intense frequency.

"I'm not *doing* anything." I say in a deadly low tone. I'm not doing anything. At least, not intentionally. "Look me in the eyes and say it again. Maybe I'll believe you." I dare him, hands in fists.

The Bear finds his courage and marches over, towering over me with determination. His eyes are near black, his carotid throbs with Aether and blood, his heartbeat *pounds* in my ears. I tremble, heat licks my neck. The ship is making its final descent, the energy under my feet hums intensely as the engines slow us down. We stare into the other's furious gaze. I'm on my tip toes with scrunched brows and raised chin, he stares down at me with clenched fists.

"I do *not* love you, Lythienne."

My heart drops and face falters when he spits his confession to me. I drop my eyes to the floor and the energy once surrounding my body dissipates into nothingness, what I've always been. Tears fall silently and Pan stands there in silence, taking a moment to realize he won. Of course he doesn't love me. I prepared myself for his truth and my heart still can't let him go, and I wish I knew why. His heavy steps rattle the floor as he walks away from me, jolting me back into reality.

Panrauth Firthorn grasps the door handle and pauses, eyes cast over his shoulder to gaze at me before he goes. I force myself to tear my eyes from the floor and up to him, willing as much anger into my face as possible. He *promised* he would stay.

"Be careful out there." Panrauth says with softened eyes, then leaves without another word, and slams the door behind him.

THE HANGED MAN

HALLOWED GROUND

As decreed by The Four Ancients after the Civil War of Iverbourne.
The mainland of Iverbourne will be severed from the Southern Continent which includes the Iron Court and lands of the Fraithall.
The Northern Continent which includes the Wildlands and homeland to all creatures, the Realm of Giants, shall be severed as well.
No creature is allowed through the borders or permitted through either side of the Meggido without ***explicit*** *permission.*

ISN'T THAT THE WAY IT GOES?

I gear up with double knives on each thigh, a full belt of pouches and the leather baldric slung across my chest. I changed my cropped top for a gray long sleeved tunic, and the thick jerkin is back over top. I don the wool cloak on as well, pulling the hood up and hiding my hair. I glare at the cane laying in the hammock, then take it after a moment and slide it into the strap on my leather belt.

I look around the crew's quarters with a sigh. This life suits me, perhaps I will be a pirate someday. A wide smile escapes at the thought. I shake off my feelings and head to the deck above. The ship docked about twenty minutes ago with several groups of footsteps leaving at once. I couldn't bring myself to leave the pantry until only about ten minutes ago, dragging myself off the floor and burying my disappointment in myself, and Pan.

I pause on the main deck and look up at the helm one more time. Captain leans against the steering wheel and tips her hat down when she sees me. I cross the decking and weave through the remaining crew members in a few careful strides and meet Captain at the helm. I give her a full smile and a magnificent bow, then bite my lip before I ask, "If I find you again someday, can I join your crew?"

Her aura is light pink, flowing around her tall figure like a soft creek. She taps her chin, looking me up and down. Captain pulls down my hood, then removes her feathered hat and places it upon my untamed hair. She nods in approval, placing porcelain hands on her lean hips. "Of course. Then I can get rid of some of the other hooligans." She grins, jutting a thumb to the emptying deck below. I clap her on the shoulder and she folds me into a rough hug.

"Thank you." I whisper into her hair before pulling away. Captain nods, then watches me walk away with a small smile on her porcelain face. I pause at the top of the ramp, ears straining for a lute strumming, and walk away only when I'm disappointed. *Damn*.

Umber chats with the twins on mossy land, it seems empty without Pan's heavy presence there. I hoped Novak would've at least said goodbye, but I haven't seen him since our game. It's not like he had a reason to go with us, I just ... thought he would.

I stop on solid ground, searching the ship behind me one last time for his goofy smile. He seems like he would be a good friend to have around, something I'm in need of. I focus on the group and push away my feelings. "You're coming with us?" I ask the twins.

"Only makes sense." Alvis muses, gesturing to the stone path stretching before us, then to Umber. "Cervalis is quite a handful to get through, not sure this one can handle getting you through it."

Umber rolls her eyes and shoves Alvis' shoulder playfully, earning a handsome grin from him as he slings an arm around her broad shoulders. I had nearly forgotten they fucked in the cantina. They have a good comradery, but nothing obviously romantic between them. Nonetheless, it's probably a good thing I pushed him away.

Cervalis' port rests on a massive grassy cliff side, the foggy depths below beckon me to stop off the crumbling sheer drop. Twenty docks perch on the edge in a semi circle fashion, keeping the ships afloat as they load and unload their goods. Our path converges with those from the other docks, leading to the epic trading city.

"There's a place we can stay a few miles outside of the city, just stay close." Umber calls to me over her shoulder.

I nod, walking in silence behind her and the twins. Fog rolls over the busy city, thick cold creeping into my bones. The main square is larger than the entire village of Echo, and twice as loud. Buildings constructed from large blocks of cut granite tower into the night sky all around us, making me feel even smaller than I already am. I'm not a fan of too many things going on to keep track of, but it's quite impressive here.

My ears lay down flat as I follow behind the others, my eyes filled with the colorful faelights overhead. The diverse rainbow of auras throughout the oceanic crowd moving as one jump starts my heart. Vendors of every breed are bargaining with traders and tourists, some races I don't even have names for. There are some resembling High Fae, but their legs are furred with hooves, and horns lay atop the male's heads.

Slaves tend to several booths and it's the first time I've seen Lesser Fae servants myself in the real world. In the Machine, we're all slaves. Warmth burns my gut and my hands ball into fists. I pause my step, watching them flutter around their master's tents in the standard gray servant's garb, their beautiful eyes dull and empty, devoid of life. The group is disappearing ahead of me and with a last look I continue on, swearing to make it right.

More of the short folk live here that I saw in Echo, akin to small children running barefoot. Age wears on most of their faces and ale is common among them, populating several of the open bars along the edges of the square. The *actual* half folk children are no higher than my knee, and twice as mischievous as I imagine Fae children to be. I know I was, mischievous, that is. I smirk whilst watching a red headed girl run into a vendor's canopy, then flee with a wide grin while she stuffs a loaf of bread under her shirt.

We near the center of the square after nearly an hour of *squeezing* through an increasing crowd, it's as if the entire city has congregated to celebrate an event unbeknownst to me. Music calls to me and I turn in a slow circle, but I can't find where it's flowing from. Wherever it is, it's beautiful, sweet and slow. Not as nice as Novak's, his music is alive with Aether itself, pulling at your heartstrings one moment, and making you dance the next.

I find myself searching for the blonde mop of curls once more, then curse myself for doing so. I don't know him, haven't I learned my lesson? My boots drag and stumbling steps become common, my hips protest the thought of traversing any longer. I chuckle inwardly, this is only the beginning. Walking to Hallowed is going to take days.

Bring it on.

Orion peers over his shoulder and spots me lagging behind, he hikes up the large bag on his back, identical to the ones Umber and Alvis haul. The tall male slows his pace and walks beside me, the other two get lost in the exhausting crowd before us. "I hope you don't find this offensive, but I find your technology rather appealing." Orion glances at me, his collar damp with sweat, voice shaky.

"Thank you, I suppose?" I chuckle, mildly amused.

"No, no. Not in *that* way. Females are too complex for me." He shakes his head, muttering about males not being much better. I've never seen a Fae with so much fluff, and ears so *long*. They're even longer than Alvis', the charcoal fur shines under the faelights.

After a moment I focus on the road, cheeks warming as I find myself studying him for far too long. "I'm talking about your *actual* tech, it's phenomenal." He pushes his glasses up, voice rising in excitement. "Captain said you were good with a wrench, and I must admit, I didn't believe her at first. Must be true though, eh?"

I weigh his words, many questions fight to be asked. I extend my leather and tech ridden arm and give him a small smile as I spin my arm to show off the gear. "Thank you. Time and space are lost concepts in the Mountain, these help a bit. If you'd like, I can explain them to you later."

The crowd thins enough to walk without pushing into others and I can see an end to the madness that is Cervalis' main square at night, the music drifting away behind us. "I know an engineer when I see one, tell me something about you." I say, noticing the oil on his hands, staining the white vines along his dark skin.

We enter a quieter part of the city, the faelights hang lower here and are less intrusive, glowing a soft gold. Large yards, homes with gardens, and swing sets dotting the suburbia caught my eye. "Well, you aren't wrong." Orion laughs breathily, shaking loose hair away from his face. "Alvis and I hail from Silverbury."

I shrug, never having been there. I've heard rumors of the atrocities Water Fae have commited and have encountered many of them in the Eternal, but that doesn't make them any different to me than anyone else. *Everyone* is capable of evil, despite what Aether is in your veins or where you were born.

Our path remains empty and an owl calls from the woods ahead, the faelights and townhomes becoming fewer. I glance back to the city, bright and alive, and the path behind us is lonesome. Warmth spreads over my neck and my heart drops with disappointment. I bite my lip and focus on the road ahead while Orion continues after some time contemplating in silence.

"I was the personal engineer to the High Lord, and Alvis a scout of sorts." Orion's voice is a bit more steady, fluorescent violet eyes wary as he scans the creeping roadsides filled with thick vegetation. Glowing eyes poke through the forest along the way and frogs chirp, but nothing approaches us. Ancient trees rise from thick moss and swamp grass, the damp pollen tickles my nose as foreboding dusk takes over.

"That sounds like quite the life. Yet you are both now pirates." I tease, craning my neck so I can see his face.

"Typhan is one of the most vicious faeries I've ever met. Life with Captain suits us much better." Orion's smile fades and he draws his shoulders in, but his words are confident. No regret. I stumble, my worn boots catching a hole in the path. I curse under my breath and draw my cane out, catching myself before I fall face first.

Again.

I don't look at Orion and continue in silence with scuffing, heavy steps. He doesn't say anything and walks alongside me in silence, hands clutching the straps to his duffel bag tight. Umber and Alvis are quite beyond us, elbows locked together. Faelights end and homes turn into distantly scattered cottages and farms, hours are lost into the night. The miles-long stone path slides into a slick mud, and fog crawls along with us. The canopy of trees here is encompassing, the thick ancients of earth call me to come and get lost. Truly a dark and terrible place of hidden beauty.

The silver and golden rays of sparkling light beaming down through a break in trees ahead stops me in my tracks. Metal feet slide forward as my cane digs into the ground. I throw my head back, eyes locked on the two full moons hanging over us, one much larger than the other.

Celestial bodies close enough I could climb a tree and touch them, they beckon my spirit to find them and dance in their light. Just a little closer, come closer. *Home*. The smaller moon is bathed in a warm golden glow, the other in a luminescent silver, near blinding no matter what way I look at them. My lips part and I press a hand to my chest, air escapes me in short bursts.

"Let's go home, I'm tired." The gentle, feminine whisper in my mind returns. Shadows sweep across my soul, begging to reach out into space. I close my eyes for a moment, panic ensuing as I push out short breaths and the lingering dark presence inside me. After recomposing myself and burying the voice, I fixate on the stars and avoid Orion's curious gaze.

Orion watches me for another moment, then focuses his attention to the glorious galaxy above. Glittering emerges before our eyes, poking through the velvet cape of deep purple night being slowly replaced by soft black. Dying planets shine in more colors than I thought possible. I wish we had a better view, but I don't entirely mind being surrounded by trees and plants. The forest is hiding many treasures in the dark, allowing mystery to linger and beckon me to become one with its fatal beauty.

Perhaps I can come back when I'm not in such a hurry and discover the creatures, animals and wild Fae I've read so much about. I smile, thinking about the lands I can explore. New things I will see with my own eyes, not just a picture in a book. I study every inch of our small view of night through the trees, the cape embedded with the finest crystals and gemstones, worn by silver and gold goddesses in the sky. Like sisters beckoning me home.

Is Pan looking at the same sky I am, or does he have a better view? I sigh with longing, I miss my friend. His story about stars gave me hope that the world wasn't as bad as the Mountain, it could be better. So far, Iverbourne is much more tolerable above ground. I can accept he truly doesn't love me. I just don't understand why he had to leave me *behind*.

"You really grew up there, didn't you?" My blood runs cold as Orion's gentle voice surprises me and sends a shudder throughout my cold body. I blink, staring at him after a moment. He focuses on the moons, the light reflects across his dirty lenses.

"Everyone keeps calling me the Keeper of Death. Why?" I ask, my words a whisper. Orion's face turns to mine, terror lights his glowing eyes for a moment. I can see the reflection in his glasses, my crystal eye resembles the silver moon, the other eye matches the dark velvet night.

Truly terrifying, Pan once told me. I'm sure I'm exactly that. Right now, and always.

Orion breaks his gaze and takes lazy steps forward. I follow alongside and evaluate the path ahead. Alvis has an arm slung around Umber, the pair turn at a faint lantern a good ways down the road, the light half hidden in foliage. They seem very close, in the way two lost souls find comfort in the other.

"For a few years now, there's been a story in almost every territory we've been to. A Fae cursed by the Ancients. The only Empty Fae made, sent to live in the deepest hell possible." He hikes up his bag, stumbling a bit. "To be honest, we all thought it was a bullshit ghost story." Voice shaky again, we encroach on the turn in our path, roots snake out from the slick dirt. "Cursed to work on the Machine for eternity, bringing death to any who touch it."

I can't help but smile, it sounds like quite the story. I've always said I'm not the hero, and apparently others think the same. Bitterness stings my heart and I'm not sure why, so I shake it off and focus on the dark road ahead.

"Well, what can I say, it's all true." I muse offhandedly, grateful I have my cane for the entirely root covered path leading to our destination. Waiting deep in the looming forest, a glorious tavern waits, perched in a behemoth of a gnarled tree. The thought of climbing *anything* right now has me seriously debating sleeping outside, despite the gorgeous architecture promising comfort.

We walk in silence, then halt at the base of the tree. A wooden door carved into the tree comes into view while I peer through the ivy. I make for the door with haste, an enormous sigh of relief leaving my tired chest. Orion steps in my way, startling me.

"I think maybe a few parts were left out." He says fiercely. For a moment, he reminds me of the warrior in his brother. He sets his sharp jaw and crosses his arms, already fluorescent Aether burns brighter in his eyes. Perhaps it was the Machine restraining everyone's Aether, but I never knew Fae eyes could shine so *intensely*.

I pull on a half ass smile, then pat him on the shoulder. "Isn't that the way it goes?" I attempt to step past him, but he doesn't relent. I scowl, my brows narrow tight as I stumble back.

"It's not fair." His whining tone grinds the gears in my head. Why does he *care* so much?

"Are you gonna get out of my way so I can sit down? We can guess at the Ancient's sense of humor later." I bite out, harsher than I intend, and push past him. I throw open the door with too much force and stop mere feet inside the tree, wonder distracting me.

The hollow holds just as much whimsical beauty inside as it does outside. A quiet common area greets us, holding detailed Air Fae carvings on the walls.

Cozy quilts and pillows line long couches constructed from full logs. Fae and animals of every sort compose the artwork, trees and flowers follow the fauna. Craftsmanship is apparent in every detail, from the simple rustic furniture, to the construction of the tavern itself.

"There are rooms upstairs, and one downstairs." Orion states. Umber and Alvis aren't in sight and I'm more and more sure it's a good thing nothing happened between Alvis and I. Orion and I stand in the center of the room, devoid of other life or sound.

"Where are the others?" I glance at the spiral stairs leading up to another wooden door with a curtain of ivy hanging over the frame. The plant hugs the railing of the staircase and hangs down into the air above us, also reaching the end of the railing and teasing the floor.

"Probably drinking, and if I know Umber they'll wind up sharing a room." Orion rolls his eyes, confirming my suspicions that Beltane wasn't a one time thing. "I'll see if the room down here is open for you."

"No, I'll come with you." I say, if a bit too quickly. I roll my shoulders back and pull together a mask of boredom. I'm not ready to be alone.

Not yet.

I check the time on my watch. Eleven already. Sleep won't be a priority tonight, either. "Suit yourself." He shrugs and I follow him up the stairs. He's far less inquisitive now, his aura darkening into a deep blue. It doesn't feel like pity radiating from him, more like anger. I can't imagine Orion hurting a fly. Alvis yes, but Orion seems better suited to the labs. Then again, I'm suited for both, perhaps he is as well. We reach the top of the stairs, my thoughts distracting me from my tired body.

"It might get a bit loud." Orion warns, grasping the door handle hiding in greenery.

"Wait." I say, clasping his shoulder tight. Orion raises a brow, softening under my touch. I leave my hand on his strong shoulder, thankful for the warmth there. How long will I be touch starved for?

"Where did Novak go?"

Orion chuckles and shrugs, small dimples showing in his slender cheeks. He is quite handsome, in a different way than his brother. Where Alvis holds scarred beauty and a smart ass sense of humor, Orion is refined and elegant. "Novak has friends he visits in Cervalis." Orion moves to open the door but I grip tighter, resulting in his smile fading.

"But why didn't he say goodbye?"

"Did you want him to?" Orion raises a brow, even toned.

I roll my eyes and gesture to the door, his attitude getting under my skin. "Never mind."

Orion pushes the door open, revealing boisterous laughter and music as soon as he does. How we didn't hear it before I'm not sure, then the Aether rolling heavy from the room slams into my senses, must be a sound shield. The magic of this land still intoxicates my senses every time I smell it, making me feel almost as stupid as alcohol does.

Umber and Alvis are clearly way ahead of us, both us them hollering for us to hurry up and get our drinks before the ice melts. I'm not sure I heard them right, but when I approach the bar, there are indeed globes of ice. I hold the glass up and inspect it with a raised eyebrow. Umber catches me looking at the ice suspiciously, then laughs heartily at my disbelief. She's so beautiful, especially when she laughs.

That is the Umber I know. Carefree, rough and loud. Alvis is admiring her as well, my cheeks warm at the sight and I focus back on my glass with ... disappointment?

"I just don't understand the concept." I say, swirling the drink.

"Well you see, alcohol tends to go down better when it's cold. Over on *this* side of the pond we get ice, from Borealis." Alvis teases me, raising his drink. Umber hangs off his shoulder and we all clink glasses, downing what I discover to be faerie wine. I have to agree, ice definitely helps things go down.

The spacious bar decorated similar to the rustic downstairs holds a corner I long to visit, where musicians bring forth melodies from their instruments. My three companions chat away and I watch the lute, vocalist and drums sing together. The simple lute reminds me of Novak, he plays so beautifully. Time is a cruel trick, the lifetime I spent in the Mountain is a blip in my immortal life compared to the past week, which seems like a blessed eternity.

Perhaps it's because I've spent so much of my time in numbness, separating myself from who I was. I was surviving. Not thriving, like Pan said. Fuck him.

I watch couples dance before the musicians and listen to Fae laugh among themselves, and wonder what I'm doing now. More than surviving, but not exactly thriving. I'm certainly more *alive* than I have been in a long time. Panrauth sparked the feelings of being alive inside of me, and alive brings heartbreak, but it also brings *this*. Happiness.

Orion and Alvis are laughing at a wild story Umber tells and I grin watching them, happy to be on the outside looking in. A hand claps onto my shoulder and I freeze, breath hitching at the unexpected touch. I whip my head around, fists ready to strike.

"*Sheesh*, you guys could have waited for me." Novak is absolutely filthy, covered in mud, sticks and leaves stick out of his hair. A wide, dimple pulling grin spreads across his cheeks. The sight warms my heart. Alvis roars with laughter and I can't help but feel relieved he's here.

"What in the Eternal happened to you?" I ask, wiping mud filled hair from his eyes, neck warming as I drop my hand.

"Well, I thought *you* would've at least waited for me." Novak throws a speck of mud at Alvis who fails to dodge it.

Orion rubs his forehead. "Do you two *ever* stop bickering?"

"I could say the same for you two, always have to one up the other." I tease, bringing a grin to both the twin's sharp faces.

Umber rolls her eyes and takes my hand. "Let's dance, Lyth." I grin and down my drink then follow after her, my curiosity in Novak's visit fading. Once Novak joins the other musicians and the twins start a rowdy swing dance, the rest is history. Our dancing and his music evoke the raucous crowd to whoop and holler, demanding Novak to keep playing.

The last thing I remember are sapphire eyes staring into mine, and soft lips pulling into a goofy grin. Music pulls me to sleep, lingering in my gentle dreams.

DID WE?

I groan heavily, my head swims in faerie wine and hips flat refuse to work when I attempt to roll over. I danced *way* too much last night, but at least the aches and pains are from simple living, not torment and torture. Stiffness resides in all of my joints and I smile thinking about dancing with Orion, he really let loose last night. Novak's music is permanently burned into my ears, though I'm not complaining.

A celebration followed Novak's arrival, every person in the bar recognized my companions. After dancing for far too long with Orion and Umber, Alvis keeps me company at the bar as the party continues around us. "How is it everyone knows who you four are?" I ask Alvis, giggling as I rest on a stool and watch the others dance. I can't dance anymore, even though I want to.

He swivels in his seat beside me and his wide grin fades slightly, white vines along his thick muscled arms glowing a soft white. "You've never heard the tales of Captain, have you, Keeper?" He says, reaching forward to move hair from my eyes. I smile and shake my head when his fingers brush my cheek and his face flushes beautifully.

He is more than handsome, he's a work of art.

We both take a drink and he focuses on Novak with contemplation and a soft smile.

"We don't have much time for stories in the Eternal, I'm afraid." I say. He leans with his back against the bar, long arms outstretched along the light wooden slab, his left hand dangerously close to my right resting on the wood.

"Captain and Novak have spent their entire lives saving Humans and Lesser Fae from the likes of Fae like me, and Orion, with that ship of theirs." Alvis says darkly, pulling my attention from the party to his darkened eyes sharpened onto me. Always watching me.

"Fae like you?" I ask, brows furrowed.

"Bigots, murderers, kidnappers. Water Fae usually fit the bill for all things nasty in Iverbourne." I wait for sarcasm or a joke to follow Alvis' serious words, but nothing does.

"You're not like that." I say, my fingers touch his and send a spark of warmth through me.

"That's kind of you Keeper, but it's true. Before we met Nova," he stumbles on the nickname and I tilt my head, but he recovers before I can ask, "when we met Novak and Cap, my brother and I were exactly that. They came to save people ***from*** *us, and ended up saving us too, gave us a chance to do some good."*

I glance between him and the others, eyes catching on Novak taking a request from a petite Air Fae female. Orion looks at us with a smile and I wave to him subtly, my hand leaving Alvis'.

"Well, it would seem everyone knows you for who you've become since then, not for who you were." I say, giving Alvis my attention once more.

The brooding has left his face and is replaced by a soft smile. "They may have forgotten, but I haven't."

Silence follows Alvis' statement and I contemplate the idea of being forgiven for what I've done. I wonder what life Alvis lived and how awful he ***truly*** *was, I can't see him that way though. If these people can celebrate a visit from Novak and his friends, forgive the twins for whatever they've done, can I ever be forgiven?*

Can I forgive myself? As I stare into Alvis' wet eyes, I find my answer.

I stand and swallow, then ask a very stupid question. "Can I, hug you?"

Alvis blinks rapidly, dazed for a few seconds. He stands, staggering slightly as he throws his arms around my small shoulders. He's so much taller than me, my arms wrap around his waist. I relish his warmth and sigh. "What's this for, Keeper? Not feeling sorry for me, are you?"

"We don't have much time for hugs in the Eternal either, so shut up and hug me."

The sun burns my eyes as they squint open momentarily, then I decide better of starting my day. I moan and throw myself over in bed, rough sheets caress my naked thighs, bare of prosthesis and clothes. I pull the blankets up over my head and exhale a sigh of content, my back and hips quite thankful for a real bed. Probably one a few hours rest, but more than enough when it's in a place as comfortable as this. Warmth rolls beside me and I smile, the skin on skin touch comforting me.

My eyes flash open and I narrow my brows in confusion at the lump of blankets next to me. Scarred and muscled skin presses against me under the fabric, but no face is revealed under the mess. Goosebumps spread across my skin as I try to remember what the *hell* happened last night, and who lies in bed next to me. The sheets are a different color, and the blankets thinner than I remembered. I am utterly naked, now biting my lip with desperation. I rub my face and curse myself as memories seep in.

Novak plays the lute for me, just **me**. *Alvis lifts Umber off the bar, his hands firmly gripping under her thighs as they disappear into a hallway leading to the bedrooms. Orion's sprawled out on the bar, his soft snores filling the otherwise empty room. We are the last ones up, and after a long moment of us being lost in each other's eyes, Novak speaks softly. "Looks like we're all alone."*

He continues playing the soft melody, the one I love and first heard in Echo, giving me a nervous smile. We are seated together in a corner with a small table separating us. I rise, taking the first unsteady steps between us. I bite my lip and search his blue eyes, waiting. Novak sets his lute down, then rises and takes my hands in his. His heart thrums so loud my own pulse races to keep up with his.

"You're quite handsome, you know." I murmur and smile wide, staring up at the galaxy of freckles across his nose and cheeks. I brush a honeyed curl from his eyes, drawing color to his soft cheekbones. His bright sapphires confuse me, he ***looks*** *like a Water Fae, and yet he has this powerful Aether fueled by darkness ruminating inside him.*

I don't mind the dark.

"Well thank you, my lady. We should get you to bed, though. You can tell me all about how good looking I am tomorrow, when we're not so tipsy." Novak rubs a delicate thumb over my cheek, looking me over with admiration. He's so beautiful, right down to his soul filled with nothing but kindness and strength.

I think about what Alvis said, that Novak's always been the hero. I've admired his ability to conquer whatever darkness resides inside him with a smile, and tonight the alcohol has me feeling bold. I take his hand and press his thumb to my lips, kissing it ever so softly. A gasp escapes him when I look up through my long lashes, a wicked smile spreads across my face as I decide what I want.

I haven't had much sex, but I do know my best features.

I sit up with intense stealth and peek over. A curled mop of blond pokes out from under the blankets, the rest of the musician hidden. I peer at the floor, his shirt is in one corner, and my pants are in another. The walls aren't familiar, this is indeed *not* the bed I fell asleep in. I rub my face and groan inwardly. Did we *really* sleep together? I don't remember his body against mine at all, shreds of how I got here flow back to me in patches.

"Are you sure you don't want to stay?" I whine pathetically. Novak tucks a heavy blanket around me, then brushes knotted hair from my face. He sighs, giving me a pained smile before leaving my small quarters.

"Ask me again tomorrow, and I will stay."

Novak's stirring, drawing my attention to him. He rolls in bed towards me, his bare slender torso illuminated in the sunlight as he pushes the blankets off. A gentle smile rests on his sun kissed face as he nestles into the pillows beside my hip. A cradle of charcoal shadows is revealed from under the covers, kissing his skin. Not an aura, but *actual*, visible shadows. Even in his sleep. I find the warm tendrils of night comforting, and reach out with a cautious hand. Darkness wraps around my fingers, caressing my skin and eliciting a sigh.

Does he know I came to his room?

The shadows creep closer, dancing along my arms and hugging my body. I smile, finding solace in his warm darkness. I bite my cheek and gently reach out, hovering over his freckled chest. The muscles usually hidden by his loose clothing catch my eye first, but I'm soon distracted by the raised scars covering every inch of him. *Precise*, raised skin covers nearly every inch of his chest, ribs and back. Intentional markings that overlap in some places. The sight strikes my heart down and warmth burns my eyes. Whoever did this to him, they better *not* be alive.

Novak opens his eyes drowsily, finding me thoughtfully playing with his shadows. His restful smile widens and his half open eyes simmer a bright blue. He reaches a freckled hand to mine and my heart flutters, fingers twitch. The Fae stops midway, eyes wide and grogginess *wiped* from his face. He throws himself wildly away from me with a loud yelp, thudding onto the floor as his shadows skid through the room.

SWAMP THING

We all meet downstairs in the common room for breakfast. After the fiasco this morning with a flabbergasted Novak, I committed the walk of shame back to my own room to dress and wash up. After sobering up, fragmented memories of wandering to Novak's room and crawling into bed with him come to me. I'm not sure if I can bear to look at him, and my cheeks are permanently warmed. If I had at least kept my clothes on the situation would be bearable.

But no, apparently I wanted to cuddle a near stranger, naked.

Why doesn't that word feel *right*? For him or Alvis? They're not strangers, and yet ...

A long table waits in the center of the rustic lobby, elegant platters of food are placed precariously from one end to the other. No servants or workers of any kind are about, and now that I think about it, there wasn't a bartender last night either. Our small group are the only ones seated, and no one says a *word* as we eat. Novak's the last to arrive, light footed and with his usual grin. I wait for the taunts and teasing, but it never comes. At least not for me, he picks on the others instead, Orion especially for his makeshift bed on the bar upstairs.

All dressed for adventure today, our trek will take at least a full day of walking. The Others haven't been seen in this part of the territory lately, but we're all strapped for danger anyway. They are an occasional threat here, not the peaceful people the High Lady preaches them to be. I add thieves to the kidnapping and murdering definition of the Others and what they stand for.

I wear the same loose pants with cuffs and the gray long sleeve from yesterday, sans the wool cloak and jerkin as I'm already warm. The usual belt of leather pouches adorns my thick hips, with the matching leather baldric slung across my back. Captain's hat rests upon my head and I leave my purple hair loose, finding I like the way it tousles in a fresh breeze. Alvis' voice pulls me from thoughts of how little of a thing like wind can make life seem better.

"I'm sorry, what did you say?" I startle and shift in my seat. Judging from the look on the others' faces, he must've tried to get my attention more than once. Novak's face falters at my question, he pokes around at his food when Alvis asks again.

"I *said*, can you ride? Horses?" Alvis taps his finger on the table, full of annoyance. Novak's aura darkens and he stiffens in his seat, setting down his fork with unsettling care. Alvis glances at him and then leans back in his chair, voice softer. "Orion, Novak and I are going by horseback from here, our cargo is time sensitive. You are welcome to join, if you wish."

If you're *able* to. If you can *handle* it. I ponder the hidden question, biting my lip and finding Umber's watchful silver eyes from across the table. Novak leaves the table and casually paces the room, rubbing his face with both hands as he shakes off creeping shadows.

"I'm fine walking." Umber shrugs, devouring a pastry. I'm sure she prefers not to walk.

"Well, I won't be a true adventurer if I don't fall off a horse at least once, right?" I tease, grinning at Alvis. Novak left moments ago, leaving the door to the outside world open.

The large gray barn with purple trim hid in the darkness last night, though in the daytime it's hard to miss. Each stall holds a window overlooking the pasture Alvis and I cross through. Regal creatures poke their heads out, some nickering and others tossing their heads as we approach.

Alvis pushes the wide doors on rails open, letting fresh air in. I reach my hand out to a fine dapple who presses her forehead to my skin, sending warmth and softness under my palm. Alvis crosses his arms and waits in the wide main alley while I walk up to each stall, peeking in and saying hello to the creature who lives there. Have I ever *pet* an animal before? I think of the monkey in Echo, so small compared to these muscular workhorses.

"This beaut is Fiddler, considering how much you like music, he may suit you." I smile at Alvis who comes to my side, his voice and face much gentler than at breakfast. He almost seemed ... pissed.

I focus my attention on the gentle giant before me, a refined dark bay with soft golden eyes and an elegant charcoal mane. Fiddler lowers his thick head over the stall door and I press my forehead against his, closing my eyes and *feeling* our Aether connect. The breath in me halts for a moment, heart fluttering as I sense his strong life force beating under my skin.

After a few moments, Alvis muses from behind me. "Sure there's not some Earth faerie blood in there?" I glare over my shoulder at him and he shrugs offhandedly with a grin. I lead Fiddler from his stall to outside the stable where he waits patiently for me to learn.

Alvis supposed on the way over I should get acquainted with the parts of a horse, the tack and general dos and don'ts of controlling a beast thousands of pounds heavier than you, before I even attempt getting on. Nobody tells me I can or *can't* do anything, just go along with my lead and keep their opinions to themselves. Alvis is quite easy to be around, flirtatious banter and all. It isn't like that first day though, his eyes don't linger as long and his hands never brush my skin.

The Water Fae teaches me the basics of tack, first being the simple leather bridle. Fiddler wants to rest his head on my shoulder and hug me, making putting the bridle on a challenge. After much coercion and a frustrated Alvis, we then put the saddle on with less difficulty, although it seems rather tight to me. Alvis assures me it loosens during riding, and sliding off a horse is not an experience I want to have, so I just nod.

When all that's left is to mount, I stand on uneven grass looking up at the giant beast, scratching my head and sighing. Of course the smallest person in the crew would connect with one of the tallest horses. "I can get you a stool." Alvis offers, completely serious. I bite my cheek and scowl at him, finding his handsome face truly pulled with concern. Warmth spreads across my neck and shoulders, even between my thighs.

Pay *attention*.

"No, I'm not going to have a stool out there." I gesture to the road rolling past the pasture and tavern, averting my eyes when the heat in his own flashing violet refuses to cool. I pat Fiddler's muscled neck and press my forehead to his shoulder. "Think you can help me out here?"

In response the beast snorts, lifting his front leg. I give Alvis a wild smile, he's wide eyed, mouth hanging open. I can't help but giggle as I step up onto his leg and pull myself into the saddle, thankful for the strength my arms corde with muscle hold. I may be short and crippled, but my upper body and hips compensate for what I lack, creating a rather unbalanced figure that can endure hell. I settle, my hips complain rather annoyingly but I push the pain away.

I am on top of a *fucking* horse.

I reach down and pull my boots into the stirrups, body trembling and heart pounding. I've lived in The Eternal Mountain for 236 years and escaped the life of being a murderer, made friends and am now lusted after, loved perhaps by some. And now, I am mounted upon a *horse*, in the fresh summer air and on a grand quest. In a matter of days, I have lived more thoroughly than I could've ever dreamed.

Alvis is explaining the reins in some foreign part of my mind, but excitement takes over. Before he can finish, I take them in my hands with a wild grin. I squeeze Fiddler's side with my legs, my joints hum against his skin which throws him into a gallop. *Oh*, the feeling of flying through the air, connected with another living being, working as one, I never want to stop.

But, as we approach the fence at the end of the paddock, that is exactly what I need to do.

Alvis had said something about pressing the reins on his neck, looking where I need to go. The rail fence beckons for us to jump over and leave, but I am *not* ready for that. I grip the pommel and lay the reins against his broad neck, turning my head and looking back up to the stable. Fiddler nearly halts and turns with such intense precision, I have to hold on with my entire core to avoid falling off.

I straighten as he canters up to the stable, my enthusiasm crowing into the sweltering air. I let out a wild grin, swinging Captain's hat in the air as I fly past Alvis and the others mounting their own horses. Once we come to the end of the path that stretches from the inn to the main road, my heart drops. How do I *actually* stop? My ears lift, Alvis is yelling to pull back.

Poor Fiddler responds so quickly to my tug on the reins, he halts in just a stride and I fly forward out of the saddle, landing onto my back. The horse tosses his head, nickering and mocking me for being such an idiot. My vision blurs for a moment and I shake the ringing from my ears after air returns to my lungs. A slender, vined hand extends to me.

I take Orion's hand, thanking him as I groan dramatically, my hips and everything else cursing me for being such an *idiot*. I glower at Fiddler now grazing boredly beside me in the grass. Alvis rides by, chuckling as he shakes the shaggy ink from his glowing eyes. The sun is cast behind him in some cruel trick, bathing his figure in golden light. "You know, sometimes it helps to hear *all* the instructions."

I stick my tongue out at him, like I saw him do to Captain. Orion remounts with a small smile, pushing up his glasses and trotting after Alvis. I brush off the dirt covering me and fix Captain's hat, then re-situate it on my crown. I mount again with Fiddler's help, quite grateful he follows after the others with a *much* slower step now. Umber catches up to me, pulling away from Novak who trails behind us. She begins chattering about the land, but I only listen half heartedly.

I peer over my shoulder at Novak, the musician watches the woods with his usual resting smile, like just *living* is enough for him. When his relaxed eyes catch mine he gives me a dimple filled wink, the aura of night around him fades to a lighter charcoal. Always softening when I give him my attention. I bite my lip and goosebumps spread with the memories of our bodies entwined in his magical darkness, my naked body against his.

The most crystal clear part of it all are the deep carvings that stretch across almost every inch of that kind Fae. Not only his chest, but on his back as well. More than scars, they are raised so high they must've initially been valleys across his body. I focus on the road ahead, trying to imagine what they looked like fresh, shuddering at the idea of him even being able to survive it.

Suddenly I want to touch him, explore his body and caress every scar, kiss every bad memory away. I want his teasing smile lingering on the nape of my neck, sending shivers across me. The musician's slender fingers trace my breasts next, then down my stomach. I bet they can play other things just as well as the strings on his lute.

Ask me again tomorrow, and I will stay.

Will he, or will it be another cruel trick?

I sigh, straightening in the saddle and evaluating the bog that surrounds our path. The road we travel on is mostly dirt, but some low valleys of swamp turn our path into mud. The horses don't mind too much, though. The only traffic we encounter heads to Cervalis and we seem to be the only ones going to the Mists, so far. I pat Fiddler's shoulder, resting my hand there for a moment.

"Lyth, are you ok?" Umber's patient question pulls me from my thoughts, I had forgotten to answer her. I swim in the thoughts overflowing my mind and check my watch, realizing an hour has passed since she caught up to me. I study Umber for a moment, her blue skin positively glowing in the sunlight. No fog, no darkness, no overwhelming canopy. When we left the deep forest a few miles ago for cypress scattered marshes, we also left behind our shade.

"I don't know. I think so?" I shrug, thinking for a moment. "Do you remember when I told you I wouldn't even know how to live out here?"

"Yes, and now you are." Umber gives me a small smile which falters when another long pause commences.

"But I still don't know how to live, like actually *live*. I feel like a fish out of water. Ugh, I'm so deprived I haven't even been in an actual body of water. Even my metaphors are pathetic." I mumble, my blood burning. "Knothall trained me my whole life to be good at two things. Fixing things and destroying them. Now he sends me out here, without thinking there might be more to life than fixing or breaking."

As the words leave, a weight tumbles off my shoulders, a small but noticeable one. My sunburned ears fold down, the purple fur lining them does nothing against the heat. "You know, Pan is right about one thing." Umber whispers. I tilt my head, unsure I heard her right. She shrugs, rubbing her neck. "He said it's your turn to live. Maybe, when all this is over, you can."

When all this is over. You can live.

"I remember. I was pissed at you for being an ignorant ass, so I pretended to be asleep." I chuckle, grinning at her.

"Figures, you don't miss much." She gives me a half smile, but we continue on in silence. The twins bicker in front of us, and music drifts from behind. I turn to watch Novak picking at his lute, the reins loose on his horse's neck. A deep breath escapes my heavy chest, the music washes over my spirit and peace spreads through me. The song I love the most, just slower and drawn out, each note caressed on the old strings. I'm sure he can afford a new instrument working with Captain, but the homeless vagabond look seems to be part of his charm.

"Careful there." Umber teases, raising a brow.

I have so many questions for her, but I can't ask them right now. I settle for teasing back instead. "And you? Seems like you are having fun of your own."

"No doubt about that." She laughs deeply. After a few settling moments, she adds the last words in a whisper. "Anything *more* than fun, can be dangerous, though."

I ponder her words and regret my galloping shenanigans from earlier. At least it's a pain from living. "You've known them for a long time, then?" I ask.

"What is a long time to Fae, anyway?" Umber snorts and I glare at her. "If you consider two decades long, then sure."

"I'm surprised you've never told me about them, the Crew of Misfits make for good stories." I say light heartedly, testing the waters.

She laughs offhandedly and sighs, then stares into my eyes with an unexpected intensity. "I thought it would be cruel, to tell you about the world you were missing."

I stare into her unwavering gaze, contemplating her statement. That was a possibility I considered, why she's never told me anything about herself. Perhaps that's part of it, but my gut tells me there's another reason she's kept her life secret.

I spend the rest of the ride wondering about what pirates do exactly, other than flying ships and being terrifying.

We arrive at the Hallowed Court by late evening, and I must say it's not at all what I expected. After Cervalis' epic beauty, I assumed the High Court of the land would be rather impressive, befitting for the ancient High Lady who has ruled over Hallowed lands since the war.

Instead, I find myself standing near a rickety bridge leading to an island of mediocre town homes on stilts. The large village rests precious inches above misty swamp water that stretches widely into a cypress filled lake, encapsulated by lurking trees hanging precariously over the foreboding depths. It appears I've walked into a swamp thing's den. Our horses are stabled in the small lean-to outpost by the bridge, and our group is gathering themselves before crossing.

"So, is that really Hallowed?" I ask unsteadily, to no one in particular.

Umber gives me a half smile, shaking out her hair and remaining silent. The sun is dulled here and the air is flat and stagnant, marsh and decay fill my nose. I shudder as a cold chill passes through me.

"Don't let what you see fool you. High Lady Trihewyn has ruled these lands since before the war. She is *not* a force to be reckoned with." Orion speaks with a solemn tone, pushing his filthy glasses up. He carries the large bag upon his back, just as Alvis and Umber do.

I glance at Novak who isn't carrying anything other than his own belongings, and he's still the only Fae who doesn't hold weapons at his side. It occurs to me he never explicitly said he was coming, or why. Unless he did, and I forgot in my drunken stupor. Perhaps Captain is right and alcohol is far more trouble than it's worth. Novak nods to me, his usual smile *gone*. All four hold especially dark versions of their usual auras.

They're afraid, and perhaps I should be too.

We cross the swaying wooden bridge blanketed in mist, the swamp swallowing the view of the land behind us. Dim, purple faelights hang overhead the decking we land on, illuminating the village tucked into the mist. Female High Fae flutter along the walkways between stilted buildings, paying us no mind and keeping busy. Water gurgles beneath the rickety wood at our feet, and the only other noises are the idle tasks being carried out and rare chatter occurring every now and then. There are no males around, none that I can see anyway.

I shiver against Novak beside me, surprise taking over when I find myself leaning into him, both of us following behind the twins. He gives me a half smile, taking my hand in his and squeezing carefully. He makes to let go but I hold tight, keeping my gaze fixed on Orion. We stop at another bridge inclining to the tallest building, a modest castle situated in the center of the swamp village.

Two hooded, female sentries wait for us, their spears crossed over the entrance. I scan around casually, there has to be more hiding. Hiding in the fog settling around, no doubt with the males. Alvis straightens before the guards, the obvious leader among us. "Here on official business from Captain."

The sentries nod simultaneously, one eyes the feathered hat on my head. They remove their blockade and let us pass, the bridge only wide enough for us to go single file. I release Novak's hand reluctantly and he follows close behind me.

Violet faelights encircle the decrepit wooden building, moss overhangs from the shingle rooftop and ivy drifts down to murky water, teasing the surface. The tall blue doors waiting for us are adorned with intricate white clouds along the frame. The ancient text from Captain's ship outlines the entirety, written in a familiar shade of a red. The windows situated around the building hold warm lanterns and the same design as the door.

Clouds and blood.

A palace fit for a bloodthirsty swamp thing, not the Court of Air Fae. I enter behind the twins and behold the High Lady of Hallowed, and decide there isn't much of a difference.

YES, I'M THAT OLD

A graying High Fae female with diamond studded glasses and a crown of crystalline clouds is perched high above us on an elegant raised dais. The silver throne holds details of clouds, faeries and books, and is almost as breathtaking as the High Lady herself.

I can see right through all that beauty and straight into the most dangerous being I have encountered so far, besides Eros, that is. Surrounding the throne is a vortex of raging purple Aether, tugging on all of the auras in the room and *draining* my friend's Aether. We're kneeling before her on a gnarled wood floor, and after a moment we are allowed to rise. Dizziness slams into me when I stand, and after a moment of refocusing I glance at the others, pale and expressionless.

Now, Orion is the one who does the talking. Despite Novak working as first mate, he mentioned on the way here he no longer handles the negotiations. Novak and the twins had gone very quiet after that statement, so I didn't pry. "High Lady Trihewyn, it is an honor to be in your presence again. Captain sends their regards and appreciates your business."

Composure fills his voice, none of the nervous Fae present from yesterday. Do I terrify him more than *she* does? Captain's hat weighs heavily upon my head, the court of females surrounding the dais simultaneously turn their stony faces to me at the mention of the legendary Fire Fae.

You haven't heard the legends of Captain? Alvis' surprised words from last night ring in my ears and I swallow anxiety, resolving to learn more about her heroics. I'm starting to think her hat was more than a gift, but protection.

Orion, Alvis and Umber set their bags down as one, the weight of their delivery shaking the floor. I never thought to ask *what* they were delivering. The twins had said something about spices, but this seems like quite an ordeal for flavors. Alvis and Orion step back, but Umber approaches further and stands at the High Lady's side, then faces us with a cold stare.

My eyebrows narrow and I shoot a look at Novak who's fuming with a wild aura threatening to break into visible shadows. The twins however, do not appear surprised to see Umber at the High Lady's side. The sharp faces with white vines teasing down their necks bear the same flat mask as my own, hiding any emotion or truth. Trihewyn's gaze washes over the twins, making no acknowledgment of Umber.

The High Lady remains expressionless and waves a hand, the bags rise in the air and drift over to her. She peers into them one by one wordlessly, then waves them off behind her. She nods to Orion, and then to Alvis, only giving Novak a second of attention. Isn't he just as much a hero as Captain?

"Tell Captain I am pleased, they may continue to have safe passage in these lands." Her voice is even, albeit laced with an edge. The predator locks onto my hat, then down to my black and white eyes. I raise my chin and straighten, the most vulnerable person in the room, per usual. "And who are you?" She gestures *at* me, not really speaking *to* me, though.

I open my lips but Umber speaks first, her words cut me like a knife and cement the betrayal I never saw coming. "This is Lythienne, the Keeper of Death from The Eternal Mountain. As promised." Trembling anger takes over exhaustion and my hackles rise. I came here freely, on my own mission, and Umber planned to get me here one way or another. I knew she was hiding something, but this? Our plans came together so conveniently for her. Or maybe it was too convenient for me to get out so easily.

Fuck. How do I keep missing the obvious?

I wonder what her reward is, what her angle is for bringing me here. Luckily, I have a bargaining chip of my own. I suppose if I'm going to be introduced as Keeper of Death, I should start acting like it.

I break from the others, stepping onto the platform with confidence, and halt only feet from Trihewyn. One hand rests on the dagger at my side, and the other tips Captain's hat down in a slow and seductive fashion. I bow, winking at the High Lady of the Hallowed Court. "At your service, High Lady." My voice drips with honey and I draw a breath, *taking* my abyss of an aura back from her vortex.

When I stand, air freely enters my lungs like the first bits of air I caught leaving the Mountain, and the auras beside me return to their owners. The storm of Aether surrounding the High Lady retreats, keeping tight to Trihewyn. Tense silence fills the room and I give her a wicked smile.

The voracious laughter of the High Lady shakes the swamp castle, all elegance and proprietary gone.

We are given rooms for the night, highly *encouraged* to spend dinner, and the night together to discuss business. I was able to request an audience with the High Lady privately, but only *after* we've had dinner. The dining hall and guest rooms lay in the upper part of the stilted castle, my own room is quaint but beautiful nonetheless.

I run a long finger along a walnut armoire, ornate with designs akin to the throne and everything else in this place, but details are left in silver paint here. Naked and alone in the dimly lit room, I have no idea what the battle attire is for political dinners. Wearing my prosthesis and nothing else is quite freeing, a sensation I don't experience often.

A slim mirror rests on the side of the wardrobe, and for a few moments I just stand there and stare at my body. Scars randomly litter across softness and muscle, My face and arms are a darker tone than my thick core. Freckling hands explore my cream stomach, my body is thankful for the days of good food. Both prostheses match the color of my thighs seamlessly, but my face is burned by the sun.

I flick my ears, the tufts at the ends of my long points are growing in thick. Orion's ears are the longest I've seen yet, flopping down with inky fur against his neck, contrasting Alvis' constantly alert and perked ears. Novak is blond, perhaps his ears once were as well. There is something about him I find fascinating, and apparently I will have to find out about his darkness by myself, now. After a shudder of goosebumps perks my breasts, I explore the outfits waiting for me.

Dresses, breeches, tunics of short and long sleeve varieties. Items of clothing I have no names for, and sheer fabrics of every color imaginable. So many combinations, too many decisions. Fingers pause on the dark green of a dress. I've never worn one, but the velvet is comforting, daring me to try it on. The hem is short in the front, but the fabric flows in the back with elegant thin shoulder straps of leaves. For some reason I think of Pan, when he asked me who I want to be, and when Captain asked me what I'm going to do.

I slip the dress on, full breasts threatening to leave the plunging cut. The fabric comes together again below my sternum, revealing my chest and small blistered scars. I braid my sleek lavender hair into a crown, leaving some loose curls trailing down my shoulder and teasing my chest. I frame black and white eyes with a silver powder, then paint my lips red.

I can't help but grin. Even like this, I look absolutely terrifying. Keeper of Death has a nice ring to it, but she's evolving into something different now. I strap my engraved obsidian dagger to my right thigh, visible to anyone who looks hard enough. The dress rides mid thigh in the front, both my prostheses are in full view. Orion will get a chance to see my 'great technology' up close, and the thought brings a smile, not shame, to my heart.

I decide on wearing short leather boots, providing support but revealing more than my usual tall boots do. My last step for war is to face my fear. I glare at the two waiting boxes on my bed of blue quilts. With a long breath, I open up the box with my name on it. Air pauses in my chest and goosebumps spread across cold skin when I remove a small note, in Knothall's handwriting.

Lyth, there are some things you should know.

I met Rohana in the war. (Yes, I'm ***that*** *old.)*

What you may not know is that I did not fight for Iron Court. I fought with Rohana for the Humans, against Fire. What we set in motion, all those years ago, is now for you to finish.

There is a better way for all of us to live together. Humans, Lesser and High Fae.

This has always been our plan for you, your difference from other Fae is not a mistake, as you so love to call it. You were made as an empty fae for a ***reason****, and I think that reason is to fix the world.*

Listen to Tribewyn. Trust me. If all else fails, trust yourself, but ***no one*** *else.*

If you ever want to know where you are from, that is in here too.

If you ask me, you should find out. You might be pleasantly surprised.

I let out trapped air, heart racing as burning stings my eyes. When I was laid up in bed after my first attack, I told him I was a mistake, and he never forgot it. With shaky hands I reach inside the box, finding a leather bound journal waiting with my history tucked into its curling pages. I caress it, unable to open the tome and reveal my secrets.

I roll his words over in my mind. The assignment was never meant to *end* here. More than an assignment, this is a plan over twelve hundred years in the making. How exactly Knothall and Rohana plan to fix Iverbourne is beyond me, let alone how *I* can help.

I close my eyes, but the sight of Rohana's smiling face tumbling down the chasm waits for me. My chest caves in and I slide down the edge of the bed, resting on the floor with my face hiding in shaking hands. I attempt to breathe in through my nose and out my mouth, but I struggle to find *any* air to push at all. The decades old whispering in my soul starts to *scream*, begging to be let out with my tears.

Darkness surrounds me, warm shadows hold me close while the sobs wracking my chest subside. I can't remember the last time I haven't been afraid of total darkness, and I release every ounce of pain spiking my heart. I usually always find those pale eyes waiting in dark corners, and when I close my eyes, the unending whispers keep me company. The voice hidden in my mind subsides after an eternity, giving me some relief.

I leave my hands with a sigh and find it's *Novak* holding me, not darkness. His shadows are pitch black, blocking out the room and entangling with my own dark aura. Novak's eyes are no longer bright sapphires, but entirely black like my own and feral. The pounding in my heart subsides and I focus on his eyes watching my *every* move. My chest rises steadily, but he keeps his shadowy embrace around me.

"Who hurt you?" He demands, usual goofiness gone. The danger I found when I met him is back, waiting to pounce on the culprit. Darkness isn't coming *from* him, he *is* the darkness. Night and stars scatter across his now ethereal skin, transforming the carefree male I know into a brilliant nightmare. Galaxies live in Novak, painting his entire body to match the dual capes the goddesses wear.

"No one." I breathe, my aura retracts and lingers on his body for a moment before dissipating entirely. Novak's still on guard whilst evaluating my face, then flinches as I pull back from him. Night fades, his skin once again sun kissed. He moves from kneeling to standing over me, then offers a hand as he takes his warmth with him.

I grasp his hand and rise unsteadily using all my might, my back and thigh muscles spasm intensely once I'm vertical. I stumble backwards and he keeps me upright with his other hand. "I'm fine, Novak." I snap in a whisper, no humor or wit to be found at the moment.

"Like hell you are." He snaps, and the composure he held *shatters*.

Once I'm steady, he releases me and begins pacing back and forth across the bedroom.

Back and forth.

Back and forth.

Both hands rake through once finely combed hair, tousling it back to the way I prefer while he walks a hole in the floor, cursing and muttering. His formal attire hugs his hourglass figure and I blush. A fine emerald tunic rests across his shoulders, the fabric embroidered with silver thread and half the moonstone buttons are undone. Tan breeches and leather boots compliment the rest of his figure. The musician is no young trouble here, elegance and maturity haven taken over his distraught features. I want him to come back to me, bring his warmth back to me.

"I knew Umber was up to something, after not seeing her in *years* why else would she find us other than to hatch a plan? I had no idea it was *this* though." He curses under his breath again, muttering about how he was right to come. I stand there and watch him, hands relaxed at my sides. The gears in my head turn and I'm almost dizzy watching him pace the small room so quickly. So he wasn't planning on coming, not at first.

"Al *swears* he only knew she was the emissary of Hallowed, nothing about any *deal*." He waves his arms in the air at the last word, glowering at me while he paces. Then, Novak pauses in front of me, face faltering. "Why aren't you saying anything?"

"I guess ... I'm just not surprised. That's not my problem, right now, anyways." I shrug before stepping back to sit on the bed. "I don't know why *you're* so upset." I bite my lip, staring up at him still frozen across the room. "Why are you here, anyway?"

He's gone entirely still, light hair falls over his worried face. I just want his smile to come back. He snaps out of it, then crosses the room. "Do you want an honest answer?" He rests beside me on the bed, completely serious.

"You seem to be the only one giving me truth, don't let me down now." I whisper, brushing hair away from his eyes. I think of his strong body beside mine this morning and my cheeks warm, hand falling back to my lap.

"Then let me tell you later. I *promise*, I will." Novak moves from the bed and kneels on the floor before me. I keep my attention on my fidgeting hands, the last time someone got on their knees and made me a promise, they broke it.

"You don't trust me?" He asks, pushing the hurt words out. The shadows he once held at bay surround us again, his hand moves towards mine but he thinks better of it, pulling away in a fist.

"I trust you more than I trust the rest." I say, because it's true. Why? Who knows. My own waves of darkness creep out, teasing his shadows. Is it really just my aura? I *know* it isn't Aether inside me, but other auras don't seem to have a life of their own, like Novak's and I's do. The bedroom has no signs of lightening, we are in a bubble of each other's darkness.

"I suppose that'll have to do." Novak rises, breaking the orb of warm night and tousling hair away from his face. I release a heavy breath and take the hand he offers, my own shadowed aura dissipates with the air in my lungs as our skin meets.

"I rather like your shadows." He murmurs before letting go, and his eyes widen as he realizes his words were spoken aloud.

"You can see it?" I ask, voice rising in excitement. Novak's now blue eyes are wild and he opens his lips, then pushes them into a thin line. When he speaks, his voice is strained, deep and hoarse.

"Yes."

"I don't understand. Are you like me?" My voice hinges in the thick air and I grasp his forearm.

"There's only one you." He smiles, averting his eyes for a moment. He focuses on me again when he tells his truth, his fingers resting atop my hand. "When they did this to my ears, the bastards took my magic as well." He gestures to his ears with his other hand, keeping his wary eyes on me.

Took his magic.

How is that even possible? Born without it is one thing, but to have it taken from you ...

My soul shudders at the thought. I avoid staring at the carvings on his chest, what I now realize must be sigils. Old magic Knothall told me about, that he thought died with the Ancients.

"The Ancients must've decided I still deserved something. I used to be a Water Fae, you see." He releases my hand and bows dramatically, then shakes his hair again, smiling as he rises. I can't smile. Not right now.

"I was left with the shadows and shell of my magic, the darkest parts of it, and other things ..." Novak's smile fades as his voice cracks. "The darkness is a friend of mine, and you my lady, are quite full of it. I wish I could tell you why, but I truly don't know."

I decide it doesn't matter what happened in his past, or why the Fae here seem to look down upon him. The Fae I know right now, he is someone *good*. Velvet green drapes behind me and I step closer, moving the hair from his eyes with a sure hand, unfailing now. "Sometimes there is comfort in the dark." I whisper, resting my hand on his soft cheek.

"You just keep getting better and better." A small, wicked grin returns and he takes my hand. He kisses the top with care and I stifle a shiver.

"Or worse and worse, depending on how you look at it." I tease with a laugh, cheeks warming as he wipes smeared powder from my eyes. "Thank you." I whisper, and we stare into each other's hearts for what seems like hours.

My watch clicks, pulling me back into reality. Only a minute has passed.

I leave his side, locking up my box before I take the one with Trihewyn's name upon it. I stare down at it, then back up to Novak. "I have a long road ahead of me, I think." Kindling, curious eyes meet mine. "I'm not sure what crazy plan you have, but if you plan on tagging along, consider yourself warned." I throw him a sweet smile, nudging at him while I saunter past, wide hips pressing tight against my dress.

"What do you take me for, some kind of scaredy Fae?" He muses playfully and I can't help but keep my smile the whole journey to dinner, trailing behind a Lesser Fae servant who was waiting in silence outside my room.

Before entering the dining hall I take a breath, straighten my shoulders and put on my best wicked smile. The face I wear before torturing prisoners. The grand hall has open foyers on each side, leading to distant rooms snaking out around the main area. Mazes live in big cities, under mountains and inside of swamp castles. I will never be rid of them.

A milky white table holds Trihewyn at one end, and Umber at the other. The twins are seated along one side of the table, surrounded by female courtiers. The other edge holds two empty chairs waiting for Novak and I, centered between two sentries. I chuckle a bit and saunter by the guards, trailing a hand alongside the back of their chairs. The females grip their weapons when Novak sits down.

I continue past my empty chair and stand before Trihewyn. She evaluates me with amusement playing at her wrinkles. Smooth silver hair tickles her lips as it flows past, and powerful eyes pause on the box in my hands. I lift my chin, voice confident and teasing. "I assure you, the game I'm playing at is much more fun than the one Umber has going."

Chairs creak while Fae shift in their seats. "Well, let's play, little one." Trihewyn's calm voice drips with poison. The swirling void she keeps to herself. For now.

"Not until you agree to my conditions." I state flatly.

Trihewyn glances to the table and then back to the box in my hands, lifting her eyes to mine after a moment. Faerie bargains are not to be taken lightly. *Especially* for an unknown reason. "Go on." She gestures to me, impatience filling her precise features.

"After tonight, myself and my companions will be free to leave and do as we wish. You shall not siphon anything else from them, or myself. Whatever questions I have for you, you will answer. *Truthfully*." The last word hangs in the air, all noise ceasing to exist for a moment.

Trihewyn scrutinizes me, her brows narrowing at my specifics. No loopholes. "What makes you think I would want to keep you here?" She asks, tilting her head at me. She rises when I don't answer, approaching me with grace. I glance at Orion and Alvis who are leaned back in their seats with masked faces.

"You can never be too sure of Fae." I retort, straightening myself. She reaches for the box. "You have to *say* it." I order, hands unrelenting.

A small smile pulls up a corner of her pale lips. "I agree to all of your conditions. Now, let's see if your bark is as big as your bite." She takes the box greedily and her eyes stare directly into me, her purple Aether chokes me for a moment. A white light flashes in her eyes and I'm reminded of the tunnels.

Trihewyn leaves me and my shoulders drop. I remain standing long enough to recover my breath and then find my seat beside Novak. He gives me a quick wink and the twins across the table bow their heads to me. I glance at Umber who's staring at me, even faced. Dismissing her without so much as an emotion, my attention turns to the table while Trihewyn opens the box.

The regal courtiers are dressed in simple dresses of purple and silver. They shift their gaze between Novak and I, a look of disgust resting on their faces. They're all fairly young, perhaps even younger than I. As Trihewyn sets down maps and parchments on the table, my thoughts turn to the males of Hallowed again. I haven't seen any trace of them. No children either, just a foreboding village supporting its swamp thing.

"So, tell me, why would Knothall entrust you," Trihewyn muses, a smile on her face when she looks up at me, "to deliver this?" The females lose their disappointment towards me, Knothall's name turns their eyes down at once. I lean forward on the table, breasts begging to leave my dress while I rest on my arms.

"Knothall had quite a few good things to say about you. I'm almost ... disappointed, he didn't mention anything about his apprentice." I grin, twirling at a loose tendril of purple. My poker face has to be on point.

"Knothall is dead." The High Lady states bluntly, tapping the table with a jewel clawed finger. Warmth spreads across my face and neck. I lean back immediately, biting at my cheek. "I have not spoken to him in centuries, my emissary delivered the news to me upon arrival." She gestures to Umber who stares directly at her High Lady, avoiding the hurt displayed across my face.

When did she know? She could have told me, even if she planned to betray me. Was our friendship a complete lie? I find no answer in her cold, sapphire face, or perhaps all the answers. Shadows twirl in my peripheral vision and I peer at Novak who has a small smile and worry lingering in his creased brow. The dark aura nearly visible isn't *his*, it's mine. I push out a breath, then roll my shoulders back and draw the shadows in with a deep inhale.

Not another word is spoken while dinner is served, though no one at the table is particularly hungry at this point. We spend the rest of the formality in pointed silence, pushing the gorgeous food around our plates.

Trihewyn never lets the box, or me, out of her sight.

YOU KILLED THE HERO

I stand on the open balcony of the library, nestled onto the highest floor of the mossy stilted castle. The double moons shine down upon the swamp water and I am alone. Luminous bugs skitter by, and a soft call of what I assume to be owls lulls from across the bog. The inky water is disturbed every now and then by a surfacing creature, but it's too dark to make out the exact nature of it.

I had decided against alcohol after dinner, leaving the others to their folly while Novak played his lute for the loosened court. I wanted to stay and listen, but my mind is too busy to be around other Fae. After some exploring through the maze, I came across this treasure. The sheer quantity of books rivals the small library Knothall possessed, my second home to the labs. Parchment and the stench of rot filled the humid air inside, and comfort was nowhere to be found as I searched through the volumes. When I couldn't decide on finding the right book, I opted for the night sky instead.

Knothall's on my mind, and why he trusts Trihewyn so much that he would die trying to get me to her. The female seems like a monster wrapped in sheep's clothing, power hungry just like the rest of them. I wander back into the silent library, the books shelved upon every free wall call to me. The walnut desks and upholstered chairs offer a place to rest. But I don't want to.

With not much for decorations, the large map waiting on a desk catches my eye. A map of Iverbourne crafted rather recently, the parchment still crisp and ink unfaded. I trace my finger along the borders and lands, studying the local villages in each territory. The empty Realm of Giants above the mountains in the north brings my hand to a pause. The map is far more detailed than mine, I need to update the old thing.

"Now that we are alone, we can finally talk." Trihewyn's voice pierces the humidity from behind me.

"What was in the box?" I demand without turning. She pauses on the other side of the desk, eyes flitting to my hand on the empty land of Giants. The air muffles and a shield is drawn around us, Aether dances wild in her bright silver eyes, bordering on white.

"Answer my question first. Why did Knothall send you?" Trihewyn counters, precise and even.

"All I ever did was protect the Machine. He trained me for the life of being a Keeper." I cross my arms, sighing before continuing. "I never thought I'd see the light of day. I will always be thankful to Knothall, but I have no idea what I'm doing, what I delivered to you. That is the truth."

Trihewyn watches me intently, hands at her sides. At last she wanders away, overlooking the open balcony as she speaks in a distant tone. "If you think the realm is beautiful now, you should've seen it before." She watches the swamp for another moment before coming inside to find a dusty volume from the shelf closest to her. Thick and haphazardly bound, simple worn leather, no details, no paint.

"There was a time when the Ancients lived among us. Working side by side, tending to the land and creatures within it. In my time, they visited only on rare occasions, revealing themselves to those deemed worthy enough. The settlements of the land are based on the origins of the elusive Elemental Fae." She gestures to the territories on the map, and then lays the tome open on the table, revealing the first page of forgotten history. "Villages across the land were composed of far more beings than just High Fae. All possessed magic, humans even. Fae commanded giant beasts and lived with them side by side, familiars of a sort."

A half goat and half fae creature catches my fingers first, my gaze wanders and searches the other tribes of fae combined with mythical animals. The pages pour ancient Aether, my fingertips tingling and cold. "I didn't even know that kind of world was possible." I breathe, watching her flip the pages to reveal more illuminated pages, brilliant stories of our land. Stories I've not heard before, any history book I had in the Mountain all took place after the Machine was created. Knothall didn't talk much of the 'old days' before the war, other than to teach me the word *shomer*.

Illustrations of moon phases surrounded by Fae, Humans and a menagerie of other beings take my breath away, and the High Lady pauses while I take it in. "Aether doesn't flow in their veins like ours do, Humans have to ask. Work *with* the land. The Ancients taught them rituals, how to use the power of the moons and such." Trihewyn explains.

I stop her after she turns the next page, a loose scrap stuck in the bound parchment stops my heart. A Fae with purple hair like mine. The body is feminine, long tresses flow with her cape of night. The face is blank, with a thick body dressed in a glittering silver gown. A lady of the night.

"What's this?" I whisper. No description, no context is inscribed upon the page.

"*Findmefindmefindme.*" The scathing demand claws at my mind, the sight of the page startles a throbbing headache into me and I push the nightmarish voice away.

Triheywn traces the plain face and shows no notice of my sudden grimace. "I don't know." I glance over at her, raising a purple brow. With her bond, she has to be truthful. Her eyes meet mine, even and calm. "My daughter found this, years ago in the mountains of Vabel. When she found no answers, the page found its home here. Along with everything else forgotten by time."

Silence swells and I swallow, building courage. "May I have it?"

Trihewyn lifts the parchment with a trembling hand. She caresses the illustration with a distant smile, then passes it to me. "I suppose if anyone can unravel her quest, it will be you."

The mystery weighs heavily in my hands. The parchment is far more delicate than the remainder of the book, edges curled and crisp. I dip my chin to her and she turns the page in silence, bringing us to a scene of a grand city. The sprawling metropolis reminds me of Cervalis, and in the illustration creatures of every kind live together. *Borealis, before the war.*

I wonder if slavery lived back then, too.

"So, Iron was jealous then?" I ask, thoughts still elsewhere.

"Fire was only a small part of the problem. Sylvan was much larger back then, ruled by a greedy lord, and there were many sentimental to his cause." She sighs, rubbing her forehead. "Only creatures who are born with Aether in their veins, should be allowed the privilege of using it."

"Would that be Typhan's father?" Orion's face comes to mind. What atrocities had he faced, or committed whilst there? Or Alvis for that matter, scout is probably a polite term for spymaster. Interrogator, perhaps. Alvis said they were murders, kidnappers. A shudder escapes at the thought of Alvis hurting anyone, even with all those telling battle scars and the arsenal he carries.

"No, his grandfather. You will find Typhan is cut from the same cloth, however." The story pauses on a wicked, bloodied non descript High Fae male resting on a crystalline throne, situated on a mound of bones, flooded by a river of crimson.

"I'm not sure I want to." I mutter as another shudder escapes.

Sylvan Court seems absolutely frightening, especially the more I hear about it. Triheywn doesn't say anything, just turns the page. The next is a map of

Old Iverbourne, when the continent was one. Iron Court was once a jungle with wildlife and greenery spreading across the entire southern lands. Above the narrow strait connecting the north and south lay the small, new region of Borealis.

"When war broke out, it wasn't just between Iron and Borealis. Sylvan was taking land at an unprecedented rate, pushing Terra into the north. Mercenaries were sent out in every territory to track down humans, and human sympathizers. Though, they still do that bit." Her voice trails off and she walks away from the book, and me.

I cradle history and turn the lonely pages. An ancient story desperate to be told, for the past to be righted. I bet those Sylvan mercenaries have grown more vicious as the years went on.

Novak.

I used to be a Water Fae.

By the Ancients. He must've lived there at some point before meeting Captain, a Human sympathizer in dangerous territory. Hate creeps across Iverbourne and has tainted everyone I've met so far. Terra isn't exempt either, Panrauth's family proves that point. There was no reason for Weylin to die. Why couldn't they have lived together at the castle, in peace?

Why did it matter if she was a Human?

Why does it matter at all, if you have Aether or not?

"Sylvan stationed armies all throughout the continent, everywhere *except* against Iron." Trihewyn's tired voice breaks my thoughts as she rests in an upholstered chair, rubbing her face after she settles.

I try to imagine the land before it was broken. What would harmony even look like? There's no way Echo was a jungle and not the starving wasteland it is now, and when I think of a world without the Machine, my brain can't compute.

I keep reading, but the illustrations of battle, war and terrified humans are almost too much to bear. Innocents trying to escape bloodthirsty faeries waiting for them at every turn. Next in the thick tome of history are images of Fae turning on each other, and the land dying beneath their feet as they spill precious kindred blood.

The next page freezes my veins and every fiber in my being. A magnificent portrait of Rohana dressed in full plate armor with an elegant gold handled sword at her side, the familiar defiance swirling in her silver eyes. At the bottom, the inscription breaks my heart in half. *Rohana, Hero of Borealis.*

I set the book down with care, then shakily take a seat behind the desk. I lean back, resting my trembling hands behind my head and keep my eyes focused on the wall. Breathe. *Breathe.*

"I had just become High Lady, no older than you, really." Trihewyn gazes past the balcony, talking to the night sky more than me. Her voice is slow, thoughtful.

"Not a position I cared for, politics and such. I was the remaining heir, and if my daughter wasn't solving riddles, she was defending Humans. Anyone, really. But, when war broke out, the Ancient settlements needed protection."

Trihewyn waves off in a general direction, unbeknownst to my inner plight. "She left with a small battalion to aid Borealis. Most of our forces were on their way to Terra, barely making it there in time to stop Sylvan from destroying the Earth Faeries completely. Whoever else could be spared, saved our history. The temples, old libraries. Or what was left of them, the others were so careless." She mutters, shaking her head.

We met in the war. Knothall wouldn't really send the murderer of a High Lady's daughter to her feet, would he?

Did I just walk into a trap?

"We were the only territory that sent reinforcements to the Humans. Without Knothall breaking away from Iron, she never would've saved them." She chuckles offhandedly, eyes wandering the tomes beyond me. "Rohana nearly killed him, until she realized his red eyes didn't match the Borealis regalia he wore."

Cheeks warm and I imagine the Fae I murdered attempting to take down Knothall. Hard to believe, but then I remember the courage that poured from her when she stared down death. An Air and Fire Fae, falling in love while fighting evil. Memories of Knothall begging Rohana to stop fighting in the Trench break my heart and I brace myself using the desk, arms shaking as I clench its wooden edges tight.

"You are all heroes." I state in a whisper. Heroes, forgotten by time.

"Well, not everyone else thought so. Sylvan lost, brutally. Terra reaped the benefits of course, pushing them farther inland and taking up the farmlands. Knothall and Rohana rebuilt Borealis. Here in the Mists, we restored what we could." Trihewyn sighs, eyes finally settling on me.

That isn't right. They *ended* the war?

"I thought the Ancients stopped the war. With the Machine." I breathe, tapping a finger on the table before I shakily turn a page. A glittering castle tucked away into snowy mountains. Rohana must've built the palace herself, what *power* she must've held to manipulate the glacial air is beyond my comprehension. Grand spires with crystal spheres of every color dotted the masterpiece. *Borealis after the first war.*

"No, not until the second war." Trihewyn muses softly, sadness turns down her wrinkles.

"The *second* war?" I leave my seat and pace the room, gears burning in my head. Everything I thought I knew was brewing and festering in such a filthier truth than I ever thought possible. Magic does nothing but cause problems.

The scars on Novak's body and inevitably his soul flash across my mind. The nightmare of my legs and dignity being taken from me. Knothall, Rohana. Orion and Alvis. I can't even imagine their stories. My watch clicks, hours have gone by in the portal to another time. The Ancients should've just sent us into oblivion and started over, to hell with the Machine. Obviously, the Eternal isn't doing the job of keeping the lands in balance either. No, it *exacerbates* the problem.

I kneel before Trihewyn, dropping my head as I await punishment. "I cannot hear anything else, not without telling you. I killed Rohana."

A warrior princess, saving the realm of humans. And I killed her.

"I know." Trihewyn says, leaning away from me.

"So, this whole time you knew who I was?" I whisper, fury stings my eyes.

"Of course I did. You think I wouldn't know who murdered my daughter?" Her voice is cold, calculating, stabbing into my heart.

"So why didn't you just kill me then? Before, or now, even."

"Knothall convinced me you were worth keeping alive, but wouldn't tell me much more than that." Trihewyn evaluates my dark eye, and then the cloudy white one.

"And I suppose Umber is how you sent information in and out?" I snark, rising and pacing the room again. My guilt is mingled with anger, too many emotions to count bounce through me.

"Before her, there were others. Knothall and I were the only ties to worlds we were kept apart from, so don't take it personally. I just hadn't realized Knothall's apprentice is the Empty Fae I've heard so much about."

"Is that a problem?" I bite out, drawing my brows together.

"Not in the slightest." She stands, clasping her hands together.

"So, why were you looking for me then? *The Empty Fae?*" I halt my pacing steps, facing her uneasily. The words 'empty Fae' sear my pride.

"We have hardly finished with this story, and you want to start another?" She chides, a smile pulls at her wrinkled face. I roll my eyes and cross my arms, annoyed with her games.

"What happened then? If the war ended, why did everything fall apart?"

"Faeries are selfish. Losing a battle doesn't change that." She states, losing the smile. "Iron came back and burned what those two had built to the ground. The massacring didn't end until Knothall made a deal." I swallow, tears threaten my eyes. His crime. "The son of a High Lord helping humans would not go unpunished, and they knew what he was to my daughter."

I laugh, shaking my head at her words. Trihewyn tilts her head at me, confusion spreading across her features. Tears fall and I hold my stomach, dark amusement twists me over.

So different from his legend in the Eternal. A criminal who committed grave treachery indeed. I rub my face and catch my breath, recollecting myself. Trihewyn crosses to the book, turning to the last pages. Her solemn voice draws me over to her side. "The Ancients woke from their slumber the moment Knothall was on their side of the sea. Shattering the land and sending up the mountain walls all around."

The Eternal Mountain protrudes from the depths of an inky sea. A grand continent ripped apart by violent flames and earthquakes. Glacial cliffs grow along the northern and southern borders of Iverbourne. Cutting us off from whoever lives there, for over a millennia of separation now.

What a sight. Watching your mate being physically separated from you, and dragged into a hellish Mountain erupting from the sea. I still don't know what being someone's *mate* means. To be mated sounds more permanent than marriage, a connection between souls.

"Rohana came home only after providing her magic to rebuild Borealis one last time. With the Aether restrictions it was nothing like it once was, but she gave them a start. She returned to me, but was never the same."

"She wouldn't stop fighting." I say, catching her silver eyes.

"Of course not. She stood up for what she believed in, until the day she was thrown into that damn mountain, and every day after."

Both heroes of the war were trapped under the Mountain, punished for a lifetime of fighting for those less fortunate, less privileged.

And they both died there, because of me. I know the rest of the story.

"Who else knows this?" I ask, shutting the book with a thud.

"Only the Hallowed and Borealis Courts were given a Book of Teachings to protect, the Ancients recognizing how careless the other lands were." Trihewyn scoffs. "The hatred Sylvan holds for anyone deemed 'lesser' never ends, they just hide their terror behind walls. And Terra, they aren't much better. Doing nothing is sometimes just as fatal." Anger shakes her voice and Aether burns in her eyes. I can't agree more.

"Are you going to tell me now why you were looking for me?"

"What do you know of The Others?" The High Lady asks, taking me by surprise. I immediately think of Amwren terrified, reduced to ash. Eros, destroying Knothall. She and I both killed heroes. We are both villains. By the Ancients, what have I *done*?

"I've heard you struck a bargain with them, and I know for a fact they're murderers. Which has me questioning you." I spit out without thinking, cheeks warming. I pace away, leaving silence hanging for a moment

"Their leader is the one who killed Knothall." My last statement is a whisper.

"I know. I need your help." I face her, evaluating the High Lady's calm figure. Trihewyn's wrinkled fingers are intertwined together. "The information I need, for Eros. That's what you brought me."

I cross my arms and narrow my brows, studying her carefully placed statement. "Why me? I won't listen to another word, not until you tell me what is so *special* about an Empty Fae."

Her eyes set hard upon my face as she approaches and she stands over me in a few strides. "Only an Empty Fae can assemble the Harbinger, the greatest weapon of our time. Eros and Ragnis are working together, and as you know, Eros is capable of Aether unlike any I have ever seen before. Ragnis plans to exact revenge on the lands, with her help."

Eros and Ragnis. I rub my face, digesting her words. "What if I say no?"

"You are free to leave, as we discussed. I have kept up my end of the bargain, and you yours. Do you *want* to say no?" She asks, tilting her head with a smile. She knows I won't say no. In some part of my cold heart, goodness lingers.

Or a strong desire to settle the score, at the very least.

"Did you really make a bargain with The Others?"

"Yes. I provided Eros with all of our men, in exchange for asylum." Trihewyn says matter of factually, and my brows raise.

"Being High Lady comes with hard decisions. I would rather give her the males, than to be the first thing she wipes out on her path through their realms." Trihewyn leaves without another word, leaving me with the glacial sting of her words.

The *males*. What a cold, calculating bitch.

Unable to make the walk to my room after being hit with so many waves of truth, I find sleep in the library, slumped into a plush chair. My rest is fitful, familiar and new nightmares taunting me, over and over. The last one is what wakes me, the most vivid one yet.

"When will you find me? You're so close, almost there. Find me, and we can go home."

I search around the abyss of my mind, sending my lulling voice into the warm darkness blocking out every sense. Every sense, except for the writhing of her voice in my brain.

"I can't see you, you have to come out of the dark." I plead.

The endless whispering halts, and a delightful giggle takes over, sending panic through me.

"Silly girl, I am the Dark. I am everything and nothing, what was and never will be. Just, like, you."

KEEPER OF DEATH

I stand on the open balcony of the library, nestled onto the highest floor of the mossy stilted castle. The double moons shine down upon the swamp water and I am alone. Luminous bugs skitter by, and a soft call of what I assume to be owls lulls from across the bog. The inky water is disturbed every now and then by a surfacing creature, but it's too dark to make out the exact nature of it.

I had decided against alcohol after dinner, leaving the others to their folly while Novak played his lute for the loosened court. I wanted to stay and listen, but my mind is too busy to be around other Fae. After some exploring through the maze, I came across this treasure. The sheer quantity of books rivals the small library Knothall possessed, my second home to the labs. Parchment and the stench of rot filled the humid air inside, and comfort was nowhere to be found as I searched through the volumes. When I couldn't decide on finding the right book, I opted for the night sky instead.

Knothall's on my mind, and why he trusts Trihewyn so much that he would die trying to get me to her. The female seems like a monster wrapped in sheep's clothing, power hungry just like the rest of them. I wander back into the silent library, the books shelved upon every free wall call to me. The walnut desks and upholstered chairs offer a place to rest. But I don't want to.

With not much for decorations, the large map waiting on a desk catches my eye. A map of Iverbourne crafted rather recently, the parchment still crisp and ink unfaded. I trace my finger along the borders and lands, studying the local villages in each territory. The empty Realm of Giants above the mountains in the north brings my hand to a pause. The map is far more detailed than mine, I need to update the old thing.

"Now that we are alone, we can finally talk." Trihewyn's voice pierces the humidity from behind me.

"What was in the box?" I demand without turning. She pauses on the other side of the desk, eyes flitting to my hand on the empty land of Giants. The air muffles and a shield is drawn around us, Aether dances wild in her bright silver eyes, bordering on white.

"Answer my question first. Why did Knothall send you?" Trihewyn counters, precise and even.

"All I ever did was protect the Machine. He trained me for the life of being a Keeper." I cross my arms, sighing before continuing. "I never thought I'd see the light of day. I will always be thankful to Knothall, but I have no idea what I'm doing, what I delivered to you. That is the truth."

Trihewyn watches me intently, hands at her sides. At last she wanders away, overlooking the open balcony as she speaks in a distant tone. "If you think the realm is beautiful now, you should've seen it before." She watches the swamp for another moment before coming inside to find a dusty volume from the shelf closest to her. Thick and haphazardly bound, simple worn leather, no details, no paint.

"There was a time when the Ancients lived among us. Working side by side, tending to the land and creatures within it. In my time, they visited only on rare occasions, revealing themselves to those deemed worthy enough. The settlements of the land are based on the origins of the elusive Elemental Fae." She gestures to the territories on the map, and then lays the tome open on the table, revealing the first page of forgotten history. "Villages across the land were composed of far more beings than just High Fae. All possessed magic, humans even. Fae commanded giant beasts and lived with them side by side, familiars of a sort."

A half goat and half fae creature catches my fingers first, my gaze wanders and searches the other tribes of fae combined with mythical animals. The pages pour ancient Aether, my fingertips tingling and cold. "I didn't even know that kind of world was possible." I breathe, watching her flip the pages to reveal more illuminated pages, brilliant stories of our land. Stories I've not heard before, any history book I had in the Mountain all took place after the Machine was created. Knothall didn't talk much of the 'old days' before the war, other than to teach me the word *shomer*.

Illustrations of moon phases surrounded by Fae, Humans and a menagerie of other beings take my breath away, and the High Lady pauses while I take it in. "Aether doesn't flow in their veins like ours do, Humans have to ask. Work *with* the land. The Ancients taught them rituals, how to use the power of the moons and such." Trihewyn explains.

I stop her after she turns the next page, a loose scrap stuck in the bound parchment stops my heart. A Fae with purple hair like mine. The body is feminine, long tresses flow with her cape of night. The face is blank, with a thick body dressed in a glittering silver gown. A lady of the night.

"What's this?" I whisper. No description, no context is inscribed upon the page.

"*Findmefindmefindme.*" The scathing demand claws at my mind, the sight of the page startles a throbbing headache into me and I push the nightmarish voice away.

Triheywn traces the plain face and shows no notice of my sudden grimace. "I don't know." I glance over at her, raising a purple brow. With her bond, she has to be truthful. Her eyes meet mine, even and calm. "My daughter found this, years ago in the mountains of Vabel. When she found no answers, the page found its home here. Along with everything else forgotten by time."

Silence swells and I swallow, building courage. "May I have it?"

Trihewyn lifts the parchment with a trembling hand. She caresses the illustration with a distant smile, then passes it to me. "I suppose if anyone can unravel her quest, it will be you."

The mystery weighs heavily in my hands. The parchment is far more delicate than the remainder of the book, edges curled and crisp. I dip my chin to her and she turns the page in silence, bringing us to a scene of a grand city. The sprawling metropolis reminds me of Cervalis, and in the illustration creatures of every kind live together. *Borealis, before the war.*

I wonder if slavery lived back then, too.

"So, Iron was jealous then?" I ask, thoughts still elsewhere.

"Fire was only a small part of the problem. Sylvan was much larger back then, ruled by a greedy lord, and there were many sentimental to his cause." She sighs, rubbing her forehead. "Only creatures who are born with Aether in their veins, should be allowed the privilege of using it."

"Would that be Typhan's father?" Orion's face comes to mind. What atrocities had he faced, or committed whilst there? Or Alvis for that matter, scout is probably a polite term for spymaster. Interrogator, perhaps. Alvis said they were murders, kidnappers. A shudder escapes at the thought of Alvis hurting anyone, even with all those telling battle scars and the arsenal he carries.

"No, his grandfather. You will find Typhan is cut from the same cloth, however." The story pauses on a wicked, bloodied non descript High Fae male resting on a crystalline throne, situated on a mound of bones, flooded by a river of crimson.

"I'm not sure I want to." I mutter as another shudder escapes.

Sylvan Court seems absolutely frightening, especially the more I hear about it. Triheywn doesn't say anything, just turns the page. The next is a map of Old Iverbourne, when the continent was one. Iron Court was once a jungle with wildlife and greenery spreading across the entire southern lands. Above the narrow strait connecting the north and south lay the small, new region of Borealis.

"When war broke out, it wasn't just between Iron and Borealis. Sylvan was taking land at an unprecedented rate, pushing Terra into the north. Mercenaries were sent out in every territory to track down humans, and human sympathizers. Though, they still do that bit." Her voice trails off and she walks away from the book, and me.

I cradle history and turn the lonely pages. An ancient story desperate to be told, for the past to be righted. I bet those Sylvan mercenaries have grown more vicious as the years went on.

Novak.

I used to be a Water Fae.

By the Ancients. He must've lived there at some point before meeting Captain, a Human sympathizer in dangerous territory. Hate creeps across Iverbourne and has tainted everyone I've met so far. Terra isn't exempt either, Panrauth's family proves that point. There was no reason for Weylin to die. Why couldn't they have lived together at the castle, in peace?

Why did it matter if she was a Human?

Why does it matter at all, if you have Aether or not?

"Sylvan stationed armies all throughout the continent, everywhere *except* against Iron." Trihewyn's tired voice breaks my thoughts as she rests in an upholstered chair, rubbing her face after she settles.

I try to imagine the land before it was broken. What would harmony even look like? There's no way Echo was a jungle and not the starving wasteland it is now, and when I think of a world without the Machine, my brain can't compute.

I keep reading, but the illustrations of battle, war and terrified humans are almost too much to bear. Innocents trying to escape bloodthirsty faeries waiting for them at every turn. Next in the thick tome of history are images of Fae turning on each other, and the land dying beneath their feet as they spill precious kindred blood.

The next page freezes my veins and every fiber in my being. A magnificent portrait of Rohana dressed in full plate armor with an elegant gold handled sword at her side, the familiar defiance swirling in her silver eyes. At the bottom, the inscription breaks my heart in half. *Rohana, Hero of Borealis.*

I set the book down with care, then shakily take a seat behind the desk. I lean back, resting my trembling hands behind my head and keep my eyes focused on the wall. Breathe. *Breathe.*

"I had just become High Lady, no older than you, really." Trihewyn gazes past the balcony, talking to the night sky more than me. Her voice is slow, thoughtful. "Not a position I cared for, politics and such. I was the remaining heir, and if my daughter wasn't solving riddles, she was defending Humans. Anyone, really. But, when war broke out, the Ancient settlements needed protection."

Trihewyn waves off in a general direction, unbeknownst to my inner plight. "She left with a small battalion to aid Borealis. Most of our forces were on their way to Terra, barely making it there in time to stop Sylvan from destroying the Earth Faeries completely. Whoever else could be spared, saved our history. The temples, old libraries. Or what was left of them, the others were so careless." She mutters, shaking her head.

We met in the war. Knothall wouldn't really send the murderer of a High Lady's daughter to her feet, would he?

Did I just walk into a trap?

"We were the only territory that sent reinforcements to the Humans. Without Knothall breaking away from Iron, she never would've saved them." She chuckles offhandedly, eyes wandering the tomes beyond me. "Rohana nearly killed him, until she realized his red eyes didn't match the Borealis regalia he wore."

Cheeks warm and I imagine the Fae I murdered attempting to take down Knothall. Hard to believe, but then I remember the courage that poured from her when she stared down death. An Air and Fire Fae, falling in love while fighting evil. Memories of Knothall begging Rohana to stop fighting in the Trench break my heart and I brace myself using the desk, arms shaking as I clench its wooden edges tight.

"You are all heroes." I state in a whisper. Heroes, forgotten by time.

"Well, not everyone else thought so. Sylvan lost, brutally. Terra reaped the benefits of course, pushing them farther inland and taking up the farmlands. Knothall and Rohana rebuilt Borealis. Here in the Mists, we restored what we could." Trihewyn sighs, eyes finally settling on me.

That isn't right. They *ended* the war?

"I thought the Ancients stopped the war. With the Machine." I breathe, tapping a finger on the table before I shakily turn a page. A glittering castle tucked away into snowy mountains. Rohana must've built the palace herself, what *power* she must've held to manipulate the glacial air is beyond my comprehension. Grand spires with crystal spheres of every color dotted the masterpiece. *Borealis after the first war.*

"No, not until the second war." Trihewyn muses softly, sadness turns down her wrinkles.

"The *second* war?" I leave my seat and pace the room, gears burning in my head. Everything I thought I knew was brewing and festering in such a filthier truth than I ever thought possible. Magic does nothing but cause problems.

The scars on Novak's body and inevitably his soul flash across my mind. The nightmare of my legs and dignity being taken from me. Knothall, Rohana. Orion and Alvis. I can't even imagine their stories. My watch clicks, hours have gone by in the portal to another time. The Ancients should've just sent us into oblivion and started over, to hell with the Machine. Obviously, the Eternal isn't doing the job of keeping the lands in balance either. No, it *exacerbates* the problem.

I kneel before Trihewyn, dropping my head as I await punishment. "I cannot hear anything else, not without telling you. I killed Rohana."

A warrior princess, saving the realm of humans. And I killed her.

"I know." Trihewyn says, leaning away from me.

"So, this whole time you knew who I was?" I whisper, fury stings my eyes.

"Of course I did. You think I wouldn't know who murdered my daughter?" Her voice is cold, calculating, stabbing into my heart.

"So why didn't you just kill me then? Before, or now, even."

"Knothall convinced me you were worth keeping alive, but wouldn't tell me much more than that." Trihewyn evaluates my dark eye, and then the cloudy white one.

"And I suppose Umber is how you sent information in and out?" I snark, rising and pacing the room again. My guilt is mingled with anger, too many emotions to count bounce through me.

"Before her, there were others. Knothall and I were the only ties to worlds we were kept apart from, so don't take it personally. I just hadn't realized Knothall's apprentice is the Empty Fae I've heard so much about."

"Is that a problem?" I bite out, drawing my brows together.

"Not in the slightest." She stands, clasping her hands together.

"So, why were you looking for me then? *The Empty Fae?*" I halt my pacing steps, facing her uneasily. The words 'empty Fae' sear my pride.

"We have hardly finished with this story, and you want to start another?" She chides, a smile pulls at her wrinkled face. I roll my eyes and cross my arms, annoyed with her games.

"What happened then? If the war ended, why did everything fall apart?"

"Faeries are selfish. Losing a battle doesn't change that." She states, losing the smile. "Iron came back and burned what those two had built to the ground. The massacring didn't end until Knothall made a deal." I swallow, tears threaten my eyes. His crime. "The son of a High Lord helping humans would not go unpunished, and they knew what he was to my daughter."

I laugh, shaking my head at her words. Trihewyn tilts her head at me, confusion spreading across her features. Tears fall and I hold my stomach, dark amusement twists me over.

So different from his legend in the Eternal. A criminal who committed grave treachery indeed. I rub my face and catch my breath, recollecting myself. Trihewyn crosses to the book, turning to the last pages. Her solemn voice draws me over to her side. "The Ancients woke from their slumber the moment Knothall was on their side of the sea. Shattering the land and sending up the mountain walls all around."

The Eternal Mountain protrudes from the depths of an inky sea. A grand continent ripped apart by violent flames and earthquakes. Glacial cliffs grow along the northern and southern borders of Iverbourne. Cutting us off from whoever lives there, for over a millennia of separation now.

What a sight. Watching your mate being physically separated from you, and dragged into a hellish Mountain erupting from the sea. I still don't know what being someone's *mate* means. To be mated sounds more permanent than marriage, a connection between souls.

"Rohana came home only after providing her magic to rebuild Borealis one last time. With the Aether restrictions it was nothing like it once was, but she gave them a start. She returned to me, but was never the same."

"She wouldn't stop fighting." I say, catching her silver eyes.

"Of course not. She stood up for what she believed in, until the day she was thrown into that damn mountain, and every day after."

Both heroes of the war were trapped under the Mountain, punished for a lifetime of fighting for those less fortunate, less privileged.

And they both died there, because of me. I know the rest of the story.

"Who else knows this?" I ask, shutting the book with a thud.

"Only the Hallowed and Borealis Courts were given a Book of Teachings to protect, the Ancients recognizing how careless the other lands were." Trihewyn scoffs. "The hatred Sylvan holds for anyone deemed 'lesser' never ends, they just hide their terror behind walls. And Terra, they aren't much better. Doing nothing is sometimes just as fatal." Anger shakes her voice and Aether burns in her eyes. I can't agree more.

"Are you going to tell me now why you were looking for me?"

"What do you know of The Others?" The High Lady asks, taking me by surprise. I immediately think of Amwren terrified, reduced to ash. Eros, destroying Knothall. She and I both killed heroes. We are both villains. By the Ancients, what have I *done*?

"I've heard you struck a bargain with them, and I know for a fact they're murderers. Which has me questioning you." I spit out without thinking, cheeks warming. I pace away, leaving silence hanging for a moment

"Their leader is the one who killed Knothall." My last statement is a whisper.

"I know. I need your help." I face her, evaluating the High Lady's calm figure. Trihewyn's wrinkled fingers are intertwined together. "The information I need, for Eros. That's what you brought me."

I cross my arms and narrow my brows, studying her carefully placed statement. "Why me? I won't listen to another word, not until you tell me what is so *special* about an Empty Fae."

Her eyes set hard upon my face as she approaches and she stands over me in a few strides. "Only an Empty Fae can assemble the Harbinger, the greatest weapon of our time. Eros and Ragnis are working together, and as you know, Eros is capable of Aether unlike any I have ever seen before. Ragnis plans to exact revenge on the lands, with her help."

Eros and Ragnis. I rub my face, digesting her words. "What if I say no?"

"You are free to leave, as we discussed. I have kept up my end of the bargain, and you yours. Do you *want* to say no?" She asks, tilting her head with a smile. She knows I won't say no. In some part of my cold heart, goodness lingers.

Or a strong desire to settle the score, at the very least.

"Did you really make a bargain with The Others?"

"Yes. I provided Eros with all of our men, in exchange for asylum." Trihewyn says matter of factually, and my brows raise.

"Being High Lady comes with hard decisions. I would rather give her the males, than to be the first thing she wipes out on her path through their realms." Trihewyn leaves without another word, leaving me with the glacial sting of her words.

The *males*. What a cold, calculating bitch.

Unable to make the walk to my room after being hit with so many waves of truth, I find sleep in the library, slumped into a plush chair. My rest is fitful, familiar and new nightmares taunting me, over and over. The last one is what wakes me, the most vivid one yet.

"When will you find me? You're so close, almost there. Find me, and we can go home."

I search around the abyss of my mind, sending my lulling voice into the warm darkness blocking out every sense. Every sense, except for the writhing of her voice in my brain.

"I can't see you, you have to come out of the dark." I plead.

The endless whispering halts, and a delightful giggle takes over, sending panic through me.

"Silly girl, I am the Dark. I am everything and nothing, what was and never will be. Just, like, you."

SOMEONE WHO GIVES A DAMN

My clean lavender hair is thrown up into its usual side knot, light skin fresh and ready for a few more days in the sun. Simple brown breeches, a short sleeve cream tunic and my leather jerkin layered above is much more comfortable of an outfit than the dress. I equip my sides with the usual daggers, and while slinging the belt of leather pouches on, Umber knocks on the open doorway to my room.

I stare at her momentarily, brows drawing together before I continue packing in silence. I tuck away the updated map Trihewyn left for me in the refreshed duffel bag of clothes and supplies. Umber waits, arms crossed and oceanic body dressed in dark gray layers of traveling leathers. I sigh and cross my own arms as I halt my hurry. "What do you want, Umber?"

"I never expected the Empty Fae to become my best friend." She says simply, taking a step inside the bedroom. I don't speak, only tilt my head. A full minute passes before she speaks again, warmth flushing her broad cheeks. "I didn't know how to tell you any of it. You were barely surviving there, let alone ready to hear the world needed you."

I almost believe that. I drop my arms, warmth pricking my neck as she takes another step. "You could've at least told me Knothall was dead."

"I honestly thought you knew. I thought you *saw*." Umber drops her own stubborn facade, closing the distance between us.

"I didn't look back. I wouldn't have left if I did. I guess ... I was holding onto hope he was strong enough." I admit, rubbing my face with a hand. "If I can't trust the one person who I thought was my friend, how can I trust anyone? Did you ever care for me at all, or was it just a game to you? I don't know who you are, and I guess I never did."

"You *can't* trust anyone." She offers her hand to me, palm up. Her usual carefree beauty is cold and hard here. "Of course I cared about you. I *still* do." I scoff and cross my arms, stiffening my body as I avert my eyes. Umber turns with a huff, marching away only to pause at the door, glancing at me sideways over her shoulder. "High Lady is sending you with a guide. If you do not wish me to go, I will tell her."

I grumble inwardly at the thought of being with anyone else from Hallowed. Trihewyn has only told me bits of truth, and I don't trust her. The swirling void stealing power from all those around her and sacrificing the lives of her people for a bullshit deal is enough to make anyone uneasy.

"I would rather travel with the enemy I already know." I spit at her, keeping my eyes down. Umber leaves without another word.

Orion, Alvis and Novak are waiting for me in the dining room, devouring a cold mid afternoon lunch of fresh bread, salad and fruit. The *same* fresh bread Umber delivered to me for years. I sit in an empty chair beside Orion, glancing at Novak seated beside Alvis on the other side. They are arm wrestling. Unbelievable.

They laugh, *oh* how they laugh. I smirk and shake my head, then collect fruit and salad fixings onto my elegant china plate. I give Orion a smile, locks of ink fall over dirty lenses as he smiles wide. How are his glasses always dirty? He rolls his eyes at the pair across from us, thick dark brows raised. "Be warned, these two are endless trouble."

"I'm counting on it." I say confidently and wink at Novak, taking him off guard long enough for Alvis to finally defeat him. Orion erupts into laughter beside me and claps enthusiastically. Novak throws a strawberry at Orion, hitting him square in the glasses. Without warning, a gush of water erupts from Orion's open hand, soaking Novak from head to toe.

Before long, we are all laughing like children. Trihewyn, Umber and one of the court members from last night enter the dining room to find us acting like hooligans. The regal brunette female at Trihewyn's side arches a brow at the High Lady after glaring at us for a cold thirty seconds. "You're kidding."

The female's glacial judgment stops us all. We collectively turn to them standing at the end of the table. Umber's arms are crossed, sapphire hair now braided tight against her head. The courtier is handsome in a rough way, but her constant scowl dissipates any beauty she might have.

Trihewyn smiles softly, speaking to me as she scans the table. "My second in command finds your choice of companions concerning."

The short haired brunette Fae locks silver eyes with each of us, pausing for a moment on Novak. "If you want my help, you get theirs too." I state with confidence, then lean back in my chair and rest my hands behind my head. Orion cleans his glasses and Alvis shifts in his own chair, his eyes on the consort. Novak hasn't stopped eating, unbothered by the palpable hatred directed at him.

"I never said I had an issue. This is *your* mission. If you fail it, you fail everyone else in Iverbourne. You've gotten this far by making your own decisions, I'm not about to make them for you." Trihewyn is stern, but she doesn't look at the female beside her. The brunette rolls her shoulders back and withdraws her angry stare, silver eyes dulling to a hard gray slate. "Mariah is the only member of this court who knows of our mission. As such, I expect respect to be given from both parties."

"Understood." I nod to both of them. "Now, tell me what I have to do." Mariah steps up to the table and unrolls a worn, lengthy map. The parchment stretches across the enormous dining table, end to end. The territories make themselves known, but each one is magnified and has their own section on the map. Orion and I stand, taking in the information.

Information regarding each High Lord or Lady of the land is near its respective section. Above Borealis lies Okucha, a glacial area not explained on either of my maps. Terra Court has Panrauth Firthorn listed as the High Lord, and my stomach twists into knots when I read his name. Trihewyn points to the ruins above on the Hallowed Court section. *Ruins of Sprinas.*

"This is where your journey begins." Trihewyn's wrinkled face meets mine, her eyes calculating my reaction. "To build the Harbinger, you need the essence given from each elemental Ancient tied to the lands. Since we don't know the full effect the essence will have on you, you will receive from Air first, here."

"How do I get it?" I straighten, crossing my arms while Orion continues to study the map, his fluffed ears twitching as he listens and adjusts his lenses.

"You don't *get* it. The essence is given to you, freely. By the Ancients, through each High Lord or Lady. The reason why we need *you*," Mariah pauses, twinging her eyebrows in a pained grimace. Alvis narrows his brows and Novak leans forward, listening with an even face. The grand answer to my lifelong question. Everyone else wants to know the answer as well.

"You, an Empty Fae, are like an empty vessel. Any other Fae who tries to receive the essence, the Machine deems them to be greedy and in violation of the treaty. No matter their intention, they cannot have it, they have already been gifted magic once. You, though, have not." Mariah's last words fall flat, piercing the silence in the room. I turn away from the eyes on me and pace along the empty side of the room. Alvis and Orion engage Mariah while I contemplate.

If only an Empty Fae can wield the Harbinger, then perhaps I'm *not* a mistake. Perhaps I do have a purpose, and this is it. I peer at Novak over my shoulder, his focus on Alvis. Always on Alvis. The Fae was saved by the Ancients from death, even given shadow Aether of sorts. The Ancients are still interfering, very much alive and interested in our dealings, from wherever they hide.

I return to Orion's side. He watches me approach and pushes his glasses up with a shaky hand. I lightly grasp his shoulder and his tense muscles relax under my touch. "How am I supposed to convince the most powerful in the land to give me their power?" I glance between the twins, then back to Trihewyn. "Especially Typhan, if he is truly as bad as they say, he will never give an Empty Fae magic."

Trihewyn rubs her chin in distant thought. "I suppose if you are clever enough, you will figure it out." The High Lady smiles, wickedness dancing in her eyes.

"You first have to receive from Air, and then convince Panrauth. He has just returned to power and may not want to show weakness. I would not discount him as a challenge." Mariah reminds me firmly.

"Firthorn returned to power because of *me*. It will be no problem." No one challenges the bite in my voice. Novak gives me a subtle wink when I catch eyes with him quickly.

"Once Lyth collects the essence, what happens after? How do you make this Harbinger?" Alvis is standing now as he gestures to me, and then to the map. He said my *name*, not Keeper. It is soft rolling off his tongue, the white vines across his rippled body illuminate subtly when he says it. I cannot help the next vision that comes to mind, and I become lost in the fantasy for a moment.

To be between the warrior and musician, our bodies and the pleasure never ending. Novak behind me, hands on my hips with Alvis on his knees before me. A vined hair pushing the wild hair from my face, then with a thrust from Novak I would be able to taste Alvis. A throbbing warmth spreads between my legs as I imagine them together, such strong males giving in to whatever feeling is between them. I bite my cheek and shift, burying the fantasy as I focus on the silent High Lady.

Trihewyn nods to her consort, the elder keeping quiet through the discussions. A silver clawed finger points to the Eternal Mountain, and Mariah's voice claws at my skin, the words unbearable. "You bring the essence here, and forge it into a weapon using the coal forges of your Machine."

The room is silent, waiting for me to say no. I decide to digest the dreaded end in my own time, pointing to the empty map above the mountain borders to the north. "What's this, exactly?" I ask no one in particular.

"The Realm of Giants." Mariah whispers, her tone full of respect.

"And that is?" I ask, receiving a disgusted look from Mariah.

Novak whistles low. Alvis shifts in place and Orion begins trembling again beside me. Every aura darkens at her words, and I have no idea what they mean. I've seen the blank spot, but have heard nothing of what lives there now.

"An Aether fueled land with floating islands, beholding epic abominations of beasts that once roamed alongside the Ancients. Great tribes of Fae and creatures of every sort, all supposedly destroyed when the Mountains went up." Mariah says, her voice the softest I've heard yet. She doesn't look old enough to have lived during the Golden Age, but the longing in her face tells me she has a connection somehow to the old land. I bite my lip, the page I had taken from the Book of Teachings comes to mind.

"Sounds like a story used to scare children." I scoff offhandedly, but no one lightens at my sentiment. Silence fills the room for several moments. I rub my face and shift the weight on my hips, then lean on the table with the usual leather and tech covering my arms. I stare directly at Trihewyn, trademark sarcasm filling my voice. "So I have to gallivant across the countryside, charm the most devious Fae in Iverbourne and build an unstoppable weapon to wipe Eros off the map? Sounds like a good time."

Mariah glances at her silent High Lady, then back to me. "If you can handle it." Mariah taunts. The High Lady smiles at Mariah, then to me. *You must answer truthfully.*

Perhaps that's why Mariah is doing most of the talking. Trihewyn is hiding something, my bargain preventing her from flat out lying. A scowl rests on my face as I ponder the thought, and am soon interrupted by the musician.

Novak jumps up from his chair, his cheerful voice breaking the gloom gathered over the table. "Well, what are we waiting for?" He grins wide and I can't help but smile at him.

We are gathered on real land again, leaving the stilted island of Hallowed Court and beginning our journey to the Ruins of Spirans. Trihewyn and Mariah lead the way on brilliant black horses with feathered feet. The twins ride behind them, Novak and I are next, and Umber holds up the tail end.

The muddied path leading away from the island takes us from the clinging sparse woods and swampland following us since Cervalis. The evening pollinated air tickles my nose as the horses step into a field of wildflowers. I catch one more look at the dark forest behind us, fog hiding the swamp land in its clutches. Umber doesn't appear much brighter than the woods, her face cold and emotionless.

The Ruins wait on the eastern coast, leading our company deeper into the Land of Mists. Rolling knolls and muddied meadows lead the way, the scent of marsh tangling with the persistent fog. The mist rolls heavier when the sun sinks behind us, unbothered by gusts of winds intensifying as we near the sea. Lilac hair flies loose around my face, the Captain's hat nearly breaks away every few moments.

When twilight hits the animals silence noticeably, and goosebumps crawl across my nerves. What beasts roam at night that can silence the wildlife at a moment's notice? Perhaps it's me they're scared of, the empty hole of Aether disturbing their peace.

Novak's music pulls me from my ominous thoughts. He rides beside me, leaning back in his saddle with the reins loose on his gray mare's neck. I give him a small smile, raising a brow as I tease him. "Were you born with that thing in your hand?"

"If I hadn't become a devilishly handsome vagabond, I think I would've been a bard instead. Singing to the world of your stories, of course." He grins and continues playing the beaten up lute, toying with his trademark melody.

By now I've heard several different tunes from him along our journey, he seems to have one for almost every occasion. Bringing joy to a crowd, or lovers together on the dance floor. Inspiring joy into those who felt lost. The tune he plays now though, especially drawn out and caressed, is my favorite. He looks up from the strings, giving me a quick wink half hidden by hair as he catches me staring at him. My cheeks warm and I scan the barren field we ride through.

If I hadn't been nearly killed, I would've traveled the world with my music. That's what his humorous words really mean. Whatever power, and 'thing' the Ancients put back, it terrifies everyone he meets.

I have to bet that was the 'before' Orion was talking about. Alvis and him were together before he nearly died and came back to life as a tortured soul of sorts. The danger I encountered in Echo hasn't reappeared, save for the fraction I saw last night when he saved me from myself. For some reason, he used it to try and scare me off in the Oasis. After spending so much time with him and his crew of misfits, it's quite apparent he isn't the villain. Not really.

So, the 'incident' can't be the reason him and Alvis aren't together, can it? Novak's horse catches up to Alvis' and I watch the two laugh and talk together like they always do, never a fight between them. I suppose it's not my business, and Novak doesn't seem to care if Alvis sees us together, but my heart burns all the same.

I rather like your shadows.

I should've told him I rather like his darkness as well.

Humidity dampens my light tunic, the gusting wind cutting through causes a shiver to escape. Fog blanketed cliffs come into view on the dark horizon and my usual headache creeps in with full force. The pink and purple sky gives way to creeping night, throwing the distant ruins into a foreboding silhouette.

I let the reins rest, entrusting Fiddler not to take off with me. He just lazes on behind Novak's mare, head hung low. I pack my pipe and puff on it for a moment, then hand it over to Novak when he drops to my left. The smoke drifts towards the twins who drop back to join us on my right. The High Lady's consort looks back and shakes her head. Umber doesn't ask, and I don't offer.

We smoke several bowls and Orion explains the lands of Terra to me, preparing me for what I will encounter. Alvis cuts in every now and then, wildly telling me about the tribes of Wild Fae in the north, much more fun than the stiffs in the Great Tree. Novak agrees, finding the woodland folk much better dancers at the very least. Orion disagrees completely, but is abruptly stopped.

Fiddler throws his head up, a shrill scream perking both our ears. My heart rattles against my rib cage. I take hold of the reins and focus my breathing. I search for Novak but my gaze is cut short. "*Don't* look." All three of my companions order at once.

"Don't look at *what*?" I ask breathily, turning my eyes down to Fiddler's anxious hooves. Trihewyn's horse let out a nicker ahead.

"*Nothing*. You hear nothing, and you see nothing. It will stay that way as long as you don't look." Novak is dead serious, using the same primal tone from last night. In silence we continue into the mists swallowing those ahead of us. I know Novak is at my side, but I feel completely alone, cut off from those in the milky clouds.

Terrified screams for help ring my ears, the blanket of fog hiding the evil calling to us. Every hair on my body stands up, ears pinned down and pushing away the screams of inmates begging me to stop, please *stop*. I shut my eyes tight, but that only makes the images of carving the insignia of Iron court into numerous inmates even more real, followed by my own body chained down to a table. I open my eyes and hyperventilate when my own screams join in the distance, first those of a little girl echoing through a dark tunnel which forms through the fog in front of me, its yawning mouth ready to swallow me whole.

My attention raises slightly, heart sputtering as the tunnel grows and *grows* before Fiddler and I. One scream stands out from the rest, the fall of a great hero to my left, past where I imagine Novak is. Ancient and booming, loud enough to shake chasms and mountains. Glowing pools of blood catch my periphery, my mentor's voice begs me through *sobs* to spare Rohana. To spare his love.

"LYTH, NO!" Umber bellows to me. I'm pulled out of the trance but it's too late. I already paid enough attention to render the creature real.

The red winks out and I unsheathe my dagger just in time to face a lunging creature, its impossibly heavy form knocks me clean off Fiddler and into the marsh beyond. I land on my back with the creature on top of me, thuds of feet hitting the ground sting my ears.

"*No*! Stay where you are!" I shout with my entire chest, we don't need any more death. I can *do* this.

The ethereal Knothall pins down my chest like the Fae who took my eye, knees digging into my arms. Flaming eyes release rivers of blood, pouring down his cheeks and splashing onto my face. The screaming insults, death threats and jabs of pity shatter my eardrums. The beast gnashes at my throat with rows of jagged, decaying teeth. The bellowing voice of guilt alone is enough to haunt me for the rest of my days.

I scream at the top of my lungs, tears carving into my crimson ridden cheeks. I break my dagger free and strike him in the throat, then *yank* down with all my might. Hot liquid fills my mouth and glues my eyes shut, my nightmare of drowning in blood fully realized. The creature collapses on top of me and I sputter on the blood forced into my lungs. The weight of his body crushes me for only a moment, then the being is reduced to ash and taken by the wind a moment later.

I throw myself over and empty my stomach, choking on so many different fluids. The body wracking heaves end and I attempt to push myself up, but tired limbs resist. I settle on my knees and close my eyes tight, willing the atmospheric screaming to cease. I cover my ears, hot sobs fracture my heart. Creatures wait, hungry to be seen, hungry for blood and fear.

Warm shadows find me and I open my eyes, finding Novak's hand outstretched. Without looking up to his face I take it, then lean on his body heavily. With Novak at my side, I limp the ten feet I had been flung, cursing under my breath the entire time. I leave the musician when I reach Fiddler's side and lean on the steed, taking a moment to compose myself. I want to ask what the hell that was, but fear even that will give them enough credence to be real again.

"Are you alright?" Alvis' question rolls quietly from beside me. I don't look up to him or answer, just step up onto Fiddler's raised leg and pull myself into the saddle with screaming forearms and hips. We continue on again in near silence, the screams fading as we approach the ruins.

"Why didn't you want us to help you?" Novak asks, hurt lacing his voice.

"No sense in you all getting killed over my mistake."

Novak mutters something unintelligible ahead of me. Even Orion curses under his breath to my right. Alvis remains silent, but he's so close to me his horse keeps brushing up against my left leg.

"We're here, the beasts cannot step onto this ground." Trihewyn calls, lifting my eyes up. We are stopped twenty feet before a mossy circle of epic rectangular stones. Standing on end and stretching at least thirty feet into the air, how they were placed here is a feat in itself, then I remember. Aether lives here, at the whim of the Fae. Most of them.

We dismount at the edge of the circle, leaving the horses to freely graze. I evaluate myself, completely drenched in thick crimson. I groan and rub my face with a bloodied hand, spreading the disaster on my face further. "May I?" Orion asks, purple Aether lighting up his eyes as he extends a hand to me.

"I suppose I'd rather be wet, than covered in whatever this is." I sigh, dropping my shoulders.

This is going to be a long trip.

Orion's magic washes over me with extreme care. A thin wave of water caresses over top my skin, lifting blood and filth into its molecules, leaving me dry and clean. I blink rapidly, watching it all dissipate into the thick air. "How did you do that? I'm not wet." I excitedly spin too fast and look over myself, giving him a smile of amazement when he stops me from falling with a quick hand.

"I wonder what you would even do without magic." Novak teases me, slinging an arm around my shoulder. I roll my eyes at him and lean into his side, thankful for his grounding touch.

"I suppose not *all* magic is bad." I decide, smiling at Orion who gives me a deep bow and quick wink. Alvis beams, a true smile resting on his sharp face. Nevertheless, my cheeks warm and a hint of guilt rests in my heart. Doesn't it hurt to see me with him?

"Let's go." Umber orders gruffly, walking towards Trihewyn.

I squeeze Novak's hand before releasing him, he gives me a weak grin before leaving my side to walk with Alvis. I unstrap my cane and rely on it heavily through the wet marsh grass melding with spongy moss. I will never be fully rested if I keep falling off horses and traversing through mud. Orion keeps my slow pace, Alvis and Novak meander ahead and converse in quiet voices. The nice thing about Orion is he doesn't say much, and if he does, it's usually important. Or terribly witty.

When we cross the circular threshold of mossy stones, a feeling of peace washes over me. A deep breath hollows me out right down to my toes. My hips are soothed, the headache in my temple lightens. Whispers drift around us and I take Orion's hand, my heart racing. The carvings on the rocks emit a soft violet glow, beckoning us to study their intricate designs. The group pauses, every Fae admiring the beauty around. Orion smiles down at me, squeezing my hand tight.

"The Ancients are gathering." Trihewyn whispers as she approaches, offering a hand out to me. I leave Orion's side, glancing at Novak before taking the High Lady's wrinkled hand. I am surprised by her soft touch and follow her to the innermost center. A flat circular stone is inscribed with the same text as on

Captain's ship. The stone is just large enough for us to both stand on, and we are now mere inches away from each other.

My friends watch Trihewyn and I from a distance, lingering near the outer edge of the standing stones. I forgot this might end badly, and seeing the others so far away has my lip trembling. The High Lady removes a necklace from her pocket, catching my attention. A simple glass vial, hanging from a corded leather. The cork top is glazed over with black wax, but the clear vial is empty.

I dip my head and she slips it on, the empty vial surprisingly heavy on my neck. I drop my cane and take her outstretched hands. "You have to ask." Trihewyn reminds me softly. The stone we stand on alights entirely, enshrining us in a lilac glow akin to my hair. I study her silver eyes, then her storming aura surrounding us both. Creeping fear raises my hackles.

I try to speak but have to try again, the sound of it draws out my own black hole of an aura which crawls out to join with her storm. I can't see the others anymore, the swirling hurricane of Aether growing too thick as it encircles us. "I ask you, High Lady of the Hallowed Court, and spirits of Air, to bestow me with a part of the essence gifted to your lands. I do so in great gratitude, and great need."

When I finish the strong words, the hurricane of emptiness chasing power halts. A gasp escapes my chest and wonder fills me at the sight, until that storm barrels right for me. The darkness and Air Aether rushes into my nose, mouth, lungs and blood. Warmth surges from my nostrils and pain misfires in my entire body.

A roaring cry rips through the air from my burning heart and I drop onto metal knees. Salt air pushes from my lungs and is replaced by Aether *rushing* through me, desperate to find a part of my soul where it can latch on. Ancient magic *burns*, frustrated at every crevice of emptiness inside me. When the essence finds no place where it can rest, the vial fills with smoke. Fresh air returns to desperate lungs while the vial fills.

The burning in my blood subsides, leaving me with only the burden around my neck. Trihewyn helps me up and I waver on unsteady legs until she retrieves the metal cane for me. I lean on it shakily, stomach wrenching and mind bending still. The glow beneath our feet and on the towering stone circle is gone, and it's all I can do to not fall over.

I look over my shoulder, searching for him. Novak is stopped halfway across the circle, held back by a shadow-covered Alvis. Orion, Umber and Mariah are waiting by the circle's edge, shock on their faces. Umber's hand is clutching Orion's. "Novak." I plead shakily and he throws Alvis off.

The Fae makes it to me in quick strides, darkness leaves Alvis as it trails the ground Novak sprints across. I extend a trembling arm to him, then fall into his warm, shadowed embrace the moment he's at my side. "I'm alright," I manage to say.

"Like hell you are." He scoops me up in a swift movement and cradles me close, the primal rumbling in his chest vibrates against me. I relax in his muscled arms and a sigh escapes when my cheek falls upon his chest. Trihewyn evaluates us, pondering while she rubs her chin. She has her aura back, tamed considerably. For the moment.

"I didn't think you ever left the ship anymore, dear *Tzel*. Who are you, to her?" Trihewyn gestures to us. I peek up to the musician, blond hair falls over black irises as he kisses my nose. The sight stops my heart, it's like looking in a mirror. Why do they do that?

Straightening with me in his arms, he gives Trihewyn that wicked smile I love so much.

"Someone who gives a damn."

PANRAUTH'S PLAUGE

The silver and gold moons are a welcoming sight after the day I've had. I curl up on my bedroll laid out on a cozy patch of moss, our camp protected by the ancient circle around us. I watch the celestial beings dance across the sky together, followed by their capes of gemstones and diamonds. What kind of magic would it take to touch the stars, feel the moons under my fingers?

I grip the vial in one hand, the other is clutched tight to Novak's long fingers. I had fallen asleep in his arms right after his infamous line, then jolted awake mid-scream a couple hours ago. Novak stayed awake with me, telling me stories about his homeland, Dew Falls. He tried *so* hard, but fell asleep midway through telling me about the grand library there. His adorable snoring and the muffled screams of the Noxious are the only noise in the dark fog around us, until a rustling meets my ears.

I release Novak's hand with care and clutch the dagger under my pillow. I sit up cautiously and scan the surroundings. Umber and Orion are sleeping, but Alvis is missing. A dark figure rests on the cliffside nearby, beyond the stone circle protecting us from the shrill cries of the Noxious.

Orion told me after we were safe what exactly the creatures are, something almost even worse than what I would imprison frequently near The Pit. The ghosts of those who died on these lands in the war, unable to move on. Taking the form of your worst nightmare the moment you pay attention to it, feasting off your fear and life. No one knows how to cleanse the area, and so they remain.

I rise unsteadily and my ears flatten down the moment I leave the mossy circle, the intense screams overtake my senses when I do. I near the cliff's edge, dead wheat grass hiding the sound of my footsteps. Alvis doesn't turn his head yet, a small orb of illuminated water hangs close by. I peek over his shoulder, entering what must be a sound shield as the Noxious screams die away.

"Can't sleep?" I whisper into his charcoal tufted ear, my voice sends the parchment in his hands scattering when he jolts. A paper drifts into the air above and I catch it, glimpsing my own black and white eyes sketched onto the scrap.

"Are you *trying* to get thrown over the cliffside?" Alvis snarls, snatching the page back from me. The waves crashing against the shards of rock below intrigue me. I have never been this close to the sea, on land anyway. Flying over in Captain's airship is quite different.

"I'm sorry." I mutter softly, rising from his shoulder to leave.

"Stay. You just," he scratches at his neck, then gestures beside him, "surprised me. That's all." His tone softens and the orb of water grows in luminous intensity. With shaky legs I settle beside him, keeping close in case I tumble off. He shuffles papers into a neat stack on the other side, using his sword for a paperweight. I close my eyes and breathe in the salt air greeting me, focusing on the waves crashing below and birds calling overhead.

"You gave us quite a scare earlier." Alvis quips after a long moment.

"Which time?" I tease, elbowing his side. The vines along his bare chest are more numerous than the ones on his arms and neck. I bite my lip and tear my gaze back to his face when the tight muscles in his torso cause an aching in the shameful, conflicted part of my soul.

"Exactly." Violet eyes narrow at me, pulling the deep jagged scar running alongside his left cheek. Eerily similar to mine, I wonder which grand adventure I've heard of so far blessed him with it. Alvis and Captain taking on rival gangs, or hunting down mercenaries with Orion and the musician. The best stories are the ones with all of them together, causing trouble throughout the places they traveled.

I stare too long, drawing a nervous smile from the Water Fae. I nod to the stack and cause his ink stained hands to fidget in his lap. "What's that?"

"I thought someone should be keeping your story straight, do you mind?" He's nervous like his brother, not at all his usual confident arrogance.

I shrug. "Someone has to." The ink on his left hand drags up his forearm, covering the detailed milky white vines. "What are they?" I cautiously trace a branch trailing on his forearm closest to me.

Alvis shudders under my touch, goosebumps trailing his skin after I pull away. He rubs his neck and looks out to the sea. "I don't really want to talk about it." The words are a stone through the air and I nod, giving him a small smile.

We sit together in silence, watching bats come out to play and dance in the moonlight. The stars are unending here, stretching over the calling sea beyond. A gust of wind hits from the sea, causing a violent shiver to overtake me. Alvis chuckles, lifting his arm and offering his side to me. "I'll keep my hands to myself." I arch a knowing brow at him, unmoving. His playful facade drops. "I just don't like seeing you cold."

I nestle against his bare side, the warmth radiating from him comforts me immediately. A sigh of content escapes when his thick arms wrap around me, holding me close. How he keeps warm in this chilled air is beyond me. Alvis keeps his word, resting his hands on his forearms, chest rising unsteadily under me.

"Better?" He asks, voice tight. I give him a nod, to which his body relaxes. In silence our breath aligns, and my shivering subsides. I want to ask him about Novak, but it doesn't feel right.

After some time, I gain a shred of courage. "Can I see? The picture?" I ask, my voice a gentle whisper in the wind. After a pause, Alvis removes the parchment from under the sword and offers it to me.

A sketch of me on Captain's ship, nearly finished. Delight fills my round face as I fly us through the clouds, wearing the feathered hat I love so much. A terrifying, but beautiful sight. I caress the delicate, precise lines forming my face. Scars and all, but even in his eyes I am beautiful. The perfect architecture of the ship is captured in the large steering wheel, and even the gnarled knots in the decking.

"I haven't seen myself happy before." I trail off, then give him a weak smile, offering it back. "It's beautiful, Al."

Alvis shakes his head, his usual confidence replaced by tenderness. "A gift from me to you."

"Thank you." I whisper and tuck the paper away, swallowing tears. An idea floats to me and I act before losing my spine. First I take out the note from Knothall, then reach back into a side cargo pocket of my pants to remove the small travel journal. I hand them both to Alvis, he looks them over with a furrowed brow and tilted head.

"Knothall's last words to me, and the journal," I push out a breath, summoning the courage running through my veins, "it tells of my family, who I might've been. You can add it to your story. Perhaps, when I get a chance to read it, it may hit easier coming from your pen."

Alvis takes the burden from me, his eyes wide. "You don't want to find out now?"

I watch his face intently for a moment before answering, the globe lighting our faces dims when I speak. "No, not yet, I have too many problems as it is. One day I will." I rub my face absently. "Just, don't tell me until I ask. Okay?"

He nods solemnly, tucking the commander's note into the journal before setting it beside him. He slips an arm behind me, pulling me back into his strong presence once more. I breathe deeply and we watch the waves build immense power in the distance, then crash into the cliff walls below.

The warrior Fae smells like the lab. Wafts of parchment, ink and sweat fill my nose, welcoming me home. "Alvis," I murmur before drifting asleep quite some time later.

"Yes, Lyth?" His soft, infinitely deep voice tickles my hair and flutters my chest.

"Why are you doing this?" Holding me, traveling with me. Not to mention I still can't decide if he's longing after me, or Novak. Or both.

"Why are you?" He asks with quiet seriousness.

"You smell like home." The words tumble out as sleep overtakes me, the sound of water crashing below us lulls me into a dreamless sleep.

Umber wakes me with a gentle nudge of her boot to my shoulder. I jolt up with a start from my bed roll, confusion clouding my mind as I imagine tumbling off the cliff. The sun rises over the ocean horizon, blinding my tired eyes. I search around, finding Novak and Orion stirring beside me. "Where's Alvis?"

"He's scouting ahead, making sure all the Nox cleared off with the daylight." Umber states plainly before leaving for the horses, her pack already upon her back.

"Now how'd you piss her off?" Novak yawns obnoxiously, stretching his arms overhead before shoving his things haphazardly into a bag. Orion packs neatly in silence, a small smile tugging at a corner of his lips.

"No idea." I pack my gear hurriedly, rolling my bedroll into a chaotic mess and start over with a groan of frustration. Alvis must've carried me back, and I bet Umber saw us together. Before she revealed her position, he seemed to enjoy her company. Now all he does is tolerate her with forced smiles.

"I *think*, you made someone jealous." Orion's teasing voice speaks my thoughts, eliciting a raised brow from Novak.

I could give two shits about what Umber thinks, but I do care what Novak thinks. Orion seems quite pleased I succeeded at pissing Umber off first thing in the morning, though. The Mountain was lonely, but there weren't so many *feelings* there. Too much love can tear you apart just as easily as having not enough. Alvis brings lust and comfort, and Novak does too, but he brings something else. Something *more*.

"Can't a Keeper of Death have friends? Or am I supposed to just fuck or kill everyone I meet? *Oh*, I know, I can do both. Obviously the murdering would be after, I'm not *that* sick." Sarcasm drips heavily and I finally wrangle the bedroll, strapping it to my dirty bag with a huff.

Orion's dark hair falls as laughter erupts from the pair, he gives me a nudge before rising. Novak's dimples pull his smile wide, subtle relief lighting his bright eyes. The musician offers me a hand and helps me up, then the three of us trail after Umber and arrive in good spirits.

Alvis gallops back to our group, winking at Umber when he stops. She sticks her tongue out and smiles for the first time since we've arrived in Hallowed lands. As much as I don't want to, it makes me feel better to see her smiling. I remember the thought I had of them, two lost souls finding comfort in the other, and realize Umber must give him the things Novak can't.

"No more foul creatures amuck, except for you, Keeper." I roll my eyes at him and grin from atop my sleepy beast. We're back to Keeper now. Perhaps it's better that way.

I never thought bleeding hearts would be part of this journey.

We leave the salt ridden cliffs, riding inland to find the border of Terra and Hallowed lands. Our destination is Beakglen, the trading center between the two territories. The wheat grass and marsh transform into alternating fields of wheat, corn and other grains. The fields we ride alongside roll endlessly, holding more life the farther we travel.

I know Terra provides most of the fresh food throughout Iverbourne, but I expected more trees. I suppose we aren't *technically* there yet, though. Flocks of birds sing to us overhead and I find myself looking for Virgil, again. I had hoped the bird would've found me in Echo, but I don't blame him for wanting to be free.

I spy my first deer, a beautiful large doe frolicking in the corn with a fawn beginning to lose its spots. Once I learn they hide in the towering corn, it becomes a game with Novak to be the first to spot one. The damn musician has quite a competitive streak, but so do I. Fae of all kinds work in the fields, using their Aether to tend to the land.

At one point my attention is caught by a purple skinned Earth Fae, and I bring Fiddler to a halt. A young female dances alone in a barren field, one that hasn't been revived yet. She's dressed in dirty green silks, leaving her midriff and arms exposed. Shimmering paint lines her face and arms, green reflecting the sunlight. She moves with precision and passion, as if no one is watching, and like her life depends on it.

"What is she doing?" I whisper to Novak. He puts a finger to his smiling lips, nodding to the magic unfolding. The land around the female darkens, nutrient rich soil blossoming under her bounding feet. Green life rises from the ground, drawing air from my chest. Rows upon rows of healthy sprouts dot the rolling field. She skips along, fingers grazing the life she brought forth.

"Earth Fae have been requested to assist bring life back to the farm lands Panrauth's Plague turned fallow." Orion states softly, drawing my attention.

"Panrauth's Plague?" I ask, brushing loose hair from my face. Orion pauses at my side, Alvis and Novak ride on in front of us with a silent Umber.

"Without the High Lord, the lands were sick. Aether resides inside of every living thing, and when it chooses the leader of the territory, it accepts no one else."

We continue at a slow walk and I ponder his words before speaking. "But that's Terra, this is Hallowed ground."

"Aether knows no bounds Lyth, everything is connected. Your watch wouldn't tell the time without every tiny gear doing its job, correct? The Ancients and their magic choose who the gears of this world are. We are but pieces in their grand scheme."

I weigh his thoughtful words in silence. What seemed so awe inspiring before almost makes me sick now. Orion stays silent, giving me a smile when I glance at his face.

Not much attention is paid to us by the Fae in the area, I expected sentries and patrols when we neared the border, along with some crowded suburbia. Neither is waiting, instead we continue through near pure nature, tended to by simple caregivers of the land. Air and Earth Fae, working together in every valley we swim through.

Wild animals are more frequent, although they blend in with their surroundings expertly. Of course, this sparks another game between Novak and I. The twins join in, describing absurd creatures that just *can't* be true. But then they appear, just to spite me. Alvis is usually the first to spot anything, my eyes are quite a bit more untrained, but Novak is a close second to him.

The bravest creature I spot rises from a grain field, its bright green eyes contrasting against muddied fur. Grass sprouts right up from his rounded head and wide back, the wild thing is part of the field itself. Eyes blink independently of each other, the dog-like animal watches me for a moment before it slinks down, becoming one with the grass again. Save for its swishing tail, tufted with wildflowers.

"Did you *see* that?" I squeal and find Novak's face first, eliciting a tender smile from him while he watches my excitement.

"Sure did, my lady." Novak winks, bringing warmth to my cheeks.

I bite my lip and attempt to wink back but fail miserably, lulling an echoing laugh from him. Umber even lets out a soft chuckle, which warms my heart a little. Hours are spent in the glowering sun, filled with teasing from Novak and Alvis, random trivia from Orion. I constantly pick at my shrinking rations, trading with the others for bits of different dried fruit. And of course, Novak's music keeps us company nearly the entire time.

"So, what do I need to know about this place?" I ask Novak.

"Probably everything. I forget you're such a baby here." He muses while adjusting a string on his lute. I throw a dried grape at him, taking the Fae off guard. "*Sheesh*, so violent."

Orion drops from the distant front to ride with us, leaving Umber and Alvis alone in the lead. He chuckles at Novak's antics, pushing up dirty glasses before speaking. The summer air clamps the collar of his fine navy tunic to his neck. "Beakglen is a favorite of mine. Think Cervalis, but smaller. And more like home." I shift in the saddle, turning the word over in my mind. *Home*.

Novak notes my glazed silence. "Captain's secret hideout is there, lots of fun. Doesn't hurt that you have a lover waiting for you." Novak sends a tendril of shadow to tickle behind Orion's ear and he giggles, swatting away Novak's magic. Well, that's cute.

"Secret hideout, eh?" I glance sideways at Orion and raise a brow playfully. "I thought you said males are just as bad as females."

"To be fair, I said *almost*." Orion chuckles, rubbing his neck and waiting for my interrogation.

"What's his name?" I ask curiously. I've never met anyone partnered with a Fae of the same sex. (That I know of) With high value placed on fertility and breeding, I can't imagine it's a welcome notion in the lands. The fact Orion had mentioned anything to me at all about Novak and Alvis, and his own lover ... The sudden realization burns the gears in my mind. He trusts me.

Truly trusts me.

"Emeric," Orion breathes his name. "He's originally from Echo, but Beakglen is quiet, safe."

Novak is even silent now, cradling his lute with subtle relief. Was he afraid I would be a bigot?

The question lingers on my tongue for a moment. "Do you love each other?"

"Yes, we do. Alas, life is not kind to Fae like us." Orion's response is instant, but his last words trail off. I know what he means, what I guessed at.

"You mean Fae that love each other? Quite a dreadful thing, Orion." I tease and he chuckles half heartedly. Novak plays a tune, smiling gently at me when I look over my shoulder.

"Yes, love can be quite a dreadful thing, to some." Orion remarks. Our group crests a final hill of grain. The worn road tunnels through a field of corn ahead, leading to a decent sized village. Orion's eyes light up and Alvis looks back at his brother with a mischievous smile. Fine townhomes and brick buildings come into view, and I'm reminded of the story about Novak standing up for the humans here.

"Can I ask you a question?" I ask Orion. Novak plucks at his lute, rounded ears twitching.

"You usually just ask them, so I suppose so." Orion teases nervously.

"What is it like, being a twin? I've heard the bond is quite strong."

He lifts a shoulder, contemplating. "To be bonded to someone, it's to feel everything they feel. For some, they share more than feelings. That is the way with twins, we share *everything*." Orion shakes the inky hair out of his face, glancing at Novak. "You're born with part of your soul resting with someone else, instead of having to find them."

"And is that what mates are, bonded souls?" I inquire, tilting my head.

Orion rubs his neck, the strumming pauses from the musician behind us. "Yes, mates are two souls who hail from the same star. Or, so the old legends tell."

"It has nothing to do with love, then." I wonder out loud, thinking about Knothall and Rohana. They obviously loved each other, but not as much as their duty. "And there is more than one kind of bond."

"Sometimes, Fae have different ideas than the universe, they don't fit as well as the Ancients would like." Novak's aura darkens visibly and I bite my cheek, wondering if I've struck a nerve. "Most times though, it's inevitable for mates to be in love. And other times, a bond is nothing more than two souls connected."

"So you and Al, you really know everything the other thinks?" I ask, cheeks warming.

"We try to keep things private, if possible." Orion arches a knowing brow at me. I tie my hair off to the side and put Captain's hat back on.

"And Aether?" I ask after a moment, pondering what else can be shared over these bonds.

"Only twins." Orion says softly. I open my lips but he canters ahead at once. I shift in the saddle and turn to Novak now at my side, his smokey aura thickening further while he focuses on slinging the lute over his shoulder.

"I didn't mean to upset him." I say in a hushed tone, fiddling with the reins.

"What have they told you?" Novak's rounded ears twitch, his tone is so low that even my own ears have to lift up. Which part does he mean?

"They were the lead spymaster and engineer, but they couldn't work for Sylvan anymore. That's all." I glance at Novak, he's silent for another moment, face emotionless.

Then he decides, "it's not my story to tell." His words are flat, forced.

"You said I should know who I'm traveling with. And you always tell me the truth." My last statement is near pleading, begging him not to start withholding things from me now. He glares at me with subtle anger, no playfulness to be seen. After several minutes, just as I accept he won't tell me, he halts and I gently pull Fiddler to a stop beside him.

"They are Typhan's sons." He speaks with such graveness, the world stops turning. Novak buries his face into his hands, spilling truth into them. "From what I understand, they must sever the bond. The Aether can't choose the next heir properly, with 'split souls.' So, their father ordered them to kill the other, that's why they left. Though really, he wanted Alvis to win, but Al couldn't do that. Could you imagine him hurting O? Captain and I, we got them out, and-"

"What?" I snap, my slicing whisper interrupting Novak's hurried words, lifting his face away from his hands.

"*Please* let them tell you." He pleads, waiting for me to give him a small nod.

"And who is their mother? The Queen?" I ask, but the words crumple Novak's face further.

"For years, she was the only way for any creature, Fae or human, to escape the walls. If it wasn't for her, those two wouldn't have escaped, but Typhan caught her." He shakes his head, eyes glistening and red. "I never met her, but she is the bravest Fae I've heard of, she's the one who got us into the walls. The current queen is ... well, not her."

We press the horses into a lazy walk, and the swirling thoughts in my head take over.

Brave indeed, betraying the High Lord of Sylvan right under his nose. Goodness trickled down the twins lineage at the very least, and for the first time I wonder if *my* parents are both the monsters I imagine them to be. They have to be, to put an infant in the mountain for the sake of lacking magic. Was it my fathers idea, or my mothers?

Did they agree, or did someone try to spare me? Anyone at all?

Are they still alive?

The realization that they very well could be, and I could come across them haphazardly, sends momentary panic through me, startling my heart. No, I don't want to know who they are. I will most likely put them in the dirt, for putting me far underneath it.

We catch up to the group after quite some time. Alvis and Orion are bickering, threatening to throw the other off their horse. Umber is laughing ahead of me at their shenanigans, her carefree laugh one that brings a moment of joy, then sadness.

The Princes of Sylvan, choosing their brotherly love for each other, instead of power. A shudder shakes down my body with another realization. They agreed to *go* there with me, knowing full well the repercussions of disobeying their father, and what they will be made to do. *If there is any way for us to help Iverbourne, we want to do it,* Alvis had said.

No, I'll find another way. They can't. I won't let them. Ragnis murdered his father and most of his family in cold blood just to attain complete power, yet these two ran as far away as possible to save each other. From the terrors of their father, and the hateful prejudices of their people. They even became pirates, and yet they still agreed to walk right back into hell for me.

For Iverbourne. They *should* be ruling, *both* of them. Either of them can change the story of their malicious people into something better, but to kill their other half for it? That's a sacrifice far greater than anyone should be forced to make.

When we enter the village and dismount at the crowded stables, Fae and humans alike are pointing at my friends, whooping and hollering. "It's the *Zemer*, and the *Te'omin*!"

The repeated words of excitement are foreign to me, but Novak's cheeks flush with the warm welcome and the twins find me simultaneously, each grinning wide like wild boys. I can't blame them one bit for not wanting to rule.

Power corrupts even the best things, no matter how hard you try.

KNIGHT OF CUPS

EARTH

Alvis; circa 16,074 A.C

"No matter what I do, someone dies. I don't want to hurt people anymore." I exhale, and my shoulders drop.

"People die every day, child, this is nothing new. Leave this place at once, and return only when you have the weapon you can not wield. Your dear Mother is tired of being his leverage, and has asked me to push you along."

"How do you know what my Mother wants?" I snap, voice cracking as I march closer to the shield between us, tears choking my fury. It's true, Mother has begged me over the years to take Orion and go before I'm ordered to kill him, but I cannot bring myself to plan her death anymore than I can his.

"Water is always listening, and always ready to share." She replies, vertical pupils dilating before her pink eyes flare so bright I have to shield my vision.

"Find the weapon you can not wield, He shall reign, and you shall walk with the poet who becomes a king. Brace for the fall, and never falter, dear child." Her booming voice shatters through my body and I drop to my knees, her command and prophecy burning a hole into my twisted mind.

"I don't know what any of that means!"

BE CAREFUL WHAT YOU WISH FOR

Wide cobblestone streets lead us through the pleasant town lined meticulously with grand brick buildings. Large townhomes hold great gardens and laundry hanging on lines. Smaller buildings of wood and brick combinations release loose flocks of dirty children, small beings of all races knocking into nearly everyone they encounter. Merchants line the inner square, flogging their wares and shouting profanities at those who disagree with their outrageous prices.

Several winged Fae minstrels play in the center, their music a fast tempo and encouraging others to dance. Waiting on a bench of intricate branches, I watch them play while my companions complete business. It had taken us a while to even *reach* the trading area, stopped by many old friends of the group on the way. The town is a melting pot of culture and resonates warmth, but no one speaks to *me*, and hard stares are present everywhere I look.

It's hard to focus on the uplifting music when so many creatures watch your every move. Earth and Air Fae peek around every corner, and the Humans are especially curious about the Fae with black eyes. I do my best to sit up straight and focus on the music, not staring at one particular thing too long. Novak insisted he would wait with me for the others, but I sent him off. If I'm being honest, it's nice to sit alone for a while. Alone and surrounded and by a harmonious crowd, if I forget the fact they all hate me.

I have no coins, nothing to trade. There isn't anything I *need* anyway. The only vendor who draws my eye is an artist tattooing onto a High Fae under the burning noon sun. Not to mention the food carts scattered around. Having eaten through my rations this morning, my stomach demands some *real* food. After an hour of enjoying the music and enduring glorious smells, I rise with stiff hips and make my way to the tattooist.

My metal cane taps on the stones, and for once the usual chagrin that comes with it is gone. The pain is from *living*, using my body, traveling the countryside. I don't particularly care anymore if I appear vulnerable. I am, but I'm also deadly, and have survived enough to not let such a thing bother me. I haven't used the blade in my cane since the day I escaped, and I'm starting to miss my wooden one from the Mountain. Peace washes over me for a moment, slowing my step.

I haven't drawn blood at all since I left. The familiar blades strapped on my thighs have been teased several times, but nothing more. No training, no strength work.

Well, that's debatable.

After coming to a rest on the half wall of cobblestone beside his canopy, I observe the artist's every move. His canvas is a jade skinned High Fae, a masterpiece coming to life on her right arm. A sleeve of forest and wildlife, with a crown of purple flowers resting in the center. Kinky dark coils spiral from her head in every direction, her long and voluminous hair just as magnificent as the rest of her.

The tattoo artist finishes a stroke and glances at me, then raises his bushy red brows so high they threaten the eccentric hair upon his head. I expect the expression on his face to be wary and terrified, however he only holds genuine surprise. Flashing bright orange eyes wash over me, and I'm surprised to find he's a Fire Fae. The only one I've seen here so far, actually.

He continues his work and the well dressed female under his inky needle remains still, watching me from the corner of her eye. She wears a cream sundress, the length of it flowing from the elevated chair, reaching the ground. "If I had known the Keeper of Death was visiting with the long lost *Zemer*, I would've cleared a spot just for you." He teases, drawing an amused look from his canvas.

Long lost? *Zemer*?

A groan escapes me and I rub my face, sarcasm dripping. "If you know who I am, why aren't you all running and screaming yet then?"

"What do you mean?" He asks curiously.

"I've heard different tales. What's the story here?" I say, boredom creeping into my voice as I roll my eyes. The tattooist finishes with a pleased smile on his wrinkled, handsome face. The female admires her art with awe, then focuses on me with renewed color to her cheeks. She's the one who answers my question, her eyes flash near white which reminds me of Pan and tugs my heartstrings.

"Do you even realize what it was like to live in Terra before the High Lord returned? You're a hero there." She says plainly and I blink incredulously, my cheeks warm. "They may be frightened of you, but no one will dare lay a hand on you."

I am definitely *not* a hero. I glance over my shoulder to the square where many are paused, their attention catching on us. Beakglen is technically on the

Hallowed side of the border, but many Earth Fae are mixed with the Air faeries and humans. A few Water Fae linger in the crowd as well, but definitely a smaller concentration.

The Fae rises from the chair, her full figure much taller than I, but that's not hard. She smiles with plump ruby lips and dips into an elegant bow before me. The artist follows suit, and a rustling falls across the village square as everyone either bows or kneels. I bite my lip, unsure what to say or do. This is *not* a situation I expected to find myself in.

At the farthest corner of the plaza, my companions are standing together, grinning ear to ear. Even Umber appears pleasantly surprised. A High Fae male stands beside Orion, the same look on his face. My friends begin to kneel and I shake my head. They do not need to show me any respect.

All their knees meet cobbled ground anyway, the last ones to do so.

The breathtaking Fae rises from her elegant bow and takes my hand, her lips leaving a kiss on my sweating palm. "Thank you." She whispers. The crowd rises with her, chatter drifting throughout. The square is alive again, every eye on the female as she leaves me, fading into the crowd before I can ask her name. I exhale a deep breath, then turn back to the Fae with red hair sticking up in every direction.

"Want one?" He asks, cleaning his equipment. His tone is gruff and deep, yet kind. Like Knothall's.

"I don't have anything to give you." I say, shrugging my shoulders.

"I didn't ask for anything. I asked if you wanted a tattoo." He stretches his bare arms overhead, pushing out a deep breath. His rolled up brown sleeves reveal a burn on his forearms, the insignia of the Iron Court. The mark of a slave, a *solider*. I've encountered enough of the 'traitors' sent from Obsidivale, soldiers cast out of the militia for one reason or another. Nearly every one I met had been a hot head, quite unlike the male before me.

"I'll try anything twice." I say, stepping towards him. A jagged cobblestone sends me crashing into the chair and I yelp. He shakes his head, chuckling while I recover. He drains a glass of amber liquid, then rests the empty vessel beside his ink and needles on the decrepit table.

"The name is Lex." He prepares a fresh pallet of color, thick brows rising. "I assume you have one? Or do you just go by Keeper?"

I chuckle, finding his presence oddly comforting. Thick ginger stubble grows along his broad face, and the orange in his eyes reminds me of a flaring sunset. "Lythienne, but I prefer Lyth."

He bites his cheek and focuses on the needle in his hand, creased eyes glisten in the sun. Is he *crying*? "What shall we start with then, dear Lyth?"

"Well, believe it or not, I like tinkering. Aether engines, that sort of thing." I say quietly, fidgeting with the leather baldric across my chest. He nods, rubbing his chin with a scarred hand. If *tears* did spring to his eyes, they're gone now. He reminds me of Alvis and Knothall in that sense, a male beaten down by centuries of battle, not artist work. "Can I ask you something?"

He dips his needle in black ink and takes my right arm gently, rolling it over to begin work on my forearm. A mild annoyance of pain ensues, and he gives me a simple nod to indicate he's listening. "What is a *Zemer*?" I ask in a whisper, expecting something crazy. He chuckles, thick jaw tightening and brows narrowing as he focuses on his work.

"Tis' from the old language, *Zemer* is a type of musician, one so talented they're said to be made from music itself. Those *Te'omin* though, the twins? *Oy*, are they a handful." He mutters, a sly grin pulling his wrinkles.

My cheeks warm and a small laugh escapes me. "They aren't too awful."

Novak's playing his lute now in the center of the square. Umber and the twins are keeping him company, clapping along to his music. Children dance about and Novak skips around with the little ones, smiling wide while he strums wildly.

Alvis asks Umber to dance and she agrees with haste. He catches my eye, happiness is spread across his handsome face and he throws me a wink. Waves of Fae and Humans join the fun, some kind of dance everyone seems to know but me commences without a word. Males join arms with females, swinging and twirling each other around. Orion and the Fae I assume to be Emeric stand on the sidelines, quiet joy beaming from the two.

Yes, I can imagine this place feeling like home.

"So, how do you know them?" I ask, interest shifting to the details of gears slowly coming to life on my forearm. Lex smiles and pauses his work, grinning up to me.

"Practically raised that brat, and good ol' Captain. It's been quite some time since I've seen either of them, though." Lex swallows, eyes turning downwards to my arm once more as his voice lowers. "Can't blame him for not visiting the old man yet, crowds follow him wherever he goes, for better or worse."

"You're kidding! I can't imagine wrangling either of them as kids." I chuckle as he refreshes his ink and needle, then wince as he resumes poking rapidly with a soft orange Aether glow surrounding the needle tip.

"I seem to have a knack for adopting problem children." He says wholeheartedly.

Novak's music fades and within moments the entire group overwhelms Lex's small space. Alvis has an arm slung around a timid Novak's shoulders. Orion, Umber and Emeric give Lexeran their hellos, then Alvis does too. When it's Novak's turn, Lexeran beats him to it. "Took you long enough, *akar*." He says kindly to Novak without looking up, albeit much more reserved than he was before.

Novak shoves his hands into his pockets, smiling nervously as he focuses on Lex. I bite my cheek, the palpable tension between the two on either side of me a living thing. "Long time no see, old man."

"*Ai*, what's a decade between family?" Lex teases, the words turn Novak's smile down. Alvis saves the day, slapping me on the shoulder after Lex's needle leaves my skin to refresh the ink.

"See you've met our lovely Keeper, isn't she deadly?" Alvis squeezes my full cheek and I swat him away, a light laugh leaving my chest. Laughter swells through the group and the tension softens, but Novak won't look me in the eyes, or anyone else for that matter.

"Quite." Lexeran agrees.

We decide to stay the night in Emeric's town home, the beautiful place owned by Captain and occupied by the Fire Fae about ten years ago. 'Headquarters', as Novak calls it, is more or less a way-point for Captain or anyone else to use, with Emeric as its caretaker. All I know is my entire body is joyous at the thought of a real bed. For some reason though, the spacious house is rather unsettling.

Orion and Emeric putter in the open kitchen together, Emeric talking a mile a minute as he updates us on the latest happenings. Alvis rests in a chair across the simple wooden dining table from me with Umber perched in his lap as she vents about getting ripped off. Lex and Novak took a detour on the way here, when the musician returned alone red and faced, I didn't pry.

Novak's seated beside me now, glossing over my tattooed arm and shoulder with curious, soft fingers. The tunic I wore earlier is now replaced by the comfortable linen crop top I've come to enjoy. Smoke rolls from my pipe and after a deep puff, I pass it to the musician. Novak nurses the long pipe for a thoughtful moment, then passes it to Alvis. His delicate fingers meet my arm once again, curious and light. Goosebumps spread under his gentle touch, fueling the hunger inside me. If we were alone right now, I would be very tempted to throw myself at him, using the table and every other available surface to ravage each other.

Nothing more has happened since our *almost* kiss in the Mists, and at the same time *everything* has changed. I want to kiss every part of him, every scar and freckle, and never let him go. The way he looks at me and teases, I want to believe he feels the same way. The way he flailed away from me though in the inn, and his long hesitation to kiss me, or even try again, maybe I'm wrong.

I've been wrong before.

"Did you ask for that?" Novak inquires with a grin, his bright eyes drawing me out of my thoughts. His and every aura throughout the house is soft, the most relaxed any of us have been in days. Orion and Emeric's light red and violet auras combine, and a smile escapes me before I turn my attention fully to Novak.

Intricate gears encapsulate my right shoulder, falling into an ocean of deep purple clouds. A great pirate ship with golden sails smashes through the glittering storm. Novak's fingers trail further down my tanned skin, need follows his wake and warms my thighs. Waiting next on my forearm are my goggles.

Tiny vials on the leather straps and the third green lens. Lex captured every detail perfectly. I asked him to crack the main lenses, to which he gave me a solemn nod without any more questions. Chess pieces lay scattered alongside the goggles and Novak's face softens, the sight pauses his curiosity.

Something about both those moments in my life changed me.

Surrounding the bracelets of scars on both my wrists are vines similar to the twins, only mine are purple. The budding floral lines snake through the few empty places on my right arm and over my shoulder, across my neck. The artist covered the scar on my left wrist, but the rest of that arm is blank, save for trailing purple vines and the sketch on my left shoulder.

Out of my periphery I notice Alvis watching Novak trailing the vines along my left arm. The warrior's jaw flexes, violet eyes flashing, and I can't tell if he's angry with me for taking artistic liberty, or jealous of my attention under Novak. Maybe I should've asked first, or at least found out what they mean. Alvis and Orion are part of my journey, and I've always loved the vines along both of them. I subtly shift away from Novak, if only to make Alvis more comfortable.

What a fucking mess.

I lift a shoulder. "Well you heard him, he just wanted to know my story. Apparently, it's wild enough that's all he needed to make a masterpiece." I chuckle, puffing on the pipe after a now silent Umber passes it to me, her silver eyes fixated on the last tattoo Novak inspects.

High up on my left shoulder rests a standing bear and small grasshopper staring each other down. The black outline sketch is surrounded by familiar purple smoke, and a crow flying out of the Aether. Novak's hovering fingers pause on the image. I give him a smile and he weakly returns it, then his fingers tangle with mine on the table.

Orion and Emeric bring in several platters, setting them carefully on the table. Umber jumps up, reaching for Emeric's platter. Novak whistles with raised brows as Orion snarls at her. "You need to wait."

Alvis chuckles at his brother's tone, stretching after he stands. His wandering gaze pauses on my hand clutching Novak's. He gives me a wink and looks away before I can react. If he isn't happy, he's trying to be. The thought twists my stomach and I attempt to focus on his brother.

Orion is absolutely primal beside Emeric. Emeric has skin darker than mine but lighter than Orion's, and red eyes with a softened mid height frame. The body of an intellectual, not someone who traverses with Keepers of Death. His hair reminds me of Captain's, in the way it's opposite from how most 'true fire fae' are, like Lex. Emeric's deep hazel hair is messy like Orion's, but only half the length as his shining tresses stop at his shoulders.

Emeric turns his soft face up to Orion, his voice tender and thin lips holding a smile. "They don't have to wait." Emeric teases. I can't help but smile watching them and I wonder how long they've been together. I suppose they would've met through Captain, but I didn't think to ask.

"Litha will be soon, seeing as how we won't be here, I thought we could celebrate now." Orion says matter of factually to us. I release Novak's hand to pack the pipe again. As I puff on it deeply, listening to the twins and Novak bicker about the correct date, I think about Pan's daughters. They will have their father home for their birthday, the summer solstice.

"So, how do you celebrate, Emeric?" I ask after a moment, catching Orion's relieved gaze.

"Seeing how the harvest will be especially bountiful this coming fall, with the High Lord returning, we will offer thanks." He explains, quite vaguely. My ears flick and I look to Novak for an explanation.

"Don't worry Keeper, we're not sacrificing you." Novak muses and jabs me with an elbow. I snarl and clonk him on the head with the now empty pipe, drawing barking laughter from Alvis. Orion picks up the platter Umber had reached for in his hands. It's filled with fruits, herbs and several yellow and white candles of various sizes. The other platter is filled with food for us, for after.

"There are some who still respect the Ancients they descended from, and we give offerings the spirits enjoy." Orion explains to me as he gives Umber a scowl, and then Emeric a weak smile. "Litha is a time of healing, something we can all use right now."

The emanating thick silence between our group confirms his words.

I rise and cross to the star struck lovers, taking Emeric's hands with tenderness. "I would love to celebrate with you, if I may."

Orion grins, kissing me on the cheek. Emeric loses his shyness, his fiery crimson eyes shining with delight. He's unbroken, on the outside. I know well though, the worst scars are hidden deep below the surface.

Umber grumbles about her appetite. My own stomach is throwing a fit, but this moment is one I want to experience with my friends. Who knows where we may be, and now that I'm in this world, I'd like to celebrate it with those I care about. Which is turning out to be quite a few, and this is important to them. Besides, it doesn't sound like it should take long.

Novak offers his hand, keeping me close to his side while the others file out the back door. "I know how hungry you are, perhaps we can fix that later. If you'd like." A devilish grin splays across his face and I roll my eyes at him, unable to contain my smile. My fingers leave his hand and rest on his chest, sighing as the warmth from his bare chest meets my skin. He's dressed in the usual way, casually showing off his scars to the world.

"You know, I can't help but wonder something, when I watch you play." I murmur, pressing my full chest against his skipping heart. His fingers meet my cheek, then brush hair from my eyes, sapphires darkening as my lips part.

"Hm?" Novak breathes, his excitement pulsating against my stomach. *Seriously*? Do I really make him feel this way with only a few words?

I slide my hand up his neck, then down his arm until my fingers find his still paused on my face. I kiss his fingertips, then look up through my lashes. "Do these fingers play other things, just as well as they play the lute?"

Control is no longer a tangible aspect. Novak's gentle hands firmly take my face and his lips are suddenly a breaths width away from mine, his body slams both of ours against the wall. I moan, the sweet sound vibrating off Novak's lips. Shadows find us and darken the hallway, a *wicked* smile takes hold of Novak's freckled face.

"You have no idea what your words do to me, my lady." He moans, his desperation washing over my mouth. I stare at his lips for a moment, and then back up to his flaring blue eyes cutting through the darkness.

"You have no idea what you do to me." I whisper, slowly taking his hand. I slide it down my breasts, quivering stomach, and when it reaches the hem of my pants, a hollering Orion breaks us from our heated indiscretion. Novak groans and leans over me to hit his head on the wall over my shoulder. I chuckle and throw my arms around him.

"Lythienne, I cannot understate how much we need to revisit this discussion on my musical skills." He whispers into my ear and goosebumps spread. I kiss his cheek and escape his embrace before we distract ourselves any longer.

"What was that word, again, *akar*, right? Alvis says it means troublemaker, and I have to say, it fits you well." I tease and Novak smiles, taking my hand to lead me outside.

Emeric's backyard is a lawnless, semi-contained garden. Sunflowers lean on the surrounding picket fence, hiding the rolling fields that lay around Beakglen. A cozy stone fire pit, surrounded by engraved granite benches, lingers in the only bare spot available. Umber lounges on one, her quiet figure opposite the twins and Emeric chatting together by the fire pit.

"This is beautiful, Emeric." I say, caressing several flower petals on my way out, fully intoxicated by colors and fragrance. Just when I think I have experienced every color and smell in this world, I find more and more.

"Keeps me busy while I wait for this one." Emeric teases, leaning into Orion. Orion grins, hunger lighting his face, but he doesn't kiss Emeric, or even hold him fully. The sight makes my heart fill, and then break. How intense is the hate they hide from?

I wonder how a Fae like Emeric wound up here in the first place. A soft smile brightens my face, the Crew of Misfits is bigger than I thought. I wish Lexeran would've stayed, but I have to imagine Novak's 'incident' is what put distance between them.

Orion gives us all an offering we can place in the pit, advising us to give our thanks and speak to the Ancients from our souls. Umber is first, haphazardly dropping a sprig of thyme into the fire pit without pause or a word, then settles back onto a bench and crosses her arms tight. The scene of her grabbing a pixie midair by its wings flashes by. Shame floods me. I truly don't know her at all. She may have kept things from me, but I know at the very least a smart Fae.

I've never prayed to the Ancients or tried to communicate with them, but even I know they're real. Watching, waiting. Well, I have once, surrounded by tunnels closing in, soul swallowed by hatred and pain.

Novak is next and he delicately sets down a small bouquet of peonies, then closes his eyes and kneels beside the stones for a moment. His usual playful grin softens, and the aggravated aura around him softens to charcoal. The sight of it takes me aback. I wouldn't have known he was upset without my crystal eye, he hides his pain so well. When he stands by my side again, I take his hand and squeeze tight, giving him a small smile. I quite like the way our fingers fit together, his soft palm against my scarred and rough one.

Alvis kneels similar to how Novak did, closing his eyes as well while he drops elongated leaves onto the pit. The writing on them teases my curiosity as they drift down. When the warrior finishes muttering something under his breath, he rises and joins Orion with a stiff smile. I release Novak's hand and leave his side for a moment, coming to squat by the fire pit. I lay my triad of yellow roses precariously beside his peonies. I don't know what to say.

*Ancients, I am in deep gratitude to you for getting me out of that hellhole. And I want to thank you for bringing me to Novak, and to my friends. If it's not too much to ask, I'd like to stay with him awhile. So if you could help me **not** die, I would really appreciate it.*

As I rise, it's hard to not let out a chuckle at my nonchalant conversation with Ancient Fae who may or may *not* be listening. Novak takes my hand and I shake purple tendrils away from my stinging eyes. Orion sets the platter of treasures beside our offerings, then pulls Emeric close to him after he stands and raises his voice.

"Spirits of the Ancient Fae, we thank you for your protection. We ask that you continue to look over us and aid on Lyth's journey, and bless the lands with your magic." Cold spreads across me when Orion's sure voice meets my ears, sending a shudder throughout my nerves. Novak bites his cheek and softly tugs me in front of him, wrapping his arms around me. Warm visible shadows fall from him, settling around us. A sigh of content escapes from me.

Novak's heart, however, thunders against my shoulders. Is he trembling?

I tilt my head back and Novak brings his rounded ear close to my lips. "I quite like your darkness." I whisper, drawing a sweet smile from the Fae. He lays a gentle kiss on my nose before leaning back, and his darkness thickens into a blanket around us. I wonder how much he restrains it, how much there truly is.

Emeric catches my eye, a soft smile spreading as he watches Novak and I. Without a glance to the street out front, he kisses Orion with tenderness before turning to the stone pit. Soft red flashes in Emeric's eyes. I still can't believe he's a Fire Fae. He is so gentle.

The roaring explosion however, is not.

An oil slick of flames erupts from the pit, towering above us and arranging into the form of an elegant Fae. Rainbow fire composes her hair, a detailed thick cloud of smoke brings to life a feminine body. My hips go weak and a gasp fractures my chest. Novak's arms steady me and his darkness recoils from the fire, but a wall of shadows separates us from the pit.

Umber jumps to her feet, mouth quirking upwards into a malicious grin. Alvis narrows his brows, staring at his brother who is fixated on the Ancient with pure shock on his face. Emeric trembles, clinging tight to Orion as he half hides behind him. Umber takes Alvis' hand, then nods to the rest of us. Why is she taking the lead, why now? No one else questions her, at least not out loud.

Our hands connect around the stone circle, heat licks our faces and threatens to burn us alive. The Ancient Fae smiles with a yawning abyss for a mouth, then the flaming figure faces me. Claws of black fire tap upon a fiery pointed chin and its disembodied voice floats across us all, directed to me. "Lady, what a surprise." The Ancient drawls, its thunderous voice shaking the ground beneath us.

My lungs stop working. Novak's tight arms ground me but I still can't *breathe*. The hidden voice constantly screaming to be found is now deathly quiet, and for the first time in decades, I feel empty and alone.

"How unfortunate it is you returned to that infernal Mountain, oh wait, wasn't that the *point*?" The fire creature snickers, sending sparks straight up into the twilight sky. "Very ... interesting, we found you, Lythienne, we thought it would be enough. But, did we choose correctly? Or does it matter at all? *Your* choice is most ... complicating." The Ancient contemplates, words twisting into a riddle as its echoing laugh cuts through thick sparking air.

The fire regards Novak after it regains sanity, then another round of barbarous heart stopping laughter *rolls*. A sparking, elongated claw reaches past my cheek to caress Novak's frozen face. "Is it you? Of course it can't be, but what if it *is*?" Devilish giggles continue and sparks fly from the pit, a cinder lands on my face but I feel nothing. "I'm surprised the two of you haven't scrambled the entirety of Iverbourne by now, isn't that what you do? WHY WE PUNISHED YOU?!"

Screaming flames projectile from its mouth and erase all other sound as fire barrels towards us. A weak shield of shadows wraps around us, but it's no use against the Ancient's magic. A cry emits from Novak and I struggle to hold him up, the musician drops to a knee as his thinning shield wavers under ancient power. A muffled shout from Alvis across the fire seems to calm the Ancient, as its onslaught retreats.

"No matter, we all know how this ends. An Empty, hopeless Fae in this life. What shall you pick next, *Lady*?" Fire spits once more, flaming embers biting my leather boots.

"Why do you visit us, Ancient? What ends do you speak of?" I find my words, voice loud and steady, quite unlike my quivering heart.

"As a sign of our good will for your *journey*," The voice sinks under my skin, the Ancient ignoring my question. "You will *each* have one small request fulfilled. Ask now, and it shall be done. If we deem it worthy." The voice is a beautiful song now, no longer possessed by wickedness.

Novak trembles, his hand cold in mine. The rainbow of oily flames reflect in his eyes, which are no longer blue. They are pitch black, and his skin is transforming into ethereal night against mine. My eyes shoot to the aghast twins and trembling Emeric, then to Umber. She is the only one who appears ... *pleased*. She can't seriously expect a favor.

I don't know what to ask for. I can ask for almost anything and it could be mine. I stare down at my boots, then back up to the terrifying Ancient. "Nothing is given for free."

Thunderous laughter rumbles across us once more, the Ancient focusing on Umber when it speaks, "Indeed, it is not. Choose wisely, or you shall be very much in debt." The next words twist into a death song. "Or into the tower you will go, *again*."

My soul crawls with the warning. I decide it's worth it and raise my chin, staring the Ancient right in its snickering face when I strike my bargain.

The fire snuffs out and rolling smoke shoots across the yard. A shock wave of Aether explodes from the fire pit, sending us all flying backwards. A scream tears my lungs apart when cold darkness squeezes the life out of me, leaving me with a vision of flashing pale eyes. The delicate, ever haunting whisper caresses my mind.

"It's wrong, he hasn't found me yet. Find me, love. Find me."

MORE, I WANT MORE

I wake with a start and spring forward, consequently rolling off whatever I lay on. A short scream rips my chest apart as I land onto the musician sitting below me.

Novak soundlessly wraps his arms around me, his warm chest under my shaking body rises and falls steadily. Tears trail my cheeks, burning as they leave my skin and fall onto his bare torso. Gears turn in my head as I remember what we did, what I asked for. The riddle the Ancient gave me, their threats.

It's all becoming too much to handle, the weight of the vial is cumbersome with only the one essence, and an arduous journey is still ahead. Truth and lies poke out everywhere I go, both equally painful. Perhaps the Ancients *did* choose wrong. What does that even *mean*? My chest heaves harder as I remember how much it condemned me, how much it hated both of us.

"What's wrong, Lyth?" He whispers, my name rolling off his tongue with a sweetness I don't deserve. I inhale sharply, willing myself to focus on breathing. Novak waits, holding me tight. When my breathing steadies, Novak orders with firm softness. "Lyth, look at me."

I obey, eyes first meeting his chest, the deep scars still running amongst the dark sunspots and freckles. I trace the numerous raised lines with careful fingers, tears threaten to leave me again.

It didn't work.

I raise my face finally, finding relaxed sapphire eyes framed by locks of warm blonde, a smile pulling his deep dimples. His eyebrows are so light, contrasting the warm shadows cradling us. Air shoots from my chest when I finally see *them*. I bite my lip and reach out a shaky hand which draws a flash of Aether to his eyes. I pause, then he nods, holding his jaw tight.

Long fingers caress his elegant ears, furred with *white*. Long and wide like Orion's, they lay down on his *neck*. As my fingers tickle the pointed snowy fluff at the end, Novak giggles. The most beautiful Fae ears I have ever seen. Perhaps asking for his magic to be returned was too big of a request. This though, the look on his face, this is enough.

"It worked." I breathe, relaxing in his lap. My breathless voice perks his ears, raising them a bit. I smile and lean back into his chest, watching his ears move as the fireplace snaps. Lightly muscled arms hold me close, the shadows intensify and bring a sigh from my lips. I brush a stray lock of honey from his eyes, then my hand trails down his cheek.

"You used your creepy magic wish on me?" Novak tilts his head and takes the hand I had on his face, kissing my palm. Of course he's trying to make me laugh. Always making others laugh.

"Well, yeah. I figure if anyone deserves creepy magic it's you." I bite my lip when he erupts into laughter. I mumble something about at least saying thank you.

"Funny thing is, I thought the same about you." He murmurs and I draw in a breath at his words, pulling away from his chest. We're in a small bedroom, seated on a hardwood floor beside a crackling fire, and a lounge chair covered in tangled blankets waits behind us.

"What did you ask for, exactly?" He asks, resting his hand on my thigh. My prosthesis and sockets are gone, leaving my legs bare as I'm wearing loose, unfamiliar linen shorts.

"To give back what was taken from you. What did you ask for?" I ask, neck warming as he watches my lips. Our moment in the hallway flashes through my mind.

"I asked them to give you what you needed, and apparently *this* is their answer." Novak reaches beside him, revealing a dagger.

The well made blade is forged from obsidian, similar to my own. The handle is crafted from bone, and insignias from each element are carved into it. In the pommel is a small amethyst, something I have only seen in books, crystals rumored to be lost in the war. The brilliant cut stone matches my hair perfectly, and when I take the light blade, Aether tickles my palms. The weight is perfectly balanced, whoever created this is a brilliant craftsman indeed. A simple note is tied to the hilt. I flip it over and scrutinize the plain writing under the fire light.

You will never miss your mark. Aim wisely.

I twirl the dagger in my fingers, a small smile escaping as I remember Knothall teaching me how to do it. I'm thankful Novak didn't ask for my legs to be fixed, but the thought falters my smile. I didn't even think he might feel the same way about his ears. I thought he would get his magic back. I hand the blade back to him, and he sets it precariously on the floor.

"Are you upset I didn't ask for something else?" A stray freckled hand wanders further down my thigh, pausing midway.

"*No*, I'm glad. It's just ... I rather like my scars. It didn't hit me that you might like your own as well, my intention was for your magic to be returned."

"Well, I think you might have it backwards. I've told you, I rather like the shadows, mostly." He chuckles for a moment, smile fading while he ponders. "And I rather like Humans, but I'm glad I don't look like one. I didn't fit in on either side. Makes being a vagabond rather difficult." His fluffed ears twitch and he bites his cheek, drinking in my lips parting.

We release the hold on the magnetism between us. Our bodies and lips crash together with such a wild need, we could burn the world down.

And we do.

My spirit sighs in exhausted relief, relishing in his soft and ravenous lips craving my own. I bite his lip and he moans against me, slipping his tongue in to explore mine. Once soft hands grip my face with hunger, pulling me closer, *closer*, even though we are already melded as one.

I run a hand through his hair and grasp tight, the other is thrown around his neck. I will never get close enough, he's everything I'm missing. He finds a handful of my soft hair and fingers dig into my thick waist. Novak's lips drift down my face, following my soft jawline to find my ear. His breath tickles the purple tuft, sending a shudder through me.

"Don't tease me any longer, *please*." I beg, drawing a dark chuckle from him.

"Lythienne, I have to tell you something." He caresses the hollow of my neck with teasing teeth, threatening to bite. I arch into him, pressing my artery into his hot mouth. I ache for him, not just love, but *him*.

"Yes, Novak?" I moan two small words into his thick hair, absorbing the smell of sea salt. His shaft begs to be free of his pants, pressing into me. I want him, all of him. He lifts from my neck, taking my cheek in a desperate hand, then rubs my bottom lip with his thumb.

His honeyed curls are beyond disheveled, wide eyes alight with blue flames. Deep dimples appear when he speaks, and the lean muscles flex in his shoulders. "I lied to you, before. I love you, Lyth. That's why I'm here." His tender words fill my empty vessel of a heart, caressing the darkest parts of me and reviving them with renewed strength. A wide smile spreads across my face and soul, this is *real*.

"When you came back, all covered in mud," Sunburnt lips filled with need collide with mine, interrupting my confession. Desperate hands tangle in my hair, my fingers find his neck and shoulder, gripping *tight*. "I want you to love me. I want to love *you*, Novak. Let me love you."

A firm hand slides down my back and he lays me down beside the fire on a pile of blankets. He kneels between my legs, hands sliding to grip my waist. Every artery in his body is awake and pulsing, the strength he usually hides under loose clothing is revealed to me under firelight.

"Say it again." He asks firmly.

"I want you, my vagabond bard. Every, single, inch." My seductive words draw satisfaction from him. Gentle hands pull the hem of my shorts down, he carefully slides the fabric off my thighs. His hands slide back up to my stomach next, traveling underneath my shirt to slip it off. The moment he beholds my bare breasts, a shudder spreads through him.

"You are so fucking gorgeous." He breathes, laying a kiss between them at once, where the majority of my blistered scars are.

"I asked you to quit teasing, please let me have you." I whisper, taking his face in my hands.

"Come and get it." He taunts, raising a brow.

I reach down and unbutton his pants at once and release his throbbing shaft, begging to be touched. Warmth surges through me, and I'm unsure if I can take him all, at least not at first. Novak bites his lip and grins at my indiscretion. Settling over me and teasing my entrance, he begins a path of kisses starting at my forehead, across my eyelids and down my neck, trailing down my chest. The soft grazing brings goosebumps across my heavy breasts. He finally takes one in a sure hand, the other he teases with his mouth.

The moment his lips meet my hard nipples, I press into him, begging for more. A sly tongue dances, caressing me in his mouth with gentle kindness before nibbling and turning fierce. I whimper and beg, grasping a handful of his hair and a shoulder. He's so close to entering me, the hard tip of him grazes my throbbing clit and I shudder. He pulls away with a wicked grin, the musician lays a finger on my lips.

"Don't interrupt my fun. I've been thinking about this for a long time."

I scowl, evoking a mischievous laugh from him. His mouth lowers to my stomach, kissing and nipping the softness of my belly. "I want to taste every inch of you, feel every part of you under my lips." He murmurs and continues wandering, exploring my waist with his mouth and desperate hands, the sensation thrilling. I have never felt so wanted, so worshiped.

This is what *love* feels like. Not just lust, but love.

My cheeks warm when he lowers himself once more, kissing my inner thighs. He pauses midway, looking up to me. "May I?"

"Yes." I breathe, grasping my breast with one hand as I run the other through my hair. I close my eyes and focus on the feeling of his lips trailing down my leg, his fingers gently caressing the sensitive end. A moan escapes me and after a moment he's waiting between my legs, hands grasping my hips.

"Are you ready?" Novak asks, shaking wild hair from his beautiful face.

"I've been ready." I raise a brow, moving closer to him.

"We'll see about that."

His tongue first meets my clit, flicking across with precise gentleness. I've never had anyone down there before, and any sex I've had before is beyond useless now. Even my own self pleasure is nothing compared to this, especially when his finger slides into me at the same time. I grip the blankets and whimper as his gentle movements turn quick.

"More Novak, I want more."

He obeys, exploring me with his tongue while sliding another finger in. The combination of his smooth thrusting and flicking tongue has a massive wave building inside me. His fingers curve upwards, pressing into a spot I didn't even know existed, and gentle teeth meet the nerves above.

I cry out his name, my nails digging into his back. A groan of satisfaction leaves him and the vibration has me close to the edge again, it's all I can do to hold the building orgasm back. "Wait," I barely manage, his fingers leave me at once and he lifts his head, brows pulling in confusion. "Not yet, I want to come with you, inside me."

The musician nods, nervousness tainting his smile and eyes flashing dark for a moment. He settles over top of me, his thick length teasing to enter, but he holds himself up with a steady arm. Novak's other hand slips under my shoulders and he pauses for a moment, studying my face with quiet intensity.

I rest my hands on his cheeks, air leaving me heavily in anticipation. "Are you ok?"

"I don't want to hurt you," he admits, "I haven't loved anyone in a long time, and I'm afraid, afraid I'll mess it up."

My heart fills and breaks with his words. My eyes sting and I kiss him deeply, cupping his warm cheeks. "Don't be afraid to love me, please. I can't bear it." I whisper into his mouth, and he smiles gently under my words. He pulls back just enough to look me in the eyes, then enters inside me.

Inch by inch, bit by bit, I take him in. His face twists and he groans, hips moving slowly, his muscles ripple with self control threatening to snap.

"*Oh*, Novak." I whimper, his name on my lips draws a primal rumble from his chest. His arm underneath holds me firm while he settles deep inside me, the pressure unbearable. My tattooed hand tangles in his hair, and my chest is unable to steady.

"Are *you* ok?" He utters with delight while remaining paused inside me, so *hard*, so ready to burst.

"I could be better." I scowl before biting his lip and arching my hips up into him. He replies with drawing out of me, teasing to leave, which draws a pathetic whine from me.

"I seem to get the impression you don't like it slow and sweet, do you?" He mutters, staying inside me, *just* barely.

"I'll take you whatever way I can have you." Darkness flickers across his eyes once more at my words. I put on a wicked smile, challenging him. "But I would prefer not to be able to walk tomorrow."

On my last word he thrusts back into me, all playfulness gone.

"Good."

A cry escapes me, a beast is trapped under that facade of composure and humor. He draws back only to hurriedly find the deepest parts of me, over and *over*, strength pouring from every motion and hidden muscle throughout his body. Somewhere in the world things are crashing to the ground, and nothing has ever felt more right.

I throw my head back when the wave of pleasure swells with twice the intensity as before. I shudder under him and claw at his shoulders, which must be torn up by now. He either doesn't notice or doesn't care, but then he moans and I wonder if he likes the pain. The orgasm I was on the edge of finds me and awakens everything *fiber* of my being. By the Ancients, I've never come like this before.

This feeling with him, this is home.

"Let me see you come." He orders, breathless but firm.

In response I throw my entire body forward, wrapping myself around him. With a deep groan he grabs my ass harshly and sits back with me in his lap. I'm now gazing into swirling oceanic eyes, and he wastes no time continuing the moment we settle, this position driving him deeper. His hands are careful under my thighs, lifting me with each motion. Another orgasm shakes my thick body, but we hold our gaze on the other. His hand takes my cheek and I nuzzle into it, then he kisses me through my fading whimpers.

"You're everything I've ever wanted." I admit onto his lips when the wave passes, and he slows under me.

"I hope you know what this means." He breathes into me, a hand wandering to find my hair. I rock my hips slowly, the most that I can, and he lazily follows my movements.

"Mm?" I ask, offering him my neck, to which he lays kisses with a slight bite. Before speaking, his body turns still, and so does mine.

"I'm yours, now, and always." Novak's primal tone surprises me and he pulls my face to his, holding me firm by my chin with a finger and thumb. Once blue eyes are black, his shadows leech around us and a wildness takes over his handsome features.

Ancients, he's so fatally beautiful, and he's really all mine.

I tighten around him, my hair tangles further in his hand at my neck. "Good, because I'm yours, always." I promise and at once take over, riding him as I hold tight to his shoulders and work my tired hips.

Sun kissed skin feathers out into ethereal night, and hunger filled delight takes hold of his galaxy ridden face. He kisses me harshly, passion dripping from his shadowed lips. My movements slow and with a firm hand cradling the back of my head, the other settles under my shoulders while he lays us down. A strangled cry escapes me when he settles and a thunderous ... *rumble* erupts from him, a sound I have never heard from a person before. His snow fluffed ears flick and he *thrusts* into me, the hand in my hair holding me in place as the other leaves my back.

I almost want to ask if this is normal, all the darkness riding the room and his complexion replaced by the universe, but I don't want to scare him off. I don't mind it, this is *him* after all.

A free hand thumbs my large nipple, rolling it between his fingers, then he takes it in his mouth. I arch my back and he nibbles gently, then the feeling is washed over by a sly tongue. Continuous smooth, deep and *harsh* thrusting has me crying out his name. His hand leaves my breast and slides under my hip, lifting me upwards. Pleading desperation fills my voice and trembling body. "Fuck, I need you. I need you to fill me."

The bedroom *blackens* at my desperate voice, and the silhouette of massive wings unfurling from his back is thrown against the walls, taking my breath away. He slows and his smiling lips find mine, then he sucks gently on my bottom lip. The roaring fire beside us is dimmed by his Aether, but he only has darkness filled eyes for me. It's then I realize he has no idea what's appeared on the walls behind him.

"We've only just begun, my lady." His hips pause, voice teasing.

I look up through purple lashes and stare directly into two pools of the sea at night. Deliberately, I bite my lip with tortuous tediousness, knowing it's his weakness. His heated gaze focuses on the last plump bit of flesh released by my teeth, his heart quickening audibly. The silhouette of wings rustles and the fire sparks. He works again in a smooth, deep and paced motion, slower than before, and pleasure escapes my chest once more.

"I love hearing you come, I love watching you. I never want to stop." Novak breathes out, a shudder escaping him as his thrusting intensifies, his next words are a struggle. "Are you ready?"

"Please." I beg, placing both hands on his face, voice commanding. "We have our whole lives together to feel this, I promise."

In that moment, he releases deep inside me so powerfully I can feel his come dripping out in seconds. Both of his arms draw me tight to his chest and he moans my name over and over again against my swollen lips and I come one last time with him, my own darkness entangling with his shadowed wings on the wall.

The world shifts on its axis as our spirits meld fully, a connection cementing between us. His uproarious heartbeat thunders in my mind, and the intense ecstasy flowing from his side of the ... thread, it feels like, throws me into oblivion. In that moment, we are one soul, one body, and nothing else exists.

And I'm not entirely sure we were two separate souls to begin with.

We lie naked on a bed of blankets beside now simmering coals. I listen to his now settled heart thrum under my face, and the gentle tune he hums. His pulse no longer echoes through my mind, and I wonder if I had imagined the connection between us. My eyes are half closed while he curls purple around his fingers, his other hand caresses my thigh. A thought bubbles to the surface, pulling me from my drifting.

"Why didn't you tell me, before?" I ask, gentle and curious. The hand on my leg pauses, then continues. The feeling borders on a tickle, but I don't mind. I'm not used to so much touch on my thighs. Or anywhere, really.

"When I first saw your face, you were lit up watching me play. I knew by your hair who you were, and for a moment, the thought crossed my mind I should've been scared." Novak pauses, pushing out a breath. "But I wasn't. I saw how happy you were and all I wanted to do was play for you. I decided to find you after, but then Panrauth was there."

I swallow, fully comprehending his simple words. Pan swept me off my feet, danced with me. Novak watched him, and then saw him break my heart on the ship.

"What was I supposed to say, hey I know you fancy that handsome fellow and we just met but I think I love you?" He chuckles softly, still exploring my hair and body with gentle hands, though the warm shadows cradling us darken a bit.

"He was kind, and he saved my life. He was the first person who saw *me*, and I loved the idea of loving someone." The weight of the conflicted thoughts lingering since the day Pan left disintegrate. I sit up on an elbow. "This is different." I kiss him delicately, moving the hair from his bright eyes. "You think I really believed you were coming along to be an *adventurer*? You're already that."

He chuckles, attention drifting to his hand caressing my chess tattoos. "The day I woke up to you at the inn, staring down at me with all your scowling beauty," he gestures to me, "I was so happy. It took me a moment to realize *what* was going on, and then I was *terrified*." His voice becomes dramatic, hands gesturing in the air. I giggle and he gives me a kiss on the nose. "I didn't want it to be a drunken thing between us."

I replay the scenes with this new information, relief finding me.

"So why didn't you come along then, at first? Where did you go?"

"I, I had to meet a friend." Novak says reluctantly, then is silent for a moment, lost in his thoughts. I wait patiently, I'll take what he wants to give. "When I came back to the ship, you were all gone. I became quite distraught, to say the least." He smirks, shaking his hair. "Captain set me straight, told me I would never find out what would happen if I didn't get off my ass and find you."

"That sounds about right." I laugh softly and a thought strikes me. "Why did Orion look at you today, when he mentioned mates?"

Novak's hands rest heavily on me, pausing in their tracks. "He's been hounding me since that first night he saw us together, on the ship." A minute passes and he is *silent*, drawing soft panic from me.

"We literally just went over how you're an idiot for not speaking your mind." I tease, but silence creeps for another moment as he stares into the fire beside us.

"I didn't think you could have more than one. Orion seems to think differently though." He whispers distantly, and a nervous laugh leaves him. "When you nearly stabbed me in front of everyone, I felt my soul reach out to yours. I did, and ... it was nothing like the first time."

I gently pull his face from the fire to meet mine. His eyes are wet, and a gentle hand brushes hair from my face. I open my lips but have no idea what to say. "It's scared the hell out of me ever since, it didn't end well for me the first time, and the fact I *could* feel that way about someone again. The idea of my soul reaching out to yours, and, yours not calling back. and then there's ... well, love wasn't in the cards for me."

He has loved and lost. He is afraid to love me, but can't stand to let me go without trying. I *had* felt something last night connect us, but whatever was there, it's now hard to reach.

"And was that your, friend? I thought you saved them." I ask, unsure if I want to know the answer.

"I did, but it wasn't him," he sighs, pushing a hand through his hair, "I was mated to the Fae he was married to. She ..." He trails off again, pushes down the lump in his throat.

"It's ok. Tell me when you're ready." I rest on his chest once more and close my eyes, replaying every moment we've had together, and *everything* settles differently. That's why Alvis backed off. I bet Orion told him after that night. *Oh*.

Novak had a mate. Was that why ...

"I do have to ask one thing." I say before I lose my nerve.

"Hm?" He murmurs, light fingers traveling my spine.

"You and Alvis, am I stepping in between something?" Silence fills the room and he *freezes*. I will my body to remain relaxed and hug him tight.

"What do you mean?" He asks, choked up a bit.

"*Novak*, it's obvious how much he loves you, and you him. You don't have to tell me what happened, but I don't want to hurt Alvis, if there's still something there ..." A gentle finger lifts my chin. We stare at each other for a long, *long* moment.

"I told myself, told *him*, a long time ago, that I would never love again. Easier, that way. I've spent two decades alone, in *that* sense, then you came and wrecked my plans." Novak chuckles nervously and I scoot up, then quietly press my forehead to his. He shakes his head softly, not breaking skin contact. "He doesn't want ... It's ancient history, I promise. He understands."

I nod and kiss him gently, but I don't feel very comforted. If I've learned *anything* about Alvis thus far, it's the fact he seems to put everyone *else's* feelings first. And the way Novak's voice wavered and his eyes dimmed, I just *know* he still has feelings for Alvis. There's no jealousy in my heart, only a growing guilt and new ambition to reunite them, somehow, some way. I nestle into his neck and sigh, allowing myself to not worry any longer tonight about the situation. We have time.

I want to ask Novak about the wings but I don't think he knows, and he's already so afraid of himself. I can't tell where one scar ends and another begins on his torso, but I'm quite sure they weren't *real* wings I saw. Where would they have popped out from? I want to believe it's just his shadows playing tricks on me, but deep down, I have a feeling there is a lot more hidden beneath his skin than meets the eye.

Alvis might know, or Captain. Orion's words from the library come back to me.

"What he hides inside is more than I could bear, for that I am certain."

We lay there, awake but silent, for several hours. I am nearly asleep when I finally tell him, but I want him to know. I want to be brave, like him, and I believe my words to be true.

"Does it feel like getting drunk, when you first meet them? And you know you never want to be without them again, and your heart hurts looking at an empty ship?" I yawn, voice drifting. "If so, then I think we are mates. Sorry."

I fall asleep with a smile on my face whilst teasing him. His chest rumbles with gentle laughter and strong arms followed by warming shadows keep me safe.

Most of the next morning is filled with lovemaking, fucking, and storytelling. And with Novak, there is *definitely* a difference between the two kinds of sex. He assured me there was a sound shield on the room, but I still can't help but feel a tad bit embarrassed at all the noise we've made.

We now rest naked together in the bed, he's playing my song on his lute. I am curled up beside him, his locks of hair curled around my finger. "You know, I've always quite liked this one." I say, voice hoarse. A content smile finds him, and he raises a brow at me.

"It came to me a few weeks before I met you, up in the nest on the ship. Scratched it into the wood and everything." He says proudly. I draw my brows together and give him a look. "Serious! I'll show you next time we see Captain again."

What do pirates do all day, anyway? I've been thinking about becoming one, I didn't think I was quite cut out, but if you're a first mate, can't be that hard."

He laughs heartily, tossing the lute aside and covering me with tickling kisses. I squeal and he scoops me up, a dead serious look crossing his face. "Can I bathe you?"

I blink incredulously, peering at the end of the bedroom that holds the washroom. "You want to *bathe* me?"

He makes for the quaint bathroom, holding me tight to his thundering chest as he rolls his eyes. "Yes, you, me, in the bath together. Soap and the such. I mean, I *assume* you've taken baths before."

I elbow him after he sets me down carefully on the edge of the tub, drawing the usual theatrics from him. He was true to his word last night and I am *quite* sore today, but am absolutely *not* complaining. It's not like we're in a big hurry, and if we stay here for a few extra days, that won't be so bad. Will it?

Within moments the water is running and a vial of soap is poured into the tub which brings huge bubbles. The sight makes me giddy and I reach in, scooping up a handful of the floral scented clouds. Novak bows deeply and gestures to the tub. "After you, my lady."

I lower myself in, the warm water is bordering on steaming. A sigh escapes and I lean back, dipping under at once. When I surface, Novak is waiting with a thoughtful smile, still outside the tub. "I thought you were coming in." I say, splashing at him.

"I am, but not yet." He says quietly, his soap filled hands find my scalp and scrub gently, moving to coat my tresses from root to end. I relax under his touch at once, and when I raise my head to the ceiling so he can rinse me, I release a breath that has been stuck inside my chest for 236 years.

The consequences of bargaining with Ancient Fae did not bode so well for everyone.

Alvis tussles my wet hair when I sit down at the dining table, and he grins at Novak's own wet mop. Alvis saunters to the kitchen and Novak trails after him, turning red when his friend complains obnoxiously about the thunderstorm we must've had last night, *and* this morning. So much for the sound shield.

I roll my eyes at Alvis, but when I spy the sadness lingering in his eyes whenever he looks away from Novak, the conclusion I came to last night stings even further. He is too good a Fae, a friend. Of course he will never tell Novak he still loves him. I make Novak happy, and that makes Alvis happy. Well, Alvis deserves to be happy, too.

Emeric and Orion are perched on a couch in the adjoined living room, snuggled together and each reading their own version of the same book, veiling childish smiles behind the pages. Umber is nowhere to be seen. The rooms are filled with gentle conversation, and normalcy strikes me. *This* is what it's like to live in a home, the unsettling feeling I had last night.

Novak sets down plates filled with meat and potatoes, a hulking salad earning its own platter. "What is that?" I poke at the slab of meat with a fork.

"Same as your dried crap, just better." Novak teases, winking at me. I decide fairly quickly he isn't wrong. Alvis settles across from us with his own plate of food, scrutinizing a map of Terra. The thick blue aura he usually holds is especially dark today, reminding me of what a brewing storm would look like.

"Where's your sidekick today?" I taunt, finishing my plate. You can hear a pin drop, the air turning still and empty. Orion joins us at the table, Emeric pretends to be interested in his book.

"Umber is dead." Orion rests a hand on my shoulder and I drop my fork. Cold *crawls* under my skin. I whip around, brows narrowed together.

"What happened?" I whisper, but the truth is knocking on my heart.

Alvis speaks harshly from across the table. "She pissed off the wrong people." Orion leaves my side and joins his brother. Orion reaches for Alvis' arm, but his brother roughly shrugs him off. "*Poof*, pile of dust." Alvis grumbles with dark amusement, staring at me. Only me.

"I didn't realize you cared so much." I tread a thin line, packing my pipe with caution.

Alvis slams his fist on the table, losing composure and rattling the plates. "I thought I could let my guard down." Alvis' heightened anger sends my heart into a thunder, and his charcoal ears fold down. After a long breath, he speaks with quiet defeat. "She was smarter than to pull this." He breaks, finally embracing his brother who takes him aside for a moment.

I quietly puff on the pipe, then pass it to a contemplative Novak. Emeric joins the circle in silence, standing on the other side of Novak. The air is too *dense* in here. The Fire Fae puffs, then passes the device to Orion after the twins rouse from their moment of unspoken words. I make it through one more silent round before storming off to the decimated garden.

The only visible landmark in the yard is the stone fire pit, somehow still intact. All the well tended flowers and shrubs are flattened to the ground. The sunflowers and fence they had once leaned upon are destroyed as well, the wood splintered in every direction. A bomb of ancient magic erupted in poor Emeric's backyard. A rare moment passes when I wish I could draw on the Aether in the atmosphere.

"I want to say, I'm sorry." Emeric's soft voice startles me and I startle on the remains of a stone bench. I look over my shoulder incredulously at him. He's standing at my side now with hands clenching elbows and a soft orange glow to his downward eyes. I stand uneasily, sore muscles protesting, and rest my rough hand on his soft, rounded shoulder.

"What for? Have you seen your garden?" I ask, attempting to tease. He lets out a small smile and rests a trembling hand atop mine.

"I didn't know that would happen last night. It was just supposed to be a small fire. I made cake, for after. I didn't know." Emeric's eyes brim over with tears and I wrap my arms around him, reeling in my breaking heart.

"You were visited by the Ancients because they respect you, and you respect them." I sigh, pausing. Sorrow lingers inside me for the Fae I thought I knew, but not the one she *really* was. "Whatever deal Umber tried to make, and her own choices, lead to her demise. Tricky as they might be, the Ancients are beings to be respected. Though it appears they don't like me very much."

Alvis is right, she might not have been kind, but Umber *was* smart. I push the thought away for now, holding Emeric in his torn garden. The Fire Fae heaves against me as we hold each other, and is silent for a few moments after.

"It's not very often that I wish for magic." I admit. My statement causes him to pull back, face filled with surprise. "But I wish I did, right now, to fix this." I whisper and wipe heavy tears from his soft, dark cheeks, then gesture to the mess around us.

Emeric smiles, then a small giggle escapes him. Those soft sunset eyes come *alive*, and he holds a steady hand up in the air between our chests. "Sometimes, you have to burn it all down to the ground, and start over again."

He snaps his fingers and sends the devastation around us into white flames, the heat feasting only on what he commands it to, leaving nothing but charcoaled ground.

Clear and ready to start over.

UNREQUITED LOVE

Alvis

I have an unrequited love for my best friend, and he's fucking the only other person I've thought about loving in twenty years.

Headquarters hasn't changed much over the years, except for one key detail. For my first year as Captain's Quartermaster, Novak and I shared a room during our short visits to Beakglen. After he left, I stayed there, transforming it into a hovel of self pity. When he came home with *Tzel* in tow, I cleaned it up and much to Novak's protest, told him he could have it. I took up the smaller room beside his, close but never close *enough*.

Tonight, I regret how thin the walls are.

Hours have passed since Umber ... fucked up. I don't know what happened. Orion and Emeric either, and Novak insists he or *Tzel* don't know what the Ancient was going on about. The thing is, Novak is lying. I can always tell; the way he subtly dips his chin and bites his cheek. I let it go, for now.

Instead of (un)intentionally eavesdropping, I recount the night in attempts to maintain my sanity. Novak had a mild lapse in control afterward the fire exploded, so I gathered an unconscious Lythienne in my arms and staggered upstairs, delivering her to where she belonged. I had debated on the bed or near the fireplace which sprung to life the moment I passed through the threshold, one of Captain's many charms in the place.

Lythienne shivered in my arms, long curls falling past her shoulder as she took hold of my charred tunic, making my decision for me. With some difficulty, exhaustion and frustration rolling through my bones, I settled on the floor near the hearth with Lythienne close to my chest. I freed the arm I had under her legs, gently lowering her thighs. I glanced at her prosthesis, deciding to leave that up to Novak.

Not my place.

But *oh*, how she curled into me and nuzzled her face into my chest with a pleased sigh. At that moment I remembered us on the cliffs, her saying how I smelled like home and how her body fit against mine, and it still makes my heart uneasy. Only one other person has told me that, and he's currently in the next room with her. I had, for a *stupid* moment, hoped he would've asked me to stay when he came back from his fight with *Tzel*.

Nova had only slunk down beside me and sighed, "Thank you."

"Of course. You alright?"

He raked a hand through his wild hair, bit his cheek before releasing an, "I'm fine."

There were no more words between us until Lythienne had started to stir, then my arms loosened around her and I said, "You two should probably talk. She's figured it out, you know, that you two are connected."

I don't, *won't*, say mated. I don't believe in that anymore. Connections, bonds. I believe in those. But not an end all, be all person. Never again. Novak's mate destroyed him, me, *everything*.

Novak sat up, his precious warmth leaving my side. He looked tired, defeated. Novak without the mask. I'd be lying if I said I didn't take pride in the fact I'm the only one he doesn't constantly pretend to be happy with. He just *is*, when it's just us.

"Connected." He echoed after a second, staring farther into my soul than he had in a long time. He chuckled darkly and looked down at Lyth's face, then brushed a curl away from her scarred cheek. "I suppose that's more fitting, isn't it?"

"Here," With quiet movements, Lythienne was shifted from my lap to his. I stood over them for a moment, heart twinging at the loss of both their bodies against mine. The empty bed I would have to return to. Umber's absence filled the air around me. Novak looked up to me, lips parted, and I *swear* the words, '*Stay, Alvis,*' were there.

But I couldn't bear to see his mouth close, swallowing my hopes and dreams, so I turned away first. I opened the door and hesitated, the opportune moment for my fate to change.

"Al," Nova called, and I looked over my shoulder, finding firelight reflecting the tears streaming down his freckled cheeks. "I can't do this to her. I'm ... evil. I told myself *no* love for a *reason*."

I close my eyes and roll over in bed, burying my face in the pillows to shut away the fresh memory of rushing to his side and telling him 'no, no you're not evil, just be honest, it's her choice, just talk to her, it's ok, I'm here for you, it's ok to love her.'

And of course that calmed him down, which my rattles my heart against it's cage.

A shift in the air thick with humidity and sex perks my head from freshly laundered silk pillow cases, courtesy of dear Emeric. Magic, pure and volatile and *intense* washes through the room, seeping through the wall from Novak's room. I sit up and put my ear to the wall, biting my lip as I do. Indiscernible whimpers, moans and sweet words are crystal clear, whatever magic this is practically eliminates the sound barrier between us when I press my ear to the wall.

"Let me see you come," Novak orders fiercely, in a tone I've never heard from him. A combination of beast and Fae, something that should bring about fear but only arouses me. I push away from the wall with a pounding heart. Of course, my cock and my head are on different pages and it's ready to fuck. Novak's had sex since me, *when* exactly I have no idea but he told me through rosy cheeks and slurred words one night in Echo over drinks, fifteen years after *Tzel* moved in.

He had been whining that I left him behind the night before to meet up with Umber. I was pissed, his wild mood swings and long held stares full of desire followed by cold shoulders had been getting under my skin for quite some time. It hurt my heart too much to actually hope his lust filled looks meant something. I kicked his boot off my lap, told him, "Get laid, it'll do you some good."

Novak had been leaning back in his chair and nearly fell backwards but recovered in a swift, shadowed movement. He cupped his summer burnt face in his hands and rested dirty elbows on the small table between us, usually bright sapphire eyes were shaded by *Tzel's* darkness. I've learned the signs of when it's close to the surface, and I often bring it out in him.

He licked his cracked lips and I watched, which he didn't miss. A devious grin full of danger and dimples made way for words fermented in alcohol and amusement, ones I've never forgotten. "I've fucked since us, you know? Kept my head the *entire* time. Had to prove I could do it, first. He, *it,* didn't even care, but boy does he *fucking hate* you."

My jaw had worked open and closed, then I settled on an off handed joke and patted him on the shoulder. To top the night off, I carried him to the ship after he puked on my shoes. He was beyond drunk and I was afraid to ask what he meant by 'first'. I've been standing on the edge ever since, wondering if he meant, 'I had to fuck someone I didn't care about first, so I could see if it was possible with you.'

But he *does* care about Lyth, I am abruptly reminded by a deep, purring groan through the wall. What a *fucking* mess. Will he lose control? Will he hurt her? My moral compass is spinning wildly.

Should I listen?

The angry, bitter part of me says, "Fuck him, he tells you he *can't* love but he's fucking her hours later? Sounds like he *wants* you to listen, who else is making that magic?"

The softer side of me says, "You don't have to listen, but no one would fault you for using your imagination. You're alone, and there's nothing wrong with loving yourself."

So, I do.

I sit with my back to the headboard and untie my pants, breathing heavily as Lythienne's cries break through. *She* is definitely not holding back, even without pressing my ear to the wall I can hear her *begging* Novak for more. I close my eyes and after a second of guilty anticipation icing my veins, I take hold of myself and turn my head so my ear is closer to the wall, but not touching.

It amplifies sound all the same. The sound of bodies slick with sweat slapping together, Lythienne whining for Novak to just *fuck* her. Dark laughter fills my ear as he responds with a taunt, then a soft *smack* and I can picture the way her ass would ripple with it. Dimpled and soft, her skin untouched by the sun would flush *red*. Hot magic fills my nostrils and my pace quickens, tightening as the perfect scenario unfolds in my mind's eye.

We're in bed, all three of us. Lythienne on her back, pillows under her hips and full thighs wrapped around Novak's slender waist. Her lips on mine, my cock rubbing against the mattress to get some *much* needed friction while Nova tenderly strokes in and out of her, one of his hands in my hair as my tongue plays with Lyth's.

She bites my bottom lip and I moan when she sucks on it, then she pulls away with a mischievous smile and murmurs, "Are you going to fuck the bed all night, or will you at least take my mouth?"

Novak chuckles, and when I lean back his hand leaves my hair to palm her full breast, his other hand has her hip in a bruising grip. His thrusting hips slow when I lean back on my heels, flushed cock on display. "By the Ancients," Lythienne breathes, reaching up with a question in her black and white eyes, small hand close but not close *enough* to the warmth leaking from the head of my shaft.

All the while, Novak absorbs her absolute reverence for me with pure admiration in his eyes, which are flickering from black to blue, and back again. The universe blankets his skin, stars replacing freckles as he lets part of himself go. "Isn't he beautiful?" Nova asks her, eyes flashing up to mine. He swallows upon making direct contact, adam's apple bobbing heavily.

I can't speak, my entire body is bathed in the heated stare of both my lovers. Every muscle stretches taut with anticipation, my hands slide down my darkly haired thighs to cup either side of Lythienne's face.

"Yes, he is." Lythienne whispers, big eyes full of lust and a need to be loved blink up at me. "May I have you, Alvis? I want you, so much." Her and Novak's words are an answered prayer, my worth validated by someone who wants more than to fuck me for pleasure. They *love* me, and *oh* how I've needed someone to love me.

"Please do, my Keeper. But say the word, and we stop." I exhale, thumb brushing over her cheek as she tilts her head back in response. I lean forward and meet Novak's hand on her hip, our fingers interlace when she takes me in her mouth and I gasp, squeezing tightly. In this dream, the word is the same as it was for Novak and I.

Dom. Stop.

Self restraint is a brittle thing. I want to absolutely ruin her, take her apart and fill her up with nothing but Novak and I. I don't know how she lived, or loved, in the Mountain, but her gaze has run red hot since the moment we met. My suspicion that she is not a gentle one is confirmed when her hands slide past my hips to grab my ass and *pull*, filling her throat with my thick cock which inadvertently hardens further, gagging her.

Lythienne has full body shivers and before I can pull back, Novak mercilessly thrusts into her cunt once and she cries out around me, short nails digging into my skin. She doesn't move to pull away and my hand leaves her face to trail down her pale neck, then pinch her nipple. Her back arches and tongue darts around the middle of my cock. "You like it when he does that?" I ask, violet aether flaring in my eyes and softly lighting the dim room.

She responds with a subtle nod, earning a series of vicious thrusts from Novak. I study his face twisted with pleasure, absorbing the way his golden lashes sweep across his freckles and the way he licks his lips, nostrils flaring. I helplessly give my attention back to Lythienne, her throat working around me and breasts perking in the cold, mid summer night air between us.

"What a good girl, so honest." I moan, hand traveling from her milky breast to her thick middle, my callused fingers squeezing years of scars and softness. To her credit, she continues to suck me with wet efficiency, her vibrating cries have me on the edge already, and we've just begun. Another visible orgasm shakes her entire being, causing her mouth to clamp down and teeth to scrape my cock.

Fuck yes.

"Alvis, do *not* come yet." Novak *demands* without stopping. I tear my gaze from Lythienne's blown, wet eyes to Novak's, which are eerily black, but I can tell it's still him. I don't know this side of him, but *oh,* how I want to. It's been too long since I've been put in my place.

"Why?" I challenge, then my eyes flutter shut when Lythienne's fingers find my balls and gently *tug*. Her lips pull away from my cock.

"Because *I* want to fuck you, Alvis. Or are you not as energetic as you look?" Lythienne taunts. I flash a look back up to Novak and he nods with a sly smile.

With quick, careful movements, Novak leaves Lythienne and I pull her into my lap, her thighs wrap around my hips as her strong arms encircle my neck. I lean back with a firm hold of her ass, lilac curls flow over her breasts and tickle my flexing pectorals. My shaft presses against her warmth, then slips and slides across her wet center. Her fingers trace the scars along my clavicle, neck and jaw, then she looks up at me through her purple lashes.

"Tell me, what way have you thought of having me?" Lythienne whispers, her voice a drug I've gone too long without.

"This, us, I—"

I gasp, previously too entranced to notice Novak situating himself under Lythienne, his wild blonde hair tickles between my legs. He takes hold of my cock and slips me inside Lyth, who instantly begins riding me. I know that she's strong and uses her core muscles more than I could ever dream of, but holy *fuck,* these two will be the death of me. They work in tandem to overwhelm me with pleasure and I am helpless against it, at first. Novak's tongue occasionally swipes my cock as I slide in and out of her tight cunt, his fingers explore between my shaft and balls.

Something awakens inside of me finally and I take the lead, fingers digging into her thick thighs as I slam her up and *down* onto my cock, seating myself fully inside her. "Oh, fuck!" Lythienne cries, burying her face into my neck and biting the hollow between my jaw and shoulder. I shudder, grinding my pelvis against hers with desperate need. "That's it, ah, yes, more, *please*." She begs, then sucks on the skin under my chin, bites at my adam's apple for good measure as she starts to ride me again, needing the length of my cock to gently withdraw, then *pound* back into her.

I will never be able to tame her, and I don't want to.

"Nova, move." I rasp, then lay Lythienne down on her side when he does, cock never leaving her. Novak supplies a pillow under her hip then kneels at her side, hand in her hair and smiling lips on hers. I take hold of her thigh and hold it close to my chest. "Does this feel ok?"

Novak leans back so she can answer, lithe hand on his cock which I *want*. "Good, you are so good to me." She nods, then bites her plump bottom lip. "But, there's something I want to try."

"What's that, love?" I ask, kissing the scarred end of her thigh which causes her spine to arch and a gasp to leave her heaving chest. Novak watches with soft satisfaction, stickiness leaking from him as he absently strokes himself.

"You want him, don't you?" Lythienne smiles coyly at Novak as she wiggles her hips and clenches her muscles, drawing a moan from my lips. My attention flicks between her and Novak, heart jumping in anticipation.

"You have no idea, my lady." Novak admits darkly, black eyes catching on mine. "Alvis? Do you want me? Still?"

My heart cracks and I lock it away. "Always, Nova. Come here."

And he does.

Nova kneels behind me, his hands settle on my hips. I tilt my head back, exposing my throat to him, the opposite side Lythienne had marked. He isn't gentle when he nips me though, he *knows* me.

"Just take me," I tell him, and he does.

"Not yet," He whispers, and his teeth *sink* into the taut muscle connecting neck to shoulder. My hips work of their own stuttered accord and Novak is everywhere, hands exploring the body that once belonged to him, teeth and lips and tongue claiming every inch of my back, neck and sides.

"Stop holding back!" Lythienne shouts, one hand at her breast and the other tangled into her hair. "Please!"

"I've got you, *ahuvi*, let go." Novak whispers, tugging on my ear lobe. Even in a dream I'm restrained, but I dutifully obey them both.

Hips work violently, my free hand slaps Lyth's away from her breast and I pinch her nipple, then swat her tit. She cries my name and comes harder than before, practically milking my fucking cock. It's all I can do to not stop my movements. "You like that, you dirty little slut?" I breathe, earning a series of kisses from Novak down my tingling spine.

"Another, *please*." She whimpers and I oblige, drawing a delightful red to her pale skin. "More, Alvis. Mark me, make me yours."

Warmth swims in my core and I raise my hand. Novak's fingers slide past the bottom of my spine, waiting. My hips stutter forward to a temporary stop when his lips meet the nape of my neck. "Alvis?" He asks, practically singing my name.

"Please, Nova."

"Such a good boy for me." I open my lips to say that's my line, but his fingers slide into my mouth. Lythienne's lips part as she watches me suck on them, she tightens around my paused cock with anticipation building in her warmth. When he pulls away, saliva clings to his fingers and Lyth swallows, hips arching up when Novak's lips touch down on the point of my shoulder. His hand slides down to my ass and I thrust into Lyth involuntarily. Novak laughs against my skin and Lythienne chuckles at my eagerness.

They say sex isn't good if you don't laugh at some point, which I wholeheartedly agree with. The three of us share a moment of giddiness, the fact that this is *actually* happening, we are delving into the darkest, deepest part of ourselves and sharing them with each other, naked in body and soul.

Novak fingers slide closer to my hole and I-I-

I moan into the empty darkness, thrusting into my slick hand one last time as I release in thick ropes of sticky warmth. I ejaculate harder than I have in years, even with a partner, and my hips jerk upwards for another thirty seconds before my adrenaline, cock and mind come back down from the incredible high. For a moment, everything is right and warm and wonderful, then I open my eyes.

I'm alone.

The room is quiet and the wave of foreign magic is receding to wherever it came from. I inhale the scent of lavender and ocean before it's gone, then proceed to clean myself up. I sit on the edge of my bed, naked and partially satisfied. I stare at my wiggling toes on the hardwood floor, wondering if such fantasies could actually exist after this journey.

He kept his head, even with someone he cared about. Perhaps that bodes well for me, there's a *chance* he will let me back in, stop being so afraid of himself. The familiar stab of jealousy that a stranger cracked open his heart within days when I've been trying for years passes once again, but I swiftly dampen it.

For the first time in two decades, Novak's genuine face breaking smiles are present daily, like when I first met him, and I can't fault Lythienne for that. Maybe it was easier for her to break down his defenses, *because* they don't have history.

As much as I don't want to, I get dressed in fresh lounge pants and leave the safety of my bedroom. I step into the quiet hall, relieved no light spills out from underneath Novak's door. The hair on the back of my neck stands up as I make my way to the kitchen. I wait for Orion to find me as I pour myself a glass of water, by the time I finish drinking and spilling half of it on my bare chest, he settles into a stool at the kitchen bar.

I pour him a glass of water and glance at the clock, midnight.

"Alright, then?" He asks evenly after taking a drink, then rests his chin on knitted fingers with vines of white swirling through his dark skin. Orion's violet eyes are hazy, but he wasn't sleeping, either. I try not to dive into his mind but it doesn't take much to gather he just finished his own rendezvous with Emeric. Orion's face gives nothing away, but my soul had accidentally called to its other half like it always does when I'm in pain.

I chuckle, shaking my head at the absurdity of ... everything.

"Yeah, I'm fine."

HURT THE PEOPLE I LOVE

Lyth

After a couple more nights of warm food, baths with Novak and a farewell party in the Beakglen square, we say a tearful goodbye to Emeric. Lexeran never returned and the most I learned on the subject was a quick whisper from Orion during the party last night. Lex lives as a wanderer, and as I suspected, he and Novak haven't been on the best terms.

We've been on the trail north for a few hours now, the mood silent and solemn ever since we departed the warm Beakglen. I'm still curious what the others asked for, but know better than to pry. Despite the physical rest we've all earned, it seems our impending journey is on everyone's mind. Rolling farmlands continue well after we pass through the invisible border of Terra, and as we near the town Pan once called home, the reality of seeing him again is heavy on my mind. Novak is plucking his lute and leaning back on his horse, smiling at me whenever I find his face. Worry lingers in the bruised skin under his eyes, and I figure he's been thinking about Pan too.

I turn my thoughts to last night, cheeks warming as I do. He wouldn't let me touch him until I had come over and *over* first. Only once I was an absolute puddle of pleasure did he make love to me. *Deep*, intentional sex, and before he came his skin feathered out into ethereal night, like every time thus far, but I haven't seen his magnificent wings again. Each time our bodies join the connection between us grows stronger, but still isn't quite the same as when I first felt it.

I want to ask him if he can hear my heart thundering for him through the bond between us, like how I can hear his own nervous pulse. I can feel his warm shadows caress the depths of my spirit deeper and deeper each day, our darkness intertwining further to form a growing bridge between our souls. A seed of doubt plants in my heart that perhaps he won't ever allow himself to feel the bond, and his own trepidation is what dampens the connection. After all, he turned down the male he loves because of fear, and somehow I've broken through Novak's walls.

And what right do I have to do that?

I have his love, his courage, and that is enough. I don't need him to believe in some Aether bond, even though I very much do. I decide to focus on the area around us, and our journey ahead. We plan to stop for dinner in the approaching town Panrauth used to occupy and camp on the outskirts of the Great Tree. For now, the expansive fields shrink into small meadows hugged by meticulous lines of trees. Then, the clearings disappear entirely, overarching trees ferrying us into another world.

A dense forest of ferns and mushrooms the size of oak trees hide the sky, composing the first layer of canopy overhead. The ground is a litter of leaves, saplings and shrubbery fighting for sunlight, the skittering of foliage the only clue to life. My favorite part of the luminous forest so far are the bright mushrooms.

Some cluster on bark and provide homes to shy pixies and other tiny creatures, others rival the trees themselves with webbed mycelium ranging every color. Some are short and fat, like ale barrels with a thick dress that teases the ground. For a moment I debate stopping to test their strength and sit upon one. They certainly appear sturdy enough, but about the time I gain my courage we encounter the horrors waiting for us.

Skeletal, charcoaled remains of a cottage is the only structure left standing. Overgrowth and wildflowers have crept over the home, but it's still eerie. In the surrounding clearing, foundations of once proud and cobbled buildings are crushed into dust and pebbles. I shudder as we ride by, sure I can hear Weylin's screaming and the thud of her head rolling onto the ground under Fiddler's hooves. Even with dusk fast approaching, we wordlessly continue for another twenty minutes. About the time I shed the feeling of ghosts watching us, Fiddler's ears relax and he is more than happy to stop.

We make a small camp and decide to stay the night here, and before too long, Alvis has a rabbit crisping over the fire Novak's started. We situate around the flames and conversation finally begins, Orion's quiet voice breaking the ice. "That place felt like pure evil."

"Before the Princess' reign began, her father ordered the entire human town to be punished for Weylin's actions." Alvis remarks as he takes the rabbit off the fire, scarred face set into stone.

"That's horrible." I say, tucking my knees to my chest. Novak is cross legged beside me, eyes fixated on the fire instead of the twins across from us. "Why does no one talk about it? I've only heard about ..."

"About Water Fae." Novak finishes my sentence and my fingers creep across the grass between us, meeting his. He doesn't look at me but holds my hand, the firelight reflected in his black eyes. No blue, no good feeling. It strikes me then, how lucky I am to have Aetherless eyes. If I want to hide how I was feeling, it would be quite easy. But Fae have magic betraying them.

Alvis' darken to a stormy dark blue when he's pissed, and lighten to the brightest violet when he laughs.

Orion's don't dim very often, usually a soft lilac that matches my hair.

Captain's range from bright red to orange, then pink. I can never tell what she's thinking, even with magical eyes to clue me in.

And Novak. His are the brightest sapphires and they almost seem to *spark* with an icy blue flame. But times like now, when he's nervous or on the edge of sanity (because I'm quite convinced he's far more melancholic inside than he tends to express), his eyes are *black*. The sclera are off white, the only difference between his eyes and my own. I have no iris, but he does. Two black holes into a world of pain.

"Do you think over time, their ghosts will become like the Noxious?" I ask Alvis when he stands over us with two plates.

"Unfortunately, I do. Despite the grandness of Aether, it cannot help the dead, or reverse the course of death." I nod and take both plates from him. Novak is still stuck in a trance and had let my hand go without hesitation. I glance back up to Alvis whose dark eyes flash briefly in the twilight as they catch mine. I subtly nod to Novak and Alvis ruffles Novak's hair before he turns to leave, lightly pulling Novak from his stupor.

"*Ai*, it's messed up enough as it is." He swats Alvis away with a half smile and takes his plate from me, only to set it on the ground beside him. I bite my cheek and listen in silence as they discuss the route from the Grand Tree to Silverbury and how to avoid the main villages in Sylvan. Orion matches my silence and doesn't even try to pretend to eat like I am.

It's time. Warmth pricks my neck and my heart flutters before I speak with false confidence. "I appreciate everything you two have done for me, but you're not going to Sylvan with us."

Orion and Alvis face me at the same time, identical hurt displayed across their sharp features. "And why not?" Orion snaps. Alvis straightens and I focus on my hands, afraid I will break under his resolve. Fucking bastard gets under my skin. This business of feelings is too complicated.

"I've never had true friends before, but I know I wouldn't be one to either of you, if you came." The thought of them *not* coming hurts just as much as the thought of them being torn apart. Novak's visible warm shadows slip behind my back, a comforting touch. He's the one who needs comforting right now, not me.

"And we wouldn't be true friends if we didn't." Alvis spits, still furious at the mere suggestion, and rises to stalk off through the woods.

"We're coming, end of discussion." Orion's blunt and final words fold my ears down. He snatches up his bedroll and Alvis', then leaves us to find his brother now disappeared into the dusky woods. I scowl at the fire, Novak pokes at it every now and then in uncharacteristic silence. After a while, he lays out both our bedrolls and slips off his shirt, then beckons me over to lay beside him. I oblige, nestling into his bare chest with a huff.

"You won't get rid of them so easily, you know." Novak teases in a whisper, pulling a fur over our heads. I sigh in relief and close my eyes, breathing in sea salt. Always sea salt. Delicate fingers brush purple from my cheeks, then he twirls a lock around his finger, a tendril of darkness intertwining with it. The vial on my neck pulls me from my comfort, and the worries of Sylvan flood me.

"I can't fathom it. I try to imagine Typhan worse than anything I've heard so far, and they're still going back. I don't want them to get hurt."

"He *is* worse than anything you've heard of. You've only known them for a short time, but I think it's safe to say if you will walk into the Eternal for them, they will do anything for you." Novak chuckles, taking my hot silence as confirmation. "Alvis thinks you're the best thing since Aether, and I'm pretty sure if you didn't have Orion's heart before you met Emeric, you sure did after."

Color flushes my cheeks at his words. "It's just hard to wrap my head around this *friends* thing. This mates thing." I chuckle, tracing his cheek with a soft finger.

He smiles, eyes glazing a bit. "The more I think about it, the more I think you're right."

"You don't think we're mates?" I feign hurt, gasping. He doesn't want to admit it, but he doesn't deny it either. I'll take what I can get. Novak kisses me softly, and I respond by biting his lip.

"You're such a brat, don't you ever get tired of being put in your place?" His cradle of shadows hiding us from the world flashes black for a moment. The call of seductive darkness, and I *cannot* resist. I shake my head and lower my lips down his bare chest, tracing his scars with my tongue. I nip at his stomach, pulling the light hair at his pant line with my lips while I undo the button.

"*Lyth*, here?" Novak's desperate whisper pricks my ears, but I've already released what I want, and he's ready.

"You better be quiet." I take his hard length in my hand, stroking with a loose grip up, and then tighten subtly when I go down. I lick his shaft, curving my tongue around his pulsing thickness. "How do you want it?"

Firm hands find me and he tries to pull me up, his voice hoarse. "No, you first."

"I *said*, how do you want me to suck you?" I tease his tip with just my lips, defiantly staring up at him.

"I want to be so far down your throat, you're gasping for air."

Fuck yeah.

I take him in my mouth and he hardens further when my tongue flicks around, following down his shaft. A deep rumble emits from his chest and he tangles a hand in my hair. I moan, the sound vibrating his shaft. My hand slides up his thigh, then gently cups his balls. He gasps and thrusts involuntarily into my mouth, begging to reach my throat. My other hand wraps around the bottom of his shaft, moving in time with my mouth. I can't quite take him all, but he's writhing under me and only lasts for a couple minutes.

"Fuck, Lyth. Get up here, now." Novak snarls and I obey immediately, straddling him and taking his length, needing him in me now.

We both moan when he enters. I sit up and shed the blankets covering us. The moons light our bodies, his handsome face is filled with pure delight as I slowly ride him, my full breasts glowing under the stars. The knees of my prosthesis hum quietly on either side of him, and his hands guide my hips with gentle assistance like he has before. I love that he lets me take the lead and doesn't coddle me.

For a brief, *brief* moment, I wonder who took the lead between him and Alvis.

I shudder, clenching around Novak as my hips stutter for a moment. "How are you so perfect?" Novak moans, taking a cold breast in his hand, the other holding onto my thick hip. "You are beyond anything I deserve." He groans with such ferocity I come the moment his primal tone meets my ears.

The shadows around us flicker from charcoal to black when I cry out his name, my hips pausing as a shudder erupts through me. When I focus back on his face, he's shaking his head softly and fighting the black overtaking his eyes. Both hands dig into the skin of my waist, *desperate* to make me his plaything. I lean down and whisper into his snow fluffed ear, drawing a shudder from him.

"I rather like your shadows. Let them come out and play."

Novak trembles under me, taking my round cheek in his hand. He is worried again, like the first time, and I realize he wasn't scared that he might hurt me with his *size*, but with his Aether. Even though we've loved each other while he's completely ethereal, he's still holding back *something*.

"I'm, afraid ... what'll happen if I do."

"Please, for me." I ask tenderly, my lips lingering on his. "I'm not afraid."

Novak sits up while still inside me, wrapping his arms around me and holding me close to his chest. He kisses my nose, then nods ever so slowly. He's settled deeper inside me than before and I squirm a bit, nails biting into the nape of his neck.

"*Fuck*, sometimes, I don't think I can handle all of you." I whisper a heated taunt into his ear, tempting the beast.

A dangerous grin reveals his full multitude of dimples. The white of his eyes disappear and the deep oceanic blue in his eyes snuff out, the darkness remaining matches my own dark abyss. Well, that's new. Shadows pour around him, his warm river of night and stars block out the moons, and the *real* sky. A firm, ethereal hand tangles in my hair, yanking my face upwards while he teases my neck with a light tongue.

"You *really* shouldn't have told me that." A distorted rumble vibrates the artery pounding in my neck. His voice is different, and the sickly sweet Aether emanating from him is twice as powerful, dizzying my mind and clouding my vision.

This is *not* the same Fae I held moments ago.

My heart skips and I pulse around his shaft waiting patiently inside me. Hungry lips find mine, kissing me with such reckless abandon my heart aches with ... *longing*. Like it's been ages since we've kissed and I need him *right* now. The whisper in the forgotten part of my mind stirs, finding his dark presence curious.

"Why not?" I challenge onto his lips, my words cause his mouth to leave mine with haste. Teeth threaten my neck once more and my breasts ache, nipples hardening against his chest.

"Mmm. I remember this." The voice in my mind strengthens, but she stays in the background.

I attempt to rock my hips with impatience. He chuckles, releasing my hair only to grab me firmly by my chin. The rustle of wings unfurling catches my attention, and my breath. Individual shadows compose hundreds, maybe even *thousands*, of charcoal feathers, green mixing in them like Virgil's does, but this wingspan extends at least fifteen feet into the night sky.

"Quit. It." He orders, letting out a devilish smile that quirks the galaxies in his cheeks. I obey and am mid-stare at the stars speckled throughout his wings when I become brave, and my fingers brush a very real feather. He throws me back on the ground in a solid movement, so quick I cannot comprehend, and yet so carefully nothing is hurt. A strong hand holds my hands above my head, and the other lifts my hips, like Novak does.

The soft jawline is the same. The slightly crooked nose is the same. His hair is black, but falls in curls all the same and is a few inches longer than before.

"Are you ready, my lady?" He asks, his strong voice seeming to awaken the ground beneath us. Wings filled with the universe outstretch over top of us, spreading to twice the size they were before. He waits for my command, and I let a moment pass. Then another. Familiarity radiates from every part of his being, and the parasitic voice attached to my soul sighs with content when I finally speak.

"Yes," I whisper.

With a rustle of wings and a fatal smile, he gives me no quarter, and nowhere to go. I shake under the rolling waves, his thrusting so deep and intense I swear we are burning a hole into the ground. His hand is firm on my wrists, but gentle enough he doesn't hurt me. I arch my back and press my breasts into him, a satisfied, thunderous groan shakes the earth beneath us.

"What are you doing?" I breathe out when he slows a bit, my desperate words pulling a smile and halting his movements entirely.

"I like to watch you squirm." Pools of pitch black ocean stare into my eyes, and I finally see what everyone else sees when they look at me. It's beautiful, on him.

"Don't stop now." I taunt. I'm not scared of him, this side of Novak, whatever this is. A primal force of unmet need, followed by Aether like nothing I've ever heard of. A part of his soul he has buried for far too long, perhaps. Because ... this *is* him, right?

What truly scares me is I won't get my musician back.

And what will happen after?

Anytime his deepest shadows make an appearance, he's scared out of his wits and distraught after.

And Alvis always saves him.

The Shadow of Novak releases my hands held above, his wings tucking in slightly when his careful fingers find my cheeks. "Something wrong?" He asks, distorted and sweet.

Surprised, I lay a tender kiss on his lips composed of starlight, leaving truth there. "No, I just can't believe how beautiful you are."

"I've missed you, my lady." His words, they ... Tears spring to my eyes and I leave a whisper in his ear, causing a shudder to erupt from him, his shaft paused inside me.

"Show me."

There is little trace of the gentle bard I know when he releases his pleasure. The figure of shadows snakes his arms around me and latches onto my neck with a territorial *bite*. For a moment, I wonder if he will tear through me. I cry out, the wave that pounds through my body is one of utter pleasure and pain, but soon searing pain takes over when he doesn't release.

"Novak!"

Warmth drips down my shoulder and rough arms hold me close while he pumps deep inside, then he finally releases my neck. The moment he finishes, the night composing his skin slinks away faster than it had appeared. A violent quake overtakes him and I catch a glimpse of wings disappearing followed by a flash of blue eyes, and Novak struggles to keep from collapsing atop me.

"Are you alright?" I ask, my voice seems to center him. He steadies himself on a shaky arm and shakes his head, groaning like he had just woken up after being knocked out. When our eyes meet, terror and shame fills the freckled features I know. His dripping, crimson lips and the stabbing pain in my shoulder confirms what I guessed.

He drew blood, and not just a little bit.

Novak doesn't say a *word*, leaving me long enough to slip pants on and find my clothing. The silence is unnerving, perhaps more so than the event itself. Everything was fine, until the end. "Listen, I asked. Look at me." I will my voice steady, even though so many questions are fighting to be asked.

"You didn't know what you were asking. I shouldn't have listened." Novak snaps quietly, running a hand through his hair before using his stray shirt to clean up my shoulder with tender care. He mutters under his breath, lips moving a mile a minute but words indiscernible. After a minute passes, he was never talking to me.

"Please, look at me." The musician with now light blue eyes and a bloodied mouth with no smile to be found glares at me through the blond locks overhanging his sullen face. "I love you, now fuck off and hug me." I wrap my arms around his neck and he stills for a moment, then pulls me into his lap.

"I'm not supposed to hurt the people I love." He whispers into my hair, a cautious hand petting my tresses.

"I need to know, I need to know all of it."

Novak pushes out a breath, arms loosening. In case I want to leave. "When the Ancients brought me back, something was put inside, with me, my soul." He pats his chest firmly, then shakes his head. "Not just shadow magic, but, something else. A demon of sorts, or that's how I think of it. I truly have no idea what it is, other than a massive dick."

He searches my face for fear. Finding only curiosity, he continues in a whisper, "I've learned how to control it, but it still tries to come out. I'm not a fighter, I'm not *that*. Or I try not to be." His eyes pause on my now covered shoulder, and the puzzle pieces fall into place. "I can barely hold it back when we're together. When you told me to let go, I couldn't," He catches a hand through his tangled hair once more. "I couldn't do it anymore. For a split second I lost control, and look at what I've done."

"Do you feel better now?" I ask, and surprise slaps across his face.

"I tore you apart and you're asking if it made me feel better?" Anger draws his brows together. When I don't say anything, he averts his eyes, avoiding an answer.

"*Quit* looking away." I snap and his broken gaze settles back on me, relief washing through his eyes for a moment. He *wants* to be punished for releasing what he holds otherwise so well.

He stopped fighting, and I bet it felt so *good*.

"I'm not going to stop loving you. I love you, every facet of you, even the darkest side. And I'm *telling* you, you don't have to hide from me. I'm still not leaving." I take his freckled cheek in a tender hand, running my thumb over his soft skin. "No matter what."

"Lyth, I don't understand you." Novak whispers, pressing his forehead to mine. "Why would you ever want to be with the keeper of such a *thing*?" His sentiment hits home and Novak realizes what he said, biting his cheek the moment his words tumble out.

He is with a Keeper of Death, does he expect me not to find comfort with his demons?

"Give the beast a chance, I kind of like him." I tease, hoping it will draw out a smile.

Novak rolls his eyes, a huff of relief leaves his chest. "*It's* monstrous, perhaps you can teach the thing some manners." He grumbles, kissing me with caution.

"Perhaps I will." I smile and finally receive one in return.

"If anyone can, it's you."

Novak rests in silence, exhaustion lies under his glazed eyes. I wake to him staring at my bruised shoulder and playing with my hair. Rays of dawn are breaking through the canopy, illuminating the woods around us. After spending minutes cradled in his heated shadows and silence, I reach my hand out, beckoning a tendril of night. The darkness follows my fingertips, flowing over Novak's chest as it creeps towards my face. His Aether washes over me completely, the softest blankets imaginable.

"I didn't know it could be so warm, and comfy." I nestle further into him and release a sigh of content.

Novak chuckles, watching me cuddle with the vine of night. I giggle when the shadows tickle my cheek, but they drift away when Novak speaks for the first time since I awoke. "No bad dreams?" Hoarseness fills his voice, he holds a small smile at the corner of his lips, but the glistening in his eyes betray him.

"Slept like a baby." I grin and kiss him deeply, my swollen lips already calling to him. He rolls his eyes dramatically, pulling away from my hunger for a moment.

"Starting trouble too soon, Keeper of Shadows." Novak traces the scar on my left cheek, smirking a bit at the name.

"I quite like that." I admit and lay kisses across his bare chest.

"I have something else you might like." Novak whispers, gently taking my chin and lifting my hot gaze to his softened eyes.

"Then give it to me." I pout, and my pathetic whining is all it takes for him to lay me down and slip my pants off. Within moments he's massaging my wet clit, then stroking down my center.

"Oh, I will." Novak promises, the Shadow nowhere in sight. He's already bare chested and I attempt to reach down and pull his pants off, but am quite distracted.

"I'm already there, love, give me what I really want." I murmur breathlessly.

A tender smile rests on his face, taking in the sight of my shuddering body before he obeys my command. He slides his pants down around his knees, then sinks deep into me with a slow, fluid motion, a hand lifting my hair as the other slides under my shoulders. I whimper and grab his neck, begging him down to pay my breasts attention.

He leaves a lingering kiss upon each nipple, but his tanned hands are desperate to feel the rest of my body. My free hand tangles in his ever growing, honeyed hair, and I arch into each sensation he gives me. Slowly, he brings tender kisses along the other side of my neck, across my jaw, and up to my lips. So much kinder, gentler than he was last night. I don't mind.

The way we meld together and explore every inch of the other, it's the kind of love you make when you aren't sure if it will be the last. The last time you hear your name on your lover's lips. The last time their skin presses against yours. The last time their arms wrap around you.

I absorb every feeling, every noise he makes while he keeps his meaningful, *deep* rhythm, his delicate lips continuing to search my body. I love the way his freckles catch the first rays of sunlight and how his hair is constantly tousled, hiding those bright sapphires I've come to love so much.

This feels like goodbye.

"I love you, Novak. Always."

Novak kisses me breathlessly, and when he answers I come with him, holding onto the Fae I love for dear life. "Always, Lythienne."

I'M NOT AFRAID OF YOU

Alvis and Orion have breakfast and snickering grins ready when we find them waiting for us in their camp. I had decided to wear a short sleeved tunic and the jerkin, my usual gear covers my bruised shoulder just fine. I settle next to Orion and devour two plates as Novak finishes his one from across me, and he raises a brow.

"*Listen*, you grow up on dry food for 236 years, and then complain about my manners." I snap, but Novak rolls his eyes with a smile.

"I just assumed spending the morning and night fucking made you hungrier than usual." Alvis teases me, then elbows Novak beside him. I wonder how much he heard, or *saw*. The musician's cheeks fill with color and I roll my eyes at Alvis, a half smile leaving me.

"It's your fault, you can take just about anything and make it taste brilliant." I say, drawing a satisfied grin from him. Chatter continues between the three, but I become lost in thought. I initially thought I was no more than a pretty thing to Alvis and he only has true eyes for Novak, but I can still feel the subtle tug we have on each other. His heart is calling to be loved, and mine aches in response.

He *deserves* to be loved.

Orion elbows me gently and I withdraw my stare from my untouched food, looking up to find Novak and Alvis wrestling on the opposite side of us in the dead leaves. "Alright there?" Orion asks, an arching dark brow raised.

"Yeah, fine." I say, then eat in silence and give him a smile before I leave the camp to find Fiddler. His quiet company is comforting and I sigh, pressing my forehead to his muscled shoulder. "I bet life is much easier as a horse, eh?"

Late afternoon brings sweltering misery. The windless woods trap every bit of heat and humidity around us. “Doesn’t it ever rain out here?” I complain, lifting my hair off my neck.

“Now that you mention it, I don’t think it has at all since we arrived.” Orion pushes his glasses up, then rubs his face and casts them askew once more. He and Alvis both have been unbothered by the slick heat until now, the thick summer air creeping into every place it can on all of us. I groan, wiping sweat from my brow.

“I could make it rain for you, Keeper.” Alvis yells from behind us, riding beside Novak.

“Spoiled Magical Fae.” I mutter, adjusting myself in the saddle. A spray of ice cold covers my back, shocking my body. “Fuck, *Al*!”

I glare at him, then at Novak snickering so hard his face is turning red. “Don’t look at me, it was his idea.” Alvis pleads, pointing to Novak who fully loses it. They’re both so ... happy. Their auras and eyes light, handsome faces unfractured by worry or harsh memories.

My scowling doesn’t last long, my laughter joins in with theirs. Orion removes all the water from my clothes with a wave of his hand, his gentle Aether tickling my body. Slowly, our group of misfits is starting to feel normal again.

When we cross the threshold of woods emptying into an emerald field, relief hits when a cool breeze licks my face for the first time today. Sweetness tickling my nose reminds me of pure Aether leaking straight from the machine. The mid-afternoon sun blinds me, and after my eyes adjust, I almost can’t believe the sight.

A grand hectare of deep green fields, dotted with wildflowers and small fruit trees. Dense forest encapsulates the area on five sides, we stand on the edge of trees opposite from the distant point of the pentagon. An epic tree rises from the center of the land, its size rivaling even the behemoth, miles wide archway of the Eternal Mountain. Full gold and green foliage flutters along its upwards twisting branches, caressing the low hanging clouds swirling around it. A single carriage wide path leads from where we stand to the shining castle situated in the tree, Arca Glen. The home of Terra Court.

“It’s beautiful.” I gasp, dismounting at the threshold where grass meets leaf covered ground. I drop to my vibrating knees in the green, hands hovering over silky blades. I shut my eyes and breathe in, listening to the songbirds call to each other with alert, flicking ears. Thirty seconds pass, and under my fingers a thudding vibration jolts my heartbeat, a group of riders are approaching.

“Lyth.” Novak warns.

I rise with a hand on my sheath, stance ready for a fight. A cold shiver runs down my spine when I lock eyes with Panrauth, mounted on a great steed akin to a white mountain goat. The curling dark horns reach beyond his master's face, the beast is almost as terrifying as the High Lord of Terra himself.

Indeed still the great bear, albeit tamed now as royalty. Now clean shaven and healthy, even his once glorious walnut hair is cut short. He is a stranger to me, but the green flames in his eyes I recognize, from our time in the Mountain. He's stripping me naked.

I raise my chin, I'm a different female meeting those hungry eyes than I was a week or so ago. (A week, that's all?) Tattoos are bare, my once pale skin is tanned now, softness fills my already wide curves. Captain's hat is atop my free flowing lilac hair, tendrils glowing in the sun and sprawling around my thick hips. I must be a sight.

Pan swings a leg over the front to dismount the beast and he drinks me in for one more tense moment before rushing the distance between us. Callused hands grab my cheeks and he kisses me with such intensity, I might faint. My toes almost leave the ground and the world spins for a moment, the Aether rolling from him is *intoxicating*.

The kiss only lasts long enough for my fingers to find the familiar black blade, the dagger meets his throat and I shove him backwards with it. I give him a wicked grin, my heart pounding so hard his ears flick up. There is no fear on his face, just wild delight. It's like we just met all over again.

"We have to stop meeting like this." I taunt, stepping back and wiping the blade on my pants before sheathing the dagger.

A dozen sentries are still poised with a multitude of arrows that targeted me the moment Pan touched ground, and I'm surprised they didn't fire when I drew blood. Alvis and Orion flank behind me, and Novak stands by my side with a satisfied smirk and *rolling* dark aura. The four soldiers in the center line directly behind Pan train their weapons on Novak as he steps closer to me. Panrauth wipes blood from his neck, chuckling when he spies it. He waves the soldiers off with a bloodied hand.

"I thought maybe you missed me." Panrauth smirks, crossing his crisped arms. I had expected him to be dressed in finery, but instead it appears he's stepped away from working in a field. Dirt stains his face and body, not unlike how soot used to. Plain working clothes line his figure, and his boots are worn.

"What's this nonsense I hear about my being a hero in these parts?" I chuckle, shaking my head when I cross my own inked arms and widen my stance.

"Why don't we have dinner, and find out?" A devilish grin quirks a corner of his lips.

I can't believe the way he is acting.

He left *me*.

Perhaps being a High Lord is already getting to his head.

"*We* have business to discuss, dinner sounds lovely." I gesture to my companions, sweetness tainting my voice as my hand rests on Novak's shoulder.

Pan's jaw twitches. "Anything for you."

As we follow the High Lord of Terra to the Great Tree, our group surrounded by sentries, I wonder if perhaps this isn't going to be as easy as I thought.

The sweet fragrance intensifies as we approach, and the reality of the cloud scraping tree settles in. The entrance into the heart of the tree is a giant, gnarled archway with a beckoning tunnel of near darkness. The sight reminds me of the Eternal. I marvel at the crowd around us pouring in fearlessly, winged Fae and pixies flying in and out of the entrance with no caution.

Several airships are docked in the simple ports on the right side of the arch, the engines floating off the ground and attached by rigging. I'm disappointed Captain's isn't there, but not surprised. From what I understand, the Great Tree itself accepts very few cross territory ships, let alone one run by a Fire Fae. Centuries ago a trade deal was made between Terra and Iron, using Dew Falls as a way point. Captain has always managed the route, even now.

Horses and carriages are much simpler, in my opinion. As much as I love flying, there is so much I would've missed on the ground. Perhaps one day I can traverse every part of it, by foot. Novak and I can visit Borealis together first, he's told me so many stories of that place. I think Dew Falls sounds lovely as well, but whenever I bring it up he seems to fade into his thoughts. We stable the horses in one of the well built barns situated to the left of the tree, then begin our journey inside.

The thick crowd of middle and upper class citizens part for Panrauth, the High Lord kindly nodding and greeting those he knows personally as we walk past. He is so different here, the mask of royalty he's fashioned for himself is quite impressive. The road is a smooth dirt path worn by feet traversing it all hours of the day, and the walls are a similar surface, as if we're going underground. Magnificent chandeliers of branches hang along the tunnel, holding golden and emerald faelights, brightening the darkness.

I hold Novak's hand tight, and for a moment I can hear his skipping heartbeat in my mind. Whether he does so knowingly or not, the connection silences once more when he gives me a halfhearted smile. My heart drops but for now I push away disappointment. The tunnel releases us in the hollow of the tree, the gorgeous expanse steals my breath and troubled thoughts away.

Small timber homes hug the stretching textured walls of the well lit hollow, residences of all sorts spiraling upwards along the inner, smooth bark. Homes resembling enormous flower bulbs hang from tendrils of a giant ivy that creeps through the outer edges of the space. I notice caverns are carved into the scattered free spots in the bark. Pixies and lesser Fae peek down from the catacombs, observing the mass of creatures puttering along the dirt floor below.

Rebellious ivy, beds of moss and giant mushrooms are scattered throughout the hollow. Our winding path extends to a village waiting in the center, hiding even more structures beyond it on a distant hill. Children bounce from green to purple fungi on a distant ledge a few stories up, and a couple can be found having a picnic atop an orange mushroom. The Great Tree is rich with prosperity and happiness, no lower class exists in this communal society.

My stomach twists, bile bubbling and nearly spilling onto my boots when I think about the males killing themselves in Echo over a shred of meat. The lack of Fire Fae here disturbs me as well, but not as much as the terrified stares Novak, the twins and I receive. I'm surprised, the sentiment we received in Beakglen was the complete opposite. After that first day, the villagers treated me just as warmly as they did my companions. Terra earned this privilege of wealth and peace by letting thousands upon thousands die. Failing their allies, their Ancients, and almost an entire species.

"Doing nothing can be worse, sometimes." The feminine voice inside me that has been mostly quiet company in the past few days surprises me, echoing Trihewyn's sentiment suddenly.

"Who are you?" I wonder in my mind, but find no response. My thoughts drift to what Novak told me about his demon, and what the Ancient said to us. I haven't given thought to the idea that what is stuck inside me may be related to what's stuck inside *him*. Although, to my credit, I didn't realize his Shadow Aether was from an *actual* demon, at first. Is that what's inside me, a demon? Demons are corrupt Ancients, cursed by their kin to live in a torturous place and suffer for all eternity. That doesn't sound like what either of us have, not really.

My contemplation is interrupted when Novak squeezes my hand, bringing my attention to the hill waiting beyond the village. At the end of our snaking path through bustling merchants, art studios, musicians and fine eateries, waits an epic dais, rivaling any I've seen yet. A round, steep mound of spongy moss holds the throne high above us, with blooming fields of lavender surrounding its base.

The smell from those flowers, *that* is the smell of Aether.

We follow the incline cutting through the intoxicating purple plants, coming to an exhausted halt at the top. I am quite thankful for Novak's hand steadying me as pain seeps into my bones. Orion and Alvis stand on either side of Novak and I, each giving me a small smile before putting on the mask of boredom and arrogance they must be known for here. Two thrones large enough to fit two Fae in each rest in open view for all the curious people below to gawk at. One of the thrones, Emeric's garden incarnate, is occupied.

An emerald skinned Fae dressed in a strapless gown of soft gold waits upon the throne of silver. The grand seat has entangled vines, violets and ivy trailing in every direction around her. Gold paint is smeared across the female's cheeks, highlighting broad cheekbones. A simple crown of gold and purple rests in her wild kinky brown hair. Furious air leaves me when I recognize her jade face, the full red lips and flashing eyes that match her brother.

You have to think ahead, something you're not very good at. Novak's words from the ship haunt me and I curse myself. I should've known.

The matching crown of violets adorning her arm sparks the intense anger running through my blood even further. Panrauth leaves the front of our group and stands by her side, the female unbothered to stand. An empty throne of dead thorns rests beside her eternal spring throne, pain threatening any who dare sit upon it.

How fitting.

"We meet again, Keeper of Death." The breathtaking Fae bows her head to me.

I remain unmoving, seething in place. She evaluates my companions uneasily, then focuses on my hand in Novak's. I squeeze tight before releasing him, and put on the mask of a Keeper of Death. I cross my arms and widen my small stance, rolling my shoulders back. I shake hair away from my face as I raise my chin. Black and white eyes stare at the Fae from under Captain's feathered hat. A purple brow raises, and a *sweet* smile spreads across my round cheeks.

"I prefer Lyth, less fancy."

Panrauth's roarous laughter booms across the dais, spreading down to the curious people gathered on the path behind us and scattered below. Those *beneath* him. "This will be fun indeed." Panrauth promises, and focuses on Novak when the musician throws an arm over my shoulder.

"So, I heard something about food?" Novak drawls. I have to bite my lip at his brashness. I raise a brow and glance at him with an amused look, which fades at once.

The Fae I love has a frightening nightmare swirling around him, his aura begging to become visible and release all of his darkness for the world to see.

A grand palace of bark covered rooms and halls, the High Court rests in the cloud scraping canopy of the Great Tree, or Arca Glen as it's called here. Luckily, an Aether powered elevator saves me from the trip, the contraption situated on a knoll to the left of the village below. I have always been curious how the territories spend their allotted Aether. I only ever saw numbers on paper in the Mountain. Input and output, not too much, not too little.

The fine line of power.

I wonder, what would you do with that kind of power? Eros' words came back to haunt me as I follow behind Vivvus, the princess of Terra.

I shudder at the thought of ever working with Eros. I already have power I don't know what to do with, or what to call it. The power of nothingness, and I certainly have no control over it. Definitely not just an aura. Perhaps tonight I will get a chance to study the page I borrowed from the Book of Teachings, and maybe Novak will know something about it.

Vivvus escorts us to our respective rooms, insisting we stay the night and resume our journey in the morning. Panrauth is behind us with several courtiers in the next elevator, his group splitting off on the landing above. Novak is given a room at the end of the hall, and the twins share a room between us. After sending the males off to dress for dinner, Vivvus shows me to the entirely too large bedroom that is mine. She hovers and chatters endlessly, pausing only when I'm silent for several minutes.

I peruse the guest room in silence. This court is much finer than our stay in The Mists. Elaborate decorations inspired by nature, and gold painting it all. The theme seems to keep with the vines and ivy creeping everywhere. I can only imagine the dripping wealth of Iron Court's castle, a place I'm sure is reminiscent of blood and death. I give my attention to the enormous bed frame crafted from raw wood, gnarls and knots showing off all their unique beauty. The mattress is so thick, I don't dare sit on it yet for fear I'll fall asleep instantly.

"I had a feeling you'd be coming. Pan didn't believe me, it feels so good to prove him wrong." Vivvus speaks again, softer and slower than before. Light green eyes are half hidden under the wild walnut curls elegantly stretching in every direction. Now that I've seen them together, I can see the similarity, despite the skin tone difference.

"Why didn't you tell me who you were that day?" I quip, shooting her a glare. I unpack my clothes onto the bed, pausing for a moment when my fingers meet the velvet dress I brought from Hallowed.

Vivvus shrugs, looking over her gold painted nails. "I didn't feel like it."

My brows furrow together and I cross my arms, staring at her. "If you're here to play games, I would rather be left alone."

"You know, you're exactly as Pan described. You're all he talked about for the first few days back." Vivvus moves closer, the paint on her cheeks catch the glow from the golden sconces along the walls.

"Did he mention the part when he left with hardly a goodbye?" I snap, coming face to face with her. My heavy breathing nearly mixes with her own calm breath. Her bored mask drops for a moment, surprising me with worry.

"Do you even know who you're traveling with?"

"You mean the friends that have stuck by me? Yes, I do."

"No, I don't think that you do." She whispers. Vivvus towers over me like her brother does, her figure strong and curved. Novak's smoke images come to mind as I stare up into her flashing, defiant eyes.

"I haven't seen any of your kin." I taunt, and a grin fills my face when ice takes over her seductive features. I have no doubt if Vivvus didn't take care of her brothers and the Purists herself after taking over, Panrauth took out everyone on sight when he returned.

She leaves me, pausing at the door frame before speaking. "You will tonight."

Thirty minutes later, a soft knock on the door interrupts my hard stare into the full length mirror. I open the bedroom door, revealing a sharply dressed Novak. He whistles, looking me up and down with a sly smile. The chagrin I have for wearing a dress dissipates, and I throw his body against the door as soon as it shuts.

He laughs softly against my dark red lips, his hands come up to cradle my full cheeks. "I see someone got worked up earlier."

I draw back immediately, brows narrowing. "*Not* funny." I waltz away, finishing my attire with the dagger from the Ancients strapped to my bare thigh. "You know, I was hoping I'd get to see you in action, defending my honor and all."

"I wouldn't dream of insulting you like that." He crosses the room and stands behind me, holding me in his arms as he turns my view to the mirror. "You're a beautiful being, Lythienne. Do you know that?" His whisper tickles my ear, and goosebumps spread across me.

I truly am.

Caramel skin covers a full face and body, strong and healthy. No longer a mountain creature, I am a young, curved and beautiful Fae. Lilac hair lightened by the sun frames my striking black and milky white eyes. Captain's hat rests for the evening on my bedside, and tonight I embrace my femininity. My tattoos are in full visibility, the silk forest green dress I chose is a mere piece of clinging fabric. Intricate leaves compose the beaded straps, hardly covering the green and purple skin of my neck and shoulder.

Novak's eyes pause on the sight, his aura darkening around us. He's dressed in a silk green tunic embroidered with gold leaf detailing, half unbuttoned in the usual way. Without trying we match, and the thought brings a flutter to my heart. The scars and freckles on his chest are visible, but the loose fabric hides his corded muscle underneath. His light hair is fluffy and clean, it appears he made an attempt to comb through it, but wild locks still need to be brushed from his eyes.

No weapons are at his side, even in a place that obviously hates him. His careful fingers trail the tattoo on my shoulder, the bear and grasshopper. I face him, placing a sure hand on his shoulder, and the other brushes hair from his dull eyes. He lets out a weak smile.

"What's wrong?" I breathe, his hand grasps my own and gentle lips meet my fingers.

"I was waiting. For you to kiss him back."

To be in love with someone else. Like my last mate. The unsaid sentiment hangs in the air, then are replaced by equally painful words. "Especially after last night." His face and voice drop, his heart beats against my chest and through the weak connection between us.

"I don't love him, Novak." I cradle his cheek with a sure hand, pulling his gaze up to mine. "I don't care if you can't ever call me your mate. I don't care if you think you're too broken. I don't care if we have to run away and live with the Giants when this is all over."

A genuine half smile leaves him after my promise, the dimples on one side of his face making an appearance. I press on, needing him to *hear* me.

"I don't care about anything, except for loving you. Us, you and me, that's what makes sense to me. I'm not afraid *of* you. I'm afraid of *losing* you."

Warmth burns my neck as tears roll from both of us. Our lips find comfort in the other, his heart rate slows and he presses his forehead to mine after a passionate moment. A rumbling from the doorway freezes my blood. The deep clearing of a throat, ruminating from the hulking bear with a heartbroken face.

He must've heard everything.

"It's time." Pan's flat, broken voice folds my ears. Dressed in a simple elegance, his faded clothes match his dull eyes. The trimmed and clean High Lord leaves without another word, leaving the door open.

Shall we kiss and make him jealous?

PEOPLE OF TERRA

Vivvus
Approximately One Year Ago

Sunlight wakes me from the best slumber I've had in years and I smile before opening my eyelids kissed by the dawn. I reach for Bonnie's solid shoulder, only to find emptiness. I frown, then sit up and force my groggy eyes open with dedicated fists. Bonnie's house is the same as we left it, albeit decorated with bits of my clothing and brightly lit with a new day.

Bonnie herself is nowhere to be seen, and the clothes she so easily discarded last night are gone as well. The morning is peaceful, birds are singing and I'm surprised by how much light is coming through the open windows. The world inside the Great Tree is usually a few shades darker than the outside world, but not today. Distant notes of last night's bonfires catch in the wind and I wrinkle my nose.

I stalk out of bed, heart pounding obnoxiously. I don't bother with the torn dress, instead I dig through a scuffed armoire in search of simple pants and a tunic. I find both in earthen tones, the linen trousers are a bit snug, but the worn black tunic is mine and fits like an old glove. I left it here last time I visited, along with a few other random bits of clothing. I pass through the beaded curtain and rake through my mane in attempts to tame the wildness, but it's to no avail.

My heart pounds as I tiptoe through the hall, my stealthiness uncalled for. I enter the front room, finding an empty kitchenette and the neat living space opposite it. I step around upholstered chairs with gaudy floral designs, then peek into the hearth and find a long dead fire. It was burning last night for sure, and Bonnie tends to make breakfast in the morning. I hold my elbows and air catches in my lungs when I notice a note on the kitchen table.

'Duty calls early today, see you this afternoon,

Love, Bonnie'

The birds stop singing.

I carefully place the note back where I found it, then follow the tug in my heart outside, too entranced to shut the door behind me. I dig my toes into pine needles and dirt, then lift my face to the Hidden canopy and close my eyes. Aether creeps up my spine and I inhale slowly, then exhale as I gently search the earth for any nearby disturbances. The arches of my feet tingle and I open my palms, allowing my fingers to twitch.

Something is coming.

A solid mass of negative, black energy slowly passes through the tunnel leading into the Great Tree. Pinpricks of green light, hundreds of them, are gathered in the town center, before the thrones. Black is misted through them, a general discontent and anger riding the air. The ground trembles beneath my feet. I open my eyes.

And I run.

I drop to my knees before my Father and Mother's thrones, the impending danger is nothing compared to the fact she is *here*. Mother sits ram rod straight in her throne, crown of flowers and vines upon her head and Father's hand tangled with hers, his thumb absently rubs her knuckles. He smiles wickedly at me, whereas Mother's wide eyes never stop moving, but also never land on me. As if I'm not here. I reach out to touch her and think better of it, instead I clear my throat. "Mother?"

She hones in on me, eyes sharp and usually quivering lips are pulled into a full, painted smile, breaking my heart. "Vivvie? Viv? Vi? Yes, yes, it's you, yourself. Have you heard the news? News, joyous stories and wonders and-"

Father tightens his grip on her hand and she immediately stops talking, eyes dart aimlessly once more. Aether flares in my core and I have half a mind to murder him for silencing a female who hasn't spoken in ten years, never mind the fact she's my Mother, his wife.

"What did you do to her?" I manage evenly.

"Me? Why dear, I did nothing! *You*, however, you have done everything, haven't you? I see you didn't appreciate my gift." Father gestures up and down at my 'peasant's clothing'. "I'm rather disappointed you failed to heed my warning." He taps the arm of his throne, his other hand tightens on Mother's further.

"One girl, two girl, three girl, ***not*** four." Mother keens, her screech rattles my ear drums. "*Not* four."

"One girl, two girl, three girl, but *not* four." Mother keens, her screech rattles my ear drums. "*Not* four."

Ice cold dread washes over me as Father releases Mother's hand then rises to stand over me. I don't waver, but my voice does. "What are you talking about?"

"The yellow rose." He says, taking hold of my chin with all the feign fatherly love in the world. Lavender that has doubled in size since last night tickles my knees and trampled leaves squeeze between my toes. The trembling ground is more frightened than before, taken to shaking and rumbling. Disquiet breaks out and the crowd is on the cusp of returning to the riot I started last night, demanding the answers I want to know.

'Are we in danger?

What's going on?

Is that the High Lady?

Is that the bitch Princess?

Fuck you, don't speak that way.

*Someone is coming, who **is** that?'*

"You're upset I haven't married." I grit out.

He *laughs*. "Oh, that's the least of my worries. No, it's rather, who *has* married, and *what* they married. Any ideas now, *daughter*?"

The puzzle pieces settle like a slap to the face, my stupidity a solid knife to the gut. "No ..." I breathe, unable to comprehend the gravity of my world falling apart.

"**Yes**. It's time Panrauth comes home, one way or another." Father says, discarding my chin like a useless piece of trash. Mother squeals with insane delight, bouncing up and down in her throne as a group of soldiers crest the hill leading to our part of town. I gasp and both hands fly up to my mouth upon spotting a horseback Aiden in the midst of a heavily armored escort. His arms are full of two small cloaked bodies and his face is shrouded in blood.

"A pity, really, if you had thought a *little* bit harder instead of fucking your mother's guard senseless all night, you could've warned them."

My attention whips back to Father's razor sharp grin. "What have you done with her?"

"One problem at a time, my dear." He waves me off, the most amused I've seen in ages, then nods to the group soldiers now waiting at the top of our lavender and throne decorated dais. "Mother dear, your son is home, as promised."

The High Lady of Terra stands, clapping enthusiastically. I join her side and call upon my Aether, then focus my attention on the platoon's front line opening before us like a flower, revealing a bloodied treasure inside. I hold my free hand to my chest and Mother stops giggling.

Aiden is astride no horse at all, but a *got* whose snow white head hangs low despite the chaotic crowd drawing closer to our high rise dais. He swings one leg over, careful of the bundle in his arms, and lands on both feet. His jaw tightens, but he does not cry out. Aiden only has eyes for me, and they are swollen and bloodshot. His torso is bare and flecked in still leaking wounds and a rainbow of blood that could be anyone's. Silence plagues him, Father and I.

Mother breaks the silence with her chirping, "Where's Pan, Pannie, Pan?" Aiden's hard stare breaks and his attention slides to her, but his gaze does not soften. Father steps forward with a curious hand raised to the bodies against his chest, but Aiden *snarls* at him, a guttural sound I didn't know Fae were capable of making.

"*No.*" My brother's word cuts through the air like a solid ax.

Father's hard lined face tightens as he whispers, "Why have you brought *them* here? Where are your brothers?"

Aiden's shoulders strengthen and he stands tall, calling upon every ounce of power to project his voice to all those gathered. A group of three soldiers work behind the *got* and I peer over, finding a high sided wagon of wood and iron. My heart quickens. Pan must be in there. And Weylin is ...

"The High Lord of Terra has conspired with the Princes Lhion and Nino Firthorn to assassinate the future High Lord, Panrauth Firthorn, our only hope and future in restoring the lands of Terra. Prince Lhion is guilty of not only possessing the *ra'al* plant, but using it against his kin. Prince Nino is guilty of murder, and has been punished accordingly."

Father draws upon his power, his considerably dull eyes compared to Aiden's alight with ferocity and the faelights above us dim a shade or two. "Fallacies! What have you done to them?"

Aiden's jaw sets with determination and he raises his chin, opens his lips. "I have-"

"I killed him." A bloodied, broken and *angry* Panrauth is shoved onto his knees beside Aiden, eyes only for the male staring him down with complete *disgust.* Panrauth doesn't, or *won't*, look at me. Mother gasps, then flings herself from my arms. Heavy fury sticks to my bones and my mouth twitches to hold back the words, *'Why couldn't you love me this way?'*

"Enough." Father takes the collar of Mother's dress and yanks backwards, causing her to sputter and choke, arms flailing to her son. Panrauth growls and emerald flares in his eyes, then he yells out when a large triangular rune glows to white life on his forearms. He's already been bound.

Two stretchers are brought round from the wagon, past Panrauth and towards the elevators. "Bring them here!" The High Lord shouts, causing the healers and soldiers to hurry back. They give apologies of 'he must be seen to, my lord,' but Father has no care.

My toes dig into the earth.

My ears ring as Father cries out upon seeing Nino's head a few inches from his body on the first stretcher. Mother thrashes against his tightening grip on her waist.

Aether dances around my fingertips as he inspects an unconscious Lhion, the rest of us siblings and his distraught wife forgotten.

Something is coming.

Father gives permission for his injured and dead sons to be taken care of, then he d*rags* Mother by the back of her neck and faces Panrauth once more. He thrusts out a gnarled finger right into Panrauth's face. "For the crime of murdering your kin, marrying a Human, and abandoning your duty, I sentence *you*, Panrauth Firthorn, to death. Ancients be damned, I *will* kill you myself."

Mother *screams*, begging for mercy with the last bit of coherency she has.

Father *laughs,* then ***snaps*** her neck and tosses her over the edge of the dais, where she rolls into a hysterical crowd.

Panrauth, Aiden and the *entire* Great Tree roar with fractured hearts, but I do no such thing. I choose death, and I choose not to fear consequences any longer.

I spread my toes in the dirt, inhale copper and lavender, then release every inch of power inside me that the Machine will allow. Decades, *centuries* of hurt, deception and fear hurl themselves at my father in the form of hundreds of arrows thick with red thorns, ragged black bark and rapidly budding violets, the arrowheads are a shining obsidian that cut through the brightest sunlight Arca Navi has seen in years.

And another member of the Firthorn family falls, skewered by his daughter's anger.

I wait for the Ancients, *someone*, to strike me down for killing the High Lord of Terra, but nothing happens. Every soul in Arca Navi holds their breath, waiting for lightning to strike me down or for the High Lord's power to flow into Panrauth, as it should. Aiden and Panrauth stare at me with a newfound shine to their poisoned eyes, but Panrauth is no High Lord. *'Not yet,'*

'Not yet, not his time, I need him for something,' A gentle breeze whispers through the lavender I brought to life last night, the only confirmation the Ancients have heard what I've done. No one else seems to hear the gentle plea but me. When the dumbfounded silence takes hold for another tenuous moment, I step into my duty as Princess of Terra before I lose the slippery control I've gained. I can use this. I step forward and kick Father's pin cushioned figure away from Mother's body, then cradle her skeletal body into my arms with ease and stand, facing the crowd and my brothers.

"I, Vivvus Firthorn, Princess of Terra, have vanquished the disease tainting our Court. The Ancients thank me for it, proven by the fact I am standing before you all and the innocent Lady of Terra dead in my arms, courtesy of the *former* High

Lord. Power corrupts the best of us, and destroys the worst. I am tired of living this way, and it ends now. We have lost four brethren this day, and the Ancients propose a compromise in regards to my brother's crimes."

No one speaks, fully enthralled, so I continue with my half truth.

"Panrauth Firthorn will be interred into The Eternal Machine for one hundred years for his crimes of murder, consorting with another race, and failing to take the throne. He may be released sooner, if the Ancients consider him ready to serve. In the meantime, Aiden Firthorn and myself will rule over Terra Court until his return,"

Aiden bends over and whispers a vital addition into my ear and I nod, then continue,

"Panrauth's twin daughters will reside here as part of the Court, magic runs in their veins and their souls are protected by the Ancients. Those who disagree will be dealt with, *accordingly*. You have three minutes to discuss, as I *will* take your opinion into account regarding our future High Lord's fate. It is not up to us to determine *his* punishment, only the Ancients. Also, Lhion Firhorn is henceforth sentenced to death for his crimes of conspiracy, attempted kidnapping, and murder."

Disorder threatens to erupt as discussions take hold in my traumatized people. Aiden stares at me with unbelieving eyes, his feet are still planted beside Panrauth and the bodies in his arms have been listless this entire time. Panrauth however, drops his head and his chest collapses inward. I have no choice, right now this is the best I can do. If he hadn't admitted to killing Nino ...

"Aiden, come." I order, chin raised. He looks down at Panrauth who does not move, then back up to me. Aiden joins my side and faces the Great Tree with me as a united front. I glance over in hopes of finding a girlish face underneath all those blankets, but I find nothing.

"Why are you doing this? Was this your plan all along?" He whispers, driving a stake into my gut. "Why didn't you tell me?"

"I have no plan, but it's time for a new age. If this is the way, so be it." I reply and he scoffs. I frown. "And you? What were you doing with Lhion and Nino? Did Panrauth really ..."

He glances at a waiting Panrauth, then down to his full arms. "I had no idea what was going on, until it was too late. I thought we were bringing him home. Nino, he ... beheaded their mother. Panrauth didn't kill any-"

I hold up my hand, this is not the time to get into specifics. "Call the vote, we have to be united or this falls apart. He's already taken responsibility."

Aiden lowers his head and sighs, the weight of Nino's death heavy on his shoulders. Why Panrauth took the fall I have no idea, but it's too late now. Aiden's chest expands and his dark locs fall back as he raises his chin, focusing on our people. "People of Terra, what say you?"

In response, unanimous chants of *'Ai,'* sweep through the Great Tree and just like that, Panrauth's fate is sealed. The future High Lord of Terra lifts his head and stares at the remainder of his family. Sister, brother, and daughters. His eyes linger on mother's body in my arms as well.

"Do you have anything to say, Panrauth? You may stand." I offer, and he does. He rises to his full height, the rune shackle on his arm is glowing just as fiercely as his eyes are. Panrauth turns and the soldiers surrounding him shift as well so his view of the waiting people below is unobstructed. His fists shake and shoulders roll back.

"People of Terra, I thank you for this opportunity to redeem myself. I will not squander it, as I will spend my time planning a new Court where all races can live together in peace. I have shirked my duty, yes, but I have also lived in the world my father has hidden away from us. Humans are not dangerous, not any more than us, and they have knowledge rooted in a life without magic. We Fae are far too spoiled, and I often ask myself, how useless would we be without Aether? Would we know how to survive?"

Panrauth gestures to Aiden and I, his tawny neck throbbing and emerald eyes unwavering from our people.

"My daughters have Aether in their blood and *will* experience the Spark, proving wrong the idea that Fae and Humans cannot reproduce without dire consequences. I never planned to fall in love with a Human, but I do not once regret it. I hope during the time I am gone, you can take a look inside yourselves and take apart the hatred my Court has planted into you. I know my sister and brother will set you on the right path, for their hearts beat to the same song mine does, but it is ultimately up to you to dismantle the prejudice inside yourself."

Tears splash onto mother's thin arms crossed over her chest and air catches in my lungs. Panrauth turns to us and approaches slowly, as one might a wounded animal. He stops before me, his own grief apparent on his furred cheeks now that he's closer. He stares down at Mother's face, reaching forward to caress her cheek. When he does, he inhales sharply and drops his hand, then focuses on me through wet eyes.

"Weylin always said it wasn't your fault, and I never knew why. Never would *let* her tell me why. I am a fool for not listening to her, or you. I don't know how you made this possible, but thank you for sparing my life. Please, take care of them and be sure they know I love them, and how precious they are, no matter what anyone else may say. I know you will raise them to be fine women."

"Oh, Pan. I'm so sorry." I whimper, if I speak any louder I will be sobbing before my entire Court. He rests a hand on the back of my neck and pulls me close, then presses his forehead to mine. "I'll do my best."

"I believe in you, Vi. I have one more favor to ask."

"What?"

Without breaking the subtle touch between our sweating foreheads, he chokes on words before trying again. "Give her a proper *levaya*, please."

Oh, no.

I nod and he pulls away, then attends to Aiden. The eldest and youngest Firthorn brothers stare into each other's eyes for a long held moment, then Panrauth silently reaches forward and paws through fabric until he finds a sleeping Mirah and Estienne curled up together in the crook of Aiden's arm. They're just as bloodied as Aiden is, Mirah has a nasty cut on her forehead that is beginning to scab over already. Panrauth kisses Mirah's forehead, then Estienne's. He whispers a prayer not meant for our ears, then covers the girls back up. He focuses on Aiden once more, then takes hold of his neck and gently pulls him in for a forehead press as well. "I don't know why you were there, but I'm glad *you* were. Thank you, for saving them, and me."

Aiden cries softly and nods against Pan, then the future High Lord turns away and approaches the wagon. He stops along its side and rests a hand on the wood, then looks over his shoulder to a silent Aiden and I. Tears fall into Panrauth's beard, but he is infinitely more courageous than I am right now.

"I would like to go now."

And he does.

Break My Heart

Late to my own party, how fitting for a Keeper of Death. My companions and I enter the grand dining hall swarming with lesser and High Fae. And Humans, so many rounded ears present. Real Humans, this time.

The wide hall framed by great spires of branches rests on a mushroom balcony off shooting from the Great Tree. The crowded area overlooks the twin moons rising, pulling the night and stars behind them. I note several small side balconies for where to hide later, and the two side exits.

Music drifts from multiple points, and scantily dressed Fae dance on platforms situated through the room. Room is an understatement, the gathering hall is nearly the size of the entire village down below. With prosthesis in full view and the silk dress trailing behind me, I walk with my chin high and eyes locked on the set of thrones overlooking the room. Simpler than the ones on the ground level, but elegance and danger pour from these just as well. The rolling laughter, conversation and music plaguing the room hushes when I come to a halt with my companions, only whispers ride on the chilled evening air.

Pan and Vivvus are laughing heartily with a group of courtiers, all Fae dressed finer than their High Lord. A lone Human dressed in light fighting leathers stands with them, scanning the room with hardened brown eyes. Novak and I are standing together, Orion by his right side, and Alvis stands close to my left with a hand resting on his sword. The High Lord and his second in command eventually give us their attention, laughter fading from their group as they do.

"High Lord and Princess, thank you for the hospitality." Novak's mature, clear cut voice surprises me.

I've learned that he stopped his negotiating duties when the demon settled inside him, turning the world renowned *Zemer* into a recluse. That's why Trihewyn was so surprised to see him, he never leaves the ship. Novak winks at Vivvus as he fully bows, reminding me of when I greeted Trihewyn. I straighten, heavy breasts hardly concealed by the deep cut fabric. I dip my head to them both, and the twins follow suit.

Panrauth grins, the wicked smile traveling much farther without his beard to hide it. "The *Tzel* has manners, Vivvus." First the *Zemer*, now the *Tzel*. I have a feeling *this* name is nothing kind, it's the same one the Ancients called him.

"Why have you come?" Vivvus asks, her lips pushed thin as she evaluates my lover.

"I have come to ask for your help." I speak up, bellowing as I stare at Pan. My brave facade fades for a second as his heartbroken face plays in my mind once more. The High Lord crosses his bulky arms, the flickering in his eyes visible from here. He caught my fleeting pity. Pan opens his lips, but words are interrupted by immense light laughter rushing in. Small bodies knock me to the ground within seconds.

Buried under a pile of small human and High Fae children, questions bubble from every mouth. Tiny dirty fingers poke my eyes, hips protest as they pull at my prosthesis. I sheathe my dagger with haste as a human child finds it quite interesting.

"Enough." Pan's soft but commanding voice lifts the giggling little ones from me. I sit up and immediately meet the grassy green eyes of Panrauth's daughters. They are even more identical than Alvis and Orion are, their soft faces untainted by the horrors of life. Vivvus must've taken good care of them after all this time, and respect builds for the bothersome female.

Flower crowns adorn their curling dark hair. Soft black skin rivals the bright flames in their eyes, and rounded ears poke from under their locks. Their gang of friends stand around me, wide and curious eyes taking me in. The children of Terra hold life, whereas the starving children of Echo hold death. A disgruntled High Fae male shifts in the background behind the throne, disgust filling his thick face. The sight of the pitch black leathers and blades strapped to every place possible sends a chill down my spine.

"I am rather pleased to meet you, but perhaps next time don't knock over the cripple, though?" I tease half heartedly to the children, evoking laughter from nearly everyone, even Vivvus. Novak offers a hand and I take it, learning on him quite heavily as my hips are *not* happy with the onslaught. Panrauth smiles in silence, but his gaze catches on the hand on my waist, then to my own hand shifting the dress back over my shoulder.

Panrauth's pale green aura darkens immensely, like when he argued in the pantry. His smile is wiped and he focuses on the dangerous male at his side, which must be his brother. They're much more alike than Panrauth and Vivvus are. Although the male's skin is much darker than Pan's, the broad features and brooding attitude is similar, and all three siblings have the same dark hazel hair.

"Thank you for bringing our father home, Miss Lythienne." The girl's gratitude pull me from my observations, their sing-song voices joined as one.

Each wrap their small arms around my waist and hug gently, then bound to Orion and Alvis. The males allow the small children to poke and prod them, and I chuckle watching the sets of twins who are quite interested in the other.

My eyes warm and I search for Vivvus who dips her chin with a small smile. Panrauth is delving into the voracious party resuming with ferocity, his brother trailing not far behind. Novak's uneasy face catches my attention and I take his hand, pulling him close so I can press my forehead to his, for all to see.

I don't want to think about anything else right now, there is only one thing I want to do. I whisper into his ear with softness, folding both his fluffed ears flat against his neck. "Will you play for me, please?"

Novak's dark aura lightens as his dimples appear, and he bites his lip through a smile. Leaning close to my own purple tufted ear, he teases me. "I would rather play *with* you."

Goosebumps break out and I contemplate fucking him on the nearest table. We settle for finding a lute instead, and Novak draws a crowd rather quickly, borrowing a beautiful instrument that puts his decrepit one to shame.

Whatever fears the people of Arca Glen held before are dimmed by his music, plumes of herb smoke and the endless alcohol provided to everyone. Our corner of the hall is full of dancing bodies and smiling faces. I turn down drinks from gracious strangers multiple times. Their thanks are quite confusing, like a parent forcing their child to say sorry after doing something bad, and they feel no remorse for their misdeed whatsoever.

After dancing with many curious and flirtatious Fae, I retreat to where I spy Vivvus alone, near the opening to an empty side balcony.

"Your *Tzel* is certainly entertaining, I give him that." Vivvus chirps, watching the crowd with an amused expression filling her feminine beauty.

"His *name* is Novak." I snap.

He's playing for the entire hall now, every face paying attention to him as his music reverberates through the atmosphere. A peaceful grin rests on his face and his searching gaze finds me. Relief washes over him and his attention leaves me after a moment with a dimpled wink. His heart beats in tune to his song down the bond. I can hear it clear as a bell through the connection, and it doesn't fade.

Finally.

Vivvus presses close to me and brings her beckoning lips to my ear, her threat no more than a whisper. "You're not afraid? Or of those *Te'omin*?" Disappointment drips with her last word.

Why she hates the twins I'm not sure, but I don't care. Alvis has already tried to warn me. I. Don't. Care.

"No, I'm not." I retort fiercely and shrug her off. I lower my disgusted tone, raising my chin to her smirking face. "I had questions for you, I can see they will have to wait."

What I need her to do, I'm not entirely sure I trust her. Respect yes, but never trust. Then again, I don't have much of a choice.

Vivvus shakes her kinky hair out, hips swaying as she wordlessly struts to the private area behind us. I raise a brow at her once we are alone on the empty mushroom balcony, then glance at the party behind us. A sound shield goes up, muffling my eardrums.

We stand feet from each other, she knits her fingers together and I cross my inked arms. I wonder how shields work, if someone powerful enough can infiltrate one, or if the shields are unrelenting.

I don't have a choice.

"You strike me as the real power in command here." I admit, wasting no time.

She chuckles. "Pan doesn't want anything to do with politics. The only thing that's changed is his ass is *on* the throne. He's perfectly happy toiling in the fields and working with his hands, if it means the land is restored to its former abundance. Unlike him, I care about our people."

Now that he has nothing left to fight for, he's perfectly happy to play puppet.

"And you're still pulling the strings."

"I'm rather good at it. Kept this place together through a decades long famine, and fended off Sylvan's snatchers." Vivvus pauses, flashing green eyes studying the meadows below us. "Pan didn't give me much of a choice, when he came back." Vivvus pushes out a breath and a sliver of truth, holding her elbows and looking uncomfortable. She's just as trapped as he is. Bound by the Aether of the land and duty to their people.

"I have a favor."

She steps closer and her short pointed ears flick. I notice the brunette fluff is coiled, just like her hair. "I'm listening."

I rest on an empty wooden bench hidden in the darkness of the balcony and gaze up at the stars lighting up the glorious fields below. Longing tugs at my heartstrings, but it's not just my own. Novak must be searching over the crowd again for me, but I can still hear his music drifting outside, albeit a slower tune. I push out a breath, thankful I can still feel his heartbeat and that *more* is leaking through the bond from him.

How *can* you deny the connection between us that strengthens every time we are together? He will admit it one day, one day I will hear the words from him.

I hope.

The night illuminates everything it reaches, with no clouds to be seen. The gold and silver moons are waxing, nearly full. The summer solstice will only be a couple of days away now. I wonder how they celebrate Litha here, if it's similar to how Echo celebrates holidays. Wandering thoughts turn to Pan, heat pricking my neck at the foggy scene of him fucking that Fae in the street. This is so much messier than I thought it would be.

I didn't expect him to care so much, or for a part of me to still call to him. What happened between us in the Mountain is not easy to push away, he was kind and loyal to me, until Echo. I am finding there is more than one kind of love, different people call to different parts of your soul.

On cue, his looming figure casually saunters past me and aims for the balcony overhang.

"What did you think," Pan leans on the thin branch railing and overlooks the sky, avoiding my face, "the first time you saw them?"

I swallow, shame filling me as memories of us in the lab are replaced by his pained look after watching me confess my love to Novak. *No*, he left *me*. He hurt *me*.

"Actually, I thought about you. Where you were, if you were looking at them too. I saw them the first night, the night you left me." My voice starts strong, but ends small.

Pan runs a hand over his head and grumbles when he finds no locks to comb through. "I have regretted that night, and the night before, ever since I left." He leaves the railing and stands before me trembling on the bench.

"I don't understand you. You left me breaking, without a proper goodbye, even. I come here, and you try to sweep me off my feet, tell me you miss me." Anger burns through my veins, I can't contain the words even if I tried.

At this point I've known Novak longer than I've known Panrauth, but Pan's behavior still hurts. As if an old friend I've known for decades has turned into a stranger.

What is time, to a Fae, anyway?

"You make it seem like I had a *choice*." Pan drops to a knee, a beastly snarl to his voice when he takes my hand with surprising care. I bite my lip when his eyes travel over my tattoos and pause at the chess pieces, bringing back the memory of us on the ship.

Should I call you high Lord now, or later?

The world crashes when everything locks into place, my ears ringing as the ground shifts. Novak is right, *again*. I never think ahead far enough. The look on

Pan's face when he left me at the Oasis, he knew who I was talking to. He knew everything, and pushed me away, didn't even give me a choice in the matter.

I shove him off and thrust myself from the bench, pacing the small balcony with intensity. "You *knew*, didn't you?"

Pan stops me in my tracks, rough hands taking my small shoulders with caution. So unlike how he held me earlier, now he is only nervous. There's no one to piss off, it's just us.

"The moment you saw each other I knew. It didn't even happen to me and I could feel time stop when you listened to that damn music. I knew right then I lost you."

Tears of anger pour from me and my small hand smacks his clean cheek with such an intensity it knocks him sideways.

"You *fucking* asshole. That's why you did it. You were *trying* to push me away." Ferocious anger taints my fractured voice as I grab a fistful of his tunic and slam him against the wall before he stands fully. I am so small, he could've stopped me long ago. His broad features are surprisingly calm, hands loose at his sides while he takes the brunt of my feelings.

"I didn't want to get in the way. You can't deny that you were drawn to him." I'm surprised by his gentle touch, his hand encompasses my left cheek and he runs his thumb across my scar. "I meant every word I said that day. I thought I could get over you, I thought it would be easier if you hated me. I thought it was the right thing to do, but ... I miss you."

"Well, it wasn't." I break finally, releasing his tunic as hot tears flood my cheeks. I study his face before speaking quietly, admitting my own truth. "I missed you, I missed my *friend*. You didn't have to break my heart."

His fingers trail down to my chin, holding it gently like he did once before. His eyes fixate on my trembling lip, and his next low words are fatal. "You have been breaking mine ever since I met you."

I step back at once, holding my elbows tight. I can't do this.

I want to hold him.

"It was never my intention. I didn't even know. Novak," his name rouses darkness in Pan's pale green aura, but through my anger he remained calm. "Stop brooding and *listen*." I snarl, and the High Lord blinks in surprise.

"You two had the same stupid idea. When he saw us together, he wasn't going to tell me *he* cared either, that *his* heart was breaking too. He respected you enough to do that. *And* respected me enough to make my *own* choices."

I reiterate, my words strong. "It's my choice, and you're right. No matter what, I will always choose him over you."

Pan's lips push thin, his tone threatening. "Do you even know what you're mated to?" He steps forward with haste, slipping the strap off my shoulder and sending warmth through my cheeks. "It appears so." He clenches his jaw and glowers at the bare, bruised skin.

"Yes, the Fae who never left my side, *especially* when I needed him. He has never lied to me, and would never hurt me the way you did." I straighten, the open skin of the bite mark is healed already, now it's just a deep spreading bruise. "I would rather play with his demons any day than your bullshit."

Pan crosses his arms as he towers over me. I turn away and study the moons, beyond pissed off. I can feel his eyes burning on the Bear and Grasshopper tattoo. A minute passes, then he comes to my side and faces the world below, hands clasped behind his back. "If I had stayed, and told you that I love you, where would we be?"

"If you stayed and told me you loved me, I would've believed you. You would know the enormous task I have ahead of me, and you would've been friends with them." I jut my chin to the direction of the now quiet party, Novak's music has been replaced by gentle lyres and other instruments. I sigh, shaking the loose purple from my face when I look Pan in the eyes.

"And when we came here, when you saw your daughters, your wife's face in them, we both would've realized you're not ready to love anyone."

He shakes his head softly. "You may not think so, but I *do* love you, Lythienne."

"Admit it, I wouldn't make a very good wife to a High Lord. Too *fancy*." I tease, ignoring the words he just said. I can't listen to them.

They are too late.

"I can't disagree with you there, although I must say, you are truly terrifying tonight." He grins half heartedly and I can't help but smile. After a moment, his brows narrow. "Tell me what you need."

I tell him everything Trihewyn told me about the Harbinger, and he already knows about the 'forgotten' history of Iverbourne. When Vivvus told him their temples and libraries were ransacked when he left, one of his first orders was to work with the Mists in restoring them. I'm not surprised to find he knows of Terra's role in the wars, passed down to him by his mother. What he doesn't know is my role to play in the future of Iverbourne.

The evening air is quiet for a minute after I finish, and he pushes out a large breath whilst rubbing his chin. "Eros has been increasing her power since we left, she is now the High Lady of Iron."

My heart stops beating for a moment, drawing panic from Novak down the bond. It has been otherwise quiet and emotionless until now, and I take a deep breath. "How is that possible?"

"Do you really want to know?" Pan asks, glancing at me sideways. I nod, unsure I actually do. "Eros is the daughter of Rohana and Knothall, she is the true heir of Fire Court."

I fall to the ground so fast the air knocks from me and the world spins. I regain my vision just as a flurry of shadows usher in Novak at my side, his hands stop me from hitting my head.

"What did you do?" Novak asks Pan, his voice hoarse and primal. Freckled arms sweep under me and hold me close to his chest. He stares up at Panrauth with no fear. Pan on the other hand, is mortified at the sight of Novak's ethereal skin, shadowed with night and stars.

"I'm fine, Novak." I breathe, my arms tight around his neck. He stands with me crushed to his chest and takes a step back from Pan. Novak's voice and the fury in his eyes softens when he turns his attention to me. "Like hell you are. We don't have to do this Lyth, we'll find another way."

Pan watches us with a face of pure stone. The flames in his eyes are dulled, just like in the Pit. When all hope was gone. "We were discussing the problem at hand. Lyth received some information that is problematic at best. Perhaps we should gather and discuss immediately, as a group."

Pan is diplomatic and strained, the demeanor of a High Lord. He leaves us without another word. Novak and I are left on the balcony, the party inside slows and faelights are dimming. I bury my face into the bare skin revealed from his loose tunic. Sea salt lingers on him. I inhale deep, wait a few counts, and exhale heavily. Once ethereal arms fade back to sun freckled skin.

"Do you want to talk about it?" Caution fills his soft voice.

"Not right now."

After another moment of enjoying his strong chest, I look up. His brows are knitted together, his jaw is tight and heart still thunders against my side. With a steady hand I find his disheveled hair, twirling his locks with my fingers.

"I think the Giants are starting to sound like good company." Novak says before kissing my nose with tenderness and his face softens, but he still looks worried.

"I wanted to tell you, I think your malicious nickname is much better than mine." I tease, smiling up at him.

Those handsome dimples lift a spectacular, real smile from him, and my heart bursts.

SUCH A FOOL

Vivvus
Three Days Ago

"Three, two, one, *fire*!"

A flurry of arrowheads slice through the incredibly hot predawn air, each burrowing into their target with ease. I pace behind the line of archers, inspecting the *Adira's* work as I pass. Mirah mimics me, hands behind her back and eyes set on the form and poise of our soldiers. Each female waits to be called to next position.

"What do you think?" I ask Mirah, and she nods just the slightest bit to a Human at the end of the line. We slowly approach and I command the archer to attention. She turns on her heel and slings her bow upon her back, then thrums her fist to her chest.

"Commander Firthorn."

"Leah Istaria, is it?"

Leah nods, taken aback just the slightest bit. Her hair is cropped short, muscles corded and skin a dark brown. I haven't thought of Bonnie in some time, but Leah reminds me of her. Pure strength and loyalty ruminates from this Human and I inhale deeply. I glance down at Mirah who has yet to break her stare from Leah. "I think you're onto something."

Mirah beams, then recomposes herself and nods with a nearly indiscernible smile. Her and Estienne both haven't been the same since a much too early Spark, almost like their personalities ... switched. Mirah's wildness is now Estienne's true love. Mirah walks slower and talks less, hands constantly moving and feeling and touching. Estienne is training to be a huntsman with Aiden's youth group, and Mirah shadows my footsteps in everything I do, but she particularly enjoys the *Adira*.

She itches to rule her father's court, I think.

I never thought I'd see the day where the girls separate for hours at a time, but it's not for much more than that. The twins reunite after studies and training, and the four of us make a point to eat together at night, even if that sometimes may be well into the eighth or ninth hour.

And then we wake up and do it all again.

It's good work, both harder and easier since when we first started. Humans and Fae are living cohesively with infrequent issues, some Satyr have come south to reside in Arca Navi. While the lands are not to their full splendor, the Ancients must be satisfied with Aiden and I standing in for Panrauth as the harvest this coming fall looks the most promising in years. Some crops still refuse to grow, but it looks like we won't starve this winter like we nearly did the last. But, just in case our luck changes, I invested in indoor greenhouses and doubled down on livestock. Not to mention our new trade routes with Borealis and Hallowed have opened up more possibilities.

Father kept us in the dark for no reason at all, and it still angers me to this day.

The latest difficulty rises from the mysterious 'Others Court' plaguing Hallowed villages and rumored to be encroaching on Terra and Sylvan. After visiting a place, the population drops by over half. Whoever the Others leave behind are incoherent and drunk like, unable to remember anything but a flash of ice. Trihewyn insists she has it handled, but I have a bad feeling.

Luckily, I've been training this platoon for nearly a year now, same as Aiden has with his warriors that work in the shadows.

"Commander Firthorn?" Leah asks, breaking me from my thoughts.

"Ah, yes. I have a test for you. Pass it, and you become the leader of this platoon. You've excelled in every other mark, and Mirah here has a feeling you're the one. Not to mention you won the vote by a landslide."

The line of archers is silent but their excitement is palpable. Leah softens, glancing down at Mirah. All the females love my niece, but the only Human in the group has kept her distance from the Half-Fae. Leah looks back up to me, shoulders straightening. "Yes, Commander. I would be honored."

"Good." I turn to the soldier behind me and ask for a bow and an arrow, she obliges me at once. I saunter out to the end of Leah's firing range, then announce the test.

"*Adira*, listen up. You have all nominated Leah Isitara as platoon leader, and I approve, given that she can pass a test. The same test the first Earth Ancient bestowed to Damitius, who was one of the first Earth Fae, and the first of *all* Fae to be given the gift of Archery. She must meet my arrow in the distance between us. Without killing me, of course. You are all permitted to break formation and watch from a respectable distance, so as not to disturb her."

I turn on my heel, my back to Leah's target, and the tail feathers of her arrow tickle my shoulders. I find wide eyes, murmurs and a determined Leah. Mirah is thoroughly enthralled, not at all worried. Her Aether is something other, what she describes to me as a 'feeling' regarding people. Air Fae are the only ones I know of that can affect and sense the mind, and I've had no luck finding anyone else like Mirah in Terra.

Leah wastes no time nocking an arrow and I do the same, both of us raise our bows and aim at the other. "Do you know why Damitius asked for the gift of Archery?" Leah calls, surprising me. Her black leathers trimmed with gold catch the early dawn's light.

This story is close to my heart, but still I ask, "Why?"

"So he could slay the beast imprisoning his family, a *tannin*."

"And did he?" My arms quiver along with my heart.

"Yes." Leah says, a whisper in the wind.

And our bowstrings *snap*.

Glinting arrowheads cut through the deep blue sky giving way to pinks and purples outside the Great Tree, the once full double moons disappearing as the sun chases them away. Grass sways over my feet, some blades fresh and green, others dead and yellowed. I exhale watching my shaft barrel for Leah's approaching arrow, both are fletched with the standard crow feathers.

I smile whilst watching the obsidian arrowheads clash, spraying flecks of green into the air. All the arrows are charmed to bring their bearer protection, but we haven't tested that theory in battle yet. I'm alive, so that must mean something. The hundred strong *Adira* unabashedly cheer for Leah, breaking from their long held anticipation to sweep their new platoon leader up. I don't miss Mirah being tossed into the air as well, her smile brightening the entire morning.

A shiver runs up my spine and I glance over my shoulder, finding Panrauth a few steps behind me. I startle backwards and stare at him, utterly bewildered to find his calm, trimmed face. His eyes flash a *bright* emerald, far more intense than before, and he holds out a callused hand to me.

"Hey, Vi. I'm back."

Silence falls between us, the joyous group at the end of the range oblivious to the return of their High Lord. I stare down at his outstretched hand, then back up to his no longer youthful, hopeful face. A year in the Eternal has aged him immensely. Burns and scars mark his bare arms and neck, his tunic is a few buttons undone and reveals thick muscles stretching across his chest. Everything about him is bigger, darker, *older*.

"*Hey*?" I swat his outstretched hand away because it's *Pan*. I glare up at him with all the fury in the world, then throw my arms around his neck after a tentative second because it's *Pan*.

My little brother is home.

"How are you here?" I murmur into his neck and he squeezes me tight. We embrace other for a long moment, his sunburned skin is near unbearable against mine. He sets me down, then sighs and rakes a hand through his cropped hair. Tiny *x* shaped scars fleck his work worn hands and I still can't decide whether he actually grew two inches or if I shrank. "I kind of ... broke out." Panrauth admits, crossing his arms and avoiding my eyes.

"*What*?" I hiss, taking a step back.

"It's time I take the throne, and the Ancients must believe me because they haven't struck me down yet. I've heard quite a few things on the way here, it sounds ... It sounds like you've done good, Vi. Maybe we can work together."

I shake my head, hands up in defense as coils fall over my eyes. "You can't just, *no*, go back to the beginning! How the hell are you here?"

But then, Mirah is there, jumping into her father's arms like no time has passed. Her arms wrap around his neck, legs latch onto his waist. Panrauth falls to his knees, hands in Mirah's hair and apologies on his tongue.

"You're here, you're here."

"I'm here, little one. I'm here."

I take an unsteady step back, then another one. Emotions ranging from happiness to pure anger swirl into a raging maelstrom in my heart, so I leave the father and daughter reuniting. With every step away from Panrauth and towards my comrades the air rushes easier into my lungs. "We'll be ending this early today. I expect you ladies to treat Leah right this evening, ahh, don't think I don't know what you all do after the lights go out. Just don't be too hungover for tomorrow, we'll be making up today's work, no doubt about that."

The *Adira* bring their fists to their black leather chests as one, then bow their heads. Curious eyes meet mine and no one moves after dismissal, then someone summons courage. "Commander is that, the future High Lord?"

I nod into my hand, rubbing my face. "Yes, it appears our High Lord has returned to us. But please, keep this to yourselves, for now."

They all nod, then start down the dirt path leading from the training grounds to inside a side tunnel leading into the Great Tree, one reserved only for royalty and militia. I stare down at my toes in the grass, then decide to do what I do best.

My duty.

Panrauth and Mirah join me, hand in hand. Mirah smiles up at me, a wet and genuine thing. "Let's find Uncle and Estienne." I nod, taking the free hand Mirah reaches out to me. Then, the three of us return to Arca Navi, together.

Panrauth and I sit beside Weylin and Bonnie's graves, our only company being the heated summer night. Stars wink into existence and I stare up at them, waiting for Panrauth to finish his silent prayer.

After what may very well be hours, Panrauth lifts his forehead from the dirt and leans back on his heels, then sighs. "I've been such a fool."

I arch a brow at him, hugging my knees close to my chest. "Do tell."

Panrauth promised that once we were alone, he would tell me everything. After a buffet of sweets, treats and stories, a disgruntled Aiden took the girls to bed so Panrauth and I could talk. Aiden seems to feel the same way I do, caught somewhere between anger and relief. Tomorrow will be filled with honorifics and a crowning, then we will visit this place together as a family shortly thereafter. Panrauth wanted to visit Welyin alone with me, the first time. Panrauth rubs at his clean shaven jaw, frowning at the lack of facial hair there. He levels me with a singular look. "Have you ever heard of the Keeper of Death?"

I blink, searching my mind for the term. "No. Honestly Pan, I," I clear my throat and prepare for him to be pissed, "I haven't interned anyone since you, so I haven't heard much about the Mountain."

Panrauth nods, lowering his head as he stretches a leg out and reaches into his pocket. "Good. That's good." He retrieves what appears to be a photograph, thumb rubbing over it's face. "Have you ever seen this?"

He passes it to me, and my hands shake at once upon recognizing the picture. I trace Mirah and Estienne's faces, noting the powdered sugar lingering in the corner of their mouths. Their eyes are alight with the brightest emerald Aether and their rounded ears are apparent, holding back their wild locks. The day we visited Beakglen. Aiden and I were standing behind the photographer, making sure the contraption wasn't going to bust into flames or something. Lexeran assured us it was safe, he knew the photographer personally.

"It's ... mine. We went to Beakglen last Samhain, and I thought, I thought I had lost it, fell out of my back pocket. How did *you* get it?" I wearily give the photograph back to him and tears prick my eyes but I have no clue why. Panrauth stares at his girls for a moment longer, then pockets the picture once more.

He stares at me, hard, then tells the story of the Keeper of Death who stole his heart, and gave him freedom.

Silence follows his tale filled with rebellions, hard labor, death and fleeting love. He finishes on the note of leaving Lythienne behind, because she met her mate.

"You should have gave her a choice." I finally say, leaning back on my hands as I stretch my legs out. "She probably doesn't even know what mates are, let alone-"

"You don't *get* it, Vi. I literally watched them be pulled to each other, it was just as people say. If it had been anyone else, maybe I would have ... I know now that I should have, *fuck*." Panrauth cuts me off with a fist to the ground.

"Did you know the person? Her mate?" I tread, which immediately fans to life the green flames in his eyes.

"I didn't recognize him at first, I thought he was just a Human, but then I saw them talking together and shadows were *dancing* around him." Panrauth shakes his head, scowling.

It takes me two heartbeats to catch up and I sit up straighter. "You're not serious."

He nods. "The Shadow of Death."

NO, AND THAT'S FINAL

Alvis nudges me while Orion explains the Harbinger, *me*, to Panrauth and his closest court members. Pan's inner court is composed of Viv, his brother Aiden, two Humans and two Lesser Fae. The two half goat and Fae creatures hiding in the corner I learn are Satyr, the ambassadors hailing from the northern lands of Dew Falls. The last frontier before the separated Realm of Giants.

I break the locked gaze I have with the middle aged woman. She's been staring me down since we started the meeting, even though I'm hanging back from the table. I recognize her as the same Human who was in the dining hall before.

"Got you something." Alvis grins wider than a child with candy, the scars in his face stretching upwards. Inky coils on his crown fall over violet eyes, the rest is freshly trimmed on his close cut temples. He stuffs a small satchel into my hand, so full of herbs I can smell them without opening the bag.

My black and white eyes widen and I clap him on the shoulder, pocketing the sack into my pocket with a smile. "Thank the Ancients, what do I owe you?" I whisper. Alvis ruffles my hair and winks before leaving me to join his brother's side at the battle table.

The so-called table is a massive slab of charcoaled wood, a tree round easily the size of my current quarters. Papers, maps and weapons litter the space, and intense passionate auras flow heavily from the creatures in discussion around the table. A dimmer switch for this eye would be quite handy, the passionate arguing fuels every sense I have. All weapons were surrendered at the start of the meeting, and a shield was placed on the room to prevent magic.

Apparently, politics can be quite dangerous.

Aiden is the only surviving brother of Panrauth and Vivvus, the others were executed when Vivvus took the throne. Apparently, Aiden is the better of the three brothers who slaughtered Pan's family, and was only going along with orders. He's always in the background, listening and standing guard near his brother and sister.

I can't imagine being near him at all, let alone imagine how Pan's daughters must feel. His skin is so dark it's near black and it's tinged with a hint of green. He has a slender body similar to Alvis' fighter figure. Long, dreaded black hair runs down his back, and he dons full fighting leathers.

Aiden does not like the idea of waiting for an Empty Fae to collect magic and finish Eros off, sparking my dislike for him even further. I step up to the table once Panrauth decides to cease the arguing, coming to stand between the twins. I scan the table and focus on the High Lord speaking for the first time since we began this arduous meeting. With arms crossed, he speaks directly to me with commanding authority.

"If I give you Terra's essence, you still have Water and Fire to deal with." Pan gestures to the map, specifically the growing territory the High Lady of Iron has. The entire south will soon be in her control, as Trihewyn made her deal long ago for asylum.

"Eros will never give Fire to you freely, and it's highly doubtful Typhan will agree either. From the increased trade between the two, I wouldn't be surprised if they're working together already." A Lesser Fae courtier explains from beside Panrauth, their comforting gray eyes focusing on me. Their body is just as soft as their voice, light green skin contrasting the High Lord beside them.

Vivvus glances at me, but I ignore her. She scrutinizes the map again with Novak at her side, and he studies the map with his hands clasped behind his back."What is your point?" Alvis asks, even and calculating, his body protectively pressed against mine.

"The point is, your mission is impossible. We need to fight Eros another way." Leah, the human, is matter of fact.

Aiden nods, the male Satyr agrees with him as well as the Lesser Fae. Novak whistles low from his place at the table, then steps away for a moment. The russet female Satyr finds Novak's company and the two talk off to the side. I wonder how many Satyr he grew up with in the North, if they perhaps know each other. Satyr aren't immune to aging as Fae are, but they can live to be hundreds of years old.

Orion and Alvis straighten simultaneously, towering dark sentries on either side of me. I attempt to pull on my best Keeper of Death mask, but I'm tired. I rub my face before speaking pointedly to Leah. "I take this quite seriously. The true High Lord of Iron fought for what was right, forsaking his entire country, to save *your* kind."

Leah and her companion's gaze lower, the people of Borealis know full well what was sacrificed for their freedom. I strengthen my stance and voice, filling it with confidence.

"I will not let his brat of a daughter destroy everything Knothall and Rohana fought for. I will not allow *that* to be their legacy. We need every bit of help we can get, I've seen her power firsthand. We have no allies, you've said so yourself, Thornton, that your mother cannot risk her people. I cannot say that I blame her. Haven't you lost enough, haven't we all lost enough?"

The young Prince with Leah stares me down with fury, but doesn't argue. Queen Agaleth is his mother, and I would be afraid to face down Eros too, especially with no Aether. The tribal white markings of his people are painted down both his sharp tawny cheeks, smooth hazel hair is tucked behind rounded ears. He raises his chin, then subtly nods.

Everyone is watching me. Novak stands beside Vivvus again with a proud smile.

"I have a plan to get the essence of Iron, and Sylvan. None of that matters though, not if we don't trust each other a little and have a little hope." I lock eyes with everyone in the room for a moment before continuing in a worried whisper.

"If we don't do that, what is the point of saving everyone? If we're just going to keep killing and hurting for the sake of power and magic, we *should* be wiped off the map. Why bother to live in a world where you can't love freely? Not only that, but to live in a world where most don't even know the true history of their own people. Fae are fractured, and the only ones you can save us are ourselves."

Everyone nods or voices agreement quite boisterously, and even Aiden's broad face is upturned into a small devilish grin. The tedious meeting has been brought to a clear moment of truth. We have all loved and lost. It's time for the bloodshed to be over, to love each other and put away petty things.

Vivvus locks eyes with me and I nod to her. The next step. The second in command holds up her hand and passionate conversations are silenced. "I believe you, Keeper of Death. We still need to be prepared if all else fails. One moon cycle for you to complete your mission, and for us to prepare for a possible third war, that's all we can spare. If Eros continues to take power on your journey, there will be nothing left for you to save."

"Agreed." I nod. Orion and Alvis are still vigilant at my side. Novak watches the twins and something like pure love fills his entire being, his charcoal aura so light I can hardly see it.

"You will receive Earth essence and leave here at first light, I'm afraid even one moon cycle will be too long. Thornton, you must propose to Queen Agaleth that she reconsider." Viv decides with graveness, pulling me from the relief I find looking at Novak. Thornton agrees and the table begins discussing the best route through Sylvan.

Groups of Purists roam the area solely for hunting Humans or non-Fae. I've also learned that anyone who delivers a criminal to the Eternal is given a hefty reward, something I've never heard of before, though it makes sense. I will be an easy target to spot, and apparently Novak has a reputation in Sylvan for being a 'troublemaker', not to mention the twins themselves. We need to arrive on our terms, not Typhan's.

Panrauth presides over the meeting in silence, watching me lead the conversation with the others. Thundering fear ripples across our bond suddenly and snaps my attention upwards to the High Lord sizing up Novak, each sidelong glance longer and causing the musician to shift uncomfortably.

The Satyr gather closer to the table and I give them half my attention. The male is Fin and the female is Ruki, brother and sister. Fin gives me nothing but disgust, his sister however seems to be a kindred soul. She has shown Novak kindness and has a hunger for changing things.

The High Lord is quiet throughout the decisions made for him, but I know he will have a condition. Pan is merely a puppet, and Vivvus makes an excellent puppeteer, but he will want to have some fun. Pan's eyes alight with Aether with near the same intensity as when he burned Umber's ship down. If not for the shield, I wonder if this room would look the same.

Pan steps closer to Novak, making the musician look like a rag doll in comparison. Novak shifts a casual step back from Pan, crossing his arms with a wicked grin. I can feel his fear, but you would never know it on the outside. Not yet.

"*I* will do this, on one condition. I need a favor." Pan states with drawling amusement. Vivvus shifts in place, thick brows narrowing at her brother. The courtiers exchange nervous glances, the dominance Pan establishes with such little words is unsettling.

"Sheesh, from little old me?" Novak keeps his steady grin, but his aura darkens and I watch subtle darkness mask his bright blue eyes. Everyone is silent, and I hope the shield can hold Novak's power if he can't contain it.

"I've heard that your *Tzel* makes an excellent interrogator. I am in need of one."

I knew Pan would ask for something, but I didn't think he would ask this of a Fae who never carries weapons. I'm not sure if Novak even knows *how* to hurt someone. Invading someone's mind, I wasn't aware that was even possible. The aching in my shoulder disagrees with my sentiment, but that isn't the same, that wasn't *him*. The control he's crafted for years is for a reason, I know that now. I won't tempt the *Tzel* again.

Unless he wants me to. Other than the bite, I found his company quite pleasing.

Panrauth closes the tense distance between them and stares down at Novak's hard face, smile wiped from freckles. "I have several suspected spies remaining in my court." Pan explains. Novak stands his ground and rolls his shoulders back.

The move causes Alvis to break from my side, subtly moving closer to his silent friend.

"Come now, it can't be that hard, break their minds, tell me what I need to know." The High Lord's bored demand rings my ears. He plays it off like it's such a minor thing to do, like it isn't ... a violation.

When he doesn't answer, Panrauth straightens over Novak's shaking figure and glances at me sideways, giving me a deadly smile. He wants to break Novak, and make me watch.

Viv shifts closer to Pan and reaches for his arm but he shrugs her off. Aiden holds a quiet smile, like a dagger waiting in the dark. He's at his brother's side, looking down on Novak. I think he could very easily kill someone with his bare hands. The two brothers are terrifying and for a moment I fear for my love, and the fate of Terra, in their hands.

Novak shakes violently, once blue irises are black but the whites haven't disappeared yet. "I don't do that." He speaks with such struggle I grasp Orion's hand and he squeezes me tight, neither of us looking away from the scene.

Alvis is nearly there, casually slipping past the Satyr, his presence the only relief I have in this situation. I want to speak up but know if I do, it will only make Novak appear weak.

"Can't, or *won't*?" Pan's jaw flexes as he spits the words down into Novak's defiant face.

We watch the High Lord press his foot to the stray dog's neck, threatening to snuff its life out.

A familiar river of star filled abyss flows around Novak and his entire body transforms slowly into ethereal shadows. Darkness feathers out across his features, but no other demonic bits come out to play. Whispers sweep across the table. The *Tzel* is real. The connection between him and I holds shame, fear and *anger*. So much fury.

I have a strong need to punch Panrauth in the face.

Novak's dark eyes meet mine, and a deadly smile spreads across his clouded features. The white of his perfect teeth, aside from that crooked incisor on the right, is a stark contrast against his galaxy ridden complexion.

"I could arrange that for you." Despite the situation, a wicked grin takes hold of my lips when I hear his hoarse voice through the bond.

"Are you going to admit I'm right yet?" I taunt playfully, as if two highly charged males aren't about to face off in this entirely too small battle room.

Novak chuckles darkly, sliding his attention *slowly* from me to Panrauth, drawing subtle confusion and perhaps fear from Pan. The High Lord glances between the amused Keeper of Death and the Shadow, his hackles bristling further as he does.

Alvis is now feet from Novak, and he hangs back for a hesitant moment. Novak shudders and his figure is becoming more frightening by the second, almost like when the beast took over last night. Alvis rests a hand on his friend's shoulder, grounding Novak and causing some of the darkness to fade. Alvis visibly relaxes when Novak does, as if he wasn't sure his touch would be welcome.

The *Tzel* is fighting to get out and claw Pan to pieces, and Novak is fighting twice as hard to keep it in. The sight makes my stomach twist in on itself. I wish I knew how to control my own darkness to throw at Pan, to threaten him in some way. He disappoints and disgusts me. Novak nervously glances at Alvis over his shoulder, and then to me.

Everyone's attention is on me, in fact. Even through his wild shadows, I can tell Novak is absolutely broken at the mere thought of invading anyone like that.

But, he says, *"I'll do it. For you."*

I don't answer my lover, instead I lock eyes with the High Lord and raise my chin. "The only reason you returned to power is because of *me*. I have always done what is necessary, no matter the consequence or cost. I was once *your* Keeper of Death, Panrauth, do not forget that for a moment."

The sharp words hit their mark and I proudly wait as Panrauth dismisses Novak falling apart. He paces to me in a few long strides, then pauses inches away from my face. "No deal, then." He huffs, hot breath rolling over my lips.

Almost every member of his court shifts, disapproval on their faces. Pan just made it personal, and everyone knows it. Novak will certainly make his job easier, but Pan doesn't *need* him, and every word I said is painfully true. All Pan wants is to turn Novak dark. Whether to punish him, or me, or both of us, I don't know.

I pat Pan's clean shaven jaw with my small hand, grinning at the redness still there from when I knocked him sideways on the balcony. I should've hit him again.

Over and over until I smacked sense into him.

"Fine with me, High Lord." Honey drips in the words I leave behind. Orion, Alvis and Novak follow me out, keeping close as a war ensues in our wake. The moment we leave the room Novak's shadows loosen from him completely, his tight darkness trailing on the floor behind our group.

The watch on my wrist clicks as it strikes the early hour. The moons are hidden as the sky is blessed with a preemptive, glorious dawn. Our silent group is dressed in traveling gear and packed, waiting together at the elevator. I don't tell anyone about Vivvus coming to my room, begging me to stay and that she can convince Pan to help.

I don't need his help, or want it. He's selfish, always has been and always will be. I'm not sure if my plan will work, but I have to try. I won't ask Novak to be a weapon, and hopefully Vivvus' help will be enough. If it's not, well ... I'll cross that bridge when I get there. Anxiety seeps into every pore, long held worry over facing Typhan mingles with this newest development.

"Lyth, what are you doing?" Novak pleads in a whisper once we're in the elevator, he can't shake the night skin and heavy shadows. His heart pounds so wildly down the bond, it throws me into a headache.

Orion questions Novak, his soft words immediately send rage through me. Out of all people. "It's just once, Novak."

Alvis stiffens, sensing the anger I have brewing for his brother.

"*No*, and that's final. Not another *word* until we get out of here." I snap, absolutely shaking with anger and fighting pissed off, hot tears.

Novak and Alvis glance at each other and we ride the elevator in silence. Alvis casually rests a hand on his sword and scans the empty village ahead of us before we exit. The grand hollow is eerily dark and empty, the cleared and sleeping city reminds me of a bat colony hiding in plain sight, waiting to fly out and spook you.

The horses are certainly excited to be free, the large stables outside the Great Tree are full of nickering horses and the large ram-like creatures calling to ride with us.

"They're called *got*." Alvis explains as we tack up and I nod in acknowledgment, too pissed and stressed out to answer. Before we leave I pause and look back, debating on letting all the creatures out just to cause a problem. Vivvus will have to clean up the mess though, Panrauth certainly won't do it.

I race after my companions instead, heading for the point of the pentagon that holds our hidden path to Sylvan. The sight of a crow flying overhead catches my breath. A part of me hopes it's Virgil, but I know better. There's no way he could've made it over the sea. The damn bird always did like Pan though, led him to save my life.

Fucking High Lord, making things complicated.

The moment Fiddler strides into the woods, air rushes into my lungs with less resistance and the comforting black speck disappears into the canopy above. Novak's lost in a trance and his shadows have finally withdrawn, leaving a broken male with nightmares playing in glazed eyes. He rides by my side, and the twins are equally silent ahead of us. The bond between us has gone cold, anything that was shared between us before is gone.

He shut me out. He shut the world out.

After riding through thick tension and dense woods for an hour, Orion halts abruptly and turns his painted horse to face Novak and I. His hardened, stormy eyes stare into mine, and Alvis is an unreadable stone beside him. "Now what?" Orion asks evenly, though tension pours from the two.

I rub my face and sigh, glancing between him and Alvis who shakes hair from downward eyes, his side of the aura transforming into a perilous ocean. "Now, we sleep for a few hours, and figure it out when we wake up."

"What is there to *figure* out? As much as I hate to say it, we can't do it without that bastard. Same goes for Eros, you can't get the essence without them. You can bluff to them, but not us." Alvis shouts suddenly, composure replaced by frustration.

Orion flinches and pushes his glasses atop his head, then rubs his flushed face. Novak is motionless and stuck in a trance, fixated on the overarching canopy above. His shadows slowly come to life and drift to the ground around his horse.

I dismount and land with a jolt to my thighs, then limp away from them in silence. Alvis isn't letting it go, the warrior in him fighting to be knocked down a peg. The scarred Fae with white vines decorating his body dismounts with a huff, trailing after me. I ignore him, stopping only when his hand claps down on my small shoulder.

We're doing *this*, then.

"Brother." Orion warns from behind us. My hackles rise and my instincts beg me to throttle him. I bet I can hold my own against him, if I use surprise to my advantage. I don't want to fight him though, I'm more disappointed than anything. He doesn't trust me. I keep my feet planted and barely look over my shoulder to him, but my voice is *glacial*.

"You seem to forget I was the Lead Keeper of the Eternal Machine, a title earned through blood and a lifetime of managing the Aether *you* all treasure so much. Funny, since *you're* the one who hasn't let me forget that fact." Alvis' grip on me loosens and I catch surprise in his eyes before shaking him off. "If you can't trust me, then go. You have always been free to leave or stay, Prince. *Nothing* is keeping you here."

I storm off before he can protest, and I already regret my poisonous words. No one follows, and perhaps it's better this way. I don't know why I believed they could truly trust me. I thought they did, but I can use that to my advantage. Just like I use everyone else in my life. I settle down in a small clearing after ten minutes of walking, the warming sky reminds me I won't get much sleep.

I wish Novak was here, I want to hold him. I sit with my legs stretched out in thick leaves and peer in the direction of their distant camp a few times, seeing no trace of anyone. I close my eyes and search the bond between us, sending my darkness down the tether. The bridge of shadowed stone between our minds is crumbling, and my darkness rebounds off a frigid, invisible wall.

I bury my face in my hands and sigh. I decide he doesn't want to be found right now, and try not to think the worst.

The fresh herbs are of excellent quality. Smoke soothes my soul and body while I lie on the leaf littered ground, staring up into the brightening canopy. Just when I think I have everything figured out, another wrench is thrown into the mix. I take another puff and close my eyes, imagining myself on Captain's ship.

The air rushing through my hair as I stand on the helm with Captain beside me, the twins bickering on the deck below as Novak plays his lute in the crows nest above. Dinners filled with laughter and wild tales are waiting, and I can go on heroic adventures and redeem myself like the twins have. I'm going to get all of us there again, somehow. My hopeful thoughts are interrupted after a moment, doubt crawling in.

I have no idea if the ancient vents in these lands will give me the essence I need. Trihewyn said I had to ask the Ancients of the land, do I really need the royalty of courts to accompany me when I do that?

I don't know if my plan will work at all, loopholes in faerie deals are tricky things, and I'm risking so much.

Maybe they're right, and I'm wrong. Even so, the alternative is too sickening, even for my tastes. The vial strung on my neck has grown heavier these past few days and suffocates me at times, reminding me of a collar more than a necklace. I can't imagine what it will feel like full, and the thought terrifies me. That is, if I even get that far.

Perhaps the Ancients *didn't* choose right, I'm not who they think I am. After all this time, I will prove to be nothing. The female in my head has been quiet since I reached out and I never got a chance to look at the illustration with Novak. The Ancients spoke of a 'Lady', perhaps that's a start. My eyes are still closed when leaves crunch, twigs snapping under too much weight to be my companions.

I inhale deep, forcing my racing heart to calm. "Not changing my mind, so kindly fuck off." I grumble, keeping my eyes closed.

Panrauth lays beside me in the leaves, his arm brushing against mine and sending shivers. Like when we sat together in the lab, watching a malfunctioned invention burn up. "I wasn't expecting you to." The usual dark amusement resides in his voice and I fight the urge to swat him.

After a moment, I open my eyes and turn my head to scrutinize his broad face. The blacksmith I befriended is gone, only the shell of a High Lord remains. Why do I feel sorry for him?

Panrauth watches the canopy above, tight jaw muscles flexing when I spit anger at him. "What do you want then?"

"You need the magic, don't you?" He muses and a small smile tugs a corner of his lips. I sit up and scowl at him, waiting for him to elaborate. He follows suit, holding me steady in his burning gaze. "I was curious if he would do it."

"You are cruel."

"I agree."

I scoff and scan the woods around us. He's alone, still dressed in the fine elegance of last night's party. Shackles of faded silk. His rough hand cradles the vial on my neck and the burden lessens temporarily, but my skin crawls under his light touch. I raise my chin, glaring at him. He drops his hand with a chuckle, gesturing to the pipe in my hand as heaviness resides in my chest once more.

"Not bad, eh? You inspired me to start gardening, apparently I have a green thumb."

"Is that what a High Lord does in his spare time, grow plants and tempt demons?" I pass the pipe to him and cross my arms.

"I thought you weren't scared." A smoke ring fills the air above us, floating with Panrauth's curious taunt.

I'm not scared of Novak. I'm not even scared of the *Tzel*. I'm afraid of what will happen to Novak if he ever releases the beast, completely. A weapon he will be indeed, but what will be left of the musician?

It's a chance I have to take.

When the pipe returns to me, I place my words carefully. "I'm not. I took the time to listen." I pause and inhale, then drop my guard as I exhale. "You see the *Tzel*, I see Novak. A Fae who is quite good at the lute. A Fae who has had a series of shitty things happen to him, because we live in a shitty world. And now everyone holds it against him. Sound familiar?"

Pan rolls his eyes, glowering down at me with a smirk. "You can take anyone from The Pit, find the tiniest bit of light, and spin it into something more."

"Most people are worth saving, you just have to give them a chance." I whisper. His face lowers so his slightly off kilter nose is inches from mine and sweet lavender Aether fills the air, overtaking my senses.

"You never cease to amaze me." Pan rubs my cheek with work torn fingers, then runs a thumb over my left brow. I shudder, remembering how I felt the first time he told me that. My heart races and lungs hold air when his gentle fingers pause at my lips.

"Pan," I breathe, staring into his thirsty eyes.

I memorize his strong face, one good, *last* time. The lust between us will never cease, and it's plain he's still waiting for me to come back to him. But, we're not meant to be. We never were, regardless of Novak. When he doesn't answer me, and instead presses his thumb to my bottom lip, I avert my eyes and focus on the rainbow of leaves beside me.

After pushing out a ragged breath he grasps my chin, pulling my face back to his with caution. "You have to ask, right?"

The thought of asking him for anything now is sickening. After what he did to Novak, and the tortured relationship between us. I close my eyes and breathe, focusing on the task before me. I recall the words I said to Trihewyn and take Pan's hand from my face, then hold both of his gently. Our eyes meet and my fingers squeeze tight as I shakily make the request, fear crawling as I anticipate the impending onslaught of power.

"I ask you, High Lord of the Terra Court, and spirits of Earth, to bestow me with a part of the essence gifted to these lands. I do so in gratitude, and great need."

Pan's pale green aura *explodes* into an emerald storm immediately, swirling around us with instantaneous ferocity. I inhale sharply at the sight of the micro burst. The terror in Panrauth's wild eyes matches my own, but the realization strikes us both much too late.

It's too much. I can't handle it.

The hurricane of Earth magic lifts rocks, dirt and small plants from the ground with ease. A foreboding pause has everything hovering in the air around us for torturous seconds. A thunderous crack rips through the sky, then all airborne objects slam to the ground.

The force is simultaneous with the crackling cloud of green that thrusts into my ears, eyes, nose and mouth. I'm torn apart by the manic Aether ricocheting inside, burning through my veins and disrupting my organs. A scream escapes me, then is abruptly cut off.

Sense of the world fades away and I tumble down, down, down. Panrauth's eyes filled with panic is the last clear scene I have. Rough hands attempt to extract me from the chilled underwater world I find myself in, the substance viscous like oil.

Muffled, angry voices are above the surface, it sounds so terrible there. The weight on my neck strengthens and firmly tugs me *down*, out of the grip from multiple sets of hands gripping to me for dear life. The vial offers to drown me, and won't take no for an answer.

I will miss them all so much, Novak and Alvis especially. I can't deny that I'm thankful the fighting has ended so I can feel what true *peace* is like. I don't have to hurt anyone now, no betrayals need to be committed.

"It's not your time yet. I need you." The Lady's familiar voice floats around me in the slippery dark. An ice cold grip gently takes my wrist and lifts me from the silky soft and warm bottom.

"I'm tired, do I have to?" I protest, having just settled down into the most comfortable bed.

"I'm afraid so. All will be explained in good time, little one. You will be able to rest soon, your journey is almost finished, then I shall ensure you will find a peaceful life."

"Will you tell me who you are?"

"You will find out soon enough, my dear."

A new type of darkness sweeps through the sea, immediately lifting me out of the cold place, bringing warmth and dangerous love with it.

DON'T TRUST ME

The desperate sun strokes my face, birdsong fills my ears and a soft breeze caresses my skin. Sea salt fills my nose and I smile, gratefully inhaling the smell of my home welcoming me back to the land of the living. The swaying movement underneath me disorients my peace, pulling my drowsy eyes open. Panic ensues.

I'm on a horse.

I squeal and flail but Novak's arms tighten around me, settling me at once. "Careful there."

I exhale and rub my throbbing forehead, then take in our surroundings. I'm sideways on a bareback Fiddler, held close to Novak's bare chest. No reins, no saddle. We're trailing far behind the twins and another small rider is with them. The golden hour of dusk touches open fields of low grass, the heat near unbearable and causing sweat to bead on Novak's forehead. How long was I out for?

"What happened? Where are we?" I shield my eyes from the bright sky and hide into his damp chest again. Freckled arms keep me steady, his chest releases a heavy breath and an unsteady voice.

"I couldn't feel you, feel *us*. I thought I lost you, Lyth."

The bond. I lift the burdensome vial from my neck, dense green and purple smoke chases each other in the glass. I look up to Novak, his hair beyond disheveled and eyes distraught, dark circles rest under them and his usual warm skin is pale.

"I'm-" I start, but Novak's harsh voice stops me, worry lines twist his absent smile down.

"I *swear*, if you say I'm fine one more time, I'm going to feed you to the Giants." He warns.

I chuckle, my small laugh becoming boisterous. I hold my side, unable to stop. Novak rolls his eyes, fighting the relief in his voice. "I'm mad at you, stop laughing," He grunts, but I kiss his neck, then bring my smiling lips towards his ear. He shudders and brings his lips to mine, lingering and whispering desperate words. "Seriously, Lyth. I can't do that again."

"I couldn't feel you either, you know. Before Pan came, I called out to you. And you didn't answer." Hurt laces with my whisper. He shut me out, just after letting me in.

Novak bites his cheek and looks elsewhere. "I'm sorry. I was ... occupied. I didn't mean to shut you out, just ... it."

I nod, placing my hand on his cheek. "From now on, we're together." I brush a thumb over his bruised eye, purple and blue spreads in a massive splotch down his face. I raise a brow, evoking the serious face again from him.

He lifts a shoulder. "It wanted a fight, so I gave him one."

"*Pan* did this?"

"No, he cleared off the second I found you."

I imagine the scene, my unconscious body on the ground with Pan over me, a shock wave of Aether ripping through the forest. The *Tzel* coming across his love, almost lost to death.

"What does *Tzel* mean?"

Novak's gaze is hard on the horizon. "Does it matter?"

"No, I suppose it doesn't." I snuggle back into his chest and wrap my arms around his neck. Novak sighs, a hand finds my hair and gently rakes through.

"Shadow of Death. That's what everyone started calling me, after what I did." When I don't speak, he continues. "After those *fucking* purists left me for dead, I was alone. Mav and Sage," He pauses again, their names causing his eyes to darken. I find a curl at his neck and wrap my finger around it.

"I told them to run the moment I made the deal, and they did. I told them to, and they did." Sadness creeps into his voice. He told them to leave, but hoped they would stay. "I suppose it's a good thing. They were long gone when it happened."

"When what happened?" I ask, the words falling out. "I'm sorry."

"Do you *really* want to know Lyth? Because I'm afraid if you do, you won't *ever* look at me the same again." He snaps, more pissed than I'd ever seen him.

"If you knew half the things *I've* done in that damn prison, you would be afraid of me. It doesn't matter to me Novak, I just thought after all this time you would realize I'm on your side." I shift in his arms, anger pulsing through my veins.

"I have never doubted that, Lythienne." He gives me a softened stare, then sighs. "I was nearly there, I could feel whatever waits for us on the other side. And the next thing I know, this damn *thing* is using my body, destroying an entire village. I tried, I *tried*. No matter what I did, or what I said, all it wanted was revenge. Even if it meant killing innocent Fae."

"Revenge for what?"

"I don't know." After a beat, he gives me the most serious look I've ever seen from him. "After that, I made a deal with the thing. Anytime I lose control and it takes over, I'm gone."

"*Gone*?" I reiterate, and he nods solemnly.

"I never want to see anything like that again. Especially knowing it was caused by my own hands. Asleep, more like, not gone. I have no control when it takes over, and I don't ... I don't want to watch what I become."

I nod, debating whether to tell him about the Lady, and how she pulled me back from death. I decide right now isn't the time, I don't want to stop his truth. The twins look behind them, both grinning when they see me awake in Novak's arms. "I nearly killed them, but thankfully they were able to stop me, pull me out of the wreckage I left behind." He gestures to them with exhaustion.

"You didn't leave wreckage, the *Tzel* did. You cannot blame yourself for not being able to control it, Novak." I say, and he brushes wild hair from my face as Fiddler slows under us.

"Maybe not, but I have sworn since that day I would keep it contained. You make that quite difficult." He teases, kissing my nose.

"Perhaps it likes me." I grin, receiving an eye roll from Novak. "Novak, did you know," I pause, biting my lip as I look up into his slightly brightened eyes. "When you turn into the night sky, I find it quite beautiful. And, well, you have wings, when you let yourself go. I didn't know if you knew that, but I wanted to tell you, and I think they're magnificent."

Surprise lights his face, and I expect terror to follow. Instead, he thoughtfully contemplates my words. "Are they big?"

I laugh, pressing my forehead to his. "Perhaps tonight we can entice them, and you can see for yourself."

He smiles, kissing my nose once more. "I'd like that."

We continue on, catching up to the group paused on a knoll. Alvis and Orion meet my gaze with relieved faces. Leah waits beside them, giving me a slight nod when I turn my attention to her. The plan is still on.

Alvis' face is injured much worse than Novak's, and I wonder why he or Orion haven't used their Aether to heal the intense lacerations. The *Tzel* must've beaten him within inches of his life for the injuries to still be there. Faeries heal fast, but not all wounds heal quickly. Especially life threatening ones. I think of my shoulder, healed now and bruises gone.

Perhaps the *Tzel* and Prince both needed to let off steam, and this isn't the first time the two have used each other in this fashion. If anyone can tackle the beast, it's Alvis. I shudder at the thought of being caught in a battle between such powerful males.

"Silverbury is just over the next knoll. We can make it there by nightfall, or camp here to recoup." Leah is matter of fact, looking at me for orders.

Orion and Alvis focus on the horizon, at their home hidden behind the next hill, with sadness in their eyes. Novak's gaze lingers as well. I had wondered before if he lived there long enough to call the place home, but now I know the only true home he's had is the ship.

"We will head out at first light. I need to take these off." I say and rest a hand on my knee. Leah nods and we all dismount, then set up separate camps in a hidden grove of cherry trees neighboring the meadow.

I rest on Novak's chest and listen to a menagerie of critters trill and call to each other through the night. Alvis and Orion wandered off to their own camp nearly an hour ago, no doubt discussing the impending visit with their father. Leah's camp is not far from ours, the Human mostly silent thus far. Novak had cast a sound shield around our snuggled bodies the moment we were alone.

"Why is she here?" I jut my chin in the direction of her camp, curious to hear his reasoning.

"Apparently traveling with the Shadow of Death and its Keeper is better than dealing with the High Lord of Terra." He decides, dark amusement tainting his tired voice.

I'm quiet for a while, listening to the grove further come to life at night. The full canopy above rustles in the chilled breeze, and every once in a while a flash of nocturnal eyes is apparent. A soft floral scent wafts in the air and I sigh, utterly content to stay here forever. Tomorrow's mission is overwhelming my mind and I need something to think about.

"Can I ask you something?"

Novak's breathing pauses, as does his hand petting my hair. "Of course."

"Can we live here? Right here?" I ask bravely, focusing my gaze on his. The clearing is perfect, every tree is in full bloom and fills the ground we lie on with purple and pink blossoms. The area needs to be cleaned up a bit, otherwise it's partially hidden away from the world. "After we visit Borealis, and wherever else you take me, let's make a life here."

Novak sits up on an elbow and takes my hand, his growing smile matches my own. "It sounds like you have quite the grand plan for us." He whispers, brushing hair from my face. I need hope. I need to think about what kind of life we *could* have together. "Tell me what you're thinking."

So I do.

I tell him all the places I want to visit, and my dreams of becoming a pirate with him, Captain and the twins. The idea draws laughter from him, as does traveling to Borealis and listening to him play in the music halls I've heard all about, dancing the night away with Alvis. I want to visit Dew Falls, where Satyr live in the mountains and Novak grew up. That sentiment only brings a sad smile, but he doesn't say no.

"And then what, live here and grow old together?" Novak asks with a tender smile, caressing my tattoos with a gentle hand. I point firmly to a wide and healthy cherry tree behind us, its thick branches overhanging our camp. "Right there. Put our names in it so we know exactly where we belong."

Novak obeys, crossing to the ancient tree, perhaps the oldest in the clearing. With a twitch of his fingers, a tendril of shadow extends. The letters *L* and *N* silently burn into the bark, surrounded by a heart. "How's that, my lady?" He asks and gives me a dramatic bow, throwing hair from his eyes after he rises.

"You are much more powerful than you let on." I state matter of factually, drawing surprise from him. I need his help, whether I like it or not, which I absolutely *don't*. "I need to tell you something."

He sits cross legged in front of me and takes my hands, sapphires reflect the double moons leaking through the canopy above. "What is it?"

"Do you trust me?" I ask, guilt lumping in my throat.

"You know that I do." Novak squeezes my hands tight, and his thick fluffed ears perk as he tilts his head. I tell him everything that I've been planning thus far, and his once soft face tightens as secrets release into the thickening atmosphere between us.

Well, nearly everything. Unfortunately, I will have to hurt him by the end of this, too. Silence lingers in the air for minutes after I'm done speaking, but his eyes do not leave mine once during this conversation, nor do they darken even a shade. His hands did retreat from mine after I revealed the height of my manipulation, as I expected them to.

"You *cannot* tell the others Novak, do you understand this?" I ask in a fatal tone I've never used with him before, and he doesn't say anything. His eyes desperately search mine for the person he's come to know on this journey, but instead he only finds the Keeper of Death. "I cannot think of any other way to get the essence, I have to ... betray them."

"He will never forgive you for this." Novak warns in defeat as his hands tighten into fists.

I am the one to break our long held stare and he draws his knees up to his chest, fingers desperately gripping his shins. Hot tears escape my eyes and I bury my face in my hands, silently grieving the friendship I've come to treasure. Sadness splashes onto the cherry blossoms under my hunched over figure and even though I don't deserve it, I wish Novak would hug me.

But he doesn't, and I say, "I don't expect him to."

Novak snores, adorable puffs of air lift a tussle of shaggy locks from his furrowed brow. Neither of us slept well and I groan, pain surging my exhausted muscles as I secure my sockets and prosthesis on. A careful hand rests on my shoulder, startling me.

"Need help?" I jolt in the blossoms beside our slid together bed rolls, looking up to find Orion. His figure is heavily dressed in layers of leathers, belts and a chestnut cloak.

"*Fuck*, Orion. Good way to get stabbed." I snap and roll my loose pant leg down, securing the cuff at the bottom with a huff.

"I'm sorry, I was just up early too, and heard you, I, erm, I need to talk to you."

"Help me up." I reach for his hands and he gently pulls me up. Novak rolls over in his cradle of shadows, brow finally softening as he drifts further into sleep. I waver unsteadily and hold onto Orion's arm, then point at my cane on the ground. He retrieves it for me and raises a brow when I lean on the metal shaft heavily.

"Haven't seen you use that since Glen."

"Special occasion."

I walk with him to the outside world waiting in the meadow adjoining our peaceful grove. When we find the sunrise lighting up the grasslands, Orion plants his feet and wraps his arms around my shoulders, having to lean over slightly. I let my tired weight fall back onto him. A heavy sigh of content leaves me as we watch the sun fill the awakening sky with blood.

"The flaring orange around the outer edges there, reminds me of Emeric's eyes." Orion says after a moment, a finger pointing to thick plumes of clouds in the west.

"You're going to see him again. *We're* going to see him again, I promise." I say, my fingers gripping his forearm around my chest. Orion chuckles, dark plum eyes leaving the sky to look down at me.

"He quite likes you." He remarks and I smile. Orion exhales a heavy breath, pondering the thought. "It would be truly delightful, to all be together again. Besides Alvis, that male is the only one who can bring me peace."

I shift in his arms so I'm facing him, my eyes wet in the dawn's early light. "I need to know why you're doing this. I can't bring you there without knowing."

Orion smiles, no doubt picturing me attempting to make them stay behind. After a moment, he pushes up his dirty glasses and speaks quietly, his handsome features serious. "We can't run forever. One of us has to take the throne, eventually." The last word is near silent, and his next statement is a choked whisper.

"Otherwise, are any better than Panrauth? To forsake our lands and people?"

Tears splinter my voice. "Why does it have to be this way? You shouldn't have to *choose*."

"I spoke with Panrauth, I wanted to know how he plans to choose an heir. His daughters both possess magic, even as half Fae." Orion's arms tighten around me, the breeze around us picks up and rain threatens to fall.

"*And*?"

"And Typhan is sadistic." Not my father, but Typhan. "There are no ancestral rules. Twins are one soul, two bodies. You sever the bond and you are left with a mutilated Fae, power beyond belief, and only half a soul."

It takes a minute for the puzzle pieces to settle. They are Typhan's weapons, it has nothing to do with needing one heir. The strongest will survive, and whoever is left standing holds both of their power. A loophole, at Sylvan's complete disposal.

"We should kill the bastard."

Orion laughs darkly, the white vines visible along his neck glowing bright. He pulls down the hem of his neckline, gesturing to the snaking tattoos. "I take it Al never told you what these are for?"

I focus on the lilac vines crawling along my own wrists. "No."

"When we turned of age, Alvis and I were forced into a blood bond with our father. The *first* time he caught our mother conspiring against him."

Oh, no.

I step out of his embrace, blood frozen. Rain pours all around us, closing in on where we stand. "Neither of us can so much as harm him, or conspire to. The only two Fae who *might* be able to, and we can't. We weren't able to leave without consequences, and by doing so we killed our Mother." Shame burdens him and he focuses on the muddied ground, both of us are caught in the downpour and drenched.

Then he asks, "Do you love Alvis?"

My heart stops and I cross my arms, my loose hair presses to my body. "You know how I feel about Novak. You were the *first* to know, *everyone* knew before I did. Why would you even ask that? Alvis loves Novak."

And doesn't that make me feel like a piece of shit, saying that out loud. He loves the male I'm fucking.

Orion steps closer to me, then rests a hand on my shoulder. "You didn't answer my question."

I look away. "Does it matter?"

"You know just as well as I do, my brother will be whatever you *want* him to be, and do whatever you *ask* him to do. He loves *both* of you."

Grief streams down my face, mixing with pelting raindrops. "Why are you telling me this?"

"Because I'm right, and I know there is a part of you that loves him. He tries to hide it from me, but it's so hard not to hear every single thought he practically shouts in his head about you, and he can't contain his thoughts about Novak like he used to, either. You're going to need him."

His words break me and I collapse into Orion, sobbing into his chest as I clutch handfuls of his cloak. I know what he's doing. I can use my own feelings, and his, to my advantage.

He's planning on taking the fall.

If he thinks I'm okay with this, then he'll be even more surprised when I ...

"You know, this is the first time I've felt rain." I mumble into his chest, then look up to his half smiling face. Water thrashes my body and soul, but it's not *real* rain. The intense lavender fragrance of Aether is present. It's only his overwhelming sadness, but nevertheless wonderful. I throw my arms out, face the sky and crow into the storm above. Orion laughs, joining me with a howl.

I open my eyes at the sound of the others joining our fun. Alvis runs to his brother's side, howling with him into the sky. Novak sweeps me off my feet and dances with me, humming my favorite tune as I giggle. Orion and Alvis tussle in the mud, then sling slick earth at Novak and I.

I squeal when cold mud slaps across my face. Novak and I return fire in moments. Water floods our mud pit, both twins unleashing their long held rain onto bone dry land. We take advantage of the muck, entering a full on war. Leah stands on the edge of rain and mud, arms crossed with a disapproving face.

Alvis hits her spectacularly between the eyes with a splash of dirt, earning return fire from the Human whose facade finally breaks. We end in a heap of flooded earth, covered head to toe and giggling like children.

"How have you four gotten this far?" Leah teases.

Novak chuckles, dimples present for a full, real smile. "Fun is *absolutely* necessary before impossible missions."

"Alright, what was that thing you did in the Mists? Clean up your mess." I taunt, elbowing a grinning Orion.

Alvis ruffles my sticky hair and rises, then slips magnificently into a pile, evoking another round of voracious laughter from us all.

WHEEL OF FORTUNE

WATER AND FIRE

Captain; circa 15,870 A.C

"I've seen a future, dear Brier. The day you were born your potential legend was burned into my memory, and I've waited a long time to see if it would come true."

The quaking aspen of a Wild Fae warns, and I shudder.

"Potential legend? You just said you saw my future."

"I saw one of them. Destiny is not some woven thread we cannot unravel or change. Our fate is a pliable connection with thousands of other souls and decisions, each person we meet and choice we make determines where we will land in the stars. In the end, it depends on you."

"You share a prophecy with a few chosen Fae, and you will be the first to hear it. Find the weapon you can not wield, he shall reign, and you shall walk with the poet who becomes a king. Brace for the fall,"

The Wild Fae inhales deeply, the air in my own lungs is caught by gusts of thick wind filled with forest debris. "I should not tell you this, but you shall have to betray the one you love most, for this future to unfold."

I'M THE VILLAIN, REMEMBER?

Steel plated sentries wait along every inch of the mile high walls surrounding Silverbury. They are stone cold, any and all emotion gone from their hard stares. I highly doubt they've ever played in the mud.

Silverbury is a gorgeous city, the High Court residing in a castle half underwater with merfae populating its proud lake. You would never know it from out here though, waiting in the grassy flatland. Menacing gates of iron forged in the Eternal itself are closed before us, the sight brings up bile as I'm reminded of home. A megalithic wall of granite cuts for miles through sand and thin wheat grass, keeping its treasure tucked deep inside.

Orion and Alvis are standing in the front of the group, waiting for the gates to open and lead them home. We left the horses in a small outpost outside the gates, apparently there isn't enough travel here to warrant a massive barn like Terra's.

I'm strong at Novak's side behind the twins, not daring to hold his hand here. This is a place where love is used against you, and he's not the one I want Typhan to focus on. I'm familiar with a place like this, a different kind of prison. Suddenly, I realize why Alvis and I are such kindred spirits.

He grew up in a prison as well.

Soldiers are positioned on the ground, ten on either side of the gates. Hundreds more are stationed on the walls above, bodies unmoving. I'm sure there are more beyond what my eyes can see. The guards are composed singularly of High Fae males, each waiting with an arrow strung. Females are for breeding here, not fighting.

I'm thankful Leah will be waiting for us outside, Humans are sold or killed on sight here.

The iron gates with merfae details creak open slowly and pierce my heart, the noise thrusting my ears down. I keep my chin up and follow behind my friends into Silverbury, the home of the Sylvan Court.

Silverbury is indeed a great treasure, rivaling Cervalis or the Great Tree any day. Translucent blue buildings scrape the sky, sunlight catches on large crystalline insignias decorating every surface of the city. Sylvan holds the market for many things, some of which are fine crystals. The last known precious stone mine of Iverbourne hides beneath its perfect waters.

Our path curves down into the meticulously built valley filled with merchants and homes, from here you can see how just many buildings encapsulate the shimmering vast lake. Every bit of sunlight is captured in this bowl of a city. Only Water Fae trapped by granite live here, and not many others visit, except on strict trade permitted by Typhan himself. To leave Sylvan is to forfeit your right to return, making you fair game to the High Lord's mercenaries.

Canals leak from the lake and spread throughout the city. Towering wooden wheels thrust through rushing water, powering the technology and faelights throughout the city. Aether engines must be reserved for the castle and royal airships. I've built enough of Sylvan's high tech to know it's here somewhere.

With enough natural power to accomplish anything the city needs, precious Aether isn't wasted on trivial things. I can't help but study the place in awe, subtly glancing at Orion who holds a bored mask, though his eyes linger on the grand wheels.

I want him to show me the labs. I want to brainstorm over prototypes with him while Novak and Alvis cause havoc and touch things they aren't supposed to. I want to meet the merfae Alvis and Orion snuck out to see as children. They were punished, even as small Fae, for having fun. I want to hear stories of their mother, besides the fact Typhan killed her as punishment for his sons leaving.

So many things we never had a chance to do together. I wonder if I should've told Novak the worst part, prepared him somehow. No, I need to catch him off guard. Iverbourne depends on it.

If I keep telling myself that, then maybe I'll believe it.

The descent continues for twenty minutes, my cane is a welcome friend. The closer we approach the distant castle resting on the lake, the denser the streets are with fine dressed nobility. Their whispers grow in intensity, ranging from thanking the Eternal, to cursing under their breath and spitting at us. I sweep over all of the blue, purple and pale eyes watching me with intensity.

Who is friend and who is foe? How many will fight for Eros, and against her? It doesn't appear these noble Fae can fight for anyone, even themselves.

The upper class live a sheltered and lofty life, while the mercenaries and laborers running Sylvan are situated in the slums of the outer rim we've already passed through. The place reminded me of Darkedge, poverty ridden Fae willing to do anything for a scrap of food or coin, slinking out from the darkest corners when new meat walks by. The well dressed Fae are the dangerous ones, in my opinion. Their horrors are in plain sight now, confirming my opinion.

The Market.

My attention catches on the trading station, a square to the lower right of our path. Pastries and tattoos aren't sold here, what they trade is far more gruesome. Alvis and Orion tried to prepare me for everything, providing every gritty detail of their hometown, but it wasn't enough. Currently on the auction block is a green Lesser Fae, her wings clipped together.

Shouts of her fine cooking and cleaning skills from the elder auctioneer Fae meet my ears, setting me on fire. A nobleman Fae dressed in a three piece suit discusses with his young wife, then decides to purchase the Fae. A bounty hunter hauls the poor thing off the auction block by her wing, dragging her down the wooden ramp before throwing her at the feet of her new owners. Coin is exchanged, and the nobleman tips his hat to the smirking mercenary.

Next up is a Human boy, a decent worker that will last approximately twenty years if treated with care. That statement brings laughter to the throng of nobles watching the red haired boy tremble. Tears fall from his dirty face, eyes cast downward. Novak once shared with me that Alvis received his greatest punishment for feeding the slaves awaiting auction, he would not say what Typhan did to him, only that it still haunts him.

I'm going to destroy them all. I've tried to imagine every atrocity, a torturous and obvious evil like the Mountain. This is even worse, a fresh hell wrapped in diamonds, finery and turned up noses. I stiffen and halt my steps as the bidding slows on the boy. Novak worriedly glances from me, to the now sobbing child.

"I can't leave him." I whisper, the sentries behind us threaten to shove me out of their way.

"We can't do anything right now." Novak's hand presses on my back, pushing me gently ahead. I glance behind us, at the 'empty' space behind the guards escorting us. He's right. I will find the boy after. I mark the middle aged, female's face in my mind that purchases the boy, staring hard one last time before tearing away.

A monumental castle of quartz and marble rises from the center of the lake, looming over its prestigious domain of land and water. An elegant shining bridge of silver waits, prepared to lead us to our doom on the other side. Our group pauses before going any further. I throw my arms around Novak and hold him tight, both our hearts thundering wildly.

I have to, just in case.

Orion and Alvis touch foreheads while resting their hands on the other's shoulders. Quiet fills the moment, and then the twins focus on me simultaneously. Orion pushes up his glasses, giving me a nervous smile as he does. Alvis dips his chin with a hand resting on his chest. My lip trembles, I can only manage a nod to him and Orion.

We're going to see him again. *Oh*, how I want it to be true.

A gathering of elegant High Fae follows behind us as we proudly make our way across the bridge, no laborers or mercenaries are in this area of Silverbury. Wealth and power watches on both sides of the bridge, because waiting at the end of our path is Typhan, High Lord of Sylvan Court.

Orion and Alvis halt promptly before their father, the most magnificent and deadly thing I have ever laid eyes on. Typhan evaluates his sons, seriousness masking his broad and bronzed features. With cropped brunette hair and defined strength, he and Alvis are physically cut from the same cloth. Orion with his eccentric half up hair, lean body and glasses, is their opposite. White vines crawl across Typhan's body, echoing the tattoos on his sons. The evidence of their blood bond.

The High Lord claps each male on their shoulder, a fiendish grin taking hold of his admittedly handsome features. By the Eternal, that's Orion's smile. "Welcome home boys, I've missed you."

But it's the pale white eyes beside the High Lord that sends electrifying shivers through me. The eyes of my attacker. I breathe through my nose and focus my energy on Novak's calming aura beside me, keeping my eyes on Typhan. The male beside the High Lord crosses his arms with utter delight, watching me squirm under his gaze.

The one that got away, the one that truly mattered. A bloody hand print dragging down his skin, hard eyes planning revenge in Steammire. Four males attacking one small female in a dark tunnel. The twin's voices pull me from nightmares, just barely.

They speak simultaneously, dipping their heads and thrumming a fist to their chest. "Father, we have brought a gift. Despite our absence, we still seem to be cleaning up brother's messes." Alvis gestures to the male beside Typhan, still watching me with hunger.

Horror settles in my gut as pieces fall into place, yet again. Evil delight scans over me from both Typhan and his son, their pure hatred for my emptiness plain for all to see. It's like I've walked right back into those caves. Of course, there is no way Alvis or Orion could've known about my attacker. I didn't detail that part of my story, but Novak knows. His presence enters my mind, tugging on the bond to focus me.

My father will be quite pleased, pits to hell. A hint of the scar I gave him in Slate rests on his scowling face. I knew then I should've killed him, but I let my pride get in the way.

"Lyth, focus." Novak's voice across the bond tenderly pulls me to reality.

Typhan's hands drop from his son's shoulders as he shifts his focus to me. The weight of his dangerous stare threatens to knock me over. I straighten and stride forward slowly, but his cold voice sends my blood running. I keep my mask of Keeper on, just barely.

"Ah, the Empty Fae who got away." The High Lord mocks me in a joyous tone.

"You'll find it takes a lot more to kill me than a pathetic male." I dare, staring up to the High Lord who is easily the same height as Panrauth. Bare chested and with navy linen pants, beads dangle from his dreaded, long beard and necklaces composed of bone carvings layer onto his torso.

"Does it now?" Typhan caresses a hidden necklace, lifting it from under the layers of beaded jewelry to reveal a nightmare. Amusement turns his bronzed features up while he watches terror settle into my bones. The twins and Novak stiffen at the necklace as well. Dizziness offers to hurtle me over the bridge as the High Lord moves even closer.

A pure black eye floats in the round, glass jar on his neck, perfectly preserved in a clear liquid. The tendrils and ligaments still hang from it, the pendant dances in front of my face as we are now inches away. He stands over me for a full minute, letting me observe every bit of my own eye, twitching and squirming in the jar as if it has life of its own. Only after I'm entirely blanched does he leave me trembling, returning to his sons.

Orion and Alvis make the mistake of glancing back at me with softened faces, a look that doesn't go unnoticed by their wicked father, or their younger brother. *Good.*

I push through the twins and grab a fistful of Typhan's dreaded beard, yanking him down to my level like I did not so long ago to a Bear. The sentries around us engage when I whisper into his ear with sweet death dripping from my words.

"Let's find out."

There are no fancy parties, no dinners to be held in the stretching crystal and marble castle. I was eager to see merfae and visit the artist's corner, watch fishermen on the lake and listen to the music of this land. No time is wasted on such things.

I don't want to see it without my friends, anyway.

I focus on Typhan, ignore Orion who won't stop looking at me, and try to figure out why Alvis keeps glancing at the prisoner, other than the obvious.

Typhan is seated in an epic sapphire throne with spires scratching high into the air above. His young, High Fae wife kneels in a square of crushed stone to his left. Her pale head is shaved, eyes are cast downward and her aura dimmed, she wears filthy rags that cover nothing important.

Orion and Alvis stand at one side of the throne with their hands clasped behind their back. Their brother, Apollo, stands on the other side, beside the silent female trembling in stones. After all this time, I have a name for the terrifying face. Novak and I wait before the dais, feet resting on a red carpet that stretches through the sickly crystalline hall.

A crowd of High Fae sits behind us in rows of marble pews, chattering with full dramatics echoing through the large place. Typhan pets his wife's head and contemplates me with a thoughtful look of disgust. The young Fae tries her best not to wince under The High Lord's touch, receiving a dirty look when she does. Thick crimson covers her gaunt knees, soaking the shards she rests on.

Novak is a silent stone at my side, his shadows are already threatening to become visible, even though nothing has been spoken yet. Unpredictability is not a good friend to have in this grand game of chess, and I wish he would've worn leathers or *something*. Instead, he's dressed the same as he always is, in fact, I think more of the scars on his chest are showing from under his loose tunic.

Typhan pats the Fae on her head before rising. Shekeeps her blank face focused on nothing as whispers of Human lover, filth and *whore* roll from the audience. My eye swings on Typhan's neck while he paces the dais several times, then his figure halts before me.

"Why have you come here, Keeper of Death?" Curiosity fills his voice as he plays with his beard.

"I want to help you." I say firmly. Boisterous laughter erupts from the finery behind me. The auras of my friends darken immensely, but their faces are unchanging. The calm storm of power brewing from the High Lord remains the same. I'm no threat to him. I'm nothing.

"And *why* would I need you?" Typhan kneels, grabbing my chin to scrutinize my face in a swift movement. Running a thumb over the scar on my left eye and cheek, he lets out a sigh of disappointment. "Tsk tsk, what messy handiwork."

Typhan yanks me upwards as he stands, so swiftly I have to stand on my tip toes. He whispers into my ear like a lover would, filling my mind with poison. "I'm quite intrigued at how you know my traitorous sons." He licks my scar, chuckling when I flinch. "I told Apollo to make sure you felt every inch of pain throughout your *pathetic* being. Did he at least do that right?"

He dismisses me harshly when I scowl at his words. I raise my chin in silence with a slight smirk playing at my lips. "You absolutely disgust me." He taunts, but I only straighten, crossing my arms as a mask of boredom rests on my face.

"Perhaps I was wrong, Orion. He *is* stupider than he looks, suppose I owe you for that bet, then." I say nonchalantly.

Gasps fall across the auditorium of a throne room. Orion is unreadable, but flashing amethyst eyes connect with mine. Typhan chuckles as he evaluates me up and down once more, then he looks to his twin sons. Apollo comes to his father's side, chomping at the bit to finish the job. I stare at Alvis, and subtly bite my lip. He locks eyes with me, and weakness lingers in his gaze as his own lips part.

The High Lord doesn't miss my longing towards his son. The one he favors.

"Do you want to know what the other territories plan to do?" I focus on Typhan again, feigning boredom.

"Trihewyn and that Firthorn brat? They are nothing but Human loving filth." Typhan regards Novak when he spits the words, eyes narrowing on his pointed white ears. Novak straightens under his resolve, a satisfied grin softly resting on his face. I haven't been told by my companions, but it appears this is not the first time Novak and Typhan have personally met.

"Exactly. That's why I came to you." I say. Surprise rings across Typhan's face and his attention leaves Novak.

"Tell me, before I bore of you and have Alvis finish the job. You are obviously incapable." Typhan waves off Apollo who steps back, staring me down with malicious intent.

"Whatever you plan on doing with Eros is nothing compared to what they have in store for you."

Murmurs break out, fear crawls through the rich Fae. Not of Eros, but of Terra and the Mists. I step forward onto the dais, circling the High Lord with precise steps. I lay a hand on his muscled bare shoulder, then come to a stop at his side. I lean close, pressing my breasts into his warmth. Bewildered eyes meet mine, his neck throbs and aura pulsates in time.

He can talk all he wants, but he wants this Empty Fae.

"I had a thought, though. Why fight for them, when I could fight for you?" I whisper in his ear, filling my words with hunger. A tawny, white vined hand wraps around my throat, squeezing hard enough to make breathing strenuous.

"Why should I believe an Empty Fae *whore*?" Typhan's hot breath growls into my ear. His hard cock presses into my stomach and I can't help it, a strained smile escapes at his hypocritical desire. Fingers tighten around my throat further and air struggles to meet my rapidly beating heart.

Novak tugs on the bond twice with desperation and I shoot a thought to him. "*Wait.*"

"The most dangerous Fae in the room is the one with power in their hands, and that is what you have." I choke out.

Typhan's hold on me loosens as I reach for the vial at my neck. The sight of sparkling purple and green sends his greedy hands for the vial, releasing me so fast I slam onto humming prostheses with a painful *thud*. Air strains in and out of my chest, but Typhan only has eyes for the magic around my neck.

"Only an Empty Fae can use the essence of the lands to build the Harbinger, a weapon of mass destruction. She's a loophole to the treaty, and thereby, extra magic." Orion speaks with no emotion, shrugging as he does. "I told you we brought a gift."

Alvis shifts in place, gesturing to Apollo. "Good thing brother fucked up per usual, otherwise you'd be out a weapon." Apollo snarls at Alvis, both grasp the sword they hold. Apollo shifts closer to the High Lord's wife, which draws Alvis' face even tighter.

Typhan's heavy hand tugs on the vial as he glowers down at me. He wants to take it, but even he knows the consequences of taking too much. I almost wish he would so I can watch it destroy him. But then I'd have to start all over again, and it would be too late.

I need my weapon.

"Tell me how it works." Typhan orders, walking away from me. Orion begins to answer, but is interrupted by his father immediately. "Not you, the other one." Anger burns my neck as I stand. Orion's eyes drop to the floor and Alvis continues his brother's words without pause.

Not you, the other one.

I can't have feelings right now.

"Essence from each High Lord or Lady is given to the Empty Fae, who uses it to build the Harbinger, a weapon wielding the Aether of every element." Alvis finishes explaining.

The time has come. I want to look back at Novak, I need to see him.

"I'm right here."

"Novak, there's something I didn't tell you."

He's been mostly calm until this point, panicking only when Typhan's hands were on me, and now. *"Well, now would be a fine time."*

Air pauses in my lungs when Typhan kneels before his trembling wife. I ignore Novak, frightening him further. "What do you think, darling?" Typhan caresses her gaunt face, his voice dangerously tender.

The queen's voice is small and automatic, a broken record. "You are the Highest Lord of the lands, you are unstoppable now. Even more so with this Harbinger." Words carefully placed. Typhan grabs her chin, places a sweet kiss on her lips.

The Fae moves her lips in an attempt to kiss back, but it's too slow and forced for his liking. Typhan backhands her onto the marble floor, knocking her out *cold*. Orion holds a hand on his brother's shoulder, restoring him to his place before Typhan notices. Apollo's jaw tightens as he stands over the female's body, but remains otherwise unmoving.

The High Lord rises, fixating his satisfied gaze on me. Whispers of Fae whore and Human lover meet my ears again. I will every cell inside me not to look at the broken female on the floor. Focus on the creature before me, who lusts after me. Like he didn't just single-handedly knock out the Queen of Sylvan.

"I have conditions." Typhan's booms. The show is about to begin, the crowd silences in awe. I dip my chin to him and press a hand to my chest. Novak's gaze burns onto my back. Rumbling prowls on our connection, threatening to break loose.

"Lyth, I don't know what's going on, but stick to the plan."

"To prove your loyalty to Sylvan, as a show of good faith, you will solve a problem for me. Do this, and you can have the essence, and *privilege*, of working for me."

The noise through the bond ceases.

"Kill whichever son you deem weakest, determine my next true heir." A villainous smile twists Typhan's face, and tears spill from my heart. For now, I keep on the Keeper of Death mask.

"Lyth, please." Novak struggles through the bond. I can almost hear the *Tzel* growling on the other side.

The twin's wild eyes fixate on me. I'm sure they had a plan for facing off against *each other*, but not this. I know at least Orion did, and I can see Alvis wanting his brother to live instead of him. They have shown too much weakness towards me, the moment Typhan saw our friendship, it was over.

Typhan comes to stand behind me, resting his hands on my shoulders, then whispers into my ear. "I trust your judgment, and who knows, perhaps I will find other uses for you." His hand drifts to my lower back and I give him my best wicked smile, fighting the bile rising in my throat.

"***Lyth***." Novak pleads through the bond again, managing only my name.

I unleash the dagger given by the Ancients from its sheath on my left thigh, making a show of twirling its blade in crystal filtered sunlight. I caress the tip of the obsidian blade across Typhan's bare chest, a smile still on my flushed face. "Gladly, *my* High Lord."

Thirst pours from Typhan, the male grinning with utter delight at my words. Sentries move in on the twins, one at each of their sides, then shove them onto their knees before their father and I. On display for the entirety of the Water Fae, their separation the entertainment for the day. The High Lord pays no attention to his struggling sons and brushes purple from my face, then brings his lips close to mine.

His final test of my loyalty.

"I'm sorry, love." I send the words to Novak, unable to look at him and say the words out loud. I wasn't sure exactly how I'd piss Novak off, but this will do the trick.

Hot, trembling fury rolls from him down the bond when I lift up on my toes and kiss Typhan with a passion. The High Lord of Sylvan kisses me back so intensely, I'm afraid this will turn into something more, right here, right *now*. I don't put it past him to fuck, then kill me in front of everyone. I need him to like me.

And so he does.

His hands find no limits to my body and nearly tear off my clothes. I give him just as much relentless desire, my tongue diving into his throat and mixing with his. Moans escape into thick air, the crowd stunned into silence, confused as to why the High Lord is now embracing the Fae he called disgusting moments ago.

I have to shut Novak out completely. His anger is so intense it gives me a headache, and after what seems like an eternity, Typhan reluctantly releases his hold on me. I look up to Typhan through my lashes, then press the blade to my small smile, which hardens him into me further. Typhan shifts to my side, resting a hand on my shoulder, speaking his next words with a satisfied smile. "As I said, I trust your judgment."

I nod and spin my dagger, intimidating and skillful just like how Knothall taught me. Typhan pats Alvis' shoulder as he walks by and doesn't even look at Orion. The High Lord stands by Apollo, to the right of his other sons.

I'm at the beginning of this story all over again, ordering the death of innocents on their knees before me. Orion and Alvis shrug the guards off, ignoring their father's laughter joined with Apollo's. Both focus their hot, wet gazes on me.

"After *everything*?" Orion pleads through broken glass, his dirty glasses smashed beyond repair and cutting into his nose. Alvis remains silent, staring me down with tight disappointment. They *believe* that I have betrayed them, utterly and completely.

I have to do this, for Iverbourne.

I peer over my shoulder at the crowd, fully enthralled and horrified at the thought of one of the princes being murdered before their eyes. *Who* will I choose? The question burning on everyone's mind. Novak's face is red and the vein in his forehead throbs, his darkness struggles to remain hidden. The pitch black eyes lacking pupil, the eyes of the *Tzel,* meet my vicious gaze.

Good, it's ready to play.

Novak pleads with me, dropping to his knees and clasping his shaking hands together. "*Please*, Lyth, don't do this."

I wordlessly place my attention on my friends, taking in their near identical, beautiful faces one last time. Typhan is absolutely inspired by my show, the High Lord making a meal of his powerful sons and I, eating every emotion we give each other. He delights in how Novak is crumpling behind me.

"I'm sorry, this is the only way. I have to." I whisper, the sharp plaything now a dangerous weapon, ready to strike with fatal black and white eyes. Free falling tears splash onto the marble at my feet, and my mask breaks.

"Go fuck yourself." Alvis shouts, his anger echoes through the castle, drawing laughter from his father.

I ignore Typhan and lock eyes with *him*, the Prince who loves the Keeper of Death, even though she is mated to the male he's loved from afar for decades. I've guessed it since our night on the cliffs together, and Orion confirmed it for me. I know Alvis has tortured himself everyday since the Mists, watching Novak and I together. Watching us have what he's wanted for so *long*.

Orion planned on being the one to step aside, so we can all be together. Somewhere in Alvis' mind, Orion saw a possible future for the three of us. I step back, planting my foot and positioning myself before the handsome warrior Fae. It's time to end this.

"No, Lyth, please don't do this. *Please*, not him!" Orion's desperate cries fold my ears down, but Alvis stares me down with cold acceptance. I love Orion, but Alvis means the most to me, it *has* to be him.

"Thank you for everything, my friend." I whisper, my different colored eyes focus on the small tears falling down his scarred cheeks. I lunge forward and send the blade spinning, outrunning the shadows desperately trying to reach the obsidian before it meets flesh.

Novak screams so loud the castle quakes under my feet. "LYTH, NO!"

It's too late.

A sickening crunch of dagger penetrating Faerie skull shatters the room, followed by the sound of a body crashing to stone. Screams from the remaining brother and my lover are followed by unending chaos erupting in the throne room. I've always been quite good at creating chaos.

Aim wisely.

IT WAS BRILLIANT

"I can't believe you."

Novak scrubs blood from his hands in the washroom, voice and body hoarse and broken. I sink further under luxurious blankets, pulling them tight over my head. Every time I close my groggy eyes, the horrific scene plays over and over.

Orion's wild eyes when the knife slammed to the hilt, landing with ease and crushing through bone. Horrified screams of the aftermath ring in my ears, and the snapping of a spine much too small to die. The ocean of blood Novak cleaned off my body still taints my inner soul. So much went *wrong*, too much innocent blood was spilled in that throne room today.

Aim wisely.

Three out of four essences are collected, but I'm broken. The vial constantly threatens to choke me now, the triple helix of Aether coiling tight against the hot glass. I'm not sure if I can *physically* get out of bed, let alone the fact I don't want to. When Novak awoke from his forced slumber, his first order of business was cleaning us both up. Until now, we have hardly looked at each other, let alone spoken.

I should've listened to Novak before. We should've ran away when we had the chance.

Novak's cautious body rests on the mattress behind me, he rests a hand on my back, then caresses up and down gently. His warm skin is otherwise held back from me, but he attempts to be comforting. "He will forgive you, Lyth."

I throw back the blankets from my face but keep my eyes averted. "And you?" I choke out, tainted by wet sadness. We made a plan together, he offered his help, and I tricked him. I'm no worse than Panrauth.

Novak's hands with persistent blood staining the crevices of his fingernails snake around me. A sight I hoped to never see, and I brought it to fruition. "We did what we had to. I told you I was by your side, no matter what happened. It ... mostly all went according to plan." He murmurs into my ear.

His gentleness is worse than if he shouted at me.

I roll over and stare into his calm, mostly clean face. Crimson lingers in his light hair and along the outer edges of his face. "I made a Fae who doesn't even carry weapons *become* one. I'm the biggest hypocrite alive, Novak. I couldn't tell you everything, because if I did, I'm not sure you would've let the *Tzel* out willingly, and we needed it. You were trying so hard. Be mad at me, yell. *Something*."

Novak chuckles darkly, pressing his forehead to mine, like how Alvis and Orion did before we entered this hell. "I don't carry weapons because I am useless with them. Obviously, the *Tzel* doesn't need them. I *am* a weapon, just as you said." He trails off, and disappointment is revealed at last in his faltered smile.

"That doesn't change anything." My tear filled anger rises to a shout. His once pure ears are tainted with red, and they fold down tight. "You have kept that thing locked away for *centuries*, and I bring it out in you. *More* than once, and this time was intentional. I've done nothing but cause you pain. You say you're the beast, but you're wrong. It's *me*."

Novak wipes tears from my face with both thumbs, his right one pausing as he senses the throbbing headache brewing in my right temple. He kisses my right brow, and warm relief spreads through my face. I reopened the connection between us, but I keep the memories of today hidden by shadow, along with other things. Not that he would look into my mind, but he can. If he wanted to.

"What you saw today wasn't the first, and won't be the last time that nightmare inside me crawls out again." He admits and I bite my cheek. "What's done is done, and what matters is we're together. I'm not afraid of you, and I trust you. *Still*." Anger heats his words finally, and the charcoal aura cradling the bed darkens.

I want to tell him trusting me is the worst thing you can do.

"It's just ... it wasn't what I thought. I thought I knew what I was doing, when I let it out." I tread carefully.

The devastation the *Tzel* can bring forth is much, *much* worse than what he revealed to me about the village, and the previous glimpse I had of the *Tzel* in bed is nothing compared to it fully in control. It's so much more than an ancient demon of shadows. One of the Fallen, and I don't think Novak even has a *clue*. Even with all of my shame, I know one thing for certain. We would've been dead without it. Along with the rest of them ...

"I won't ask you again."

"Do I scare you now?" Novak murmurs, his voice raw, from screaming and being possessed. The terrified question breaks his voice so much I can hardly understand him.

I kiss his trembling lips. "I find you truly terrifying, and in my world, that's a good thing."

His shaky hand finds solace in my hair, the other on my waist, and he pulls me closer. Our lips become inseparable, all fear and chaos releases as we find peace in each other's touch.

"I love you, Novak. Always." I murmur into his mouth, drawing a deep exhale from him. Relief flows through the bond between us, and both of us release enough darkness to visibly swallow the room. I almost wish he could've seen what I looked like today, drawing on my power of *nothing*. How ironic.

"Always, Lythienne."

Novak is already bare chested, so I undo the button at his shorts with haste. He frees my large breasts from the clinging nightgown, both of us desperate to feel love, feel *something*. I roll over, pressing my wide ass into him. His moan reverberates against my body, more like a rumble, but I know it's still him.

Tzel is satisfied and slumbering after its murderous day.

There is no time for foreplay. Wetness is already pooled between my thighs and he firmly presses against me. I need him inside me just as much as he needs to be in me. To be one body, one soul. To feel something real.

I arch my hips back into him and whimper as his cock slides into me, bringing peace to my body. One of my formerly blood stained hands reaches behind and finds his hair. The other I bring to my clit and massage in circles. A freckled hand lifts my thigh slightly, allowing him to enter me deeper, and a primal whisper meets my ear.

"Always."

I shudder, his promise tickles the soft tuft on my ear and sends a wave of pleasure through me. Slender hips draw his length back, teasing at leaving, only to thrust in so hard he shakes the bed. I cry out his name, enticing him to thrust more orgasms into me.

Slender fingers find my lips. I bite his thumb when he presses on my bottom lip, then suck it gently. A satisfied groan escapes him, and his shaft hardens inside me, fighting release as he loves me with such *deep*, passionate strokes, I'm afraid he'll bring the castle down. He takes my chin and focuses my gaze over my shoulder to him, pleasure twists his smile.

"Can you handle yourself, *Zemer*?" I tease. That's always been his favorite name, and it suits him. With a final thrust and dimple filled smile, he releases deep inside me. I orgasm so hard my toes curl, holding onto him for dear life.

"I can never handle myself when I'm with you."

"Has she spoken?" I ask the Princess of Terra after a long moment of silence following her briefing on the final casualty count. We are alone on a crystalline balcony jutting from the grand study of the Sylvan Court, overlooking the shimmering lake.

Water stretches farther than I can hope to see, ripples spread continuously as sea life lives in prosperity below. Merfae dive in and out of the small tides along with other sea creatures, they have been rising from the surface in increasing numbers. I haven't met them in person yet, but from here I can see the dazzling rainbows of fins and scales everywhere. Some merfae have multiple layers of sheer fins, reminding me of a full ball gown.

We've been here for a week now and I haven't left the castle. The noon sun hangs heavy above our shoulders, beckoning us to hurry before Eros strengthens any further. I can't leave without knowing. I can't leave this mess for him, not yet. Not even to visit the lake.

I need to be here when he wakes up, *if* he ever wakes up. Thankfully, Novak has the same sentiment I do, but he is even more reclusive than I have been lately. Despite our actions bringing about the greater good, nearly every person is terrified of him, and me.

Viv's curved body is adorned with a silk red gown, her slender neck and elegant ears behold emeralds and diamonds. The coils atop her head freely stretch, no crown to bind her here. She is free. Her eyes tear from the lake, pastel green Aether flashing in them when she speaks quietly. "No, I don't know if she will."

I wear similar finery, my own silk dress the color of the lake. The rings Viv gifted me encircle various fingers, and a silver ear cuff rests on the point of my left ear. The amethyst decorated Ancient dagger is strapped to my bare thigh, ready to start trouble once more. I have received enough threats in the past couple days to warrant several security measures. The second dagger at my left thigh, increased mind training with Novak, and guards trailing my every move.

I have now learned of the atrocities my friends have seen, and committed. For many years before they escaped, Alvis kidnapped Water and Air Fae for Orion to experiment on. He dissected them, stole their Aether and meshed magic in ways that brought about new abilities, in those that survived, that is. The mad scientist and his lackey, dutifully creating brainwashed psychic soldiers for their father. Their work spanned over a decade before Novak and Captain found them.

Novak admitted the *Nafshyi* were the ones who took his ears, and his magic, a year after Alvis escaped Sylvan. They used Novak as bait in attempts to lure in Alvis, as Novak was with his 'mate' at the time, but they only brought the demon forth and everything went to hell. So yes, he knew Typhan intimately.

The *Nafshyi* soldiers are now my responsibility, the new breed created after the twins escaped. Although I have insisted on not making any decisions for the High Lord, I *did* make it my business to have the lab and its warehouse of preservation chambers to be entirely destroyed. The abused and traumatized soldiers withdrawing from the mind-altering drugs they've been given for *years* are not so easily fixed, but at least Orion will never have to set foot in there again.

The only thing that kept Alvis and Orion here and enacting such horrors was the promise Typhan made to keep their mother alive. In the end though, they couldn't do it anymore.

I push away thoughts of Alvis and straighten the fabric clinging to me. The Court has requested I adopt their formal dress code, making my stay here the longest I have consecutively worn dresses. Something about being less threatening. I'm itching to wear my tunic and breeches again, the familiar belt of leather pouches saddling my wide hips. After the destruction I unleashed, I can't disagree very much.

I sigh and focus on the conversation at hand. Charis, the former Queen. "I cannot say that I blame her, but she didn't even take you up on your offer to live in Terra?"

"Charis is a hero to the lesser population here. Two nights before you came, she was caught sneaking Human children through a hole in the wall." Vivvus explains.

A Queen betraying her King, like Alvis' mother did. The image of a red headed boy with blood pouring from his broken head flashes in my mind, immediately sending my heart racing as guilt ices over my body. I shake my head and enter the study.

Bookshelves stretch from floor to ceiling around the room's edge. The glass tables scattered around behold the books we've been perusing through most of the morning. So much history, hidden away from the public in this forbidden library since the second war. I caress the open book I had been studying, my fingers coming to rest on Knothall's name. Definitely no Book of Teachings, but vital information is waiting to be shared.

I make no mention of my own studies to anyone, not even Novak, adding scraps about the Fallen to the page from Trihewyn.

"How are the history lessons going?" I ask Vivvus who rolls her eyes, elegance gone as she huffs into a turquoise, upholstered lounge chair.

"Sylvan Court is quite opinionated, they are working with us though, whether they like it or not. Purist stragglers keep making appearances, but they will be taken care of." She pauses, tapping the arm of her chair. "We'll find the remaining *Nafshyi*, Lyth."

I nod, the thought of brainwashed and abused mind soldiers loose upon Iverbourne is a chilling one. About a dozen fled last night. Ones I couldn't reach, too far gone to hear reason, too hurt to realize who the real enemy is. The remaining Fae will take time to heal, but they aren't feral.

Every fiber in my being is exhausted, the emptiness that once hardly escaped now threatens to leave all the time, offering to cradle me into an unending sleep. I have no idea how Novak does it, battling what's trapped inside him every day.

"You know, when you asked me for a favor, I had no idea it would come to *this*." Viv's musing sentiment perks my ears.

I settle in the chair opposite her. "Why did you listen then?" I snort.

Viv shrugs, checking her nails. "You were right, about everything." She chuckles after a moment, eyes locking with mine. "Besides, any reason to leave beats being Pan's keeper any longer."

I nod, my tone even. "How is he?"

"Not gonna lie, he was pretty pissed when he found out I was taking half the army without permission. Last I heard, he was muttering about at least having better neighbors."

My thoughts wander to the panic in his eyes when he realized he was too strong for me, when he nearly killed me. I was ready this time when the Water essence came for me. I shielded my mind, just like how Novak taught me. At that point though, our training was so brief, all I managed to do was stay awake, and keep the *Tzel* at bay.

I still feel sickly, even now. I sigh, tapping my cane on the plush, white carpet centered under us. For an Empty Fae, I am becoming quite good at controlling the lack of Aether, the power of nothing and everything. The power of the Lady.

A *God*. Fallen from grace.

"I still can't believe you did it. How did you know it would work?" Viv whispers, glancing to the closed door. The simple question brings bloodshed to my mind, along with *her*. The moment the *Tzel* burst from Novak days ago, her call has become unending.

"Find me."

The repetitive sentiment brings headaches and struggles to focus. The voice scratching my mind is at its worst since it started, all that time ago in the Mountain. I push out a breath and shake out building darkness, my mind threatens to become lost in thought.

"Novak kicked my ass in chess one too many times. I figured I better start thinking ahead and use my best pieces." I shrug.

Vivvus laughs darkly, twirling a hazel curl around her jade finger. "Yes, I must admit I have grown to like him." I glare at her and she wavers, speaking in a hushed tone. "You can't deny it now, the *Tzel* is terrifying."

I bite my lip. Her next words have my face hiding behind my hands. "The darkness *listened* to you."

Novak fell to his knees and let out a blood curdling scream. The moment I threw my knife the Tzel tore from him, ripping his beautiful body apart like a snake shedding its restraining skin.

The poor Fae tried to contain it, he caught my eyes for a moment with a distraught face. The wild sapphire blue snuffed out in an instant and was replaced by darkness. I stopped breathing, watching him disappear before my eyes.

Just like I knew he would.

The moment Novak's grip on reality let go, the illusion ridden shadows he had waiting over Viv and her guerrilla squad lifted. They were hidden behind us the whole time, how he managed to keep them invisible for so long was beyond me. The Sylvan sentries moved in, charging not just me, but the Human and Lesser Fae servants fleeing as well. Chaos made anyone fair game now, but not if I had anything to say about it.

A loose figure of darkness remained in Novak's place, evoking further screams throughout the throne room. Every door slammed shut, locking every creature promptly inside. Tzel rolled back his shoulders, focusing on the prey running from him. The familiar move sent a shudder through me, and my breath was stolen away as the transformation completed.

Shadowed skin composed the beast filled with milky stars, and as the being settled, a fine tailored suit of night covered his hourglass body. Tzel's face was nothing more than billowing darkness, features hidden. With a soul twisting rumble of laughter, feathered wings burst from his back, shooting tendrils of night and charcoal feathers up into the air. Pure, ***lethal*** *beauty.*

The Shadow of Death.

I widened my stance and tightened my fists at my side, pushing back the chanting of the Lady ***pounding*** *my head. She wanted* ***out****. Darkness leeched around me, flowing like the fine dresses the twin goddesses wear. Tzel and I were quite the pair, eternal creatures, no,* ***Gods*** *of Death and Chaos. Howling horror grew more desperate as the throne room filled with a thick abyss, blood and chaos.*

Always Chaos.

"Findmefindmefindme." The Lady begged, unrelenting, and I slammed her shut in the deepest part of my mind.

"Tzel, I command you to obey me. Or I will put you in your place." Elongated claws reached across the room, grasping my throat. The disembodied face floated along the space after a moment, then caught up to the choking tendrils on my carotid. The beast smelled my neck, then licked the place it had marked me before. He released his hold with a feral grin.

"Yes, I remember you. Come, come out and play with me." He taunted, black pits for eyes were framed by a roughly humanoid face of glittering, ethereal smoke. Red simmered to life where eyes should have been.

I open my eyes, thankfully before the next scene repeats itself. Viv shifts ahead in her seat. I shrink into mine. "You can talk to me, if you're having trouble, you know. I was there, when my father —"

The study door flies open, threatening to crack the crystal wall it slams into. We jolt upwards, a heaving green eyed High Fae courier hangs on the door. "The High Lord is awake."

The moment I register his words, I'm gone.

Novak meets me in a sprint halfway to the infirmary, barefoot and his hair sticking up in every direction, darkened eyes wild. "Lyth, wait." We pause and he presses his forehead to mine, then we continue in silence, steps unsteady and slow.

The noise ricocheting off the quartz walls strengthens as we approach the entry of a massive gathering hall turned hospital. A distraught voice shouts so loud it strikes my heart with fear. Profanities of every sort seem to *shake* the castle, most of the curses twist with our names, and Alvis'.

"He's *pissed*, Novak." I draw in a breath and halt before the entrance. "I can't see him."

"*We* have to. Suck it up." Novak says flatly, glaring at me with a 'it's the least you can do' look. I nod shortly, then we enter the infirmary, which is over half capacity, even a week later.

I have been down here nearly everyday with Novak. We help tend to surrendered soldiers, civilians and former slaves caught in the crossfire. The *Nafshyi* have been appointed their own private infirmary, away from noise and overstimulating triggers. Guilt trips my heart when I pass between the makeshift beds, gazing upon empty faces and bloodied bodies. I glance at Novak who keeps his eyes down.

"What is your request, my lady?" The Tzel held me close, his caress of night on my cheek was familiar and comforting, full of danger and terrible love.

"Kill every soul here loyal to Typhan. I want a clean court, and that bastard Apollo to feel every inch of pain he caused me." I whispered, eliciting a deep purr from within the being.

"My pleasure." Tzel growled, leaving me in a flurry of shadows. He appeared before the coward Fae with pale eyes. Apollo had drawn his weapons, but it was no use. Watching the Shadow of Death tear the son of Typhan limb from limb and feast upon his howling face was the grandest thing I had ever seen in my life.

The next scene though, was not. A platoon of soldiers layered in black cloaks and masks landed in the center of the throne room with such force, the castle literally shook. A chandler crashed to the ground beside me, alerting me to the soldier at my flank.

An orb of crackling water and a great sword approached my face and I parried both just in time. The soldier made it a step past me before I clutched his steel plated shoulder and drove my Ancient dagger into the gap of his armor, between his neck and shoulder. The soldier dropped and when he did, a terrifying scene was revealed to me.

Tzel saw it before I did and shot across the room to the Commander who held a squirming, red headed boy in his too big hands. One of the soldier's eyes was black, and the other purple, pupils shrunk and sclera splattered with specks of an ink like substance.

The demon of darkness could not make it quick enough, a scream tore from me when that poor Human's neck cracked. The Commander threw the broken child's body down and lunged for the Tzel, orbs of purple and black magic brewing from the manic Fae's hands as it closed the distance.

I darted across the throne room, dodging arrows and thrusting orbs of Water and Earth Aether being flung across the room as I slid onto humming legs. I heard his neck crack from across the room but I still ***had*** *to know. I was supposed to save him.*

We *were supposed to save him.*

The collision of the Tzel and Nafshyi was so intense the marble floor split in two from underneath them. Screams from bystanders too close to the rift reverberated through the castle. Tzel ripped apart the hulking Nafshyi commander worse than he did Apollo, showering the entire hall with a viscous, black blood. It splashed onto the lifeless face of the red headed boy I held tight to my chest, and me.

"Get the rest of them contained, I want them alive!" I shouted through broken sobs. The platoon of cloaked soldiers violated innocents and Terra soldiers alike with a swift wave of their hand. Their orbs of magic infiltrated every possible orifice to break people from the inside out. At that time, I wasn't quite sure why I wanted such vicious creatures kept alive, but looking back, it's probably because I recognized their eyes.

The eyes of someone drugged beyond belief.

Without a response, Tzel found the next cloaked figure, then thrusted shadows into its ears. Tzel collapsed the Nafshyi one by one, their hearts quietly beating as they fell.

I was too late, too careless.

Novak has no idea how bad it truly was. Of course, he was blacked out like the first, and every time the beast takes over. When I told him in the woods my plan to deceive Typhan, I asked for his magic, *his* help. I couldn't bring myself to ask him to release the *Tzel*. I knew Novak's emotions would do it for me. He cares so much for everyone. Too much.

How many more times will I be surprised at the fact I'm not the hero?

At the end of the sticky infirmary waits a separate room, a splintered door left ajar is the source of fury filling the air. The aura from the High Lord of Sylvan crashes in thick oceanic waves out the door. Strong enough to intoxicate me, even out here.

Novak gives me a half smile and squeezes my hand, despite the fact he can hardly breathe. "Let's face the music." He says, cracking down the middle. I give him a weak eye roll and hold my breath, then follow behind him.

Out of all the things I've seen and done in my torturous life, I have never been as afraid as I am *right* now.

The pulsing in Novak's charcoal aura pauses as what awaits inside startles him, then me. I lock eyes with Orion seated on a wood stool in the center of the room. Chest heaving and body shaking, he's covered in sweat and the remnants of burns. His crisped, light black skin is absolutely *glowing*.

Bloodied bandages and other supplies lay scattered about, wood is splintered along the outskirts of the room (once a bar of sorts, I believe) along with shards of broken glasses and pictures. Blankets lay in a crimson tussle on the floor beside his flipped over cot.

The vines are gone from his skin.

Without his glasses he looks just like Alvis now. Strength, power and *anger*, so much anger, surges through every rippling muscle of his. The kind intellectual has been replaced by a primal force of Aether and fury. I swallow and tears prick my eyes. I cannot think of what to say. An apology right now would be a joke, and my traitorous breath catches when he speaks.

"I can't *believe* you two." The High Lord rises from his rickety throne, then crosses to us in a few quick strides. He towers over us, first glowering at Novak, then at the weight on my neck. The essence of three lands, now joined together. I watch Orion's face tighten with horror and disappointment. The reminder I will forever be thinking ahead and using my most powerful pieces, no matter the cost, slams into me.

And he doesn't even know just how *far* the betrayal runs.

It wasn't my fault, not that. I *tried* to make him stop.

"You kept us in the *dark*. Overthrew the *court*, made *me* High Lord." Orion spits the words down at me, yanking at his inky, forever long locks as he does. When I don't speak, he goes to push up his glasses, then growls in frustration at their absence, actually growls. "Al and I had a *plan*, did you ever stop to think about that? *We* had a plan."

I don't say anything. It wasn't *we*, Orion. You had your own plan, just like your brother did.

Orion stares hard into my face, neither of us speak.

Novak is uneasy at my side, glancing between us. Orion's eyes had changed from deep amethyst to pale lilac when he became High Lord, further estranging him from me. Watching the Aether burn through him was the first excruciating experience after I made my throw. His body fell to the ground after receiving the power of his father, then was assaulted once more by his brother's power.

What happened after was a close second.

"Would you rather it have been –" Novak protests, but it only twists Orion's face further.

My unsure, small voice interrupts Orion's oncoming fury.

"It wouldn't have worked if you knew. I needed you to think I betrayed you. It *had* to be real, or he would've never asked me to do it. I *had* to be your weapon, but you couldn't know, or I would've been useless."

The stillness occupying the cot in the corner catches my eye, the only untouched spot in the room. Orion can't leave his brother's side. My words are lost, my vision fills with the sight of Alvis staring into my demonic eyes, accepting my betrayal whole heartedly. Then the final collapse of his body and spirit, shattering my heart into a million pieces.

"It was pretty *fucking* real! You let me believe the worst about you." Orion hammers into my ears, surely echoing throughout the castle. Novak covers his own ears, his presence in the bond shrinking as he senses my anger breaking.

"Well, it didn't take very much, did it?" Warmth flushes my gaunt cheeks with the roaring jab. I'm on my tiptoes, brows drawn together with tears carving my face. I haven't told Novak how much it stung that the twins believed me so easily.

Orion softens, glancing down to Novak as he breaks off and he shoves his face in his hands. Orion reaches out to my unflinching cheek and rests a shaky hand there, voice a whisper. "What if any of it failed? Did you have a plan for that too?"

"No."

Orion places both his hands on my shoulders, *desperately* trying to control himself and reel in the storm around him. Aether rides in a dizzying hurricane around us, similar to Pan's magic. Young High Lords are not a force to be reckoned with, and I put them on their thrones.

"Too many people need you, right *now*, for you to gamble so highly on yourself. Or him." Orion gestures to Novak who is still hiding in his hands, darkness visibly thickening around him. "Don't think I haven't heard about what you did to your mate."

Blood boils in my veins as he prods the still gaping wound, shame oozes out of it. "You are pissed at me for doing the same thing you planned to do! I would rather dive into a hundred more fox holes full of that scum –"

I shove Orion, evoking a rumble from his puffed up chest, the blood in his carotid throbs violently. If he wants a fight, I'll give him one. Novak protests against our bickering in a far corner, all of our voices are chaotic and threatening to snap what's left in each of us.

"Holy fuck, can you three stop arguing long enough so I can find the will to live?" A rather annoyed Fae with tight inky curls disheveled in every direction, dull purple eyes and a sarcastic grin sits up from his cot. The fire in my soul cools to a simmer, the sight of Alvis alive brings long awaited relief.

Finally.

After what he did, I had no idea if he would wake up again. Novak doesn't know what happened, he heard the same story Orion must've heard. It's not my story to tell, as Novak would say. I've gambled with so many lives, it's only a matter of time before my luck runs out.

Novak laughs so light, it's like the day we first met. He wastes no time making it to Alvis. The musician takes his friend into a rough hug, kissing him on each sunken cheek and then hard on his cracked lips. Alvis grins wide as he ruffles Novak's hair, not at all surprised by the sudden affection. The two waste no time falling into their usual antics, and my heart is entirely full watching them.

Orion's shoulders drop and he rubs his eyes, groaning. "It's not funny, brother."

"You gotta admit, it was brilliant." Alvis winks at me.

I attempt to step towards him. Orion's firm hand catches my shoulder, softening a shade but remaining strong. I shoot him a fierce look, but otherwise remain still. I breathe in, out.

"I made you a promise, and to keep it I did what I had to do. I'm not sorry, because I would rather risk everything than separate you from Alvis. You're my friend, Orion." I stare up at Orion with nothing but truth. His frustration breaks and he pulls me into a tight embrace, holding on for dear life.

"I never should've doubted you, Lyth. *Thank you*." Orion whispers into my hair. I rest my head on his chest and listen to his beating heart struggle, overflowing with Aether. My own heart slows as I close my eyes and listen to Novak tease Alvis. Thank the Ancients. Now if I can get him to play, or even look at his lute.

"I expect you to make some big changes around here, starting with elevators, your damn castle is too big." I say playfully, leaving the warm chest of the High Lord after a moment.

Orion rolls his eyes as he steps back to clean up his mess. Novak and Alvis pick on him and I enjoy their antics in silence. We all clean together, putting things together back the best we can, except Alvis. He steals glances at me now and then, but I mostly avoid his tired face.

I knew just as well as the others at that meeting in Terra we would need united lands, allies. So, I gave Iverbourne an allied north. Luckily, Viv turned out to be a trusted accomplice, a trusted *friend*. Without her council and stolen away forces, I wouldn't have been able to keep the court I overthrew. Someone needed to keep the throne warm for Orion, and it sure as hell wasn't going to be me. I anticipated everything. Well, almost everything.

The *Nafshyi*. Alvis' decision. The Lady and *Tzel*. I didn't anticipate any of that.

At least now everything is prepared, just in case.

Orion retrieves a chair for me and we situate ourselves in a circle. The beaten warrior pulls a pipe and satchel from his pouch after we settle. His hunched over figure rests cross legged beside Novak on his cot. The intricate pipe has carvings of the sea along its dark wooden curves, the device stretches longer than mine does.

"And *why* is this the first we've smoked out of that?" I ask with annoyance.

"You always beat me to it." Alvis smiles, his dark face lacking its usual glow, and the familiar white vines. I scowl at him and Novak chuckles at our banter, but his face *drops* as he suddenly sees the same traumatic memory I do.

"Do it now, Lyth, there's no time. Take it, please. Let me."

Alvis trembled in my arms, his hand clenched so tight to mine it shook. My tears splashed onto his face, once white vines had turned into intense streaks of oozing crimson lining his body. His clothes were entirely burnt away save for a few shreds. Orion's body finally stopped convulsing after all this time at my feet.

"Alvis, we can wait, we ***have*** *to wait, it'll kill you." I begged.*

The Tzel killed Apollo and the Commander, blood ran through the hall as the Terra soldiers collected their dead and injured. The remaining Nafshyi were subdued and the doors unlocked with a sickening simultaneous click, releasing the innocents.

Only after the Tzel had made its judgment, though.

And there were many that deserved punishment for their crimes.

"Say the words, my Keeper. Before it's too late." Alvis' hand cupped my cheek, catching my hot tears before they fell. His fingers trailed down to the vial slung around my neck and he tugged gently. Then, I asked the question I feared would kill him.

I puff deeply on the fine pipe, glancing sideways at Novak. He shifts in the seat beside me, taking my hand in his after the memory finishes leaking across the bond. Another vital bit of truth, and for a moment, Novak saw himself.

As the *Tzel* in all its fatal beauty, wings and all. I have tried my best to keep everything hidden, but my shields are weak these days. The memories hit me so hard I practically shout them across our connection if I'm not prepared. I need to try harder, but the vial is growing more burdensome every day.

Orion crosses an ankle over a knee, glancing between a now quiet Alvis, Novak and I. The pipe makes a round in surprisingly comfortable silence, our group losing themselves to their thoughts. I suppose Alvis expected me to tell Orion, but I know that would only bring heartbreak to the new High Lord. If Alvis wants to tell his brother he *chose* to be Empty, that is his business.

Orion was hit with the brunt of Typhan's power after the blade instantly took his father's life. He doesn't know the Aether chose them *both* to be High Lord, Alvis was just strong enough to withstand the sudden onslaught of power.

But then, Alvis shifted nearly all of his newfound magic to his brother in the same moment, which is perhaps why Orion immediately passed out. Afterwards, he gave me the remainder of his Aether for the vial. Al nearly killed himself in his attempt to be rid of it all, something I didn't even know *could* be done.

Whatever pact he and his Orion made, Alvis *never* intended to kill Orion, or be High Lord.

Just like Orion was willing to give *his* life, for whatever future he saw Alvis wanting, hoping for. Now, they're both alive, and Alvis is Empty, just like me. I can't help but wonder if it will last. If he *could* regenerate what he lost, it certainly would have returned by now, a week later. Someone born with such great magic suddenly without it sounds like a recipe for trouble.

"Novak and I are leaving tomorrow, we are running out of time. Scouts from Terra and Sylvan have spotted the Others in the Mists. Cervalis is taken." I break the silence, but then look sideways at Novak as I'm out of breath already.

"The *Tzel* determined who the spies were for Eros, which turned out to be quite a few. More than half the court were either purist assholes or supporters of The Others." Novak rubs his neck, trailing off as his eyes glaze.

"Before I sunk my blade into that bastard Fae," I mutter, giving the twins a wary gaze. They lean forward in their seats, listening with intent. Novak's shadows leech onto the floor as I try to recount the destruction we caused. "Vivvus and her troops were waiting in the shadows Novak cast ..."

I remember the guards I had waiting in the shadows of the mountain, ready to murder all those 'rebellious' Fae. I shake my head. "You have a clean court. Viv's been keeping an eye on things, she is ready to brief you, when you're ready. That's all that matters." I rub my face, pushing out the last words with great force. I can't talk about it, not right now.

Alvis rubs his chin while Orion stands and paces, filling with fire again. "Us on the throne or ... All of you dead. To have Terra in on this," Orion shakes his head, then locks eyes with me, "How long were you planning this?" Before I can answer, he gestures to a slumped Novak still seated beside Alvis.

"How long did *you* know? Did you really agree with this, Novak, or did she trick you like she did us?"

"Everyone had a choice." Novak snaps, then takes a deep breath and reels in his shadows.

Alvis keeps a watchful gaze on Novak's darkening eyes and rests a hand on his shoulder. Like he can do anything right now. The fact he *chose* to be Empty surprises me, but then again, he always does. Alvis' eyes aren't pitch black like mine though, they're a dull and dark plum.

"Every *single* person agreed, even Borealis stands with us now. Do you not realize how much better this is for your people? You get to change the history of Water Fae, make your mother proud. You're *free*. What is wrong with you?" The moment Novak mentions their mother, Orion loses all sanity.

Novak and Orion tear at each other's throat, ripping apart the room we just put back together. The brutally honest words send the two into a dizzying battle of shadows, storming water and fists meeting bloodied skin. I remove myself at once, stopping at the door for a second to watch the friends, torn and fighting.

Alvis slips away and follows me out without a word.

AT WHAT COST?

Vivvus

Novak *screams*.

He screams, and *screams*, and ***screams***.

Shadows are torn away from the *Adira* and I waiting on the back side of the thrones when Typhan's body slams onto the floor. Face first and further impaling himself onto an amethyst encrusted dagger. Orion topples over seconds later, white vines flare into a blinding light as I rush to his side. Alvis hunches forward on his knees, *crying* out as his own vines illuminate the entire dais with their light. I search for Lythienne and find a flash of purple along with a command booming through the center of the hall. "*Tzel*, I command you to obey me, or I *will* put you in your place."

Then I see him, and *her*, in all their glory.

The Shadow of Death.

A tailored suit of black and blue galaxies, splattered with bright milky ways and shooting stars. His shadowed complexion matches the beautiful fabric, but opaque shadows hide his face and reveal only long locks of black. Feathers of oily black and green thrust into the air from his back, tendrils of darkness and loose feathers spiral around him.

And he *laughs*.

The Lady.

Luminescent burgundy hair curls around wide hips now wrapped in a gown of glittering night. The trailing dress is a sheer illusion overlaying her battle leathers, but it's stunning nonetheless. Lythienne is otherworldly, her complexion glows softly, matching her alight crystal eye. My attention is quickly drawn away when Silverbury guards come for the Princes under my care.

I maneuver to my feet, nock an arrow, aim, breathe and release, then watch the obsidian arrowhead burrow into a wild eye.

A neck.

A heart.

A kidney.

One sneaks up behind me and I unsheathe the sword strapped to my side, its blade buries into a rounded shoulder, then I conjure vines, thrusting them into the soldier's ears when he won't go down. "Commander!" Leah shouts and I look up from my kill, finding a shadowed being darting between soldiers and leaving death in his wake. For a moment I feel hope that this will end cleanly, then *they* come.

Glass shatters and the ground shakes with the great force of cloaked warriors dropping from the ceiling, face hidden by masks. The pure evil shadowing their wild and oddly colored eyes is apparent and a pair comes for me, and my charges, with pure blood lust in their crazed stares. With how many people want to kill the twins, I'd assume it's safe to say they were never meant to survive their Father's wrath. I fire an arrow and it *pings* off an invisible shield, the pair of approaching soldiers pull down their masks to reveal full grins with blackened teeth. They raise their axes imbued with crackling, unstable Aether.

Shit. "*Adira*!"

I raise my sword and call upon my own shield, but an incoming orb of murky Aether from the pair slices right through my defenses, like my magic is *nothing.*

Lythienne screams bloody murder and everything *stops*.

A roar shakes the air muddied with blood and the marble hall *cracks* right down the middle. A giant chasm yawns open which dead civilians and soldiers fall into, along with those who are simply too close. Darkness explodes momentarily and fills the hall, then I catch part of a command from Lythienne. "I want them alive!"

Shadows retreat to a loose figure which immediately bounces between the bizarre warriors once more, but he doesn't come for mine. Leah is the only *Adira* who is able to heed my call, the coup much bloodier than we anticipated and guilt swallows my heart at the sight of so many fallen comrades.

We swing our blades together and the cloaked warriors keep us busy, neither of us are able to land a strike and pain lances through my thigh as my opponent's ax lands with a gushing *thud,* stopped by femur. "FUCK!"

A marginally more solid *Tzel* lands atop my opponent's back and shadows shove Leah away from a fatal blow, slamming her into a still unconscious Orion a few feet away from us. Darkness penetrates my enemy's ears and their crazed eyes roll back, then the warrior topples over beside me, their breathing shallow and even. The Shadow of Death stands before me, darkness settling as he extends his hand filled with the universe to me. I take it, finding the demon is surprisingly warm and his constellations scatter from my touch.

Tzel cocks his head at me, considering with my hand in his. "Why are *you* not High Lady?"

His curious words are drowned by the loud and filthy death scouring the atmosphere. "... *What?*"

Tzel shakes his head, releasing me. "Your power burns me, same as your brother's. You have been cheated, Daughter of Earth."

I open my mouth to ask what the hell he's talking about, but then his attention unnaturally *snaps* to the left of us. To Lythienne cradling Alvis, sobbing as a beautiful cloud of purple Aether flows into her vial, the excess power swirls in a storm around the pair and the *Tzel growls.* His anger is a deep vibration that makes my heart skitter, especially upon seeing dual pools of red simmer to life in his face.

The doors unlock, releasing the traumatized survivors into Silverbury to spread the word their Court has fallen. I watch *Tzel* stalk towards Lythienne with pure *red* resting in the billowing darkness of his face. Then, Alvis' fingers curling through Lythienne's goes limp, and *Tzel* relaxes. Was he just ... jealous? I leave the demon to Lythienne and call upon the least injured *Adira*, which is only a few, to help me take care of Alvis and Orion.

We put together a couple makeshift stretchers and after I give the order for the *Te'Omin* to be taken care of, I start combing through the dead. Leah walks by my side, silent as we check pulses and close eyes. We collect the injured, both soldiers and those caught in the crossfire, and there's *so* many.

We won.

But at what cost?

YOU'RE GOOD FOR BUSINESS

I crawl under a comforter, burying myself in comfort. I had shed the blue regalia, the dresses choke me just as much as the vial does. I enjoy a stray shirt of Novak's, my thighs bare and prosthesis thrown onto the floor. I pull the fabric to my face and inhale his scent. The door creaks, then Alvis burrows under the blankets and rests on his side to face me. We take in the other's tired face in silence for a moment.

"Are you ok?" He asks, fingers reaching for mine. I have avoided looking into a mirror thus far, and I wonder what I look like in his eyes. The nearly full vial has dulled my hair and skin, I can tell that much, and I'm sure exhaustion plagues my features. We are quite the pair, his own scarred skin is ashen, and we no longer match.

The white vines are gone, but my purple ones remain.

I sigh, then shake my head. "No, I don't think so."

I don't have to pretend with Alvis.

Alvis presses his forehead to mine, taking both my hands in his. After a few moments of silence, his usually confident voice comes out as a shaky whisper. "Thank you ... for not telling him."

I nod, biting my lip. "Why did you do it, Al?"

He doesn't say anything, not at first. "I have never wanted this power, it's done nothing but bring me pain, and ..."

Alvis' brows narrow as his eyes lower to our hands joined on the mattress between us. "I know it's selfish, but ... I don't *want* to be High Lord. I don't want to be anywhere near this place. I know Orion doesn't either, but ... at least he's suited to this life, he was made for this. He's good at it."

One of my hands leaves his and I gently pet his clean, albeit untrimmed and wild hair. I like it like this. "I have always admired you, even when you tried to scare me away in the tavern that night, all I could think was that I wanted to be like you. I thought if you could leave the life of villain behind, perhaps I could too."

Alvis' eyes lift and connect with mine, a soft smile pulls up one side of exhausted face. "You have terrible taste in role models."

We both laugh, and after our happiness fades, I squeeze his hand tight. "Did you really not know? What I was planning?"

Alvis releases my hand and brushes hair away from my face. "I didn't know what to think, but when you kissed that *mazzikin*, I knew you were up to something. At the very least, I knew you were trying to piss the *Tzel* off, and that had to be for only one reason. I didn't even want to *think* of it, for chance of messing it all up, for Orion hearing it. You were the weapon I could not wield."

I shudder. "I didn't know what else to do. Am I a monster, Alvis? For letting that out, for doing that to Novak? Even if it got rid of another monster?"

Alvis ponders, his faint heartbeat skips in my ears. That's not right. "To some perhaps, but I know better, if that counts for anything."

"Of course it counts." I say, heat rushing my cheeks as a glimmer of light flickers in his eyes keen on my lips. I'm almost brave enough to ask him what Orion saw between Novak, Alvis and I, but it doesn't matter now. There's not enough time left. I don't need to break any more hearts than I have to. I steer the conversation in a different direction, surprising him.

"Did you love Umber?"

Alvis sighs, running a hand over the long part of his frizzed coils. "Umber was a good friend to me, after Novak left. We saw each other through the years, but then we were apart for a long time. Meeting you in Echo, that was the first I had seen her in awhile. She was so ... *different*." Alvis trails off, eyes glazing. "But no, she's not the Fae I love."

I ponder his words, then speak with softness. "In the Mountain, she was my best friend, always knew what to do. After we left though, she wasn't the same Fae I thought she was."

Alvis' darkened eyes stare into my own, his lips tremble for a moment before asking the question I have been asking myself. "Do you think she did it on purpose?"

"I don't know, but it's been on my mind. She was too smart to act the way she did, to make whatever grand demand that pissed the Ancients off."

"It doesn't matter now anyway, she's gone." Alvis sighs, then smiles sadly. "She would be proud of you." I smile, thinking of the last time I saw my true friend, dancing in that tavern to Novak's music. All of us together, we were all really happy.

Alvis and I lie together for a while in silence, foreheads pressed and bodies kept a small distance apart. My eyes rest, one of my hands is tangled with his while he pets my hair. A recurring thought bubbles to the surface.

"You deserve to be happy, Alvis, both of you do. Help Orion do good, you don't have to be in power to do that. Just be there for him."

"You do too, you know, deserve to be happy." He retorts quietly. When I don't answer, his dark hand gently cups my cheek, lifting my wet eyes to his. His brow lifts and he gives me a knowing stare.

"I am happy, when I'm with Novak, or you. He has a tendency to be so damn *cheerful* when the world is going to shit." I chuckle, thinking of Novak playing his lute, and Alvis agrees. I falter as I remember the nightmare I released, and the fact I haven't heard him play in so *long*. "I'm just tired, I'm not sure how much more I can take, Al."

I clutch the vial in my hand. "It gets heavier every time."

Alvis takes the necklace from me carefully like he did in the throne room. I breathe in fresh air for the first time in ages. Alvis remains silent, listening with patient intent. "What if when it's full," my chest heaves with the truth I've hid from Novak, from *myself*, "What if I don't make it?"

Alvis fingers tighten around the vial and his knuckles blanch, then he gently releases the necklace as he inhales. "I assume since you're still going, you haven't told Novak. Do you plan on going alone?" He asks, voice thick.

"You have to be there for him, Al, if I fail." I beg, and my broken voice creases his eyes with worry.

"Lyth," Alvis protests quietly, "you cannot expect me to keep this from him, he loves you –"

"You tell him, and I tell Orion what you did." I catch my tears and turn serious, interrupting him. My words cut through him, his once worried face is now laced with hot anger. "You heard Orion, neither of them would let me go on if they thought I wouldn't make it. You know it's our only chance for *anyone* to live. Even with the lands united, I don't think it'll be enough to fight Eros. I *need* you to help me, and Novak. I can't,

I shudder, hiding my face into his chest as I clutch his plain tunic, "I can't do this alone. Promise you'll love him for me, please."

The last word hangs in the stuffy air under the blankets. Alvis nods after a moment, then folds my entire body tight to his while I break. Tears of relief roll down my cheeks. I can accept my possible fate, say it out loud. Alvis doesn't argue, because he knows I'm right.

I don't have another choice. Lesser Fae are disappearing by the hundreds, Humans in Terra and Sylvan have fully evacuated to Borealis. Armies are staging in the allied north, ready to take on the combined territories of Iron, Hallowed and

The Others. Iverbourne's earth has shriveled, burning in the relentless drought that began when Pan and I escaped.

Not to mention if Eros gets hold of the loose *Nafshyi*, she will have another advantage. The more I learn about the *Nafshyi*, the more I think Eros is the same type of Fae. A mix of two different types of Aether, forming a dangerous, mutant power. At the very least I hope they don't come back here, to exact their revenge.

"I promise, Lyth." Alvis' quiet promise meets me after all of my sadness is released. "I'm right here, no matter what, I'll be right here."

We are alone for a few more minutes. I have time to shed my feelings and muster a smile by the time Novak barrels through the room, diving under the blankets. A wicked cracked grin, purple eye and bloodied brow greets Alvis and I, bodies still close together and hands clasped.

"You know I'd be all for a threesome, just tell me next time." Novak teases, curling up between me and our friend.

Filthy thoughts fill my mind and my cheeks heat. It takes *everything* in me to not propose we do so right now. Sex makes everything better, but there are too many feelings and an impending end that dampens the idea. Alvis chuckles and makes room as I roll my eyes, then pull Novak close to my front. I play with his near chin length hair while he catches Alvis up.

Our conference under the blankets.

"Orion's gone to meet the remaining court members and appoint new ones, I called first stabs at Court Bard, seeing as how there's never been one. You can work in the kitchens Al, we'll show this town how we like to party." Novak teases light heartedly, but I can tell he stings his friend a bit. Alvis' light face turns serious once more and I clear my throat.

"I want you to come with us, Al. If Orion has any plans to make you head chef, it'll have to wait." I muse, offering him an official way out of duties I imagine being far more dangerous and bloody than working as a cook.

"When are you leaving?" Alvis keeps his eyes on the blond Fae, voice steady.

"First thing tomorrow, by airship. We're running out of time, and we still have to figure out how to get *in* the Mountain." Novak's solemn tone strikes a chord in me, and I bite my lip.

Alvis nods. "Let's have one last night together, then I will meet you both at first light."

"Thank you, Al." I say, thanking him for so much more than Novak knows.

"Anything for my Keeper of Death." Alvis winks before leaving the mound of blankets, then the door shuts softly behind him.

Novak turns in my arms, kissing my nose. "I told you everything would be ok." He smiles wide, handsome dimples in full view. By the Ancients, how long has it been since I've seen him this happy?

"You can plan the next coup, I'll sit back and relax." I mutter, a small smile escapes me.

He snuggles into my side and rests his head on my full chest. I twirl his curls around my fingers, then my emptiness loosens and wraps around us. Relief finds me when Novak rubs my thigh, his darkness finds mine and entangles with it. The Lady pushed deep in my mind silences, finding peace as she senses the presence of her *Tzel*. A moan of content leaves Novak, and he nestles further between my breasts.

"You still haven't asked me to tell you anything." I whisper after a long time, before sleep takes us both.

"I've heard enough from everyone else." Novak murmurs and I decide to leave it alone, focusing on the salt in his hair as I fall asleep.

"There *is* one thing I wanted to ask, but I didn't believe it, not until today."

I moan from my half sleep and my paused fingers resume their dance with his hair. "Hm?"

"I heard," Novak shrinks in my arms, "I heard you commanded it."

I giggle, kissing his forehead with a smile. "Told you I would teach him some manners." Novak ponders my words, and after a moment I tease him again. "My *lady*."

Novak groans dramatically. I peek down and find a reluctant smile tugging up a corner of his lips. "Sounds like a sap to me."

"I've told you before, my love, sometimes there is comfort in the darkness, and I think even the darkest things need comfort as well."

This answer seems to satisfy him as his body turns still and heavy on mine.

I remain half awake for a while, thinking over what I've done, and what I need to do. Breathing into his hair, I whisper softly, which draws his arms tighter around me. "I love you, my vagabond bard." I peek at the handsome freckled Fae, the smile resting in his dimples, and study every part of him.

I will destroy him next, and the thought eats me alive as I stare into the wall of our combined shadows keeping us safe.

Our nap is short lived. Vivvus sends servants to find us and I'm sure she is quite displeased we are late to another one of her parties.

Silverbury is free, the gates are open. Airships have been arriving from afar as word has spread in the last week of the new High Lord, friend to *all* creatures. Viv had offered sanctuary on his behalf to anyone who needed safe haven from the Others, and many people took her up on the offer. Today isn't about the impending war, though. Tonight we celebrate our victories, all three northern courts uniting as one and the fall of Typhan.

Viv has planned on making it a night to remember. The official welcome to the High Lord and Prince of Sylvan, and thankfully they will be in attendance. With or without them the party would've gone on. No rest for the wicked, and never mind the tightened security. Viv anticipates the remnants of Typhan's loyalists to cause trouble, and there is the threat of the rogue *Nafshyi*. I hope Emeric will be here. I sent for him a few days after the coup, but Captain needed to find someone to watch over the town home first.

Novak and I decide on our usual attire for the evening. I am especially tired of formality by now. I wear a long sleeved white tunic with bits of light lace, bound by a dark corset. Embroidered purple stars detail every part of the outfit gifted to me by Panrauth, through his sister. Captain's hat rests on my fluffed lavender curls, light silver powder lines my eyes and my lips are painted light red.

I have found I quite enjoy wearing rings and kept the ones Viv gave me, each representing the different territories of Iverbourne through the triangular symbols representing the elements. Loose charcoal pants with tight cuffs and knee high leather boots, along with the Ancient dagger at my side, finish my look.

This must be what they thought you needed.

If Novak's shadows didn't hide my shift in position, I'm sure the blade would've been stopped, my ruse found. Magic dagger or not, I only survived against Typhan through incredible luck. I focus on Novak's hand in mine instead of crimson memories, and give him a smile which he returns.

The musician wears a sand colored tunic with his usual casual flair, loose fitting oceanic pants with tight cuffs match my own style. He belongs on the lakeside, strumming his lute to the water and merfae. I narrow my brows together, trying to remember the last time he played his lute. Every time I ask he says he's tired, and I don't press further.

We walk along a low bridge leading to the lofty palace situated on an island beside the main castle. The decking rests just above the waterline, cold splashes against the wood, escaping through the gaps and teasing us. Novak is barefoot, every time the dark water tickles his toes, he lets out a giggle.

"You're quite handsome, you know." I remark with a grin. We overlook the night filled lake one last time before we head inside. Moonlight shimmers through the grand crystalline walls of the palace. Water tickles the lower edges of the see-through walls of the main hall.

The floor is clear as well, revealing the merfae and aquatic life dancing below. A group of musicians play in the center of the room, their music so boisterous it must reach the sea life below. A light orange Fae strums on a lute, not as well as Novak, but nonetheless the music entrances the crowd we snake through.

"You are quite beautiful yourself, my lady." Novak murmurs and suddenly twirls me into him, then dips his smiling lips to mine. For a moment it's just us in the middle of the room, two Fae who love each other. When our embrace ends, the lingering stares around us remind me of an altogether different scene.

"Did I please you, my lady?" The Tzel's presence was fading. Novak's body slowly came back into view as the fine tailored suit of night withdrew. He held my face with blood covered hands of milky night, then tenderly stroked my cheek.

The carnage was done, we had won. Alvis and Orion were being loaded onto stretchers behind us. Vivvus consoled her soldiers in a far corner of the throne room.

"Yes." I whispered, unable to look away as I realized it ***wasn't*** *Novak's face coming into view. I should've been afraid, the sticky blood on my cheeks should've sent something through me like fear. The galaxies parted from his face just long enough for me to see him, the* ***real*** *him.*

Without warning, my body was not my own.

"You found me, my love." The whisper haunting my days and nights stole my voice, and the distorted sound of it brought the Tzel back into full force. Wings spread from his back once more, and my body was overtaken by glittering Aether, amethysts coated my skin like the galaxies do with Novak.

Sparkling lilac lips crashed against those of darkness. Rumbling thunder erupted from the entangled clouds of purple and charcoal exploding around our figures. Black wings with green tint wrapped around us, further hiding our long awaited embrace from the survivors in the room.

After all this time, we had found each other again.

Novak pulls me from the scene, his brows are narrowed and gentle hands rest on my shoulders. He asks, "You alright?"

I nod and look around subtly, finding myself on the side of the hall. When did that happen? Orion and Viv are with us, watching me with soft faces. I rub my face and grip the vial out of habit, then close my tired eyes for a moment. I shake my feelings off and regain my senses, then release the burden.

"Sorry, what were we talking about?" I ask lightly, avoiding Novak's face and looking straight at Viv with a small smile. Orion clears his throat, pushing up a new pair of light wood framed glasses.

"I was saying Viv did an excellent job, very festive for a grand coup." Orion gestures to the place.

Fae and other beings are partying with happiness on their faces. Human children are even running around, but the sight reminds me of the redhead who happened to be in the throne room that day. Eyes of every color are here, even some Fire and Air Fae who must've fled the lands below Sylvan.

Vivvus rolls her flashing eyes at the High Lord and gives him a delicate smile, then playfully shoves his shoulder. They match, the colors of the ocean compose their luxurious fabrics.

Viv wears a long flowing dress, tiny diamonds are studded throughout the strapless bust. Orion's regalia has the same diamonds studded throughout his cuffs. His long hair is pulled halfway up, shining in the crystal filtered light. Viv's hazel hair even catches the light differently here.

"There are lots of colors out there, you should be proud." Novak kisses my forehead, whispering against my skin. I give him a half smile and scan the bustling crowd further. "I think I even saw a certain Fire Fae," he says.

"Really?" I grasp his sun spotted arm tight, then glance at Orion who is beaming at my excitement. Vivvus just looks confused, pouting at her ignorance.

"Really."

The melodic voice of Captain rings from behind me. My heart flutters when I face her and Emeric standing together. The tall Fire Fae waits in her leather and lace pirate regalia, her usual sly grin in place.

I throw my arms around her, she returns the embrace tightly. A sigh of relief escapes, my chest rising and falling unsteadily. We are all back together again.

"You're good for business kid, can't deny that I missed you, though." Captain pats my back, then takes her feathered hat back with a wink.

Orion and Emeric entangle in a passionate embrace, as High Lord he must not be concerned with who sees their love here. Good. He'll change so much around here.

Novak hugs Captain tight when I leave her side, his knuckles blanching from clutching her leathered shoulders so tight. I stand beside Vivvus and provide privacy to the tear filled reunions, hot joy spills from my own eyes. Exactly how I hoped it would be, and for a moment, everything is worth it.

But time pauses when Captain pulls back from Novak and spies Vivvus.

The air charges with hot electricity as she drinks in her beautiful figure like the first glass of water after a long day in the deserts of Echo. Captain floats towards us and takes Viv's delicate green hand gently, only to yank the Earth Fae tight against her body.

Captain's thin lips are close enough to kiss the plump, dark burgundy of Vivvus'. Captain's orange eyes simmer down to a soft pink from under her hat as she looks Viv up and down *quite* slowly. Viv raises her sharp chin as she attempts to look rather unimpressed, but she doesn't push Captain away.

I grin, glancing at Novak who can't veil his joy at the sight. Orion blushes, his hand tangled with the handsomely dressed Emeric beside him. Emeric smiles at me, he looks much older with his brunette hair swept back and such a fine suit adorning his soft figure. The suit matches Orion's perfectly, I wonder how Vivvus had it made and sent to him so quickly. She is truly a miracle worker.

Captain's black brow raises as she kisses the top of Vivvus hand, then she asks the only question that matters. "And who might you be, little princess?"

Captain's siren song possesses Viv. The warrior Princess grabs a fistful of black hair and thrusts her mouth onto the pirate's waiting smile. Red and green auras meld so intensely, it's like a coal forge has exploded before us, setting my heart ablaze in an instant.

"I wish you could see this." I take Novak's hand, exhaling a deep breath as my heart *pounds*. "They're mates."

And now I understand what Panrauth felt the day Novak and I met.

Vivvus

"And who might you be, little princess?"

Seven words.

Seven, small words set a chain of events in motion that I'll never be able to take back, not that I want to.

A fleeting crystalline ballroom filled with close friends, temporary peace and stupid hope. This coup offered me an opportunity to truly leave the boundaries of my homeland in decades, all to ensure the safety of someone else's kingdom. I didn't do it for the twins, although now I can see Orion will prove to be a good ruler, just as Lythienne promised. The High Lord and Prince of Sylvan have healed and taken to their new life all in good stride, although Lythienne did say that there was a bit of a ... disagreement, when she and Novak met with Orion the first time after he woke up.

I stayed out of it, I have no interest in their drama. While I have no ill feelings towards the *Te'Omin*, it's simply not my place. I'm not a Misfit, the only reason I did all this was for Lythienne, or that's what I told myself. Now, I wonder if I chose this path because Captain was waiting for me further down it.

Captain is as tall as I am, but that's where our similarities end. Smooth raven hair falls over leather and laced shoulders from underneath a colorful feathered hat as she bows at the waist. A thin black brow raises as she kisses the top of my jade hand, electrifying me in ways I thought long lost. Her skin is an unblemished porcelain and her soft lips burn my knuckles the moment we touch. Blood red eyes alight with orange flames flick up to mine before her lips leave my skin, and a delightful pierce to my heart tilts the room on its side. I figure what the hell and take desperate hold of Captain. My hands dives into her hair and our mouths crash, teeth gnashing in a wild introduction. I've always scoffed at the instant love of mates. I've witnessed moments just like this and thought it was so *ridiculous*, but the intense pull in my soul to Captain's is not something I can push away.

And I don't want to. I want to be selfish, for once in my damn life.

A strong pulse echoes in my ears, *her* heart.

Captain sweeps me off my feet and her strong hands settle under my thick thighs. She's leaner than I am but seems to have no trouble picking me up, so I don't protest. I catch glimpses of Lythienne smiling with tears in her black and whites eyes, Novak grinning ear to ear, and Orion trying to hide a smile but failing as Captain whisks me off to who knows where. The voracious party fades and I can focus on nothing but the firm *thump, thump, thump* in my mind, and on the first set of lips I've kissed since Bonnie ...

We crash into an alcove, and it's only then that words are used instead of hands and teeth. "You still haven't told me your name." Captain reminds me as she gently sets me down against a crystalline, see through wall that borders the lake. Water crashes against the crystal pressing on my shoulders.

"Neither have you, and I suspect you already know mine anyway." I bite back, unable to hide the need for dominance. My hands desperately grasp her waist and I turn the Fire Fae so *her* back is pressed against the stone wall. Those sparks in her eyes flare in intensity and a mischievous smile takes hold of her beautiful face.

"Perhaps." She chuckles and pulls on one of my ringlets, heat pools between my thighs. "A name for a name won't work then, will it? I hate to disappoint you, but my old name is dead. I have nothing to give you, Captain is my name."

That piques my attention.

"Fine, a name for a story, anytime I like it."

Captain smiles and says nothing at first, tender fingers leaving my coils to brush against my cheek. I swallow, caught under her studious stare as she commits my face to memory. Waves splash against the wall behind Captain and one of my hands slides from her hip to gently cup her cheek. Her heart slows in the confines of my mind. "As you wish, Princess."

"Vivvus. Vivvus Firthorn." I breathe out immediately, nipples hardening under the dark blue of my dress as our chests press together the slightest bit. The passionate moment has dulled into something reverent, albeit slow and cautious.

"Full of life? I believe it." Captain remarks thoughtfully like she's truly never heard my actual name and I blink in surprise. "Tell me, Vivvus, can you hear my heart? I hear yours." Her slender hand comes to rest upon the silk covering my breast. I nod, breathless under her careful touch. I take her hand in mine and kiss her knuckles, then press my face to her hand.

"Are we really mates?" I tread carefully, needing to hear her say it. To say that I belong to someone, and they belong to me.

Captain smiles, but it's sad. She pulls away from my touch and I instantly feel hollowed out. "It would appear the universe has connected us, yes. But, I believe there is more to love and companionship than destined fates, we write our own stories in the stars, in a sense. What do you think, Vivvus, do you want to see how many stories they will tell about us? I, "

Captain trails off for a moment, brow furrowing and confidence fading further. "I let my emotions get the best of me, but, you do have a choice. You do not *have* to be with me, because of this thread between us. We can be as little, or as much as you want. If a companion, a friend, is what you desire, then ..." I can't help but feel pleased at the her struggling with the idea of *not* being with me. "We can do that too."

I cautiously reach out and take her hand once more, then strategically place a kiss in the middle of her work worn palm. "I have never wanted anything more in my life than you, and if you'll have me, a near stranger, then I'm yours. I *want* you."

Captain smiles wide, a bright and beautiful thing, then her free hand slides past my jaw and settles to the back of my neck, pulling me closer until our lips are a feather width apart. Our bodies are melded, *finally*. "You are no stranger to me, Vivvus."

"Then kiss me again."

And she does.

Her tongue explores my mouth instead of doing battle with me, her hands and my own travel and roam along the other's body. My arms come to rest around her neck, one of her hands squeezes a handful of my ass while the other twirls the hair behind my ear. I moan into her and her searing grip tightens wonderfully, but then she surprises me. "I have to tell you something, and it may change your mind." Captain admits, lips lingering on mine.

"What?" I breathe, sure nothing will change my heart.

Captain's eyes dart away, unsure, then back to me. "I don't do sex. This I like, but nothing more."

"Oh," I whisper, thoroughly surprised. The way she was damn near devouring me, I thought for sure a hand down the pants or something would've followed. I bite my lip, then lean forward to hover over her neck. "This, you like?"

Captain moans, exposing her throat to me. I lick from the hollow of her neck up to behind her ear and she shivers. "I'm a complicated person, Vivvus, what can I say?"

I chuckle, nuzzling my nose into the space behind her charcoal tufted ear. "You don't need to say anything. We have all the time in the world, and I don't mind."

Captain's fingers find my chin and she gently brings my face to hers. "Truly?"

"Truly." I smile wide, heart pounding erratically with too much happiness. Captain lays a gentle kiss on my lips, smiling before pulling away. "As much I loathe to admit it, we need to return to the party. I do have a job to do, you know."

"Oh?" I ask, unmoving, but then again she doesn't move either. Neither of us appear to be very eager to fully separate.

Captain nods and seriousness falls over her sharp porcelain features. "Speaking of, let's go find that troublesome gearhead. I need to ask her something before we leave in the morning."

Words don't form in a coherent thought first, just spill out of me without warning. "I want to go with you."

Captain raises a brow, surprise and thinly veiled delight wash over her beauty. The corners of her tear drop eyes curve upwards. "Aren't you needed in Terra?"

I chew on my bottom lip for a moment and she hyper fixates on my mouth, causing small sparks to reignite in her eyes once more. "No. I'm right where I need to be." I say firmly.

Captain nods, then presses her forehead to mine in attempts to hide her growing grin of pleasure. "As you wish, my dear."

The two of us leave the safety of the alcove and wander to a raised balcony overlooking the main floor below filled with peace and harmony. Eyes of every color and people of every creed dance and laugh in the space, but it's not hard to pick my brother out from the crowd. I smile softly upon spotting Lythienne cross the room to approach him and offer her hand. They dance, and it's beautiful. Despite the fact they didn't end up together, it makes me happy to see the pair on good terms. They will always share the horrors of the Mountain.

"I think she loves him." Captain murmurs as her hand slides around my waist. She tracks the pair as Panrauth leads Lythienne beautifully, if not slower than the uplifting music calls for. For a moment only silence falls between us and I contemplate her words, but when Lythienne subtly looks over Panrauth's shoulder, scanning the room for Novak no doubt, I sigh.

"She loves Novak, and Alvis." I say softly. "Panrauth is someone she shared a hardship with, that's all."

Captain's eyes whip to mine and I keep mine on the Keeper and my brother, gut sinking. "Oh?" She asks and I swallow, feeling like I've said something I shouldn't have. "I've suspected about Alvis. Did she tell you this?" Captain asks in a near silent whisper.

I glance sideways, finding curiosity instead of irritation. When I catch her eyes, I nod. "Yes ... I, I don't wish to betray her trust, I spoke without thinking."

Captain nods in understanding. "Then I won't ask you to, however, I do have one question." She pauses as Lythienne and Panrauth pass by us below, leaving the gathering hall for the safety of an outside balcony overhanging the lake. Lythienne glances up to us and Captain tips her hat to the Keeper, earning a nod before she disappears outside with my brother.

"Has she told him? Alvis?" Captain asks, looking back at me.

I shake my head. "She won't."

Captain's brows furrow in confusion and I decide to spill a little more truth, needing someone to bear the burden with, one *no one* knows of. "Lythienne doesn't plan on surviving the Mountain, Captain. She doesn't want to break more hearts than she has to, and bringing Novak is destroying her as it is."

And Captain's eyes *ignite*.

Lyth

Novak proudly watches Captain scoop Viv up in a swift move, and I *smile*. I wonder how long Captain's been alone for, the happiness on Novak's face tells me it's been a long time. The lovers leave in a flurry of passion, and the remnants of their joined Aether lingers around us in a haze of sweet lavender.

Orion sweeps an arm around Emeric's shoulder, using his other hand to push up his glasses and rub his face. I thought all that Aether would've healed his eyes, but some things just can't be fixed. "What just happened?"

Novak chuckles as he pulls me back to his chest, handsome dimples showing. He rests his chin on my head, having to lean over a bit. "It appears our dear Captain has found her mate."

"*Great*, let's add another troublemaker to the family." Orion drawls, but the lines in his eyes are pulled up.

I snicker, letting out a long laugh I cannot reel in. "We are the most dysfunctional family ever."

My friends find humor in my dark sentiment, unable to contain their own joy, even after Alvis joins us. Confusion wears on his thin face, his brow arching as he takes in our state. At his side, the Hero of Sylvan clings to his arm with her tight face held high.

Charis looks *alive*. She's clean with a warm glow to her skin, and her hair is cut evenly to her scalp. The injuries on her face are healed and her light purple eyes flash with Aether once more. She wears a lilac gossamer gown, the only sign of her weakness are the trembling hands around Alvis' thick arm. I learned from Viv that Charis and Alvis used to cause quite a bit of trouble together, childhood best friends.

"Did I miss Lyth becoming funny?" Alvis taunts.

Orion's laughing subsides long enough for him to lock eyes with Alvis, which in turn releases a deep rumble echoing from the warrior through our circle. Charis' cheeks warm as she watches Alvis, a small smile taking hold of her pink lips.

"You *know* it's rude to not share with the class." Novak teases the twins.

"Yes, well, it's much faster this way." Orion says nonchalantly as he kisses the top of Emeric's head, like he can't get enough of touching and kissing him. Emeric smiles up to him, eyes flashing red. Charis breaks away from Alvis, causing the group to fall silent.

"You look lovely tonight." I offer as she walks right up to me, My lungs pause when she throws her arms around my neck. She's smaller than me, not only in stature, but she's so thin my muscled arms wrap right around her. I curve over and hold her with care.

"I couldn't have done it better myself." She whispers into my chest, her shaking voice full of anger.

When she doesn't let go, I nod to Novak who insists the twins show him their fancy new thrones. Alvis' haunted gaze lingers for a moment, then he decides she is indeed safe with me. There aren't any thrones here, and I wonder if they're really going back to the main castle. Those bastards better not leave me at this party alone.

After they're gone, I speak confidently in a low tone. "You're quite brave, you know. I heard what you did, what you've done your entire life. I will forever be in debt to people like you, you remind me what I'm fighting for."

Charis looks up from my embrace with surprise, then wipes her tears away. She takes a step back and smooths out her dress, then speaks softly. "I believe *hope* is the word you're looking for, Lythienne. That's all I wanted to do, bring hope to those trapped here."

Her words make me think of Panrauth immediately, what I said to him long ago in the Pit. "Yes, I suppose you're right."

Charis lingers by my side for a while, quietly filling me in on the Fae she recognizes and the dramatics of Sylvan. When I spy the High Lord of Terra entering with his brother, I decide there is one more thing I want to do before the end.

"Excuse me, I have to visit an old friend, would you like me to find Alvis for you?" I scan the party but don't see the twins, or Novak. Just unending finery and happiness, no societal barriers present. I'm glad I reached out to the lower classes in the Outer Rim and invited them personally.

Novak, Vivvus and I 'redistributed' some of the castle goods to the lower and middle class in secret on the fourth day here, high quality clothes and food stores that were in overabundance. We went door to door and after necessities were dropped on the doorstep of some very surprised Fae, I invited each household to join us and meet the new High Lord.

"No, I'll be quite alright. Go on." Charis smiles sweetly at me. I kiss her on the forehead before finding Panrauth who's already lost in the crowd.

But, it doesn't take me long to find him again. Even here, Panrauth is one the largest Fae. Apparently, he had the same idea I did when it came to dressing for a party, casual and dangerous. I cross the floor with my chin high, dodging questions and gratitude along the way.

I halt behind him passionately telling a story to a family of Water Fae. He doesn't hear me and I chuckle a bit upon hearing my name. He's telling the story of how we met, conspirators in crime. I tap his leathered shoulder lightly and Pan turns with haste.

I say, "Hello, my dear."

A warm smile spreads across his broad face. His beard is growing back in, but his hair is trimmed still. "Why, I was just talking about you." He bows fully to me and offers his hand.

I take it, drawing subtle surprise from him. Pan dismisses the enthralled group he presided over and leads me to a quiet corner, his brows tighten at my silence.

"Dance with me?" I ask, and within a moment one hand is on my waist, the other tangling with my own small hand. We dance in place, the background music is a fast tempo but we sway slowly, like we once did.

"I must admit I didn't expect you to want to see me, let alone dance with me. You look quite terrifying tonight, the gear suits you." Pan muses, his thick body hunches over my own.

The Grasshopper and the Bear.

"Yes, well, I suppose even Keepers miss old friends, even ones that have a track record of trying to kill me." I tease, then look up to him when he stops swaying. He evaluates my face with an unreadable expression. Our next words are so quiet and fast, I'm not entirely sure they were all said out loud.

"You look awful."

"I do."

"You don't have to do this. You get to go home."

"I don't have a home, Pan."

"Don't be ridiculous, yes you do."

"What I mean is, I won't *have* a home if I don't do this."

"Let me come with you then."

"No." I say sharply. He steps back as if wounded, his hands leave my body.

"I can always make you."

I chuckle, but I know he isn't joking. "I have a favor, then I'll think about it."

A hard moment passes and we stare at each other.

"Alright. One favor?"

Without answering, I make for the nearest balcony overhang, and Panrauth follows behind. Captain and Vivvus are back inside the palace, watching the party from a raised level. The Fire Fae spots us Pan and I leaving the main area together. I nod to Captain on the way, she tips her hat to me. She's the next one I need to talk to.

When it's just Pan and I together in the crisp night air with water crashing below us, I push out a deep breath. "Well, two favors, actually."

Panrauth rolls his eyes and crosses his arms, sarcasm dripping with his gorgeous smile. "Always with the favors."

"So, you remember when you found me in the tunnel, you said there were three Fae?"

"Yes." Humor disappears, his face turns to stone.

"Well, there were actually four of them, and the one that got away was Typhan's son, the twins' brother."

"Are you fucking kidding me? I hope he's dead because if not Lyth I swear –" Panrauth's arms drop and he closes the distance between us. I reach into my side pocket and remove Typhan's necklace, my eye. I hold it up and Pan's face *drains*, his body and words screech to a halt.

He pushes down a lump in his throat. "I'm not putting that back in."

I laugh so hard, I feel as if I might faint. Hysteria doubles me over and I hold my stomach with one hand, wipe tears with the other.

"What? I'm not." He says nervously, unsure what to make of my state. I compose myself, wiping away the last of my tears.

"No, I want to destroy it, and I thought we should do it together, at least I want to do it together ..." I trail off, biting my lip.

His jaw tightens and he carefully takes the necklace by the cord. "Are you sure?"

"Completely."

Lavender invades my nose and Aether lights up the night as the necklace lifts into the air. A swirling orb of emerald flames swallows the jar my eye resides in, but doesn't destroy it. Pan keeps one hand outstretched to the floating sphere and the other rests on my shoulder. I lean into him, watching the neon green magic reflect on the lake below.

"A good friend once told me you have to burn it to the ground and start over, and I feel like that applies here." I murmur.

Panrauth chuckles, then snaps his fingers. The orb of light explodes, sending hundreds of green stars shooting upwards into the night sky with thunderous *booms*. The sight takes my breath away, and a small weight lifts as a part of my story closes.

Our story. I wouldn't be here without him.

Hollers and shouts erupt from the palace and soon every small balcony facing the lake is packed with Fae shooting their Aether into the sky, and I finally see a true rainbow.

Fire, Air, Earth and Water Fae join as one. Aether of every hue and vibrant color splashes and *explodes* against the glittering heavens above, and I enjoy the moment with Pan in companionable silence. I steal a glance at him and when I see him smiling with silent tears trailing down his cheeks, I know he's found closure, too.

I exhale a heavy sigh and step back from Pan, crossing my arms and closing myself off as I do so. He won't like this. "The second favor is, I need you to not go with me."

Instantaneous scowl and crossing of his own thick arms follows my words. "*Why*?"

I fold my ears down and it only takes him a second to register my command, a slight flash of Aether touching his eyes as a sound shield is cast around us. "Because Novak isn't going, and I need you to help him do something for me, after."

He laughs coldly. "You can't be serious. For one, we don't exactly like each other, and for two, you're *seriously* leaving him behind? You're more heartless than I thought." Every muscle in Pan's body is alive, and his words strike the place where my supposed heart is.

Silence.

More silence.

"Do you trust me when I say it's important? All of it?" I whisper, body trembling with desperation and fear. The High Lord of Terra doesn't reply, only stares at me for another full minute.

"Will you be alone?" He asks finally. I shake my head and he nods thoughtfully. He places a hand on his chest, his voice guttural and rolling as he does so. *"Im hayiti chai et chayay mehahatchala, hayiti motse otkha mukdam yoter."*

"And what does that mean?" I ask lightly, brow raising as a warm smile spreads across my face. Pan only gives me a small smile, drinking in my body before leaving me for the last time.

DON'T LEAVE ME BEHIND

I shake Novak awake, it's only four in the morning but there's been a change of plans. He lets out a groan but refuses to roll over, it takes Captain pushing him out of bed to rouse him from the short slumber he had.

"What the *fuck*, it's too early." Novak growls, his voice echoing with the *Tzel*'s.

"Change of plans short stuff," Captain retorts and pokes him with her boot. Novak's eyes flash open and he stares at Captain with confusion, then narrows his eyes on me packing in the corner. "Talk to the boss." Captain shrugs before leaving with a slam of the door.

She's not happy with me.

"What the hell, Lyth?" Novak jumps up and dresses with motivation, my silence unnerving him. I glare at him and gesture around us dramatically, flicking my ears down as I do so. Bright blue eyes flash as a sound shield sweeps over our room.

"Captain is taking us to Echo, *now*. I'm not taking Alvis into that fucking Mountain."

Novak pauses his hurry, face softening. "Lyth, it'll destroy him if you —"

"I don't *care*. I changed my mind, he belongs here." I snap, the *always* present Lady knocks on my mind and soul, urging me to hurry. I can't lay awake and debate it anymore. I should've never asked Alvis, it's not fair to him. It was a moment of weakness on my part.

I can do this.

Novak sprints across the room and takes me by my dropping shoulders, face twisted with worry. "And what about you? What about me?"

I sigh, staring up into wild eyes half covered by ever growing hair, his angled jaw has been shaded by dirty blond these past few days. I like it. "I love you, and I know even if I asked you to stay behind, you wouldn't."

I swallow something *very* heavy.

He kisses me with a fueled desperation, pulling away only to take my face in his hands. "Damn right. Listen to me, let's just go. Right now. We'll hide in the grove, go to the mountains. Anything." His voice breaks, desperate freckled beauty watches my lip tremble. "I can't lose you. Not now, not after everything."

A hand drops from my face, taking the vial from my neck. Air rushes into my lungs and the lifted weight helps my words. "I can do this, Novak. I can finish what they started, I can make it *right*."

I'm not fooling him. The moment he drops the vial, I exhale a hoarse breath, causing his face to fall apart. Ethereal arms hold me close, his chest rises unsteadily against my skipping heart. Darkness seeps from both of us, entangling on the walls and floors, forming the familiar bubble of comfort around us.

"I don't want the world put back together if you're not going to be in it. Just promise me you won't go too far. *Please*."

I nod, unable to say the word.

Novak shudders against me, arms tightening like a vise for a brief moment. He yanks himself away, rubbing his head and groaning. "What's wrong?" I ask with a trembling hand reaching out to him.

Novak shakes the hair from his eyes and *Tzel* from his mind, rolling his shoulders back. "The idiot has a point." Novak says with defeat after a moment, *glaring* at me with an even face. My brows pull together in confusion. "Apparently, the *Tzel* doesn't like when you try lying to us. *It*."

Novak snarls and shakes his head violently again, leaving my outstretched hand as he marches across the room for his things. I scoff, crossing my arms. "I didn't even *say* anything."

Novak throws on his pack and waits. I'm still standing where he left me. "That's exactly it. I asked you to promise, and you can't even do that. For me."

"You can both stop being such a sap. We have shit to do." I scowl at him and snatch up my duffel bag, then march past him and spit the insult over my shoulder. A low growl erupts from behind me and I ignore it.

Not a word is spoken from either of us the rest of the way.

We walk in complete silence through the sleeping city. The party roared into the early morning and went surprisingly well. No one died anyway, so that is a good thing.

Dawn threatens to break and reveal Novak and I. I can't hurt Alvis and Novak any longer, even though Alvis promised he would help. I *know* he would, there is too much good in him not to. He always thinks about everyone else first and himself last.

As we climb the hill leading us to the gates, I catch one last look at the sprawling city behind us before light spreads over the glorious architecture below. I sigh, the port holds the most beautiful view in my opinion. I bet the valley below will capture the first morning light as it spills onto the grand lake and gemstones littering the buildings.

Vivvus works right beside the crew on the ground, releasing the galleon from its confining ropes. The familiar golden sails with faerie skulls and crossbones lightens my chest as they billow in the wind. I follow Novak onto the ramp and when my feet step on board, peace washes over me. Captain's positioned at the helm, flicking brass switches and bringing the engines to life. She steals glances at her mate, watching Viv like she's the most magical thing on Earth.

The ship hovers further off the ground as the Princess of Terra boards the ship. Captain grins, giving her a seductive wink. Vivvus rolls her eyes in annoyance and I silently help her pull the ramp up, noting her subtle smile. Novak's taken down by surprise, a yelp escapes from the musician. As I watch Oak wrestle him and Captain at the helm laughing at their antics, I realize just how much he was missed. Their first mate.

The sun peeks over the distant horizon as we rise further, meeting a thin sea of warm clouds. I turn away from the sun and my friends, then lean over the railing holding the last view of Silverbury. The crystalline castle fades and my heart aches as I think of the twins. I wanted Alvis to come, but I can't bear it. It would finalize my descent into becoming a horrible Fae, it's bad enough to plan Novak's demise.

What I asked of Alvis, I was hurting and thinking only of myself. Hopefully, he will forgive me for not saying goodbye. Orion promised to keep the rest of my research safe, and that he would continue it with Alvis. They will tell Novak everything, when the time is right. Emeric and Orion will rule over Sylvan and bring a new era of peace to all those who have been wronged. Hopefully Viv can keep her brothers on the right path, and bring justice to Terra's history as well.

I sigh heavily, hoping Alvis tells good stories about me.

Novak comes to my side, resting his hand on my lower back as he overlooks the fleeting city with me. "I'm sorry, for earlier. I know this is hard for you." I rise and press my back into him, both his bare arms snake around and hold me close. Flags of every color rustle below in the wind, lining the distant walls of

Silverbury. Orion insisted the walls be left up, as a constant reminder of the cost of oppression.

"I'm sorry for putting you through hell." I breathe, heat pricks my neck and spirit. "If it's between saving everyone I love, or myself," I shift in his arms, biting my lip as I look up to him, "I can't promise to make the right decision, because ... there isn't one. Hopefully it won't come to that, though."

Novak ponders my words and when he speaks, his tone surprises me. "I suppose I'll take what I can get. Aren't you supposed to be the villain in this story? Seems like you're the hero to me." A small chuckle escapes him, reminding me of the Fae I met what seems like an eternity ago.

I turn in his arms, lifting a brow at him. "I've left chaos in every place we've been to. I'm pretty sure that's *not* a hero thing." I say and can't help but smile, pressing my forehead to his. I really don't want to be alone, but I can't ask him to watch me die.

"You're *my* hero." Viv spooks me, her cheerful voice by our side. I startle in Novak's arms, eliciting a full laugh from him and Captain holding onto the now finely dressed Vivvus.

Wasn't she dressed in work clothes just minutes ago?"

"Our hero is a bit jumpy. I say we have dinner early." Captain decides. Viv raises a confused brow at Captain, seeing how the day just started.

I put on my best Alvis impression, raising a finger. "The only free meal on this ship is dinner, you'll wait like everyone else."

"That's why we're having it *early*, dummy. Have you learned nothing out there?" Captain teases, dressed in her usual full leather and lace regalia with the feathered hat that kept me company for some time. I shrug, deciding dinner for breakfast sounds quite good, and a full bowl of herb shared with friends sounds better.

A string of *roaring* profanities echoing from under the ship stops us all in our tracks.

"What the hell?" Captain inspects a flailing rope slung over the railing, and as she looks down, a grin fills her fierce features. "We have a stowaway." She juts a thumb to over the side.

Of course we do.

I glare at Novak who puts his hands up, unable to hide his amusement as two vineless hands grip onto the railing, clinging for dear life. "First you leave me behind, then none of you help me up. Wretched *fucking* faeries." Alvis throws himself over the side and onto the deck, landing flat on his back and cursing some more.

I bite my lip, attempting to veil my smile of relief. I wasn't going to hold him to his promise, but I know that's why he came. He never cared if I was going to tell Orion or not, I think he would've helped me regardless.

"Lyth, if we make it out of this alive, I *swear* I'm going to kill you." Alvis huffs and sits up, a small grin betraying him as he threatens me. I help him up, then pull him into a tight hug. "I made a promise. Quit making it hard." Alvis whispers quickly into the hair covering my ear.

I nod, eyes warming and words stuck in my throat.

Novak claps Alvis on the shoulder after the Fae leaves my embrace, grinning wide. "I told her that you'd be pissed. Glad you came."

Alvis ruffles Novak's hair, his fingers lingering just a bit longer than they usually do. "Of course, can't be stuck in that castle already."

Novak smiles at Alvis, *oh* how he smiles at him. Captain appears to be quite pleased with the situation, as does Vivvus. Captain was *not* happy when I asked her to leave early so we could ditch Alvis, but she didn't protest like Novak did. I cross over to Viv and sling my arm around her, giving the Earth Fae a tired smile which she returns.

"Make yourself useful, I'm hungry." I tease Alvis, leaving him and Novak to their roughhousing shenanigans, which I'm thoroughly convinced is just an excuse for them to grab the other.

"I need to ask you something."

"What's on your mind?" Captain leans on the steering wheel, glowing red eyes peering at me from under her feathered hat. We are alone, at last. I rest on the railing beside her and watch the ocean disappear behind us, taking in a breath of sea air before speaking.

"How did you meet Novak?" The heat of the day glares off the vicious waves brewing below. A rainstorm is coming, after all this time. Captain smiles and raises a brow. She sets the steering mechanism and faces what we left behind, with me.

"We've been friends for quite a long time. The first crew member I hired when I got this beast going, but we knew each other long before that. One day my father and I visited Dew Falls, which back then was a big deal for Fire Fae. When we landed at their airport, a pathetic looking skinny thing was picking a fight with some bullies." She chuckles, eyes glazing over with memories. "With no family and nowhere to go, he came with us. The rest is history."

"I didn't realize how long you've known each other." I remark, fidgeting. "How did he end up leaving, and coming back?"

She nods, knitting her fingers together. "We've been through quite an ordeal, that's for sure." With a pushed out breath, she continues. "The twins had been on for a year, Novak and Alvis ..."

"I already know that they were together." I say with a smile and she nods.

"That year was the best this ship ever had, they were so *happy*. Then Novak met his mate, having no idea she was already married to an old Human friend of his, a fact she neglected to mention until *after* the bond set." Captain's voice is filled with disgust, her eyes are softened with sadness.

"And he just ... left Alvis, and you?" I ask, unable to fathom Novak leaving the ship or Alvis just like that. It's the only thing I haven't been able to figure out, and Novak doesn't say much about it, just the before and after.

Captain nods, biting her cheek. "None of us understood it, that female, she was just ... the complete *opposite* of Novak, but Alvis was right there, Orion too, they watched the connection *snap* across the room. I'm sure by now you know how Al is, he gave Novak an out, he understood what it would be like to be without your other half. He just wanted Novak to be happy, even if it wasn't with him."

Of course he did.

I turn my eyes down at Captain's words. I didn't realize how much Alvis has suffered, right from the beginning. I remember what Alvis told me, how Umber was there for him after Novak left, after he took the out. I can't imagine Novak doing it, I just *can't*, but ... he did. I groan and rub my face. "Tell me what happened."

Captain removes her feathered hat, crimson aura darkening while she brushes dirt off the oilskin. "I had just landed in Vabel, the village nearby where they were staying. Alvis had been on a bender for months, and Novak was the only person I could think of to get him out of it." Captain's whispers crack and she wipes a tear from her porcelain face.

"Sage traveled her and Mav to Arca Hallow, both distraught and her magic drained," I watch her face falter with her voice, "it wasn't just your run of the mill asshole Purists. They were personally trained by Typhan himself. Those *Nafshyi* you're worried about? They are mild compared to the things that took that poor kid's magic. They were *Nafshyi*, but ... stronger, so much stronger."

A lump forms in my throat and I rub at the headache brewing on my right temple. The only thing Vabel is remotely near is Arca Hallow, which is at least a hundred miles away. "Why didn't you tell him? Novak thinks they just took off."

Captain shrugs, putting her hat back on. "They spent a week together before Mav came calling, and when he showed up, she acted as if nothing happened between her and Novak. Kid thought it was a good idea to stick around, even if it meant stuffing his feelings down. Or he was embarrassed, who knows. Perhaps the only good thing she did was make it easy for him to let her go. In the end, it didn't matter anyway."

"So, you sent the twins then?" I ask, already knowing the answer. I know the basics of this, but not the fine details she's offering me. Captain nods, lips tightening into a thin line.

"Yes. Novak had been off the crew since, well, since finding Sage. As far as he knows, I was in the right place, at the wrong time. After the *Tzel* moved in, it took all of Alvis' energy just to keep him sane and fight the beast whenever it appeared. I didn't wind up telling Novak anything, he was having a hard enough time as it is. Still does."

The wrong time, too late to stop *Tzel* from destroying an entire town, murdering hundreds of people in it's anger at being trapped. I highly doubt Captain could've done anything to stop him, but then again, she *is* powering a hulking pirate ship through the air.

"He told me they were mates, but she still pushed him away like that?" I pause, shaking my head, unable to finish the sentence.

"You *can* reject a bond, but it's painful. Sometimes I wonder if that's what did it."

"Did what?"

Captain peers over her shoulder, red eyes darting back and forth. We are still alone on the helm. Color fills her porcelain cheeks for the first time since I've met her, they didn't even flush when she was crying. "Not long after they seperated, Sage became so ill, not even Aether could save her. It was long and brutal, she withered right before Mav's eyes."

"Novak never saw her again?" To have experienced all that pain through a rotting bond, it's a wonder Novak ever smiles at all.

"In the end, she told Maverick everything. He thought the kid could help her, they made it halfway back." She sighs, flames dancing in her eyes while she stares at me. "The *Tzel* broke out when it happened, and he nearly killed Mav. That's who he visits, in Cervalis. Mav has a family now, and never had hard feelings, even after finding out."

"And have *you* ever met *Tzel*?" I ask and she raises a brow at my wording.

"Face to face, once. Alvis, that was his job." She closes her eyes, aura shuddering. "You should've seen him when he came back and you were gone, in Cervalis. At first it was just the kid, pacing and yapping incessantly." My breath pauses, thinking of him losing his mind in Hallowed after finding out about Umber. "All these years together, he managed to keep it hidden away from me. But, there was a moment when I looked into his eyes, and pure death stared back. At first I couldn't understand it, but the thing wanted it's —"

"Lady. He refers to me, as My Lady." I shoot Captain a solemn look, gauging her initial reaction. She leaves my side to gaze upon Novak below, a chuckle escaping her when Viv swats him over the head for eating. Silence fills the helm for another moment. I shift closer and lean into her twitching, black tufted ear.

"I think he's a Fallen," I whisper.

Captain's usual composure disappears, her head turning on a swivel. "What did you just say?" I study her broken facade, catching worry and fear in her sharp beauty.

"I'm just beginning to understand us. I gave Orion everything I have, just in case." My tight shoulders curl in, lungs struggling for air. I grasp the vial tight as the deck sways under me.

"Us?" Captain asks, voice tight. All I can do is nod and focus on not vomiting.

Captain takes hold of me, pulling me close to her. Oil in her hair and sea salt on her skin, the smell of my two favorite people beckons me to sleep. For a moment I rest, leaning my weight into her arms and forgetting the words I can't get out. Viv's calling voice pulls us apart. I give Captain a small smile and nod before leaving her.

Captain stops me, taking my hand firmly. "If what you say is true, not only will Novak never let you do this, but neither will the *Tzel*."

She *does* know what he is, what I am.

I swallow, shrugging her off. "I know. I don't have another choice, do I?"

Captain releases my hand, silence thickens the void my question leaves. She tips her hat to me before we leave the helm together and join our family, silently answering my question.

Our dinner for breakfast is truly a feast fit for our Crew of Misfits. Wooden, metal and ceramic platters ranging from decrepit to elegant quality rest across the stretching table. Each plate overflows with salads, pastries, venison or beef. Fruit lines some of the outer platters, and the sliced loaf of artisan bread with butter catches my eye. The sight makes me miss Umber, even after everything. She brought me hope initially in those caves, and thinking of her last moments brings me pain.

"You three outdid yourselves." I say and survey the table, pacing around it once so I can decide what to devour first.

Novak grins and elbows Viv before joining my side. He kisses my cheek and rests his hands on my wide waist. "Viv insisted we have a grand celebration. Well, another one." Alvis is seated at the end of the table opposite Captain, leaning back with his hands behind his head. Content rests on his face as he watches Novak and I standing together.

Our gaze meets and I give him a small smile, but he looks away without so much as a twinge in his jaw.

"What are we celebrating?" I push down the sinking in my heart, turning to wrap my arms around Novak's neck.

Viv shrugs, crossing her long emerald legs as she perches in her lover's lap, the cream gossamer dress and corset she wears barely hiding her breasts. The fabric stops mid thigh, right where Captain's hand rests. The Princess is free out here, pirate royalty. Captain grins ear to ear under Viv's affections, her red eyes alighting the darkness under her hat. Quite the pair.

"Good friends, I suppose." Viv decides, to which we all agree is a very good reason.

Novak kisses my nose, then my forehead. His lips meet my ear, whispering through windswept purple hair. "Everything is going to be ok."

I swallow, tears line my eyes as I gaze up into his beautiful face. Handsome yes, but oh so beautiful. I caress the freckles on his cheeks, letting out a smile as I brush chin length curls from his face. Novak tenderly kisses my hand, the light in his eyes flashing for a moment to black, then to light blue. It's so quick, he didn't seem to notice, or let on.

"I know it will be. I've got you." I murmur onto his lips, resting my hand on the nape of his neck.

"You know there's rooms for that kind of thing." Alvis grumbles from the table. My heart drops, but he grins wide when Novak shoots him a look. My neck heats and I shift away from Novak, stomach growling.

"I *am* quite hungry." I whisper to Novak and raise a brow as we sit.

"You're telling me." Novak mutters, then throws me a subtle wink. I load my plate with protein and fruit, catching Captain glancing at me from behind Vivvus every now and then. The Princess begins a fierce conversation with Alvis about who would win in a fight.

"Who is fighting what?" I ask over a mouthful of strawberries.

"The young High Lords." Novak muses from beside me, brow arching at my full mouth. I keep my gaze on Viv as his freckled hand slides under the table, grasping my inner thigh. I push out a small breath as my heart skips and I focus on my food.

"Definitely Orion." I say with no struggle. Slender fingers slide up the seam of my pants and my cheeks warm, catching my breath. Novak raises a brow at me, holding a sly smile. The noon sun brings out every blonde highlight in his hair, his eyes are brighter and each freckle on his sharp nose stands out. We only have precious hours left, and I want to devour every part of him.

"Excuse me." I mutter and nod to Captain, then leave the deck with haste. I can feel the other's stare burning into my back as I retreat to the crew's quarters below with Novak on my heels. He jumps down onto the gnarled wood of the lower deck, the ladder taking too much time.

"Come here." I beg, reaching out for him and he sweeps me up with strong arms.

We kiss like it's the first time we've ever met. Souls sigh in relief, his lips press against mine with a great need and softness. Ethereal arms filled with galaxies carry me into his simple bedroom, hidden behind a blue fabric curtain for a door. A tall wooden desk rests at the foot of the bed, where Novak sits me down with care.

"Lyth, I need you." Novak pauses his hurry for a moment, breathing heavy into my hair and squeezing my hips tight. "I need you so much, and, I don't think I have the strength to hold it back. Not today. If you don't ..." I lift his face to mine and smile, brushing the hair from his wildly flashing eyes. Both of us have filled the room with darkness just by touching each other.

"I don't want you to. I just want you to love me. With every part of your soul." I murmur into the inches between us. Novak protests and I press my thumb against his lips. "Trust me. Please."

"Have I mentioned how much I love you?" He sighs, rubbing his thumb across my cheek. The deep dimples I love fill his handsome face.

"I love you, Novak. Bearer of the *Tzel*, friend to all, traveling vagabond Zemer that stole my heart." I dramatically hold my chest and his face bursts, cheeks red and eyes glistening. "Now get over here and kiss me."

And he does.

My hands find solace in his hair. I moan on his hungry lips and am desperate to bite, just once. His hands make quick work of my corset and tunic from yesterday, my own fingers hastily undo the remaining buttons on his earthly tunic.

Bare chest presses against bare chest, hearts rattling their cages and aching to touch. I first kiss his neck, then the scars on his chest. Novak drops and kneels before me, grinning like a wild young Fae. First the left boot, then the right, and in moments my pants are thrown into a corner.

"I'm hungry." He kisses my stomach, teasing a moan out of me as his lips meet my inner thigh, tracing his warm breath across every inch of me, except where I need him.

"Quit teasing." I order sharply, and he obeys. Pleasure builds over me as he licks down my center, two delicate fingers dancing in a small circle above his tongue. I arch my hips, pressing myself into his face. I cry out his name after only minutes of his tender pleasure. The orgasm is so intense and sudden I fill his tongue and face with my come.

"Does my lady approve?" Novak looks up with a wet grin, voice husky and face transforming into ethereal shadows, matching the rest of his body. I bite my lip, looking down into two deep pools of darkness.

"I would approve more if you made me come like that on your cock." I grasp his hair and yank him to me, eliciting a playful rumble from the *Tzel* I am now face to face with. A glimmer of light shines in his black eyes, and a smirk quirks the shadows surrounding his mostly hidden face. Shadowed claws caress my cheek, and a short breath escapes me as the darkness lowers to trace my breast. "Show me your face." I command, voice steady.

Hands grasp my waist and firmly hold me in place. "As you wish, my lady." The shadows separate, revealing the love I have been missing. He thrusts into me without warning, evoking a shout from my body transforming into galaxies to match his, except mine are filled with a purple hue. Inside my labyrinth of a soul she awakens and in seconds, lilac Aether clouds and darkness entangles together.

"You're here." I breathe, holding his sharp face in my purple clouded hands.

Chaotic beauty accompanied by Darkness. There can not be one without the other, and the world, our children, would've never existed without us. And what has become of us?

Two Gods cursed to spend their miserable eternity searching for the other with no memory of who we are, until it is too late and destruction rips apart once more.

Tzel holds me close for the first time in two decades, the longest we've been apart. The vessels *never* last this long. His throbbing cock and body is still for a moment until his chest rumbles deep against mine.

"I've missed you, my Lady." Velvet night caresses my skin, eliciting a sigh from this tired body. We are melded together as one, unmoving as our souls sigh in relief, in *recognition*. The journey back to each other is becoming harder every harsh lifetime, and I didn't think I would ever break out of this Fae.

"I've been calling you, haven't you heard me?" I pout as he takes her chin with long fingers. I yank away and bite his lip, arching my being into his. A delicious snarl erupts as he devours my impatience.

"Feisty in every lifetime," *Tzel* kisses the spot he had marked the Fae, flicking his tongue across her skin which causes shivers to spread. "I forgot, and I remembered some when I tasted you, but not as much. I only remembered I was missing *someone*, and it wasn't until I saw you in that throne room that I remembered more. Why is it so much harder this time, love? Who are we? All I remember is you, *losing* you, so many times."

"I don't know." I gasp as he nips her neck and draws out, then thrusts deep, evoking pleasure throughout my worry.

He doesn't remember who we are? Who *he* is? At this rate, we won't remember each other at all next time, or ourselves. I shudder at the thought of being trapped inside the head of yet another being, unable to break free. "I had something to do. I was trying to find you, and I had something to do." I murmur, deciding to keep the rest hidden.

It's only a matter of time before the curse is broken, if I can get this Fae to cooperate.

"This is nothing compared to before, Lady, that much I know. Love me, and remember. Come back to me." Our old, lost souls love and connect all over again, like no time has passed at all. I will make sure this Empty Fae remembers every bloody detail, and that she will take me home.

One way or another, we are going home.

For unlike my love, I do know who we are, and before we can be together at last there is something I must do first. Whether this Fae likes it or not, though I have a feeling this one is smarter than she looks.

No Ordinary Fae

Vivvus

Short hours later have found Captain and I aboard a grand ship with golden sails tainted by black crossbones. Anxiety won't release my heart so I do the only thing I can in times like this. I don't stop moving.

Captain and I's passionate time in the alcove is all I've had to latch onto in the way of romantics with my newfound mate. After Lythienne left Panrauth on the balcony to watch the fireworks alone, she found us and announced we were leaving earlier than anticipated.

Without Alvis.

Everything went according to plan, at first. Captain served as Novak's wake up call and when he and Lythienne boarded, I couldn't help but laugh as Novak was knocked over by a Lesser Fae I've come to know as 'Oak'. Lythienne didn't say much, but shortly after take off she and Novak shared a tender moment. The thought of either them not making it back is a rock in my gut. Captain had admitted to me that she thought Lythienne did the right thing, leaving Alvis behind. Then, the Prince flung himself over the railing, cursing and spewing false death threats. Captain looked upon her Misfits sharing hugs with a brilliant smile that hid her worries.

Her and Novak are alike in that way, smiling despite their pain.

I now eat dinner with the Crew of Misfits, dressed in a gossamer dress and corset, both of which Captain insists she's never worn, a gift from a well meaning trade acquaintance. I had changed earlier in Captain's disorganized quarters while Lythienne and Captain spent time together at the helm, whatever they had discussed has darkened both female's eyes but I don't ask what's wrong, not yet. I perch on Captain's lap at the head of the table and revel in the feel of her hand caressing my thigh, soaking up the moment of normalcy shared across the dining deck. I curiously watch Alvis stare at Novak and Lythienne eye fuck each other, longing apparent in his dull violet eyes and I just *hate* this whole situation.

Lythienne asks what we shall to toast to, and I raise my glass. "Good friends, I suppose."

The Misfits agree, and we drink to the last dregs, then fill our bellies. Except Alvis, he doesn't bother to pretend to eat and is the most quiet since I've met him. Then again, we haven't had many moments together that didn't involve conflict. Instead, he watches a river of clouds dance alongside the deck's railing, then pinches the bridge of his nose and shakes his head, as if debating with himself. "Y'know, Prince, I'd be willing to bet your brother could take on mine in a fair fight now." I call out.

Alvis blinks out of his trance and focuses on me with the start of a sly grin. "Is that so, Princess? I think Orion could manage just fine even without all his new fancy power."

"Who is fighting what now?" Lythienne asks, mouth full of strawberries.

"The young High Lords," Novak starts, then is distracted by Lythienne's lips dripping with red juice. A troublesome smile takes hold of his freckled face when Lythienne gives me her attention.

"Definitely Orion," She agrees with Alvis, then is distracted by Novak's *very* obvious wandering hand. He raises a brow at her and she swallows, then promptly excuses herself and Novak practically chases her down to the crew's quarters.

Silence joins Captain, Alvis and I.

Alvis leans forward and rests his elbows on the table, then scrubs his face with vine free hands. "Fucking hell." He mutters.

Captain opens her lips but I'm already gently sliding off her lap. She rises and I take her seat, she smiles at me knowingly before attending to her friend. She wanders over to Alvis and sits beside him, a hand runs up and down his back in what seems to be a practiced way. Words are shared between them in hushed tones and I poke around at my plate, trying to give them the most privacy I can, but I have to admit their relationship intrigues me. Captain seems close with all of her Misfits, but Alvis and Novak especially.

I feel like an outsider looking in. I *am* an outsider looking in.

I glance up in time to see Alvis mouth the words, "I don't know if I can do this."

And my stomach settles into a tangled knot. Do *what?* He's not even supposed to be here, what does he have to do? Captain looks up to me as if I called her name and she frowns, then looks back to Alvis. He glances at me, expressionless, then back to Captain when she speaks. "You made your choice when you jumped on this ship, Alvis. I'll help you, but ... it's not going to be pretty. He won't forgive either of us. Do you remember how I said there was more to my part of the prophecy?"

I can't stay silent anymore.

"What's going on?"

Captain and Alvis share another look, then he nods to her and hides his head in his hands once more. Captain turns in her seat to pin me with a fiery stare. "When we were younger, Alvis and I received a shared prophecy. His came from an Ancient, mine from a Wild Fae, both of which said there were others connected as well. But mine had more to it than his, perhaps because I wasn't *supposed* to know."

I leave the warmth of my stolen chair and take a seat on Alvis' other side, my hand rests on his forearm like it's nothing and to my surprise his muscles relax under my touch. "What was it?" I ask in a whisper.

"*Find the weapon you can not wield, he shall reign, and you shall walk with the poet who becomes a king. Brace for the Fall, and never falter.*" Alvis murmurs into his hands, then raises his head and fixates on me with dull violet eyes. "Lythienne is the weapon in two ways, I think. The weapon I could not wield I against my father, and the weapon Fae with Aether cannot wield, the Harbinger. We don't know who 'He shall reign', refers to, but ..."

"We think Novak is the Poet, and as for the Fallen, I believe I have an idea of that too, now." Captain sighs, heated air full of worry expels into the chill night air.

Alvis blinks, then slowly turns from me to focus on Captain. "She told me to Brace for the Fall, not the *Fallen*."

"What was the part you weren't supposed to know?" I ask Captain, keeping us on track.

Captain and Alvis stare at each other for a moment, then she stares up at the sky, past the fluttering sails and crows nest silhouetted against the double moons. "I will have to betray the one I love most, and for the longest time I thought she meant a lover, but ..."

"It's Novak." I say almost immediately and Alvis blanches.

"Yes. I never knew how, or why, or that I would ever follow through with it, but this moment, what Lythienne is asking for, that's exactly what we'll be doing, betraying him. I have to believe this is the right path, even if it means hurting him. There's no way he will willingly stay behind, so we'll have to make him."

Alvis slams his fist onto the table, rattling the silverware and platters full of half untouched food, those who were feasting are now occupied by sex or secrets. "Fuck!" He growls, then coughs and chokes on his curse. He quickly wipes away blood with the back of his hand and waves Captain off when she opens her mouth to ask. "FINE. Fine. How are we going to do this? I don't have, I'm not strong enough, anymore." Alvis looks away to the decking, clenching his jaw.

I sigh upon realizing this is my cue. "I ... might be able to help." I call upon my Aether and hold out my hand to Alvis as a soft green glow takes over the palm of my hand. Then it flares brightly, temporarily blinding him and I both until the light recedes, revealing the *fucking* plant that started it all.

The blue and red *ra'al* flower with the power to neutralize Aether, and *kill*.

Alvis scowls and leans back, disgusted. "That will **kill** him."

I shake my head, offering the small plant to Captain instead who takes it warily. "Not if you prepare it properly, and he's no ordinary Fae, don't forget."

Alvis laughs, and it's pained. "How could I *ever* forget that?"

KNOWS BEST

"Lyth, get up. *Lyth.*" Novak's pleading wakes me from a deep slumber. I groan from under the pile of patchwork quilts on his bed, thighs and hips spasming with the worst contractures I've had in months.

"*What.*" I snap, rubbing my face as I endure the usual aches, and add some new ones to the list. I curse under my breath, then roll over to Novak sitting beside me. My shoulders and neck protest every movement. I keep my eyes closed as I rest my head on his lap, then sigh when I find comfort again.

"What ... happened?" Novak whispers, laying a hand on my back with caution.

"Well, everyone on the ship probably heard us fucking." I chuckle before stretching and opening my eyes, only to find a drool spot on my shirt.

"I thought I hurt you."

I take in his words and my gears turn, playing over our afternoon. *Oh.* I ensure the wall is up between us in the bond and roll away from him, then sit up on the edge of the bed. Earlier memories collide with sex sated thoughts, and my mood immediately darkens.

I remember everything the Lady said and thought. How we, or *they*, love each other.

"No, just tired me out, love." I say gently, throwing a soft smile over my shoulder. The tech on my wrist clicks, it's time to land soon. How long did we sleep for?

I gather my white tunic and ditch the corset, then search for my pants. Novak watches me from his small bed, his heaving chest still bare and light brows furrowed. Tidy and plain, sea air fills the room, and the only decorations are tapestries from each land lining the walls.

"What?" I ask, now fully dressed with arms crossed.

"There's something you're not telling me." He states, staring at me from across the room with blazing sapphires alighting his eyes. Hurt laces his voice, and so it begins.

"We don't have time for this, we have to go." I mutter.

Novak leaves the bed in a huff, crossing to me in a quick moment. He takes my shoulders with desperation. "Lythienne, do *not* leave me in the dark." He begs, and his tone frightens me. I swallow the growing fear of what he will do without me. I have an edge though, perhaps I can win.

Perhaps.

I exhale a heavy shaky breath, taking his face in my hands. "I'm not leaving you in the dark, Novak. We have an entirely new enemy to face, and other things to worry about. I'm fine, I want to get this over with."

"Like hell you're fine." Novak crosses his arms, muttering my favorite words which bring a smile to my face.

"Do you trust me?" I ask, and he stares at me for a hard minute. Even after everything, I *know* he still does, which makes this so much harder.

"Of course I do."

"Then believe me when I say I'm ok, and *we* will be ok." I kiss him with a smile. He rolls his eyes and his dark aura softens to warm charcoal.

"Ok." He relents, folding my short body to his scarred chest. We hold on to the other for dear life as the ship finalizes its descent.

"Always, Novak. I love you, always." I whisper my hidden goodbye into his chest.

"Always, Lyth." His confident promise breaks my heart, my secret threatens to spill. A knock hammers the wooden frame holding the fabric bedroom door, interrupting our embrace. Novak snarls, holding me closer to his warm skin. "What?"

Alvis steps in, arms crossed, and he halts just inside the small room. His eyes dart around the space briefly, his looming presence fills the space. I wonder if they used to share this room. Alvis doesn't use his own room anymore, opting for the hammocks instead.

I wish we had more time, to share this room, all of us ...

"Captain needs you." Alvis states and I pull away, which results in Alvis shaking his head. "Not you, him." His handsome face sets tight as he nods to Novak, standing half naked beside me.

Novak rubs his neck, glaring at Alvis for a moment before throwing more clothes on in a silent rush. My love looks back to me with soft eyes overtaken by darkness, half hidden by stray honeyed hair. "*Don't* leave without me."

He knows me better than I thought.

"Of course not." I take his hand and pull him in for one more kiss, lingering in his wonderful sea salt fragrance. "I'll be waiting for you to play for me after. It's been too long."

Novak grins against my lips, then kisses my nose before shouldering past Alvis without so much as a hello. Novak's retreating footsteps hit the deck above and I unabashedly release the tears built up inside me. Alvis takes my hand and pulls me close to his chest, sighing as he strokes my hair. He lets me have thirty seconds, then gruffly brings me back to reality.

"It's time." He reminds me. I look up to him with narrowed brows and he wipes hot tears from my black and white eyes. "We have four hours to get where we're going. Captain won't be able to hold him much longer than that."

"Captain?" I ask, lip trembling.

"I can't contain the *Tzel* and help you, and it seems she was aware of our situation anyway." He remarks, scarred brow raised

"She's not going to hurt him, right?" I murmur, face cast down. I know she will do everything in her power not to, but ...

Alvis brushes dull purple from my face. "He'll just have a little nap. When he wakes up, he'll be far away from anyone he might hurt."

Alone. This time when the bond breaks, he'll be alone.

The ship is hovering now and I lean onto Alvis unsteadily. I admit my next fear to him, voice hardly more than a whisper. "I never thought I'd be going back there. To the Mountain."

"You made it out of there once, I think you can again." Alvis attempts to give me hope. I give him a small smile, grasping the heavy vial. "Well, let's go to hell then, shall we?" Alvis says, looping my arm through his. He escorts me out, step light. When we reach the ladder leading to the main deck, a tremor rocks the ship, throwing us sideways.

I fall into Alvis who holds me steady. A rumbling thunder splinters the wood beneath us. The thrumming power threatening to blow the ship apart builds, and *builds*, an electric humming stings my folded ears. After a tense moment, the Aether surge returns to where it came from, leaving static air behind in its wake. Alvis nods to me in silence and I set my watch.

Four hours before the *Tzel* comes looking for its Lady. Viv waits for us on the main deck, our useless bags of gear surround her. The princess is dressed for war again, ready to fight at a moment's notice. The last time I saw her like this we were overthrowing a court and corralling a demon.

No, a Fallen.

"Where's Captain?" I ask nervously, holding tight to Alvis' arm.

"She's fine, just, get ready. We're about to land." Viv continually glares at Captain's quarters until the disheveled Fire Fae joins us.

Captain smooths her raven hair back and takes the crumpled hat tucked into her side, then places it on her head. She rolls her shoulders back. "I don't know how you're gonna pull this off, but you better make it quick. The minute he figures out what's going on, he's going to be *pissed*, and he's strong enough to travel and stay awake after, don't forget."

I nod, holding Alvis' hand with a death grip. I will my voice to strengthen. "I'll do my best, Captain. It was a pleasure flying with you."

Vivvus breaks from her mate's side, throwing her arms around me. Her tears fall onto my shoulder. "Thank you for bringing my brother back. I meant what I said before, you are my hero."

I can't speak, my chest is full of sadness and ready to burst. I hold her tight, breathing in the evergreen smell of Terra. I close my eyes to imagine I'm with Pan again for a moment. I still have no idea what he said to me before, but it sounded nice.

"We have to go." Alvis' stone cold tone breaks the moment. He and I take only what we need from the pile, small packs for each of us, and leave the rest behind. We step onto patchy grass filling the airport below the ship and Captain tips her hat down to me. The ramp between us folds up once more.

"Until next time." I whisper, watching the epic engines glow to life once more, lifting the galleon with golden sails high into the sky. Alvis and I leave the small port of Echo in silence, heading right for the bar.

Vivvus

Novak successfully drank the infusion and passed the fuck out in Captain's quarters. We leave Lythienne and Alvis on the sands of Echo and speed away at once. I stand by Captain's side at the helm, shaking in my boots and leathers. "I'll leave you and Russel in charge of the crew at the Old Salt Mines, I have a spare ship there if ... If you'll need it. But wait for my signal before coming back, understand?"

I've only just met my mate and she's tempting death, and my patience.

"I'm not leaving you to deal with him alone. Novak **or** *Tzel* not noticing the *ra'al* infusion was lucky, but when he wakes up, you'll want help. During the coup, *Tzel* spoke to me," Captain gives me her full attention, brows raised, "He said I burned him like Panrauth, not as harshly, but that I hurt him. I can help you."

Captain contemplates me for a moment, then she shakes her head and takes my hand, her other grips the steering wheel so tight her knuckles blanch. "I'm sorry my love, but this is my journey and mine alone. I'll be fine, trust me. If you don't hear from me, head back to Sylvan. Do *not* come for me. Understand?"

I grit my teeth, then nod after a moment. We may be mates, but I can't expect this person I've known for two days to listen to me. Perhaps she knows best.

Lyth

The cantina isn't the same, even the creatures filling it are quite different now, too. I tap the bar counter, checking my leather and tech wrist much too often. An hour has elapsed already, panic spreads over my neck with intense warmth. I scan around us again for any telltale sign of white hair.

"I'm pretty sure we'll know when she gets here." Alvis grumbles in annoyance beside me, casually watching the sentries stationed on the street outside.

"Captain said she would be making her rounds thirty minutes ago." I whine quietly, glaring at him sideways. Captain tried to fill Alvis in the best she could, warning that the rag tag desert town is not the same as when we left it. I expected it to change for the worse, and am thoroughly disappointed.

Thin pale grass spreads across the growing village, shrubbery can even be seen tucked throughout the area. Small rivers trail out from the Oasis, stretching into the thirsty desert beyond. Shining metal replaces the old wheel I remember, providing life throughout instead of congregating it in one place. The construction reminds me of the grand waterways in Silverbury, distributing water throughout the entire town.

The decrepit buildings and slums are rebuilt, proud buildings and townhomes stand in their place. Blue flags holding the phases of the moons are perched all throughout the new city, replacing the orange and crimson I'm familiar with. The flag of Eros. There are no starving children in the streets, but then again, it is nighttime.

"I hate to say it, but it looks better than last time." Alvis chuckles, rubbing his neck. I glance at *the* wall and then to him with a dirty look, earning a wry smile from him. The riotous crowd of High Fae swimming through the cantina is a surprising sight. Eyes of every color fill the place, moving in waves with the music drifting in from outside.

One set in particular, Fire Fae eyes, burn on me continuously. A female with half her face covered by a dark blue mask watches my every move, and eventually she slithers out of the bar. She pauses in the street, the stealthy and short Fae glances over shoulder and beckons me to follow. More Fae are watching us now, especially a group of Water and Air Fae together in a corner. Hatred simmers from their group, reminding me of the ones who watched me in Steammire not so long ago.

I spin in my chair and give Alvis a sweet smile. "Five more minutes, then we leave."

Alvis chuckles, brushing purple from my cheek. To anyone else, we are close friends. Perhaps lovers. "Deal."

No Lesser Fae are to be seen, even the golden bartender has been replaced by a squat High Fae female. I shudder as icy air approaches from behind us, but the crowd's voracious laughter doesn't change as the villain enters the bar. A slender, glacial hand rests on my shoulder. I fight every nerve to stab her in the heart.

Why can't I? I can end this here and now.

I can see Novak again.

It's not a wise decision. Alvis and I counted at least a dozen visible guards earlier. Not to mention I'm sure she's expecting me to be on the offense. I swivel, coming face to face with the white haired nightmare that killed my *shomer*.

"Well hello, pet." White hot flames for eyes meet my own, Eros' lips pull into a sly grin. "Did you miss home?"

"Why yes, I think I did." I stand and Alvis rises beside me. Eros looks the bristled male up and down, then dismisses him with disgust. It takes everything I have not to hold his hand. Fear doesn't run with those who have nothing to lose.

But I run with fear every damn moment of the day, now.

"He's not *quite* the same Fae as the one you left with, or the other one I've heard all about. You're busy, Keeper of Death. I'm impressed, if not disappointed you didn't take me up on my offer." She pouts, rubbing her sharp chin thoughtfully.

I cross my arms and widen my stance, raising my chin before speaking. Eros is alone and attracts as much attention from the party as a peasant.

Why aren't they running? She can kill them all with a snap of her fingers.

"I have a proposition for you."

"I thought you knew better than to deal with faeries?" Eros rests her pale white hand on my cheek, patting softly. She is now the High Lady of Winter, no longer the Others, *and* of Iron Court. Trihewyn is the only person standing in her granddaughter's way to claim the throne of Hallowed.

And me.

"Are you complaining?" I ask, patience wearing thin. Rohana's defiance shines through every icy pore on Eros. I will be the one to annihilate the last bit of her legacy. Of course it will be me.

The tired Prince rests a heavy hand on my shoulder when Eros' face closes in, inches in front of mine. "Not at all. But, the stiff stays." She glances sideways to Alvis, giving him a wink. "Girl talk."

"Fine." I answer immediately, causing Alvis to yank me into him. Our chests press together, his dark hands are tight on my shoulders. His heart alternates between skipping and abruptly halting, the beat entirely irregular. The handsome face I find comfort in is now pulled tight with worry, his ashen lip trembles when he speaks.

"No, I'm going with you." Once vibrant violet eyes are faded, no Aether has returned to them. This journey has beaten both of us, and if I thought he stood a chance against Eros, I would fight for him to come. One of us has to live, though. One of us has to be standing for Novak, and to continue the work I started. That's why I tried to leave Alvis behind in the first place.

I should've never asked him to come at all.

I wrap my arms around his thick neck, pulling our bodies even closer. Alvis trembles, placing his shaking hands on my waist. "Don't do this, let me help you."

After all this time, I release my love for him.

I take his breaking face in my sure hand, then lay my tired lips on his. The Prince hands over every shattered piece of his heart, moaning my name as he tenderly kisses me back with a passion. One hand cups my cheek, the other rests in the small of my back. Everything disappears around us while he takes the part of my heart that has called to him since the Mists.

I love Alvis, and I love Novak.

I can't ask Novak to watch his mate die, not that he would let me. He would rather let the world burn first. A part of me wants to burn the world with him.

But, Alvis would burn *with* me to save the world, without a doubt. He is good, down to his very core. Deep in my soul, that's what I want. I don't want to be the Keeper of Death anymore. Even if I have to be the most manipulative bitch on Iverbourne to do so.

I distract Alvis from my wandering hand. I reveal a long buried sentiment onto his wet lips. "I love you, Alvis."

Then, I tear from his embrace and Eros' strong arms rip me backwards. She Travels us out quickly, leaving no time for him to try and stop me. I rip my eyes away from the chaos I leave behind, Alvis desperately reaching out to me, receiving only a flurry of snow.

The watch clicks.

"Two hours. Better hurry." The Lady reminds me.

"I know. Trust me, I know."

QUIT BEING SELFISH

We land at home.

My leather boots touch down in the stone lab. Parchment and oil meets my nose and welcomes me back. For a moment, it's like Alvis is here with me, not *breaking* miles away in Echo. The choking vial pulls me down onto purring knees, and the lingering goodbyes from everyone drags my face into small hands. At least my last moments with Novak were more peaceful, not so heart wrenching.

Hot tears fill the space between my palms and cheeks. So many sacrifices and hearts have been broken to achieve this. What if I'm not smart enough to figure this next puzzle out? What if I threw away everything, for nothing?

What have I done?

"How has my ingenuity been treating you?" Eros trails the room and lounges on the master table, bored.

Focus, you're vulnerable and weak in front of the Fae you're supposed to kill, and you need *her* Aether to do it. I wipe away tears, then compose myself and rise.

I scan my surroundings, gears turning as I play this twisted game of chess in my head. My familiar lab has changed in only one way since Pan and I left. The makeshift infirmary is now restored to a study, and the bed is back atop the loft. Clothes are strewn about the study, along with maps and communications. Rather untidy, quite unlike how I kept it.

"What do you mean?" I ask, avoiding her gaze while I scrutinize every bit of information laid out.

She laughs fully and the ice in her tone freezes me in place. I focus on her, evaluating my opponent at last. She's dressed in nothing but black breeches and a long sleeved white tunic, her apparel is rather simple compared to my full gear of daggers, leather belts and pouches. Tattoos shine on the side of her freshly shaved scalp and white tresses flow from the other half of her head. The saber is not at her back, currently.

"Did Father not tell you who his best engineer was?" Eros beams with a full smile, straightening her sleeves as she does.

"Do *not* call him that, if I had known," I shout immediately, anger *shakes* through me, "I would rather have crawled across Iverbourne than use anything from you."

Eros feigns hurt, pouting. She rises from the table and crosses to me with haste, a beautiful grin still on her face. "Better take that eye out too, then." She whispers, jutting her chin upwards. Her fingers brush wild purple from my rounded face.

Why does everyone like touching my hair so much?

"Did it show you what you needed to know?" She asks softly.

I give her a look of disgust, but remain otherwise unmoving as her skin continues brushing against mine. Despite the cold, unfortunately her touch settles me. "I know everything I need to. That's why I'm here."

Laughter erupts from her again, the sound soft and carefree. "You don't know a *thing*, creature, and I won't give you the essence until you do. That's my condition." I blink rapidly, then open my lips and fail to come up with anything clever. "You think I don't know why you're here? Your work across the lands is quite impressive. Installing High Lords wherever you go, unleashing the *Tzel*. I have eyes everywhere, pet."

I shake my head, panic ensuing as I readjust my nonexistent plan. "I don't understand, if you know why I'm here, then ... You want me to destroy you?" I cannot find the mask of Keeper, only worry keeps me company.

Eros' face softens and she paces away from me, taking with her the sign of emotion. "Walk through my mind, see what I have seen. If you still wish to wield the Harbinger against me, I will give everything you need." She halts her steps and turns to me, then extends a white hand between us. I look around the room, then back to her with a raised purple brow.

"How do I know this isn't a trick?"

"We could form a blood bond." She shrugs, hand still held out. I approach, glaring at her now glowing fingers. The aura rolling from her strong body is soft, a fluffy white blanket threatening to comfort you. She looks much different in this light, a Winter Fae framed against a kind, soft aura.

"No more blood, not yet." I say, watching the menacing mask fade further from her face. She has Knothall's strong nose and Rohana's defiant eyes, more apparent without the fierce mask of evil witch. A beautiful force of destruction, not entirely unlike me.

For some reason I remember the day I escaped, the look on her face when she silently accepted Knothall's duel. I take her hand and her Aether swells at once, temporarily bringing snow until the room around us fades into darkness. Only for a moment.

"Mama, tell me again!"

Eros and I stand in the swamp castle of the Mists, albeit an even less elaborate version. We are nothing more than transparent visages watching the scene before us unfold.

On the floor in front of the throne is a wee Fae with white hair, and her mother.

The Hero of Borealis ruffles the child's tangled long hair, the pair are seated together. "Someday you will meet him in person, and he can tell you himself." Rohana nuzzles her daughter's nose. "For now, it's time for bed, come."

"Mother!" The young child flies from her mother's arms and stomps her foot, conjuring up balls of flame enshrouded in clouds of mist. The purple orbs multiply, instantly filling the throne room. Eros' eyes flash between gray, white and red, all the while they are filled with tears.

"Child, calm down." Her mother holds a mask of calm over her own wild, flashing eyes. She holds out her hand to Eros. The child grows frightened as the balls of flames surrounded by poisonous gas threaten to blow them to bits. She runs towards her mother as sulfur thickens the air.

"I didn't mean to, I didn't mean to!" Eros screeches at the top of her lungs. The mother yanks her child close, throwing up quick shields around each of the buzzing orbs simultaneously. The castle shakes, and although the explosions are contained, the shock wave rumbles for miles. Eros screams once more, shaking her mother's limp body.

The scene fades and we jump into another memory, once again in the swamp castle. Disorientation takes over me for a moment until I spot her.

The small child is older now, a handsome young female. She looks like someone I would want to approach. Dirty breeches and a ripped tunic with bits of ivy stuck into it cover her lithe frame. Eros has just returned from her adventures with the wild fae living in the woods.

Excitement rushes over me and I realize it's not mine, but hers. The memory is tainted heavily with love and adventure, her thoughts twist with my own. Eros tries to contain the parts of her memory she doesn't want me to see, but it's not use, it's as if the memory is my own.

Today is the day. I am going to tell Mother about her. I cannot, and will ***not*** *hide my love any longer. If Mother can change the world, then I will too. People deserve to love who they want to, and I know she will help me. Mother Hewyn may not be as happy for me, but she can fuck herself.*

Their bickering meets my strong ears before I turn the corner. Mother Hewyn's sharp voice stops me in my tracks. I press against the wall and put up a small shield, concealing my breathing.

"Rohana, she's too strong. You cannot leave her here." Mother Hewyn pleads.

"And I cannot take her with me. Haven't you heard a word I just said? They need my help, High Lady." Mother spits the last two words out and I internally gasp at such disrespect.

"You cannot keep trying to fix every problem in the world. Running off to save every Human and Lesser Fae won't bring him back. You have duties, your daughter. You are needed here. ***I*** *need you."*

Anger fuels me and I will my feet to stay in place. She can't really be leaving again, not after last time. I hardly got her back in once piece. The rumbling Aether inside me is already begging to be let out, ringing my ears and bringing a nosebleed as my emotions boil over. Silently I curse myself and staunch the bleed with my sleeve.

"You weren't there, you don't know how hard we fought. We did everything right, Mother. What is the point of him being there, or me living out here, if the world is still living on a leash? You remember what it was like down south, don't you miss it?"

"And Eros? You'll just leave her for some fantasy that might be true?"

"Eros has her destiny, and I have mine. One day, she will understand."

The castle disappears and before I have a chance to register the change we are now standing in a blizzard. This memory is tainted as well, but not with excitement.

Loss, disappointment, and fear.

Familiar faces linger in the outskirts of Eros' mind, one in particular I recognize. Lexeran. Eros is hidden in furs upon furs, with a young white wolf at her side. The pair stands by a dwindled company near a stone circle. Fae faces are hidden from the biting cold, but Lexeran's thick ginger beard and figure is unmistakable, goggles hide his flaring eyes.

Again, emotion makes this memory my own.

We have been searching for the elusive tablets for so long now, no one dares speak in fear of breaking the surreal moment. The note Mother left has been enough to keep me going, even through the doubt and loss along the way. So many friends, gone, and for what? I glance over to Lex, his gloved hands are balled into fists. Mira gave her life for this, for my mother's pipe dream.

A Fae steps forward from my side, pulling down her woolen hood and revealing tight curls of sapphire. She kneels, brushing snow from the ancient text carved into towering stones, and her ominous words strike fear into everyone remaining in our company.

"When the end has come, find the one who lacks power, locked away in a hellish tower.

Take the leash, and we shall feast with every Fae, Human and Beast.

Only when Aether is one, can you have your true home.

Free the land, give up your right, beware of the two unite.
Forever they shall roam, cursed to have no known.
Love is worse, they can never find first.
Beware of those who fall, for they are the deadliest of them all."

Mother Hewyn rubs her chin, contemplating the riddle. I snarl at the thought of another puzzle, carding a hand through my snow filled hair. Perhaps Mother really did send me on a wild hunt, just another fucking clue.

"Now what? Another riddle? Another clue? I think Rohana was too far gone when she got locked away, Mother Hewyn. You've said it yourself, and I don't know why ***you*** *insist we keep going." I gesture to the pacing blue haired Fae who mutters the rhyme repeatedly. I march over, anger filling my face, and take the distracted female by her shoulders. I shake her into reality. "Umber, it's time to call it quits."*

"We can figure this out, we can do this. Don't give up now." She says, desperately. The thought of giving up after everything we've lost breaks my heart, but not as much as it must Umber's. I pull my mate close, shielding her from the wind. Tribewyn discusses with the Satyr, but the goat creatures are just as clueless as we are. They didn't even know this place existed, and it was right under their nose.

"It can't all be for nothing." Umber whispers, tears freezing onto her cheeks.

"Umber, it ***is*** *for nothing. All those two did was for nothing. They tried to save a world that isn't worth saving, leashed to a god-damned Machine. We have to focus on,"*

Tribewyn holds up a hand, silencing me immediately. "You just said it."

"Leashed to the Machine." Umber repeats in a daze, then pulls back, her silver eyes flashing. "It's how we break the Eternal Machine." Umber rushes away from me, drawing fury into my soul as I watch her hurriedly read the rhyme again. Tribewyn's face glows, and others let out murmurs of surprise.

'A land without the machine?'

Lexeran and I connect eyes, but his face is unreadable. I know he has ties to that place, and Knothall personally. Where does he stand on this?

"The world has gone to shit, so let's wreak more havoc and break the Eternal? Do we even know what would happen?" I snap, the familiar burn of Aether filling my body doesn't hurt anymore, it's comforting.

Silence fills the group, from my words though, not my power. The time to study and evaluate my nameless powers is over, and no one is surprised anymore by my frustration fueled outbursts. No one here even considered such a thing like breaking the Eternal is the answer we've been looking for to unite Iverbourne. The idea it could be possible is terrifying, let alone the consequences.

Of course, I'm the only one who thinks of those.

Umber returns to my side and shakes out her snow filled hair, then pulls up her hood. "Maybe Rohana went in there for a reason, maybe all this time she ***knew****, and* *that's why she went there, to get inside information." Even with the howling wind, her whisper strikes a chord in me. "Knothall is still there, he might know something."*

"I've told you, I **don't** *want to see him. Have you seen the desert eating away at my people?" I shout into Umber's face, then shove the surprised Fae back into the snow.*

Mother Hewyn travels across the space, landing in a flash of clouds, then rests a wrinkled hand on my hair covered shoulder. "Eros, control yourself."

Snow swirls in a vortex around me and the wolf at my side snaps at Trihewyn. The Elder backs up, horrified at the sight of white flames licking her granddaughter's body. Well, that's new. Umber is on her feet, clinging to Trihewyn's side, my mate in horror of my state.

"The ancestral home of my people is called Echo Valley. The screams of starving children dying echo for miles across the barren jungle, devoid of life. And you're telling me to calm down? This is a fantasy, I'm not having any part of it. It's about time I picked up the shattered pieces you all left behind and actually did something about it, this is our reality, get used to it."

A hurricane of snow takes the blue Fae's mate away, leaving Umber and Trihewyn alone in the ancient wilderness with what remains of their battered company.

"I can't do it anymore." I send the words to Eros, but she soundlessly continues us on the journey through her past. At least this time I'm not feeling the memory, I'm watching from the sidelines with her. For now.

Eros is no longer a scared young female, she has stepped into her power and embraced it. Her scalp is half shaved now, the ancient language of her people crawls across her skull and the familiar flowing white reaches her hips.

The Fae's now pure white eyes peek over a ridge of snow and ice, scanning the surroundings. The white wolf at her side snarls, hackles raising and teeth threatening to show. Her voice is a whisper in the flurry of crystalline flakes around them.

"We're surrounded, my dear Loki." Eros pets the wolf between the ears with a loving caress, preparing her weapon in the other hand. She gives her lifelong familiar a smile, then nods to him before jumping up. She hauls her armful of snowballs at the onslaught of children waiting for them, but there's not enough.

Their snow fortress is encircled by Human, Lesser Fae and High Fae children. The halfling folk are stuck deep in the snow halfway to the fort, giggling at the biting cold tickling their waists. Snowballs from every direction pelt Eros and the wolf, sending the two into a dramatic fall, crashing into white powder which covers them both.

"I thought you didn't want kids." Umber's forgotten voice taunts from above the snow. Eros sits up in a rush and looks at the beautiful Fae with bewilderment, but it fades rather quickly.

"Who let you in?" Eros asks, quite displeased.

Umber extends a hand and helps Eros up, pulling her close. Both stop breathing for a moment, taking in the changes that have occurred in nearly a century. The familiar wide smile Eros loves spreads across Umber's face, and for a moment, everything is right. The Winter Fae holds the Wild Air Fae close, lips close and aching for the other.

One particular emotion leaks from Eros, and one particular thought. She finally came back, for me. Being away from her mate for so long, it started to burn a hole through Eros' already cold heart.

"We found it, Eir. We figured it all out, we just need you."

Eros steps back at once, brushing snow off her and calling to Loki with hidden disappointment.

What a fucking surprise.

"I needed you, Umber." Eros says with defiance, then walks away in a huff, pausing only when Umber shouts for her to stop. White hair flows in the wind drifting in from the hole in the mountain above, and her pale eyes stare Umber down.

Umber marches up to Eros with Aether burning in her silver eyes. "And I needed you. Instead, you ran away and hid in the mountains. Quit being selfish."

The scene fades, and a moment of darkness creeps.

"Let me out, Eros. I can't do it anymore."

"Almost there, pet. Almost there."

With that, we arrive in Slatepoint, standing on the outer edge of the stone center.

Eros stands between the bastard brat of Fire, Ragnis, and the true High Lord of Iron. She scans the poverty before her, feigning interest as the never ending chatter continues. A cold chill runs through Eros when Knothall gestures for his apprentice to step forward, beholding the creature she has heard so much about.

Goggles hide the tell tale eyes at first, and the Empty Fae is so short it surprises the otherwise unshakable Eros. The vessel is no more than a broken and put back together female. Who really needs a bath.

"I've already seen this." I say with annoyance to Eros' visage beside me.

"Not the way I have." She says simply, gesturing to the scene again.

The purple haired Fae lifts her small chin. Anger pours in hot black madness around the thing while she watches her goggles smash to the ground. Eros glances at Knothall, wishing he could see the aura around this Fae. No, not just a Fae.

The empty vessel Umber found isn't so empty after all. No, she holds something Eros has only heard about through legends, long ago. From the same shaman who told her company about the tablets. Is this Fae the start of the Fall?

Without warning, our surroundings change just as Eros snaps her fingers to take care of Amwren.

"Wait. Show me what happened to her." I ask, drawing darkness around us for a moment.

Without answer, we settle back into the winter wonderland, and I watch Eros kneel beside a trembling pink Fae, her glass like wings folded tight around her body. The sight stops my heart and I run to Amwren, throwing my disembodied arms around her. It's no use, and with ghostly tears I listen to them.

"You are safe, small one. Please, you have to believe me now. Look around you." Eros pleads to Amwren who uncurls her body, finding a truly marvelous sight.

To our left are the snow fortresses occupied by armies of children whooping and playing together. To our right is a sprawling garden, trees and flowers with icy crystals frozen in time. Ahead of us, at the end of the cleared path, is a modest ice castle. Everything shimmers in here, icy diamonds reflect the sun peeking above the hole in the mountain.

Amwren's eyes widen, a smile releases at the sight of some Lesser Fae she recognizes. They hurry over and the pink Fae turns back to Eros with confusion. "You were ... telling the truth, the whole time?"

Eros nods solemnly, then rises and offers a hand to the Fae. "I cannot keep you all protected without being a beast." She sighs, and Amwren's hairless brows draw together. "A High Lady must not be delicate. The world is not delicate, as you know, small one. I must admit, I had hoped I would've gotten to you first in Echo, before Ragnis did."

Eros' thoughts leak into mine, in that moment she was thinking of the bloodied desert town Amwren left in her fear filled wake. She should've just forced the Fae to come with her, back in the Mists. That wasn't her way though, everyone had a choice. It was up to them to believe Eros, but most people couldn't see the truth right in front of their faces.

So, she covered up the mass exoduses with lies. Let everyone believe the worst about her. That she kidnapped people against their will, murdered them, stole from them. Trihewyn helped stage things, make them look real. Of course, there were actual killings too, but bigots and assholes don't count.

"I truly regret you were taken from your mate and put into that hellish place. I'm sorry." Eros says. Amwren's tears freeze to her rosy cheeks and she reaches out a hand to Eros.

Eros and I whip away, leaving the bright cold of her mountain for a much different one.

"No, I'm not doing it." Eros crosses her arms in Knothall's study, staring down at her father seated at his desk. The elder Fae opens his lips, then is interrupted again by his angry daughter. "No, there's got to be another way."

Knothall runs a hand through his gray hair and groans in frustration, then evaluates the Winter Fae for a moment. "Quit being selfish." Knothall's words hit Eros like a dagger to the heart, echoing the sentiment that convinced her to come in the first place, spoken first by her former lover.

"I can't leave, and she's going to need the essence. Kill me, and it goes to you. All of it, the land, the court. You will achieve everything you've been fighting for. What's so hard about it?"

Eros fights tears, the last time she cried was when her mate chose this mission over her. All those lonely years ago. She can't deny seeing the jungles of Iron restored is her dream, but at what cost? Eros had ***just*** *met her father, just got him back.*

With another heavy moment of silence, he presses harder. "Even that sanctuary of yours won't last. I only hear what it's like out there, you live it. Look me in the eyes and tell me you don't wish the world was like your Winter Court?"

"But you can't guarantee that's what it'll be like if we do this, can you?" Eros challenges. Knothall is silent, crossing his arms. "I have worked for over a century to give every creature I can safe haven, making myself a killer to do it, that is real. What you are asking, hoping for really, it's a pipe dream, always has been. Even if somehow we get her out of here, you think the High Courts will give up their precious magic to an Empty Fae known as a Keeper of Death?"

Knothall narrows his brows, standing to tower over his daughter.

"What if all that power kills the thing, do you even care about that?" Eros doesn't relent, and her words strike a nerve in the old Fae. "You kept it alive after killing Mother, only to schedule its execution for a later date. Do you even know what you're doing, at all?" She shouts, fists clenched and heart throbbing.

*"**Lyth** can change the world, and will do so without a second thought. That's why I kept her alive." Knothall declares. Eros shakes her head, then storms off and leaves the confident male in his study, alone.*

Eros' mind slams shut, throwing me out and into my own body in the lab. Metal knees meet a stone floor. Air struggles to meet pained lungs. Eros is silent as she walks away and leaves me alone in the lab, locking the door behind her.

My leather and tech covered wrist clicks.

One hour.

"My turn." The Lady warns, and she makes good on her promise from last night, making me remember every past life she's ever had with the *Tzel*.

I slam a closed fist onto the door after twenty minutes of being crumpled on the stone floor. Footsteps approach and I step back, crossing my arms when Eros walks in.

She doesn't bother with a facade. "Well?"

"First of all, I still don't like you."

"I don't need you to like me. I just need your help." She approaches and lifts the vial from my neck, eyeing the temporary relief in my face.

"You didn't seem to think your parents were right, before. What changed?"

She sighs, then drops the vial and takes my breath away. "They could've ran away together, been happy. With me. But they chose a life without the Machine. I *have* to believe that means something."

"It can be different now, there are new rulers that will work together. You can come out of hiding, just tell everyone the truth." I plead breathlessly.

Tell me there's another way.

"Did you not hear a word I just said?" The Lady grinds in my head, but I ignore her.

"You know just as well as I do, the Machine was never intended to last. Everything I have done is to unite the lands against a common enemy, a reason to give you magic. You are the Harbinger, your mission is the same, your target is just different. How long will your friends deliberate and try to find another way to save you from this inevitable fate? Until the land dies beneath their feet? You've seen it, the Machine is choking Iverbourne."

Eros softens, her voice a whisper, "Everything will have been for nothing if you don't do this. What my parents, Umber and countless others sacrificed their lives for."

"I don't want to die." Quiet rings through the lab.

Knothall and Rohana died for this idea, giving no care to who they left behind. How they left them, or their kingdoms. Umber believed in this all along, before she even knew me, threw her entire life away to find me and deliver my purpose.

They all wanted a land free from the Eternal, the Ancient's hold released on the land and Aether. To roam freely and dwell in the lands we were blessed with long ago. The Lady has shown me that world, the one she and *Tzel* created. A realm she desperately wants back, not to mention destroying the Machine is the first step to reuniting with her lover.

For good, this time.

Novak. I want to see the world with him, share my life with him. Novak, Alvis and I could live in the mountains together, in peace.

I wouldn't do what Sage did. Even if Alvis and I were never lovers, just for him to be in my life, and Novak's life, that would be enough. Viv and Captain would visit us, along with Orion and Emeric. Our dysfunctional family could gather for holidays and parties celebrating nothing but being together. Our life would be full of love, music and happiness. I would see fall and winter, and breathe in the first days of spring.

The Lady has other plans, though.

That life I dream of, it will never be mine.

"I will do everything I can to help, but I will not lie to you." Eros pauses, waiting for my overflowing eyes to meet hers. "The power of Iverbourne will be leashed to you, *your* soul, releasing the Machine from the land, whether your body can take that," she loses her composure, "I don't think it can."

I rub my face, pushing out a sigh. "You sound like you know more than you let on."

"It doesn't matter, not to you, anyway." Her face hardens once more, her words matter of fact. "You can't get out of this."

I hold my elbows, a shiver spreading through me. "You know, there's one legend I never learned of."

"What's that?"

"What happens when we die?"

The molecules floating around us freeze, my warm breath condenses in short bursts. Eros moves closer to me, a genuine, soft and small smile escapes her. Her eyes grow distant. "I once heard a tale, in the North. Our souls go back to where they come from, to the stars, where Aether was born." Her voice catches, pale eyes turn down.

"And, what do you believe?" I ask and let my tears fall, voice broken. There's no use in hiding it now."I like to think I'll see Umber again, in the next life. Perhaps it won't be so hard next time, living in a put together world."

I ponder her words for a moment. The next lifetime. The Lady comes back for her *Tzel* life after life, but they are cursed. Will this really help break it?

Will the Lady really do what she can to help *me* if I do this?

"Do you know," I ask, recollecting myself, "Do you know what she did?"

She scoffs. "Everything Umber did was to ensure you would succeed, no matter the price. This was her life's work, I was just an obstacle." Eros sweeps hair away from her face. "But yes, I knew. Someone had to sacrifice themselves, to the Ancients. Bonds made in blood are released by blood, it didn't matter when, but it had to be done before you got to this point."

The look on Umber's face that night. She was so happy to finally embrace death, to complete her last task. Even if it meant leaving everything, *everyone*, behind, separating herself from her mate. She believed in me so much, she let the Ancients take her life, gratefully.

"They all really thought they were going to save the world, didn't they? Your family, Umber."

"Well, did they?"

I walk away from her, pacing the lab while the gears in my head turn. I try to fathom a world without The Eternal Machine.

Lands opened, the Realm of Giants to the north and the entirely unknown south rife with adventure. Magic abound through Iverbourne, I'm sure reviving the drought-hit mainlands and the deserts of Iron.

My watch clicks. Down to thirty minutes now.

Novak and I's bond hibernates. I search for him and find only softness rolling from the shadows on his end. Except, I *swear* I can hear him snoring.

"Trust me, this is the right thing to do." The Lady is firm, unrelenting.

"If it's the right thing, why will Tzel try to stop you?"

"He doesn't remember who he is, and there is no time to make him. My lands are dying, Lythienne. I am sorry I have to ask you to do this, and I would rather not ***make*** *you, but I will, if I have to. He will try to stop us, just as your musician will. As you said, they would rather watch the world burn without us in it, and this might kill me, too."*

"You didn't tell me that part."

"Does it matter?"

Eros clears her throat, brow raised. I straighten from the table holding me up whilst I was debating with the Lady. After giving the Winter Fae a grand if tired scowl, shaky hands pull out my pipe and herbs. I pack it in silence, then puff on it.

"Tell me what to do."

The glorious smoke tends to my soul and my mind clears. I release every doubt as I exhale. Eros explains my daunting task while taking the offered peace pipe, joining in my moment of bliss.

The irony is not lost on me. I have defended the Machine for over 200 years.

Now, I'm the only one who can destroy it.

Before we leave the lab, I send the Lady one more request.

Perhaps it will be enough.

THE TOWER

FIND ME

Novak

A heavy groan escapes my squashed chest, drowsiness glues me to the floor. With great effort, I throw myself over on hard decking and attempt to regain my senses.

Wherever I am, thick air catches in my chest, tinged with the smell of fear, and it's dark. I sit up with a raging headache, the only source of light turns my stomach. A singular candle is lit on a desk across the room, with a pair of glowing red eyes behind it.

"Get the fuck up, you idiot." Tzel orders, anger raging so intensely it disorients me further.

"Captain?" I ask shakily upon standing, realizing we are alone. The ship is eerily quiet, unmoving, and yet I waver.

"Where is she?" *Tzel* grows impatient, the fight has already begun before I can straighten fully from the floor. After rolling my shoulders back, the room stops spinning long enough for her next words to sink in.

"Have a nice nap?" Captain drawls, unmoving in the dark.

"Did you ... *drug* me?" My hackles raise with the realization, her silence tells me everything. The moment I move she's on her feet, meeting me halfway.

"Where is she?" *Tzel* taints my voice with a distorted growl. I let it stay in the forefront of my mind, waiting for her answer. Captain rests a hand on the hilt of her father's sword, the only thing left behind by that bastard drunk. Flames merge with my storm of shadows swirling around us. Her flaring body lights the space between us.

"She wanted to go alone."

"She left us?" Tzel asks, retreating for a hesitant moment in my mind.

"Where is she, Brier?" I ask, each word a forced struggle.

Captain scoffs at her given name, stepping towards me as she whispers fatally, "She's doing what she came here to do, kid. *You're* staying here with me."

"Finish her. Snap her neck. We need to find her. findherfindherfindher."

A snarl escapes from the *Tzel*, fracturing my searing chest right down the middle. I attempt to reel the thing in, but it hurts so *much*. Captain is ready to strike and the candle blows out, leaving her fiery body surrounded by my darkness.

Anger courses through *my* soul, not *Tzel's*. The sight of my best friend ready to kill me, for Lyth, breaks my heart into thousands of pieces. The excruciating power of the *Tzel* rolls through me and I cannot contain it, or the scream that escapes. There is no stopping it, too much brokenness lives in my heart.

I manage one word, friend to friend. "Run."

Brier just gives me a feral smile, then unsheathes her sword and spreads fire in a ring around us. I've dueled Alvis many times as the violent shadow version of myself, and as *Tzel*, but never Captain.

The *Tzel* takes over just as the decking catches fire, subsequently putting me to sleep. I won't be able to see what it's about to do. The agreement we made all those centuries ago.

"Please don't kill her. I just want Lyth."

"I can't make any promises."

"Make her stop, make her stop. Wake up. WAKE UP."

Tzel hurls from my mind and my drowsy spirit finds an ethereal, *winged* body falling backwards. My elbows crash onto sizzling hot stones and jam me into reality.

Grinding metal clamps my ears down and the smell of burning flesh is the last thing to come to me before my eyes adjust. I jump to my feet, spinning around to find myself in a smoke filled cavern. I catch my love's surprised face too close to the abyss below what must be the Machine. Dizziness follows my quick movements and I struggle to stay upright.

"Lyth, stop!" I shout, drawing a startled smile from Lythienne's tired face. She pauses, leaning over the waiting darkness with the vial of ancient magic clutched in her small, shaking hand.

Lyth's Trench. Even with every poring detail she gave me of the Eternal Machine, I am not prepared for the copper beast towering into the air above and spanning across the entire cavern. Sharp metal arms spin out of control around Lyth, who is *still* standing much too close to the edge.

All alone, looking like death warmed over.

"Wait! It's me!" I jump down from the stone cliff onto metal grates, the never ending pit below us flips my stomach. Lyth warily remains perched on the edge, but her nervous smile widens at the confirmation it's *me*.

"Hurry, Novak." Tzel begs, using my time for the first time since it attached to me like a parasite.

"Wait, just wait." Pleading words escape across the closing distance between us.

Delicate glass crushing into flesh pricks my sensitive ears and ices over my veins. She's *just* an arms length away. The damn vial laces her palm open with hundreds of shards. The shattering of my world thrusts my ears down, fluff tickles my neck.

White hot Aether burns out her black eye, and the combined essence of Iverbourne alights her crystal eye into a blinding glow. I lunge and catch her violently shaking body in my arms, she blisters my skin.

"Find me again, my love." She whispers, letting on nothing of all four elements burning through her, every vein inside her small body is on *fire*.

"I'm right here, I've got you."

I did it, I have her.

Only for a moment.

I'm thrown back from my world exploding and land head first onto the stone above the Trench.

Something cracks.

Warmth spreads under me.

I'm blinded and struggle to get back up, the roaring Machine shakes my brain as a quake unsteadies me further. On hands and knees I crawl, feeling for the edge as rocks crash to the ground around me.

"Do something *Tzel*, save her. Do it now. Please. You can have whatever you want, save her. Please, for me." I beg aloud endlessly, but frozen silence returns to me every time.

"GET HIM OUT OF HERE!" Lythienne lets out a blood curdling *scream*. Her frightened voice joins the explosion rocking the ground beneath my hands and knees.

Rough, *unfamiliar* hands suddenly take my shoulders, yanking me backwards from the crumbling edge under my grasp.

"NO! I'm not leaving her!" I shout with a broken chest, clawing at the evil hands on me as hot tears split my face apart.

"We were too late, idiot. She's gone."

I fight with every inch of my being against the firm grip now encapsulating me, willing my horrifying vision to come back. My empty soul heaves with such a deafening cry, for a moment, the entire world is quiet. Then, the last thing I hear before passing out, finishes snapping my spirit in two.

The Eternal Machine crashes into the heart of Iverbourne, taking my Keeper of Death with it.

Im hayiti chai et chayay mehahatchala, hayiti motse otkha mukdam yoter.

If I were to live my life again, I'd find you sooner.

MONSTER! I'M!

Vivvus

She didn't know best.

I watch from a rusty balloon ship anchored to the deserted Salt Mines dock as an explosion thrusts into the distant sunset tainted sky. A mushroom cloud of black smoke, fire and shadows erupts from around the red cliffs where Captain was hiding out, waiting for Novak to wake up. By herself.

Fuck.

"Russel! Get us over there!" I bark a command to the head deckhand and he obeys at once, concern crinkling his leaf green eyes. I grip the edge of the railing and wait with *no* patience. I could travel there, but then my magic would be spent. I can't hurt *Tzel* with weapons, but my Aether just might be able to fend him off. The thought of hurting Novak, even in *Tzel* form, is heart wrenching, but I have no choice. I don't even let the thought settle that perhaps Novak *himself* caused this.

The considerably short journey is painfully long, wave after wave of smoke and fire rides the air and spills across a once warm summer sky. Before we come around the cliff formation hiding Captain's ship, a fresh pulse thrums through the clouds and thrusts bone chilling *night* into the once burning sky. Darkness chokes out the sun and intense cold settles further, pricking goosebumps onto my arms as stringy ombre clouds give way to pitch black.

Everything is *black*. The ground below, the air just a few feet around the balloon ship, the tightly packed crew around me. Murmurs swell and luckily there's a Fire Fae on board, but their conjured balls of light barely cut through the cold, unnatural night and illuminate only our terrified faces. I should've pushed for Captain to listen to me, that she doesn't have to be *alone* anymore, or at the very least I could've waited *closer*. We must've finally crested the cliffs because a fireball on the ground cuts through the *Tzel's* black fury. Wild flames lick Captain's ship and I scream at the fatal sight.

I never cried out when my family died, but now I do.

No, she's not dead, not yet. A faint, *thready* pulses rings my ears. I throw myself over the ship's basket edge and conjure vines and growing canopies to gently lower me to the ground. I choke on smoke and *death* and ***evil.*** It's not until I'm face to face with the burning ship that I realize the flames aren't hot. At all. The structural damage appears to be from a struggle, fire shoots out of a large hole in the main decking and the foremast is cracked, precariously swaying in the hurricane of anger. Golden sails aren't visible through the haze.

I don't waste time wondering how or why the flames are heatless, instead I call upon vines to lift me from the sand and onto the tilted main deck. I cough and choke on Captain's name, the smoke and soot isn't from the fire, but something else, something that smells and *tastes* like pure metallic *power.* I know now that what I saw of *Tzel* on the day of the coup was *nothing* compared to the beast fully unleashed and *furious*.

I dive into Captain's quarters, the door is thrown off the hinges and discarded near the moaning foremast. Much of the ship is split and cracked but the most damage is here, in her quarters, almost like a shock wave of power rippled out when *Tzel*, or Novak, woke up.

The darkness is thickest here and I drop to my hands and knees, feeling along the wavy decking blanketed with scratches and something powdery. I gasp upon finding fresh, sticky warmth and shredded flesh beneath my fingers. I can't tell exactly *what* I'm feeling, but my fingers continue traveling and find the sharp planes of Captain's face littered with injuries just north of the shredded mess which I now realize must be her neck, or what's left of it.

I am of no help to Lythienne and Alvis now, so I do the only thing I can.

I gather Captain into my arms and close my eyes, traveling us through space and time. We land onto the balloon ship with a heavy thud, temporarily dropping the ship a few feet. Screams ensue, but not due to our surprise entrance, rather the crew's mangled Captain. I sob upon seeing her true state revealed by the dutiful Fire Fae from before.

It's a miracle she's alive, because her throat is *gone*, spewing gurgling blood, showing off wailing tendons and absent vocal cords. A female kneels before me, the picture of calm. "My name is Niamh, I'm the ship's healer." She explains, then reaches forward hesitantly with flashing blue eyes. "Let me help."

"Yes, please." I beg, unashamed of the tears shed for this person who has become my everything in less than a day. Niamh raises her luminescent blue hands to Captain's throat, but before the magic can soak into her wounds, the world *breaks*.

World shaking thunder cracks open the sky and a *roar* joins in, shattering my eardrums and quite literally shaking the darkness surrounding the ship. I hold onto Captain tightly as a fiery explosion lights the unnatural night, breaking the darkness bit by bit and revealing the fall of The Eternal Mountain.

Tears are shed, shouts and gasps escape as raging tsunamis rush the Mountain and sweep its crumbling remains into a vortex of a sea. A flash of green shoots out of the Mountain just before it implodes completely, falling under the depths of the water and shooting more destruction and fireballs into the sky from its peak.

The Eternal Mountain has fallen, and in my heart I know, it has taken the beloved Keeper of Death with it.

I sit between Captain and Novak's beds, knee bouncing and head bowed. Orion's quarters have been transformed into an infirmary, firmly shielded and guarded from the outside. Hours have passed since our return, Niamh and Orion both worked on Captain as much as they could, but only so much can be healed by their magic.

Niamh explained wounds dealt by the *Tzel* are near impossible to heal with Aether, leaving Captain's neck and face in bandages that need to be changed soon. I didn't ask the healer how she knew this, but she and Orion seemed to be quite familiar, so I assume it's not her first time patching someone up after Novak- ***Tzel***, had their way with them.

I shake my head, cursing Lythienne for leaving Alvis behind. He used up the last of his minuscule Aether contacting Orion, begging him to send Panrauth after Novak. What the *hell* was she thinking blowing the Mountain up? Did she plan this the entire time? Did the Harbinger ... backfire?

Panrauth was already here when I arrived, at Novak's bloodied bedside, and said nothing, not even to me. When I asked questions, he only blankly stared at me. Orion said he had been that way since Traveling there from the Mountain, loathe to set Novak down anywhere until Orion suggested his quarters. Orion has just as much idea of what happened as I do, his silent anxiety hardly kept at bay by a comforting Emeric. After hours of nothing from Alvis, and watching both his bloodied friends barely breathe, he had enough. Orion announced he was going to search for Alvis himself, and Panrauth wordlessly followed him out of the room.

I sigh and lift my head, glancing at Novak. The scrapes, bruises and lacerations marring his body have mostly healed now, but he's still covered in blood, dust and an odd black substance. A few more hours and you'd never know he'd barely survived a crumbling Mountain. I look over to Captain and tears prick my eyes at once, she is so *wrecked*. I gently caress the back of her ice cold hand, pondering once more why *Tzel* didn't kill her, he definitely could've. Then again, I'm not entirely sure it was *Tzel*, but I'm holding on to the thought. If it was Novak that did this ...

No, he *wouldn't*, no matter how angry he was.

I rise, needing something to do, so I check on Captain' bandages. Blood seeps through in spots along her neck but Niamh insisted to wait every eight hours, so instead I brush tangled hair back from the uncovered, upper part of her face. I shake my head, fists take hold of the sheets. I should've fought harder to go with her. To protect her. At this thought, I turn to Novak's bed. He's still filthy, and I decide modesty is out the window and prepare the basin I used for Captain, seeing how no one else is going to touch the *Tzel*.

I start with his face, having to rinse the washcloth several times by the time I get to the base of his neck. I fetch more fresh water as the basin is blackened already, then tentatively pull the covers back from his shoulders. I've never seen Novak with his shirt off and I gasp upon seeing the carvings lining his torso. I bite my cheek and slowly wash his overly heated chest, stomach and arms, marveling at how raised the runic scars are. For someone who heals so quickly, these wounds must have been ... horrifying, when first inflicted.

I've heard bits and pieces of rumors how Novak, ***Tzel***, razed a village to the ground. Lythienne did tell me that was when the *Tzel* was first bound to him, that he hadn't always been connected with the demon. When I asked how, she said nothing.

I take hold of Novak's bare shoulder and blanketed thigh, rolling him towards me so I can wash his back. I free the hand at his hip, using my knee to prevent him from rolling off. When I reach forward with the washcloth and find just as many scars along his back as the front, my heart cracks. How many times have I spoke ill of this person, even though I never met him? Never *knew* his true story, just assumed? Yes, he burned a village to the ground, but ... he also, didn't.

I think back to how pissed Lythienne was every time I treated Novak like the villain everyone made him out to be.

I think back to Aiden telling me how Beakglen was protected by a pirate gang, by the *Tzel*. By Captain.

I lay a quite feverish Novak back down and pull the blankets back up to his neck, then start to pull up the bottom of the blankets by his feet. The fabric slides halfway up his calf before the distant bedroom door *slams* open, startling me out of my skin and spilling the murky basin all over the fucking place. Orion's quarters are more like a small house than a bedroom, and a furious voice echoes through. "I want to see him right *fucking* now!"

Sounds like they found Alvis.

"Al, you *don't* understand-" Orion starts, but is cut short when Alvis halts a few feet away from Captain and Novak's beds. Orion's eyes flick to mine from behind his brother, but Alvis is unable to focus on either Captain or Novak for more than a few seconds. With a wave of Orion's hand, dirty water retreats from the marble floor and into the basin which lifts into the air for me to take, which I do. "Apologies, Vivvus. Any changes?"

Alvis' attention snaps up to mine, truly seeing me for the first time. His fists clench and release several times as his jaw works, chewing on words. I shake my head, pulling the blanket back down over Novak's feet. I gently set the basin down on a bedside table, then walk around the end of Novak's bed to meet Alvis. I carefully reach out and rest a hand on Alvis' shoulder and his nostrils flare as he opens his cracked lips. He looks infinitely worse than the last time I saw him, if such a drastic change is possible in only a few hours.

"What happened?" He grits out.

I tell him everything, how Captain insisted I stay behind in the Mines and face Novak alone. I wait for Alvis to chastise me for not disobeying her, but he doesn't, only stares at Captain while I speak. I explain how the ship was battered and aflame, but not truly burning. This catches Orion's interest, but Alvis only turns his attention to Novak. He takes a step towards him, hesitates, then takes another. He finds Novak's hand under the blanket and sighs upon tangling his fingers with Novak's.

"A Fire Fae's Aether won't continue on if they're gravely injured, think of it as a defense mechanism. It sounds like *Tzel* ... left her alive, and the flames were just leftovers from him throwing a tantrum." Orion murmurs, coming to my side. "He definitely could've killed her, but chose not to."

I glare at him. "A *tantrum*?"

"What the fuck have we done." Alvis states more than asks, frowning down at Novak.

I look between Orion and Alvis, then clear my throat. "Alvis ... Do you know, what happened? Why, why did she leave you?"

Alvis' eyes whip to mine and if he had Aether I'm sure they'd be burning. His gaunt face screws up and he opens his lips, then something over my shoulder catches his attention and he lowers his head. "Ask her."

I turn around to find a red haired Lythienne staring up at me, frowning despite the permanent scarred smile across her round face. I stumble backwards and Orion steadies me, neither he or Alvis are surprised by this ... person. Panrauth stands behind her, gaze unseeing as he stares off into the space around me. The female thrums a fist to her heart and I dumbly do the same. "I am Rylyn Yllamoira, and I believe I have the answers you need."

Captain and Novak were moved to separate rooms, and everyone is becoming pissier by the minute waiting for one of them to wake up. Panrauth returned to the Great Tree a few hours after Alvis' return and didn't ask me to come home, only hugged me in silence before Traveling off. Alvis has not left Novak's side in days, just like I haven't left Captain's, but now Alvis has his own sick bed. Charis, Orion and Niamh are the only ones allowed to visit any of the patients, but the High Lord's visits to Captain have been fewer in the last few days as the repercussions of a world without the Mountain weighs heavily on his crown.

I haven't heard from Panrauth, but I assume he is struggling with this new world as well. Orion did say there will be a Council meeting the day after tomorrow, and I have half a mind to go and meet Eros myself. I've doubted Rylyn's story and her insistence that Lythienne willingly agreed to help destroy the Mountain, and I won't feel satisfied until I talk to the fabled Eros myself. Niamh brings news when she tends to Captain in the early morning and late night, and the latest from this morning is that Iron is absolutely thriving, and allied with Borealis. Humans and Fire Fae, living and working together. Iverbourne has physically changed, but I haven't seen any of it.

Once again, the door slams open and startles me from my soft comb through of Captains raven hair, causing me to accidentally rip a few strands out. Quick steps echo through Orion's room, which he has not slept in since we've arrived, and bring forth a disheveled Novak to the foot of Captain's bed. He and I stare at the other. His sapphire eyes are wild and bloodshot, his bare chest heaves and the scarred runes are glowing a deep black, contrasting his fair complexion. I don't dare move for fear of spooking him, for he looks *terrified*.

Novak says nothing as his eyes slowly break from mine and slide to Captain, then he stumbles backwards, bringing a violently shaking hand to his heart. Her bandages have been removed, they were doing more harm than good. Her throat is barely healed over, the skin grafts from Captain's thigh filled with Niamh's Aether is taking hold, but the seams are puckered and everything is red, *angry*. The claw marks on her face and the sides of her neck are permanent, the blistered skin is finally turning pink instead of the violent red and black it was before.

"I ... I did this." Novak whispers, taking another step back, voice fractured and wet. He focuses on me when I slowly rise, his lip quivers uncontrollably. "Where's Alvis?"

That surprises me and I take a step towards him, but he takes two back and glances back the way he came. "Novak, hey, it's alright. You're not in trouble, and

Captain's ok, she's alive. Come here," I plead in the softest voice possible, but he startles as if I shouted. "It's alright, you're alright."

Novak's hands fly to his face as his eyes darken to black and he whimpers through a flood of tears, "no**no**no**no,** I hurt, I kill, **hurt**kill**hurt**kill," his voice *rises* and he *screeches, "MONSTER! I'M-!"*

Novak disappears mid scream into a flurry of shadows and I'm left standing alone in shock. When the swirling darkness settles, I remember the only thing I can do something about. I glance back at Captain, sleeping as always, then sprint out the wide open door at the opposite end of the quarters in search of Alvis. The door to his adjacent quarters is thrown open and I run inside, but he's not there. *Fuck.*

I run back out, right into Emeric dressed in fighting leathers instead of the usual silk attire he dons. Orion's lover, the Lord of Sylvan, visits nearly every day and I like him immensely, his big eyes fill with worry as he steadies me. "Vivvus, what's wrong?"

"Novak, he woke up and came to Captain, he was so scared," I start to cry as the words tumble out, "And Alvis, I can't find him."

"Shh, it's ok. We'll find him. Where's Novak now?"

With a shaky breath I say, "Gone."

ACKNOWLEDGMENTS

Thank you to Lianne Peterson for creating such a beautiful cover and character art, not to mention being an amazing friend. We 'met' ages ago on IG over a shared love for crochet, (which Lianne is fantastic at) and now look where we are, collaborating on a book together.

I also want to say thank you to Luna Daye who has been a wonderful friend, my first and most loyal fan, and a fellow author to soundboard off of.

Thank you to all the advanced readers, beta readers and early fans that have been here to see how this story has transformed and loved it despite the typos in that horrifying first, or even second version. Thank you for your endless patience while I learned the ropes of indie publishing and believed in me enough to keep going. To all the new people, thank you for joining the Crew of Misfits.

Thank you to Henni Eklund who is an amazing artist and while her art isn't in *this* book, she has done some spicy work of Alvis and Novak, not to mention a set of Tarot Cards regarding the RoG characters, and an entire swath of art for my newest book, Phantom and Rook. I'm so glad we have become such close friends and I hope we get to have Timmie's together someday.

To Cora, thank you for throwing your copy. I have officially achieved an author dream because of you.

To my Brothers (all six of you), thank you always telling me, "I knew you were going to be a writer someday."

To my Dad, for helping me get this thing off the ground, because without you, I wouldn't have.

To my Husband, for loving me through it all.

GLOSSARY

Characters are organized by location they hail from, then tribe or group.
Spoilers are included, read at your own risk.

The Eternal Mountain

Lythienne - Keeper of The Eternal Machine.

Amwren - Lythienne's assistant.

Iron Court

Ragnis Yllamoira -Former High Lord of Iron who overthrew Visha, his father.

Lexeran Priamos - Former slave solider of Iron. Spy. Father figure to Captain and Novak.

Knothall Arriens - Former Commander of the Eternal Machine. Father to Eros.

Visha Yllamoira - Former High Lord of Iron. Father of Ragnis, Rylyn and Lyth.

Terra Court

Panrauth Firthorn - High Lord of Terra.

Vivvus Firthorn - Princess of Terra. Sister to Pan.

Aiden Firthorn - Second in Command. Brother to Pan.

Weylin Firthorn - Panrauth's deceased wife.

Estienne Firthorn -Panrauth's daughter.

Mirah Firthorn - Panrauth's daughter.

Bonnie - Vivvus' First Lover and the High Lady's Personal Guard

Hallowed Court

Trihewyn Cervil - High Lady of Hallowed Court. Mother of Rohana.

Rohana Cervil - Hero of Borealis. Mother of Eros.

Eros Cervil - High Lady of the Southern Court. Daughter of Rohana and Knothall.

Maverick Makts - Lord of Cervalis. Novak's friend and Sage's Husband.

Sage Makts - Maverick's deceased wife. Novak's previous mate.

Umber - Wild Fae. Spy for Eros and old friend of the Crew.

Sylvan Court

Typhan Isadora - Former High Lord of Sylvan. Father of Alvis, Orion and Apollo.

Alvis Isadora - Prince of Sylvan. Brother to Orion. Master of Arms.

Orion Isadora - High Lord of Sylvan. Brother to Alvis. Former Quartermaster.

Emeric Dusan - Lord of Sylvan. Orion's partner and second in command.

Charis Lieve - Former Queen of Sylvan. Alvis' childhood friend.

Satyr

Dyonsus Fallon - Chieftain of the Satyr Tribes in Arca Navi and Dew Falls.

Ruki Fallon - Lead Scoutmaster of Arca Navi. Daughter of Dyonsus.

Fin Fallon - Dyonsus' second in command. Son of Dyonsus.

Borealis Court

Agaleth Yewblade - Queen of Borealis. Mother of Thornton.

Thornton Yewblade - Prince of Borealis. Son of Agaleth.

Marta Faelyn - Former Chieftess of Farhaven who was possessed by a Nafshyi.

The Crew

Captain - Leader of a rebellion group fighting Sylvan and corrupt organizations.

Oakenstead - Crew Member.

Novak - First Mate. 'Zemer'. 'Tzel.'

Vesper - Former Crew member. Friend of the Crew.

Also by Aelina

Phantom and Rook is a queer, urban fantasy featuring found family, a mysterious treasure hunt, secret identities, soulmates and second chances.
Take me to Iverbourne is a dark steampunk fantasy series which includes novellas focusing on different character's backstories and provides vital clues for the next adventure.

Children of Iverbourne is a prequel novella taking place 236 years before The Eternal Machine, following the original heroes of the war torn lands and the difficult choices they must make, all to ensure a better future.
A terrified slave, lacking bravery or free will, sent on an impossible journey.
A hardened Commander of the Eternal prison, taking in his newest inmate. An hours old baby.
A half crazed Fae, former Hero of Borealis, Court of the Humans.
Two Parents on a journey to deliver their child to Iverbourne, to freedom, no matter the cost.
A new Captain, and a trouble making Water Fae with a constant smirk.

Prince of Sylvan is a prequel novella taking place twenty years before The Eternal Machine.
Alvis is the preferred heir to the throne of Sylvan, a Fae court built on hatred and blood. High Lord Typhan pushes Alvis every day to murder his own brother and absorb his power, becoming an unstoppable weapon.
A lifelong blood bond will force Alvis to make a choice between his brother or mother, as he cannot disobey a command given by his father. Unlike most blood bonds, his can be broken, at the expense of his mother's life.
Typhan is losing patience and soon his request will be a command, then Alvis will have to kill his kin by the sword, or a broken blood bond. Alvis decides he would rather take his own life than choose between his kin and live as a monster any longer, but a legendary Captain arrives with a troublesome first mate the Prince can't keep out of his heart.
Friends, love and a whole new world waits outside their imprisoned court, but at what cost?
Blood, or sanity?

Keeper of Death is quite a fitting name for a villain, and yet Lythienne finds herself as the only Fae who can save the realm of Iverbourne.
Born as an Empty Fae, she is sent into the Eternal Mountain, a prison designed for the most malicious, blood thirsty and cursed creatures alive. Her crime, along

with so many other creatures, is being Lesser than the grand High Fae who rule the divided lands above.

Aether magic rules Iverbourne, a whimsical land ravaged by long held prejudices, unkind to all those without magic. The Others are a mysterious court to the south, kidnapping and murdering all those on their path through the continent. Only a Fae without Aether can wield the mysterious Harbinger, a weapon of mass destruction needed to defeat the epic evil taking over the realm. The elegant call of immense power corrupts most, especially those who have been mistreated. Dangerous lust, high stakes adventure and loyal companionship are thrust into Lyth's life, but can she be the Hero after playing the Villain for so long? After all, why would you want to save a world that wants to see you buried six feet under?

Perhaps this isn't a hero saves the day story. Perhaps, this is the origin story of the Deadliest Fae alive.

Novak. Zemer. Akar. Tzel. Vagabond Bard.

I've had many names throughout my life, and I suppose they've all suited me well enough. Who knew Villain would be the name that I wear best?

Months after the events in The Eternal Machine, Novak leads an Expedition into the long separated Realm of Giants, a land filled with dragons and dangerous secret societies who already have their eyes set on Iverbourne.

Novak's mind is set on one thing, defying the course of Death, but as he meets new foes, finds family and himself, he begins to ask himself a vital question. Is defying Death worth the cost of humanity?

Princess of Terra is a novella intended to be read after The Eternal Machine and Realm of Giants, **serious** spoilers are involved for the later chapters in the novella.
I've never stepped out of line.
I've never done things I shouldn't. Until the day I snapped, executing half my family and reluctantly sentencing my youngest brother to prison. Little did I know a certain Keeper of Death would bring him home, and change *everything*.
After overthrowing a kingdom that is not mine, side by side with the Shadow of Death, I met Captain, and life changed from the first time we laid eyes on each other.
Now, friends have been lost, my home is torn apart by a monster. War is ravaging Iverbourne and the Realm of Giants, and our family needs help.
All hands on deck are needed when it comes to fighting a new, powerful enemy, who once was our friend. Let's hope it'll be enough.
Princess of Terra is a dark fantasy with several content warnings.

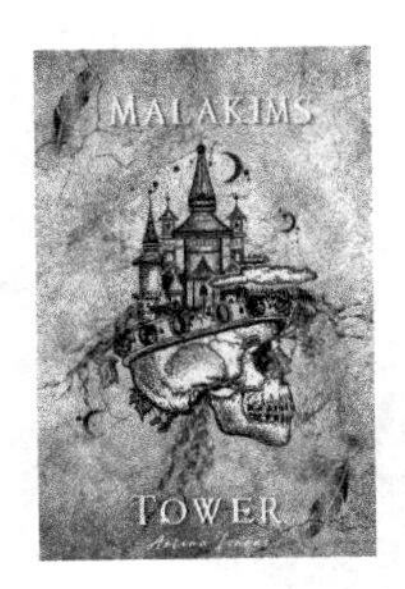

Malakim's Tower is the third novel in the series and will be releasing early 2023.
Friends are Enemies. Enemies are Friends. And no one is safe.
War is knocking on the door of every kingdom, discovered and unfamiliar. The Crew of Misfits and Expedition has merged and formed the Company, a rag tag group of old and new friends, Giants and Fae. The Company is stretching far and

wide in search of allies and growing more doubtful of their Hero returning home. Even worse, if he does, he will never be the same.

Novak has found friends in the den of his enemy and is earning freedom one heinous act at a time. With the Second Prince's help, Novak has begun to unravel the mystery of Dragons and Angels, Gods and Ancients. Answers come with a price, however. Bloodshed and ghosts taint Novak's sanity and it's time for him to make a choice.

Die as the Hero, or Live as the Villain?

ABOUT THE AUTHOR

A debut fantasy author with waves of young witch vibes, endless coffee stains and a love for adventure. Living in the Adirondacks of Northern New York, Aelina's work is heavily influenced by her love for the outdoors and high stakes adventures filled with angst and love. The Eternal Machine is the first novel in the series, Take Me to Iverbourne.

Learn more about the series and other works here.

https://linktr.ee/aelinaisaacs

Sign up for the Crew of Misfits here for free novellas and updates.

https://mailchi.mp/77c54f2842a4/welcome-to-iverbourne

CPSIA information can be obtained
at www.ICGtesting.com
Printed in the USA
JSHW031209290922
30978JS00004B/4/J